Jordan Pond

Rangers of Acadia

Kari Lemor

RYCON

RYCON PRESS

Rangers of Acadia: Jordan Pond Copyright © 2022 by Kari Lemor

Cover Art by: Karasel
Photos: depositphoto
RyCon Press

First Electronic Edition: Feb 2022
ISBN- 978-1-954056-14-5

First Print Edition: Feb 2022
ISBN - 978-1-954056-15-2

What's lost can be found again...

Five summers ago, Chelsea Woodridge met, fell in love with, and married ranger Theodore Lapierre in beautiful Bar Harbor. It was perfect, until her father's manipulations cost her not only the man she loved but their child, spiraling her into a fog that lasted for years.

Theo loved Chelsea the instant he saw her and thought the feelings returned. Her visit with her father has him questioning her love when instead of returning, he gets a note of rejection. And several months later, a newborn on his doorstep.

With her father dead, Chelsea returns to Maine, where she'd been happiest. Theo's presence brings back the pain of the past but seeing the daughter she thought was dead devastates her. How could Theo have thought she didn't want her own child? More importantly, how could her father have lied to her about her baby?

Rebuilding the marriage may take more than either can manage. They shared love once, but Chelsea still holds secrets. Ones that can't be revealed if she wants to have a life with Theo and their daughter.

Books by Kari Lemor

Love on the Line – light romantic suspense
Wild Card Undercover
Running Target
Fatal Evidence
Hidden Betrayal
Death Race
Tactical Revenge

Storms of New England – small town contemporary
Elusive Dreams – Erik & Tessa
True Dreams – Sara & TJ
Stolen Dreams – Alex & Gina
Broken Dreams – Nathaniel & Darcy
Lost Dreams – Greg & Alandra
Faded Dreams – Luke & Ellie
Forgotten Dreams (Christmas novella)
Sweet Dreams (Christmas novella)

Last Chance Beach World - small town contemporary
Secrets Under the Sun

Rangers of Acadia- small town contemporary
Jordan Pond

Coming soon 2022
Masquerade Under the Moon (Last Chance Beach)
Otter Cliffs (Rangers of Acadia)
Donovan (Last Man Standing)

For my wonderful husband, Jim, who suggested we visit Bar Harbor when we got engaged and again for our honeymoon. This visit started a love affair with Mount Desert Island that we shared with our children, and now our grandchildren.

Acknowledgements

I have to thank Teri and Jennifer for all the details and information you passed along as I cobbled this story together. My family and all the support they give to me and my writing. My TEAM, Meredith and Kris for all the assistance in so many areas. Em, my faithful editor who doesn't let me get away with neglecting all those commas. Donna and Susan who read the early draft and gave wonderful feedback and suggestions. To Kimberly who gave me the idea for this series. Special thanks go to Seana Kelly for allowing me to borrow Aiden and Katie. And to the most beautiful of places, Jordan Pond, I will always love you!!

CHAPTER ONE

"This place is perfect."

At her softly spoken words, Theodore Lapierre turned to stare at the woman standing on the edge of Jordan Pond. The cleanup crew wasn't due for another half hour, but this part of Acadia National Park attracted many visitors. He couldn't blame anyone for wanting a few minutes of the pristine beauty before a hard day's work.

The petite brunette sighed as she gazed out at the crystalline water of the lake, her shoulders rising and falling. Five years ago, he'd met another brunette here, one that had changed Theo's life in ways he'd never expected. After all this time, the thought of her still pierced his heart.

Strands of stray hair escaped her ponytail, and the woman at the lake edge tucked them behind her ears. So reminiscent of Chelsea, except her hair had been shorter. Man, he had to get his head back in the game. He couldn't be taking a dangerous trip down Memory Lane when he had the Earth Day hordes showing up soon.

Laughter at his back caught his attention. A few dozen people had started the trek down the gradual hill from the Jordan Pond House, rakes and shovels at the ready. Was this woman here for that or simply appreciating the view?

Before he could step away from the lake, she turned.

He froze.

His heart pounded in his chest as he took in the upturned nose and tiny ears decorating the beautiful, urchin-like face. Chelsea?

Closing his eyes, he shook his head. It was only a figment of his imagination. They'd met during an Earth Day cleanup. No other reason for him to be envisioning Chelsea here. Her opinion of him and this place had been made clear.

When he opened his eyes, she was still there. But now *she* froze, her mouth open in a tiny bow. Just like—

"Theo?" Her eyes narrowed in question as she took a step toward him.

It *was* her. Why? What was she doing here?

"Chelsea." Not much else would come out of his mouth with the fist-sized obstruction blocking his throat.

As she maneuvered over the pink granite rocks littering the shore, he took note. Even with the passage of time, she was as enchanting as ever. Maybe a little thinner and definitely paler, almost gaunt, like she'd been sick. Concern saturated his body. He shouldn't feel anything for her. Not after what she'd done.

"I didn't think you'd still be here." Her voice hadn't changed at all, soft and feminine so it flowed over him like a winding breeze.

"Where else would I be?"

"You were applying to the FBI. Said you would only be here for a year or two."

Did she seriously think he'd still join the FBI after the little package she'd sent? "Yeah, well that obviously never materialized."

"I'm sorry."

"For?" Why the heck had she come here? His insides twisted with too many dire thoughts.

"That the FBI didn't work out. You were excited about it."

That's all she was sorry about? Seriously? But if she didn't know he still lived on Mount Desert Island then… "Why are you here?"

Pointing to the crowd slowly making their way down the hill, she said, "The Earth Day cleanup. You know Jordan Pond's always been my favorite place, and I wanted to get it back in shape after the winter."

"Why now? It's not like you cared about it the last four years."

Her eyes darkened, and pain radiated out from them. *No, don't start feeling sorry for her or concerned.* She made her choices and had to live with them.

"My father passed away a few weeks ago."

Saying he was sorry would be the polite, well-mannered thing to do, but he honestly wasn't sorry that low life had died. It was five years too late. Maybe things would have been different. Maybe he could have—

Stop. No need to play the what if game. You can't rewrite the past.

"Well, I hope you brought some gloves," he said, glancing at the volunteers who had almost reached them. "This winter was harsh and did a lot of damage to the trails."

Tugging on the brim of his Acadia National Park cap, he marched toward the boat ramp where everyone was told to meet. Knowing how much work had to be done, he'd worn his oldest uniform and had foregone the traditional park ranger hat for the cap. His fleece was needed for now, but it would probably be gone once they got going.

"I'm going to let you run this show." Rico Montenegro, the other ranger working the cleanup, dropped a box of industrial strength yard bags on the ground at their feet.

Theo grinned, trying to ignore the fact Chelsea had moved closer. Her proximity was causing havoc to his system.

"That means I can give you the boardwalk side to supervise, huh?"

Half of the trail around Jordan Pond was a flat, graded path that skimmed the side of the lake. The other half was a narrow boardwalk created by large trees, halved and propped on other stumps. It wended through the woods yet remained within sight of the water. Some of these planks might need to be replaced. depending on how much damage they'd taken over the winter. It would definitely be the harder of the two jobs.

Rico eyed the small crowd. "I don't care which side I get, but be kind with who you put on my team."

Gauging the few dozen volunteers gathered around, Theo suspected the group of teenage girls wearing skimpy shorts, snug, revealing t-shirts under their unzipped fleeces, and Uggs were most likely the ones Rico wanted to avoid. The girls were probably here because of him. The man's dark good looks attracted a fair amount of young female visitors wherever he was stationed.

Theo wasn't exactly dog meat, but anytime the college girls showed up, he flashed his wedding ring and made it known he was off limits. His gaze moved to Chelsea, who stood by herself staring at the water. Did she still have her ring? Wear it? It had surprised him he'd never gotten divorce papers. That wasn't something he was going to initiate.

Checking his watch and seeing it was a few minutes past meet-up time, Theo cleared his throat. "If you could all gather over here, I'd like to get started."

Everyone crowded closer, and Theo sized them up. The four giggling college girls. A number of local couples, ranging in age from thirty to fifty, dressed in typical hiking gear. Two guys in their twenties who kept eyeing the college girls. Yup, keep them apart. Several other men and women who didn't appear to be together. And then Chelsea. Rico's group would be the best place for her. No way he could handle having her nearby the whole day.

"We're the park rangers who'll be leading you today. This is Ranger Rico Montenegro and I'm Ranger Theo Lapierre. We'll be splitting you into two groups, so we can tackle both sides of the pond."

The young girls sidled closer to Rico, who looked decidedly uncomfortable. The man was a bit of a loner and the last thing he'd want was to deal with that crap all day.

"You'll all need gloves as was stated in the volunteer form you filled out." Why hadn't he taken a closer look at the list of volunteers? He'd left that detail to Rico. Grabbing the clipboard his friend carried, he glanced down the names, and sure enough, there it was. Chelsea Woodridge-Lapierre. Seriously? She'd kept his last name? Had actually *taken* his last name? What did that mean?

After calling and checking off the names on the list, he and Rico took turns explaining what the task was for the day and the rules regarding the wildlife and vegetation. Get the biggest obstructions out of the way and collect any trash and debris. They wouldn't finish it all today but would do as much as they could. The volunteers grabbed shovels, rakes, and trash bags. Pointing to the two young men, a few couples, and some of the single stragglers, Theo told them to move near the path. They'd do that side with Rico. His crew would take the boardwalk.

As the volunteers grabbed their gear and headed toward their destinations, Rico raised an eyebrow and smirked. "Thought I was getting the hard part today. Plus, you took the gigglers. Looks like I'm going to owe you big time."

"And I'll collect, too."

Rico stashed the clipboard in his backpack. "I noticed the cute brunette is named Lapierre. Any relation? She can't keep her eyes off you."

"My wife." Typically, he didn't get into details about the relationship he and Chelsea had had, but one night after he and Rico had downed a few too many beers, he'd spilled his guts. Rico had a few secrets of his own, so it evened out. They trusted each other.

"Why's she here?"

Theo shrugged. "Don't know. She seemed surprised I was still on the island."

"Want me to take her with my team?"

Never any prying questions from him. That's why he liked the man. It would be best if Rico worked with her, since his senses were on overload from simply looking at her. Then again, they always said, "Keep your friends close and your enemies closer." He wasn't sure which category Chelsea fell into yet.

"Nah, I need to see what she's up to."

Rico slapped him on the back, then indicated the radio on his belt. "Let me know if you need rescuing."

As Rico marched away, Theo shrugged into his backpack and picked up the small chainsaw he'd brought. There were always a few large trees that couldn't be pushed out of the way or lifted.

By the time he crossed the small stone bridge and made it around to the path on the boardwalk side, his crew had already started removing the most obvious debris.

"Any small twigs and wood that can be used as kindling can be stacked on the side of the path. I'll pick it up later. For now, we want to concentrate on clearing the trail." Anything too heavy or too far in, he'd get with a boat at another time.

His eyes automatically searched for Chelsea as he passed some of the workers. Sensibly, she'd worn jeans, work boots, and a hoodie. Like she had the first time they'd met. He'd been fairly new at the park and had dressed in his best uniform, out to impress. It had gotten ruined with the mud, sticks, and rocks he'd needed to climb over and through.

Something about her had kicked him in the gut as soon as he'd set eyes on her. It wasn't only her beauty. It was a rare peace that she exuded when she'd looked at the lake. As if standing here was all she ever needed to be fulfilled. That had been proven wrong soon enough.

Shaking his head, he started tugging on the larger branches that had dropped during the winter winds. Chelsea was doing the same. One especially large branch was giving her a hard time, so he grabbed the chain saw and trotted to her side.

"This one needs to be chopped up."

"Thanks." She stepped back and smiled. It about knocked him over.

"Where are you staying?" And when was she leaving? He pulled on the cord to start the machine. It roared to life.

"At my grandmother's cottage."

Theo gripped the handle tighter and pushed the spinning chain through the center of the wood. Cottage? Hardly what he'd call the four-bedroom ocean front house her grandmother had lived in. It had remained empty all these years. Not that he'd admit to driving past on occasion. It was his job to keep an eye on the park. The cottage in Seal Harbor wasn't precisely on park land, but it was close.

The buzzing of the chainsaw drowned out any other conversation. He didn't want to sit and chat with her, but he was curious what she'd been doing for the past four years.

Once the large branch was in smaller pieces, Theo tipped his head and jogged down the path toward another volunteer. The floral scent of Chelsea alone was doing his head in. He'd never make it.

──────◆──────

Chelsea Woodridge pulled the cap off her water bottle and took a long swig. She'd forgotten how much hard work cleaning up the pond was, but it felt amazing. Being back here on Mount Desert Island had lifted her spirits. Even seeing Theo again, and his constantly scowling face, hadn't dampened her excitement.

What in the world was he still doing here? The Park Ranger job was supposed to have been a steppingstone to getting into the FBI's Environmental Crimes unit. It's what he had wanted and talked so much about. Why hadn't that happened?

And why had he changed his mind about *them*? Had he only married her so they could have sex? That didn't make any sense. There had been plenty of other girls hanging around him that summer who would have been thrilled to jump in and provide the service.

Turning back to the path, her head started to swim, and she stumbled. A nearby volunteer, a blonde woman perhaps in her forties, caught her arm.

"Are you okay?"

Chelsea propped herself up against a tree and nodded. "Yeah, a little dizzy. Must have moved too fast."

"Have you eaten at all today? We've been at this since early morning. I don't remember seeing you stop for lunch."

Because she hadn't brought a lunch. It was stupid, but her grandmother's cottage—her cottage now—wasn't in the best shape, since no one had been there for ages. The electricity hadn't even been turned back on yet.

"I had a small pastry this morning with some tea. I didn't want to be late, so I guess I forgot the lunch thing. I brought water and made sure to drink it."

"Here. Have some crackers and cheese," the woman offered. "My name is Kelly, and this is my partner, Tammi." She pointed to another woman with short, curly brown hair.

Tipping her head at the two women, Chelsea took the offered food and nibbled. Ever since her father had died of a heart attack a few weeks ago, her stomach had been off. But then she'd also been off her medication. Should she go back on? No. For the first time in she couldn't remember how many years, she finally had a clear mind. It was confused about so many things but didn't feel cloudy, and her body didn't feel sluggish. She did need to remember to eat better.

"Thank you. That must have been it. I'm Chelsea."

"Have you been here before?" Tammi dragged the rake through some of the undergrowth.

"I used to come up here every summer to stay with my grandmother, but she passed away five years ago." No need to go into the details of her relationship with Theo. Apparently, he didn't want to rehash anything. He'd been avoiding her today. How could she have been so wrong about him?

After taking another sip of her water, she resumed clearing the debris from around the planks. Kelly and Tammi stayed close by. To make sure she didn't pass out? That was sweet but probably unnecessary. She needed to start taking care of herself. She'd been under her father's thumb for too long.

"We own a little sandwich shop, The Brown Bag Cafe, in downtown Bar Harbor," Kelly said as she took a small hatchet and chopped up some of the larger branches into kindling-size pieces. "Since it's still early for tourists, we don't fully staff it every day, but you make sure to stop in and get some food. We can even pack it in a cooler for you if you don't have a fridge to store it."

"I will. Not sure how much of anything works in my grandmother's cottage. I only arrived yesterday." And she'd slept in a sleeping bag on top of the bed she'd used as a child.

Tammi pulled a card from her bag and slipped it into Chelsea's back pocket. "Our cell number is on the back. You need to find someone to help with any work, call us. We know lots of people on the island."

They spent the rest of the afternoon chatting while they worked. Theo checked on them occasionally but did most of the chainsaw work that was needed. As he tromped past a few times and talked to Kelly or Tammi, she had an opportunity to look at him.

His hair was a little longer than he'd worn it before and curled a bit on the ends. It was still that beautiful dark color with some lighter highlights at the temples. A few more laugh lines surrounded his chocolate brown eyes, but his face was as handsome as ever. And he'd bulked up since she'd last seen him. All the hiking and trailblazing he did on the job?

His thirtieth birthday would have been a few months ago. What had he done to celebrate? Did he have anyone special in his life? No way someone like him had stayed single. She automatically touched the ring under her glove, on the third finger of her left hand. Why had she continued to wear it once they weren't together? The last few years were so blurry, she didn't even know how long she'd been married to him. Her father had never mentioned the divorce, or if he had, she didn't remember. But he always took care of every little aspect of her life. He must have taken care of that, too.

She didn't even remember telling him about getting married. He'd known about Theo, for sure, as she recalled how mad he'd been when she'd wanted to go back to Maine and all the stuff he'd bought to make her feel better when Theo had told her not to come back. That it had simply been a summer fling and a mistake.

It hadn't felt like a mistake. It had felt perfect. But her judgment wasn't always on target, and she had to live with that fact.

A whistle blew, and Theo's deep voice called out that it was quitting time and to grab any tools and head back. Once they were all gathered at the boat landing again, he and Rico thanked them for all their hard work.

"We'll be clearing this site for the next few weeks. Anyone who wants to continue is welcome. We only ask that you let us know. Rico has the sign-up sheet."

Many of the volunteers shuffled toward the parking lot while she waited to speak with the ranger. She wanted to keep helping. Needed to keep helping. Her body was aching and complaining louder than it ever had, but she was determined to do this.

The group of teenage girls crowded around Rico, who chiseled a smile onto his features as he checked off the dates they would return.

"Thank you, ladies. I need to organize with the rest of these volunteers." His dismissal was professional but clear.

As they wandered off, still looking back at the attractive man, she stepped closer. "I'd like to sign up, please."

Rico glanced at her, then down at the paper. "Chelsea, right? What dates are you available?"

"I'd like to come back every day until it's done."

Peeking toward where Theo had gone, Rico then looked at her, an unreadable expression on his face. "Every day? You might want to take a break a few times."

"I don't have anything more important to do, and I love Jordan Pond. I'd rather be here than anyplace else."

That got him staring at her strangely again. What had she said?

"Okay, got you down. If you can't make it, please call the ranger station to let us know. We'll be moving farther down the trail, and we want to make sure we can account for everyone."

"Sure." Stepping over to the side so Kelly and Tammi could sign up, she picked up her backpack and dug inside for her car keys. It had felt strange driving again after so long, but she'd made sure to practice at the estate in Westchester for the last week, so she'd be confident in her drive all the way to Maine.

As she slung her bag over her shoulder, she caught sight of Theo climbing the hill toward the restaurant and gift shop. A blonde woman with a young girl was ambling down. The little girl broke free and dashed toward Theo, who picked her up, swung her around, then kissed her neck. Giggles rang all the way down to where Chelsea stood. The sound brought tears to her eyes.

They were too far away to tell how old the child was, but she was young. Guess Theo hadn't waited around to move on to the next conquest.

Pain shot through her heart and her stomach clenched, thinking of the past. Another reason she'd wanted to come up here. In a month, it would be the end of May. Four years from when she'd lost the most precious thing in her life.

Theo slung his arm over the blonde as they trudged back up the hill. The child's dark head bobbed back and forth on her father's shoulder. Their child most likely would have had dark hair, too. Would she have had brown eyes like Theo or blue like hers?

Shaking her head, she knew she had to get rid of these thoughts or she'd end up curled in a ball on the ground. Memories flashed through her, anyway.

"Where's my baby?" Her mind had been fuzzy from the anesthesia, but she reached down to her stomach and knew her child didn't rest there any longer.

"I'm so sorry, my dear," her father had said, his voice as brusque as ever. "There were complications."

"What complications? Where's my baby?"

"It was stillborn. I'm sorry." He couldn't meet her eyes.

"It?"

"She. It was a girl."

"No!" she cried, tears streaming down her face. "She was fine when we got here. Kicking up a storm. How could she have died? I want to see her."

"That's inadvisable, Chelsea. You know with your condition it could cause all sorts of problems."

"I don't care." She shook her head and tried to get out of the bed. The IV line pulled at her hand. "I have to see her."

Her father patted her arm and gently pushed her back down. "I'm sorry, but it was several hours ago, and they've already disposed of it. I thought it best in the circumstances."

"Disposed? You disposed of my child? My baby!" She was truly hysterical now. How could anyone do that? "And it's she, not it."

Her father nodded at a nurse by the door who did something to the IV, then left the room.

"I will not let you see the body, but if you need to have a small prayer service, we can arrange for it at the house once you get out of here. Now rest."

The nurse must have added something to her medication, because she couldn't keep her eyes open. Dread settled over her as she drifted off. If her baby was gone, then what was left for her?

It had been the last straw. Losing Theo had been one thing, but then losing her daughter, their daughter, had caused a nervous breakdown that had taken a long time to recover from. If she had ever truly recovered. They'd never gotten around to the prayer service. By the time she'd been well enough to even think about it, her father had insisted it was too late to keep dwelling on and wouldn't do anyone any good. Her father had always gotten what he wanted. What he didn't know was that she'd built a special little monument in the garden for her baby and prayed near it all the time.

Moving slowly toward her car, she took one last look down at the lake. Jordan Pond. It had been the only place she'd ever felt totally at peace. After they'd gotten married, she'd even told Theo she wanted to name their first daughter Jordan. He'd insisted on Jordan Marie after her middle name, too. Now that dream was as dead as her child.

"Can we have pizza for supper, Daddy?"

Theo glanced down at his daughter and nodded. Good suggestion. He didn't have the energy to cook tonight. Cleaning up the pond was grueling enough. Having to be on his guard around Chelsea all day had drained every ounce of strength he had.

"Sure, peanut. What do you want on it?"

His daughter danced around, the blue bow in her hair dangling from a few loose strands. She looked up at him and grinned. Same smile her mother used to give him when they'd first met. Today, it twisted the knife deeper.

"Bacon. And lots of cheese."

"I should have guessed. Okay, go put your backpack away and your lunch box in the kitchen while I call Pepper's."

After making the call, Theo climbed the stairs to his room and changed out of his uniform into a t-shirt and his most comfortable pair of jeans. His daughter bounced from her room across the hall.

"I get a piggyback wide down the stairs?" she asked, popping up and down like a Whack-A-Mole.

Crossing his arms, he grumbled, "How come you always get the ride? Why can't you give me a ride?"

Her hazel eyes looked around like she was giving it some thought. "You're too big, Daddy. Maybe when I grow up I can give you a wide."

"Hmm. Makes sense. So I guess that means for now you get the ride." He crouched down. "Hop on."

Her tiny arms wrapped around his neck, and he tossed her higher as he slid his hands behind him to hold her. The feel of her warmth almost undid him. Every day, he thanked God for this gift. How could someone not appreciate that?

As he trotted down the stairs, his mind roamed to Chelsea. God, what the heck had made her come back here? Yes, she'd always loved Mount Desert Island, but that obviously hadn't mattered in the last five years.

Passing through the living room, his daughter steered him over to the fireplace mantle and picked up her favorite picture.

"Hi, Mama. Hi Daddy," she said to the picture he still kept of Chelsea and him on their wedding day. Call him a masochist, but he never could find the balls to get rid of it. He'd worn his dress ranger uniform, and she'd gotten a fancy sundress in a light peach lace from one of the boutiques in town. It had been a perfect sunny day, and they'd been so blissful.

Then, everything had crashed down around them. He'd never even seen it coming. Like her showing up today. It had taken him completely by surprise. His first thought was she had come to take their daughter away. But she seriously hadn't even asked about her. It was like the child didn't exist. Cold-hearted wasn't the way he remembered her. Obviously, he'd been wrong about that, too.

The child on his back pressed a kiss to the picture, like always, then kissed his cheek. "Let's get some pizza, Daddy. Can we eat it there? Please."

He was so wrapped around her little finger. Depositing her on the ground, he took her hand to lead her to the SUV and said, "Anything you want, Miss Jordan Marie Lapierre."

CHAPTER TWO

Chelsea's phone jingled in the pocket of her hoodie, and she slowed the rake. Before she answered, she glanced around the area to make sure Theo wasn't nearby. Heaven forbid he see her slacking.

"Hello." Perfect. It was the power company finally letting her know they could get her electric back on today.

"Everything okay?" Tammi asked once she'd hung up. The two ladies were back and working her side of the pond again today. The way they hovered, she wondered if they'd asked to be near her. They mentioned they didn't have any children of their own, but it seemed their maternal instinct was kicking in. It was kind of nice. She hadn't had anything like it since her grandmother had died.

"Yes, thank you. The electric company. I'm finally getting power today. Hopefully, I can get some groceries, and you won't have to keep bringing me food." They'd packed extra lunches the past few days and shared with her. All she'd had were crackers and a piece of fruit.

Tammi planted her hands on her hips and tossed her short, dark curls. "What? You don't like our food?" Her grin showed she was kidding.

"I love your food and am so appreciative that you brought it for me, but now I can buy some of my own and keep it in a fridge that works."

After checking for any messages, she slipped her phone back in her pocket. It was a new one she'd gotten before driving up here. Her old one had been acting weird ever since her father had passed away. No matter who she called, it only ever dialed her father's number. Of course, she'd barely used it in years. Luckily, this one worked fine.

Her muscles screamed and ached as she continued to move old logs and rake dried leaves. After four days of doing this, you'd think they'd be used to it by now. However, almost five years of basic inactivity had taken its toll. Strolling around the estate gardens didn't count.

Whistling drifted her way, and she immediately bent to haul another old log off the path. The day had gotten warm for late April, and Theo had removed his fleece, leaving him in only his gray, short-sleeved ranger's shirt. It fit so nicely across his shoulders, shoulders that hadn't been as broad five years ago. Memories of exploring them with her hands and lips surfaced, and she lowered her face to hide the color that suffused her cheeks.

Obviously, Theo wasn't having the same flashbacks if his demeanor with her was anything to go by. Her work had been as good as anyone else's, better than the college girls who ogled Rico every day, but Theo never seemed to tell her this. He complimented everyone else on their work. Maybe he simply didn't want to talk to her. Was she a stupid decision in his past that he didn't want to think about?

When Theo passed by, she tugged harder, but the log wouldn't move. Her foot caught a rock, and she started to fall backwards. In half a second, Theo was there, grabbing her around the waist and holding tight. His heart beat rapidly against her back, and she reveled in the warmth of his arms. It was the same feeling she'd had with him five years ago. It hadn't changed.

Abruptly, he set her on her feet and stepped away. Well, maybe it had changed for him.

"Thanks," she mumbled, not wanting to see the look of disdain on his face she knew would be there. Instead, his eyes held curiosity and perhaps a bit of concern. For her?

"You've lost weight."

"I was…um…sick…for a while." She shrugged. *Please don't ask any more questions.* It wasn't something she wanted him aware of.

His expression softened for only a second, then tightened again. "Then, maybe you shouldn't be out here trying to do all this."

"No, I need to." Why had she said anything? Her father had told her to always keep vigilant. *You don't want to go the way of your mother.* "I'm fine now. The fresh air is good for me."

It was. Her home in Westchester had had fresh air aplenty, but being out here in the open spaces, doing something worthwhile, was renewing and invigorating.

His gaze raked up and down her body, his expression still neutral. "Take a break if you need to. You've been going harder than anyone else out here." Then, he stalked off.

At least he'd noticed.

The rest of the day passed quickly as more and more of the trail was cleared. They had almost reached the midway section where the little wooden bridge crossed over a small stream. Her heart raced as despair jolted through her. It was where she and Theo had exchanged vows.

As she stepped closer to the bridge, Theo's whistle pierced the air. Time to end for the day. Grabbing the rake she'd been using and shrugging on her small backpack, she turned to follow Kelly and Tammi. It would take them a half hour or more at a quick pace to hike back to the boat ramp. Her mind flitted with memories of her wedding day while her eyes stayed focused on the damp boardwalk.

By the time she got to the end of the trail, she had worked up a sweat. And here was Theo heading toward them. She doubted he'd get close enough to smell her, but being near him was something she'd dreamed about. All her dreams since she'd arrived here had been about Theo. Over the last four years if she was being honest. Might as well throw delusional into her list of health issues.

"Thanks for coming out today, ladies. Appreciate the effort. Another few days and we'll have this baby licked and ready for tourists."

Waving to Kelly and Tammi, she dropped her bag and took her gloves off to find her keys. Theo had handed the chainsaw off to Rico and crouched to dig into his own bag. The urge to be near him overwhelmed her, and her feet moved of their own accord.

"Did you lose something?" she asked, needing to hear his rich voice again. Maybe to simply punish herself for still wanting him.

Looking up, he scowled, then ripped his gloves off, shoving them in the side pocket of his bag. He retrieved a small radio, clipped it to his belt, then hauled his bag over his shoulder. She did the same.

"The gloves were too bulky. They were getting in the way."

Since he obviously wasn't interested in chatting, she dipped her chin and was about to leave, but a sparkle caught her eye. He wore a ring on the third finger of his left hand. So he *was* married.

Rubbing her own ring, hoping he hadn't seen it, she threw him an awkward smile, then started past. The design on his ring jolted her in place. It was the ring she'd given him on their wedding day. The antique one that had been her grandfather's. The one that matched hers.

"You're still wearing the ring." Her eyes glazed over, and her head began to swim. "I thought you would have gotten remarried by now."

"Kind of hard to get married when you already are." His eyes narrowed, his mouth tight.

"So we're still married?" In her mind they had been, but she'd assumed…

"Legally, sure. Can't call it a real marriage, can we? You saw to that."

What had she done to make him not want the marriage? In her mind, they'd been perfect. But then her mind was always the problem, wasn't it?

"But you still *wear* the ring?"

Fingering the piece of jewelry, he shrugged. "Keeps the tourists from getting too close if I don't want them to." He glanced at the college girls trailing behind Rico as he lugged gear up the hill. "I don't need another summer fling."

Fling. That's what he had called it in his text. The one that had ripped her heart to shreds.

He glanced down, then focused his eyes on her. "Why did you put Lapierre as your name on the volunteer form?"

It was her turn to shrug. "I don't know. When I think of this place, I think of you." Turning, she gazed out on the crystal-clear water of the lake. The mesmerizing liquid usually eased her stress, but it didn't do much today.

"I don't get you, Chelsea." His rough voice snapped her back to attention. "You use my name on the form, yet you seem surprised we're still married. How did you not know this? Did you sign divorce papers? Because I never got any."

His anger drilled through her, causing her to shake and look anywhere but at him. Or maybe it was *why* she didn't know.

"I looked through my father's papers at the house but didn't find them. I don't remember signing any, but I was sick for a while. I wasn't sure if he made the arrangements."

"Did you ask him to make arrangements?"

Shaking her head, she blinked back tears, keeping her emotions in check so Theo didn't see. "No, he usually did stuff like that without telling me. Maybe he didn't know where you were."

Dark eyes bore into her as Theo turned to stalk away. "Oh, he knew."

"Daddy, can you tell me that story again?"

Theo perched on the edge of Jordan's bed and fixed the covers.

"What story is that, peanut?" He had a slew of them he'd made up to entertain her if she wasn't in the mood for a book.

"The one about Mama."

Seriously? Where was this coming from? Had he exuded some vibe, making her want this specific story? Was there some psychic connection to her mother that told her she was close by?

"You sure you don't want another one? How about The Little Mermaid? The book's right here."

"No, I want the Mama story. Please, Daddy."

The power those little eyes had over him was intense. Sighing, he nodded.

"Once upon a time there was a handsome park ranger," he began, and she giggled.

"Daddy, you so silly." She reached up to hold his face.

"What?" He tried for stern, but a grin slipped out. "You don't think I'm handsome?"

Another giggle escaped.

"It's my story. I can make the park ranger handsome."

"You are handsome, Daddy." The hero worship in her eyes killed him every time. What would he do without this precious little girl?

"So this ranger lived in the beautiful Acadia National Park near the Atlantic Ocean. He had lots of friends but was still lonely. Something was missing from his life."

"It's Mama," she whispered.

"One day, as the handsome ranger was gazing out at the shimmering waters of Jordan Pond, he saw the most stunning woman. He thought he was imagining things. No one could be more beautiful than the lake. But the woman turned and smiled at the ranger, and right there he lost his heart to her."

"But your heart wight here, Daddy," Jordan assured him. If it wasn't for her, he would have doubted it.

"The ranger was pulled by the beauty of the woman. She said she was a princess from far away and had come to see for herself if the water of Jordan Pond was as magical as she had heard."

"It is." The soft words floated up to him from the dark-haired child.

"'It is', the ranger told the princess. 'It brings peace and harmony to all who gaze upon it.' The woman never wanted to leave. The ranger stayed with her, and they did lots of fun things during the summer."

"Pirate's Cove," Jordan yelled.

"Yes, they played mini golf at Pirate's Cove and then got ice cream across the street at Udder Heaven."

"What kind did they get?" Jordan's eyes got big. She knew the answer but loved hearing this part.

"The handsome ranger got coffee ice cream, but the princess wanted something truly special. Since they were in Maine, she wanted to try Moose Tracks. And you know what?"

"She loved it. Like I do, Daddy. We both love the same kind of ice cream."

"She did love it, and they got it every day. After a while, they decided that they loved each other, too. They went to the wooden bridge on the northern edge of Jordan Pond and vowed to always love each other, no matter what."

"And do you, Daddy? Still love Mama?"

"I do, peanut." God help him. Blinking back the moisture from his eyes, he finished the story.

"But the princess lived far away and had to go back home. The handsome ranger begged her to stay, but she couldn't. She promised to come back some day."

Jordan's expression was rapt as she waited for him to continue. Why couldn't this story have a better ending?

"Even though the princess couldn't stay with the ranger, she sent him a special gift as a reminder of their love and so he wouldn't be lonely. A piece of herself in the form of a tiny baby. One that would grow up to look exactly like her."

"That's me, Daddy."

"It sure is, princess."

Jordan rolled her eyes. "I'm peanut. Mama's princess."

Pressing his lips to her forehead, he stroked her hair and tucked her in again. "Good night, my little princess peanut."

As he got up, Jordan's tiny voice crossed the room. "Daddy, when is Mama coming back?"

"When she's ready." It was the same answer he always gave to that question. Luckily for him, she hadn't asked it too often. Shutting the light off, he whispered, "Love you, baby girl."

"Love you, Daddy." Her words were already slurred with sleep.

As he crossed the hall to his room, he thought about the question she'd asked. Her mama was back. They hadn't spoken much in the past four days. Maybe he'd avoided her for that simple reason.

After kicking off his boots, he moved toward the dresser in the corner of the room. It had been the one Chelsea had used during their two weeks of marriage living in this house. He opened the top drawer and pulled out some wispy fabric, then held it to his nose. The nightgown she'd worn. The scent had faded over the years, but the feel of it still evoked strong memories, memories he couldn't suppress anymore now that Chelsea had shown up again.

Easing down on the bed, he dropped his head into his hands and sighed. It was stupid and masochistic of him after what she'd done, but he couldn't deny it. After seeing her the last few days, seeing how thin and pale she was, seeing the pain in her eyes and wanting to take it away. Like in the story, he still loved her.

———————————◦○◦———————————

Why did Theo still wear his wedding ring? It was the question that had been running through Chelsea's mind all night long. He'd said it kept the lady tourists from getting too close. *If he didn't want them to.* Did that mean he'd let some of them get close? How close? And how many?

He'd had plenty of admirers the summer they'd been together, but he'd only had eyes for her. She hadn't been the prettiest or the one with the biggest chest, and he hadn't even known about her money until after they'd gotten married. It seemed he'd simply wanted *her.* Life wasn't always what it seemed.

Steering her car past the town of Bar Harbor, she headed north toward Hull's Cove. Fog misted the air this early in the morning, but she'd wanted to catch Theo before he left for work. Rico had hinted that he wouldn't be at the pond today due to some meetings he had to attend. Did the other ranger know her past with Theo, or was he simply guessing due to their strange interactions?

After passing Pepper's Pizza, she steered the car left and wondered if she wasn't crazy for doing this. Would he even be living in the same house? What if he had someone else living there with him? Yes, he'd said he was still married to her, but that didn't mean he hadn't found a replacement. Like the blonde with the little girl.

Slowly, she drove, trying to remember exactly where his street was. It wasn't easy in the fog, though the mist was lessening as she got farther away from the ocean. There it was. She remembered that huge rock on the side of the road with the weirdly shaped tree behind it. Her stomach tightened and her mouth grew dry as the car inched closer to the house, the small two-story surrounded by trees with the adorable farmer's porch on the front.

A car sat in the driveway. It was an older model SUV, the one he'd had when they'd gotten married. He still lived here. Pulling her Volvo to the side of the road, she took a deep breath and opened the car door.

Her legs barely held her up they shook so badly. Shoving the keys in her pocket so she wouldn't drop them, she inched her way up the stairs.

With hands shaking almost worse than her legs, she somehow managed to get to the top and knock on the door. Would he be mad she'd come to his house? Would some scantily clad woman ask what she was doing here? Maybe this hadn't been a good idea. No, she needed to know what had happened, and discussing it while cleaning up the lake trail wasn't feasible. It was too public. Maybe he'd be thrilled she'd come and get divorce proceedings going. Her stomach cramped so much at that thought, she almost doubled over.

The door clicked and opened, and Chelsea squared her shoulders. A soft, "Hi," had her gazing down at a brown-haired little girl wearing a pair of flowered overalls.

"Hi." Her lungs stopped working. Why couldn't she ever get over this reaction she had to children? Lots of people lost babies. It didn't stop them from living. "I'm looking for Theo Lapierre. Is he home?"

"Yep," she said bouncing up and down, opening the door wider for Chelsea to enter. Turning, she yelled, "Daddy."

Daddy. He had a child. And she didn't. How was that fair?

"Thanks for dropping her off, Angie," Theo's voice drifted in from the kitchen.

"It's not Angie," the child yelled back, then glanced at her again, her expression puzzled.

"Who—" Theo stopped in the doorway, holding a child's lunch box, his eyes wide and almost…scared.

"Chel." Their eyes met and something passed between them that hadn't been there this past week. What was going on? Was it because she showed up at his house? Was the scantily clad mom going to show up next?

The sound of a car pulling up front and a door slamming roused her from the trance she'd been in. Theo seemed to realize it too as footsteps pounded up the stairs.

"Sorry I'm late. I—" The blonde woman from the lake pushed through the screen door.

Before the apology could be finished or introductions made, Theo shoved the lunch box into a small mermaid backpack, then thrust the bag into what she assumed was Angie's hands.

"Time to go, peanut, or you'll be late for daycare. Love you." He all but dragged her to the door.

"Daddy." The little girl's face twisted comically. "You know I can't go until you kiss me."

Theo's eyes flew to Chelsea, and fear radiated from them. Leaning down he reached for the child, who tipped her head and giggled.

"You know where."

He planted a kiss on the child's neck. Not exactly what you would expect, but...Chelsea raised her hand to her own neck, then stared at the girl. Yes, there it was. A heart-shaped birthmark. Like the one on her neck. And her mother's. And grandmother's.

It had been Theo's little joke. It showed him where to kiss her.

Ice filled her blood, and her heart pounded so viciously in her chest she barely saw the woman and child leave. How could this be? She'd wished and dreamed for so long that there had been some mistake and her baby was still alive. Almost four years old. That's what age her child would be now. About the same age as the little girl who'd just left.

The child who had a birthmark exactly like hers. Theo's face swam in her vision as the room spun in circles. Her baby was alive. And she'd been with her father this whole time. The world went black.

Chapter Three

What was Chelsea doing here at the house? Had she come for Jordan? Five days of cleaning the trails without a word about their child and suddenly she shows up here.

After hustling Jordan and Angie out, he turned back to the woman who'd changed his world in so many ways. Color drained from her face as she stared out the door, then her eyes rolled back in her head. What the heck?

Her body crumpled, and he caught her before she hit the floor. How had she lost so much weight? Pushing her hair out of her face, he touched her forehead, then felt for a pulse. Rapid and strong.

"Chelsea. Chelsea?" Should he put her in the SUV and get her to the hospital? Who knew how long it would take for an ambulance to get here? He tapped the side of her face, and she began to stir. Thank God.

Her eyelids fluttered open briefly, closed, then opened again, panicked.

"My baby. You have my baby." Tears streamed down her cheeks as her voice cried out.

"Chelsea, what…?"

"You stole my baby!" Her shoulders rose and fell as sobs ripped from her lungs. "She's alive. How could you do that to me?" Her cries echoed loudly through the room as her body trembled.

"What are you talking about?" What was happening here? Why was she hysterical? "I didn't steal anything. You wanted nothing to do with her." The day Jordan had arrived here was ingrained in his mind.

Rearing back, Chelsea's eyes narrowed, then glazed over, focused on the doorway Jordan had walked out of. "They told me she was stillborn. That she died."

Stiffening, it was his turn to stare. Was this true?

"All this time—" Emotion saturated her words. "—I thought she was dead. And you had her. You *had* her." Lifting her hands, she pounded on his chest as the tears rolled down her face.

What she said wasn't making sense. How could she not have known?

He let her continue the abuse, wondering if he deserved it. Her whole body shook uncontrollably, hiccups interspersed with the sobs.

After a while, the blows weakened, yet she still rocked back and forth crying, "My baby, my baby."

Finally, she collapsed against him. "I never even got to hold her."

The high-pitched words shredded his heart. Her pain was palpable and tore into him like a machete. Rubbing her back, he let her continue. Hysterical cries lessened to soft whimpers, though the tremors didn't subside. The words, "my baby," were whispered over and over again like a mantra. God, he wanted to rip out her father's heart and stuff it down his throat. Pity the man was already dead.

Drawing her in closer, his own heart pounded a rapid beat in his chest. "Did you honestly not know about her?"

The eyes she turned toward him were filled with agony. Her lower lip trembled as she shook her head. "My father said there were complications, and she was stillborn."

"You never saw her?"

"They put me under for the birth. By the time I woke up, it was a few hours later. He said—" She collapsed into sobs again.

He wouldn't argue that no reputable doctor did this to a patient. Her father had enough money to buy not only a few doctors but a whole hospital if he wanted.

Burrowing into his chest, she sniffed and tried to catch her breath. God, what the heck was he supposed to do? If this was true…he didn't even know what to think. He'd been so angry with her for so long and now…

"I'm not imagining it, am I? That little girl…is my baby girl." Her eyes begged him to say yes.

All he could manage was a nod. This scenario had never entered his mind. Mostly, he'd thought she'd show up and finally be interested in their child. But to not have known about her…

"How did you get her? What's her name? I have so many questions, I don't even know where to begin."

The stream of tears hadn't stopped, but her breathing was slower. They were still sitting on the floor where she'd collapsed.

"Let's get a bit more comfortable, huh?"

Helping her up from the floor, he settled her on the couch, then reached in his pocket and fished out his phone. After sending off a quick text to his boss saying he'd be late, he sat next to her and picked up her hands.

"Her name is Jordan Marie."

That set off a fresh round of crying. They'd talked about giving that name to their first daughter.

"My father told you I didn't want the baby? How could you ever think that of me?"

"He didn't tell me. He sent some flunky to deliver her when she was only two days old. The message was you were too young to be a mom and needed more time for yourself. I was so flabbergasted with having to take care of a newborn, I didn't have time to question anything. All I knew was that you hadn't wanted to stay married to me."

For the first time since she'd shown up this morning, Chelsea looked strong as she sat up straighter.

"What do you mean, I didn't want to be married to you? You were the one who regretted what you called a *fling*."

"I never said that."

Her eyes blazed, then doubt crept in. It was obvious as soon as she started to question herself. Maybe now wasn't the time to get into too many details of their failed relationship.

"Do you want to see baby pictures of Jordan?"

Her head bobbed up and down rapidly. The baby book was on the shelf next to the fireplace. After getting it, he opened it to the first page and scooted closer to Chelsea. Her sweet scent was driving him crazy, but she had a right to see her child. How had he never suspected? Was he that stupid and gullible that he believed her father? Had he had so little faith in Chelsea?

Flipping to the front of the book, he pointed to the pictures of their child when she'd first arrived here. "I took her to the pediatrician right away. I wanted to make sure she was healthy."

"How much did she weigh?' Chelsea touched the picture lovingly, her eyes never leaving the page.

"She was six pounds, five ounces. Small. The doctor had wondered if she was early. I couldn't answer that question."

With a sigh, she whispered, "She was almost three weeks early. I figured I got pregnant right after we were married."

"I did the math, with and without an early delivery."

Her head whipped up. "Did you think she wasn't yours?"

Reaching over, he rubbed her back. "I never questioned who her father was. I know you were only with me that summer. It was *after* you left that things fell apart."

She didn't seem to hear him as she turned the page and looked through more pictures. Jordan's first solid food, first steps, first birthday. Then, later as she made friends and grew bigger.

"I missed so much." Chelsea's voice wobbled, and tears trailed down her face again. Pulling her against him, he stroked her hair and pressed a kiss to her forehead. God, he'd missed her. What in the world had happened? They'd have to hash it out at some point, but right now she seemed so fragile.

After leafing through the pages of the photo album, she flipped back to a few of the earlier ones. "You've given her lots of love, haven't you?"

"She's the most precious thing in my life." His throat felt scratchy and dry.

Her head bobbed up and down as she leaned more heavily against him. The occasional sniffle wafted his way, her fingers still stroking the pictures. The deep emotional turmoil must have depleted her reserves, because after a while, her eyes closed. Her breaths evened out. Asleep.

Easing her to a more comfortable position, he propped a pillow in his lap and laid her head on it. They'd been here before. Memories surfaced of him playing with her silky hair and smoothing it back from her face. Her hair was longer now yet still as soft as ever. The little heart-shaped birthmark called out to him from under her ear. It was so he always knew where to kiss her. That had been their little joke. He'd kept it up with Jordan.

No matter how much he'd hated what she'd done, or what he thought she'd done, he could never find it in him to hate her. Too often, he blamed himself for pushing her into marriage when she was so young. She'd barely been twenty and had recently lost her grandmother. Maybe, in the back of his mind, he'd hoped she would grow up enough to take responsibility and come back to them someday.

It was one reason why he'd kept the picture of their wedding day on the mantle. He'd never spoken ill of her to Jordan either. What he'd tell her when she was older, he wasn't sure. But he had never wanted it to be that her mother didn't love her. Now, he knew it was the truth.

When he'd first seen Chelsea last week, fear had run rampant through him, thinking she'd shown up to finally take Jordan back. With her father's money, he'd never stand a chance, no matter what the circumstances. Then, when she hadn't even mentioned the child, he didn't know what to think. Now, he knew why.

What he didn't know was why she never called or returned any of his calls or texts. His first priority was making sure that Jordan wasn't hurt in any of this.

The sound of a car pulling up shook him from his thoughts. The tread on the stairs sounded like Angie. Looking at his watch, he realized almost two hours had passed. She must have done her class with the Junior Rangers, then come back here.

As she opened the screen door, he put his finger to his lips and shook his head. Anger crossed Angie's features, but she stayed quiet. Maneuvering out from under Chelsea, he indicated the porch, followed Angie outside, and eased the door most of the way closed.

"What is she doing here?" Angie whispered viciously.

Leaning back against the porch railing, he crossed him arms over his chest and sighed. "Did Jordan say anything? Does she know who Chelsea is?"

"I didn't tell her if that's what you mean. But that little girl has looked at the pictures of her mother every day for years. She'll figure it out."

"Chelsea didn't know about Jordan."

Angie's eyes narrowed. "What do you mean she didn't know? How do you not know you're pregnant?"

"Her father told her the baby was stillborn."

"You buy that?" Angie had seen his pain for the past four and a half years. Chelsea wasn't her favorite person.

"Look. After you left, she passed out. Woke up hysterical about how I'd stolen her baby. The last hour or so, all she did was cry. There's no way you can fake that kind of anguish. It got worse when I showed her pictures of Jordan from the album you put together."

Angie's gaze roamed the woods across the street. "Time she'll never get back."

"Yeah, something like that. God, Ange, I don't even know what to do." His voice cracked.

Moving into his arms, she hugged him tight. She'd been his rock throughout all this. After taking his fill of her comfort, he stepped back.

"I have several meetings today. I've already missed the first one, but I don't want to leave her alone or wake her up and send her on her way. She's not in any shape to drive or be by herself."

"I can stay," she said, glancing at her watch. "I have another Junior Ranger class this afternoon at four. Can you be back by then?"

"I need to get through this meeting with Norma, and I'll take the rest of the day off. Thanks, Ange. I owe you."

Rolling her eyes, Angie waved him away. "If what she says is true, seems I'll need to change my attitude a bit regarding her."

"Make sure she's okay. I'll be back as soon as I can."

"Will you bring Jordan?"

That was a good question. One he didn't have an answer to yet.

***

The creak of old wood drifted into Chelsea's brain, and she opened her eyes. It took a second before she realized where she was. Theo's house. Where she'd seen her daughter walk out this morning. Her actual child. The one she'd given birth to almost four years ago. The one she thought was dead. Had been told was dead. How could her father do that to her? Her response to the tragedy had been devastating.

The stairs creaked, and she looked up to see the blonde woman from this morning stepping down. Theo had called her Angie.

"How are you feeling?" the woman asked, setting down the laundry basket she carried. She and Theo must be close if she did his laundry.

Sitting up, she tunneled her fingers through her disheveled hair. "Like I was bashed around in the water of Thunder Hole."

"You must have been tired. You slept for a few hours."

Chelsea glanced at her watch and saw it was after eleven. The last few days of physical labor at the lake, added to the stress of being around Theo and remembering their ill-fated relationship, must have taken its toll on her. Of course, she hadn't slept all that well in her grandmother's house which was still musty and dirty. She'd started cleaning but hadn't gotten far.

"Where's Theo?" After folding the quilt he must have covered her with, she arched her back to stretch.

"He had a meeting at work he couldn't miss. He asked me to keep an eye on you."

Because he didn't trust her? Or had he been concerned? Since she hadn't been around in years, the trust thing was more likely.

"I'm sorry to keep you from your work. I'll go now. Theo should have woken me."

Angie picked up the laundry basket and trundled toward the kitchen. "He didn't want you driving in your condition. Come on in here, and I'll get you some lunch."

Chelsea followed behind, confused. Why was Angie being nice to her? Was she so confident in her relationship with Theo that the ex-wife—actually, the legally married wife—showing up didn't bother her? Probably figured now Theo could get the divorce he must want.

"There's no need to fuss over me. I'll be fine." That was a lie. Her daughter had been within a few feet of her this morning. Her nerves were frazzled, and her stomach clenched in a ball so tight she wasn't sure it would ever come undone. What would Theo want to do about their situation now? There wasn't a chance in the world she'd simply back off and leave them alone again.

"I'm not fussing. You look like you could use a good meal, and Theo has some soup he made yesterday that I can heat up."

Settling herself in a chair at the table while Angie proceeded to the alcove off the kitchen, Chelsea looked around. It wasn't all that different from when she'd lived here. All two weeks of it. There was a new stove and refrigerator, the kinds she had mentioned she liked. The walls had been painted a soft yellow, also something she'd talked about doing when they lived here together. Had he done that on purpose or had Angie wanted those changes, too? What exactly had he told her about their relationship?

"Angie." The blonde looked up from throwing clothes into the washing machine. "I don't want you to think that because I showed up anything will change between you and Theo. He obviously got over me and now has you. I understand that."

She was proud of herself. The words came out calm and reasoned, though her first inclination was to scream, to tell her that Theo was hers and so was Jordan, and pour out all of her pain and resentment onto this innocent bystander … her replacement … no matter how kind she was or how good of a mother she'd been to their daughter.

The laughter that tumbled from Angie's mouth surprised her.

"Theo and I may be tight, but not that tight."

Had she read the situation wrong? The woman was doing Theo's laundry for Pete's sake. If that didn't say intimate, she didn't know what did.

"I'm Angela Cote. My dad and Theo's mom are brother and sister. He's my cousin."

"Cousin." She'd never met any of Theo's cousins. His parents either, since they lived in Ohio. They had been planning to have a big bash once she got back from telling her father. It hadn't happened.

The microwave beeped. Angie pulled a bowl from it and set it in front of Chelsea. It smelled delicious. Could she get it down?

Once the washing machine was spinning away, Angie grabbed a cup from the cupboard, poured coffee into it, and sat across from her at the table.

"I guess I should say I'm sorry." Angie stared into her mug.

"For what?"

After taking a long sip of the hot liquid, Angie looked up. "I hated you so much for what I thought you did to Theo. Tore his heart out, stomped on it, then abandoned your child. I didn't know."

The lump in Chelsea's throat grew bigger, so she only nodded. After taking a few bites of the delicious soup, she had calmed her heart enough to speak.

"How is Theo?"

"Now that you're back or before you showed up?"

"Both."

Sighing, Angie said, "He's adjusted to being a single dad well enough. Of course, I help him and so do a bunch of the other rangers and some of the people from town."

"I bet he's an amazing dad."

"He is." Angie's undiluted smile spoke volumes. "He loves that little girl intensely." Angie tilted her head. "She looks exactly like you."

"You think so?"

"Very much."

Did she dare encourage Angie to continue? "And now?"

"How's he doing?" Angie shrugged. "Confused. He told me what you said had happened."

Biting her lip, she said, "I'm still not sure exactly what did happen. All I know is that the baby I had, the one they told me died, is alive and living here." God, the tears were back, and she had no control over them. Story of her life.

Angie's gaze went everywhere but at her, obviously embarrassed. Chelsea was ashamed of how quickly the emotions reared their ugly head, too. The blonde stood and placed her cup in the sink after rinsing it out. Maybe it was time for her to make her exit.

But she needed to know one more thing. Something she wasn't sure she could ask Theo. The answer might break her heart, and she didn't want him seeing her broken again.

"What has Theo told Jordan about me? Does she think I deserted her? She never even knew how much I wanted her." The sobs could not be held back. They rushed forward, and she covered her face with her hands. Angie would know what she was doing, but Chelsea wouldn't have to see the disgust on her face.

A soft touch on her shoulder pulled her from her anguish. Angie's sympathetic expression wasn't what she expected.

"Come here. I want to show you something."

A tissue was thrust into her hand as she rose and slogged to the living room, following Angie toward the fireplace. Chelsea wiped her eyes and blew her nose, then watched as Theo's cousin picked up a framed picture.

"Theo keeps this right here, so Jordan can see it always."

What? It couldn't be. Their wedding picture? Why on earth would he still have that on the mantle?

After handing Chelsea the picture, Angie picked up another one. It was a close-up of her sitting at the ocean near Otter Cliffs. It had been the day Theo had asked her to marry him. The rapturous look in her eyes showcased how much she loved him.

"Why does he keep these here? It doesn't make sense."

"You'll have to ask him. But he's never said anything bad about you to Jordan. Not that I've heard. Every single day, Jordan kisses these pictures and says hello to her mom and dad."

She bit her lip to keep it from trembling. Theo could have said all sorts of rotten things about her if he'd truly thought she had dumped their baby with him and run. How could he have thought that of her? Hadn't they talked about having kids? Yes, it had been in the future tense, and they'd wanted to get established in their marriage first, but she'd definitely wanted children.

For now, she had to concentrate on getting through seeing her child. Would he even let her?

A tone sounded. Angie retrieved her phone from her pocket and answered. Her vague responses of "okay" and "probably" didn't tell her who the caller was, but the way Angie's eyes centered on her as she spoke told her it must be Theo.

Lowering the phone, Angie asked, "Theo wants to know if you're up for a meeting with Jordan."

The room started to spin. That old feeling of panic set in, but she fought it off. Chelsea held on tight to every ounce of strength she could muster.

Taking a deep breath, she looked at Angie and said, "Yes."

CHAPTER FOUR

"Is everything all right, Theo?" Dina Brannon, the administrative assistant to his boss, asked as he exited Norma Eldridge's office. "You didn't make your earlier meeting, and I wondered if something was up with Jordan. Is she sick, poor dear?"

Theo glanced at his watch and exhaled. He'd wanted to pick Jordan up early and get back to the house. Leaving Chelsea after her reaction this morning hadn't felt right.

"Because if she is," Dina continued, "I'd be willing to come over and help you out tonight. I know it must be hard taking care of a child all by yourself. I could even bring a bottle of wine to help relax you after."

"Thanks, Dina. Appreciate the offer." Not really, but he couldn't afford to tick off the person who basically ran headquarters. "But no, it wasn't Jordan."

"Are you all right then? Is it anything I can help you with?"

Might as well let her know. Part of it, anyway. The island was small when the tourists weren't here. She'd find out soon enough, regardless, then be upset that he hadn't told her first.

"Jordan's mom showed up at the house this morning." No need to tell her she'd been at the lake all week.

"What?" Dina's eyebrows couldn't possibly get any higher. "Why is she here? Is she looking to get back together? Make sure to tell her you have moved on."

Even if he hadn't? He'd been stuck in limbo for so long, and Dina knew that. Every time she asked him out, he'd used the excuse he was married.

"Legally, she's still my wife."

"Well, maybe now you can get that divorce. Let her know exactly how you feel about someone who abandons a poor, innocent baby. You've done such a great job as a father, but you know a little girl needs a mom. One who'll stay by her side and help her figure out the way to dress and wear makeup and navigate all those social niceties."

Dina sure knew about clothes and makeup and the effect they had on people. Men, especially. If he hadn't been hooked on a petite brunette with pixie ears, he might have looked twice at the buxom redhead. Or maybe not. Dina was too pushy sometimes.

"Jordan's not even four yet. I have a little time."

Stepping forward, Dina placed her well-manicured fingers on his arm. "Know that I'm here for you if you need me."

With a contrived smile, he moved toward the door. "Thanks. I appreciate it. Norma knows I'm taking the rest of the day off. I have to deal with this situation."

"Call me if you need a shoulder later. I'll be home." She waved as he marched out.

Taking a deep breath, he got behind the wheel of his SUV and started the engine. Get Jordan, then head to the house. How would he tell his little girl her mother had finally come home? Had she come home or was she only visiting? Was she planning to stay or head back to her fancy estate in New York? He needed to know before he left his daughter open for more heartache. *Like your heart isn't in the mix, too.*

Rico had texted him this morning to let him know Chelsea hadn't shown up at the pond. He figured Theo would want to know. When he'd texted back that she was at his house, Rico had only replied, *"Okay, let me know if you need anything."* It was great having a friend who cared without sticking his nose in everywhere.

"Daddy, you early?" Jordan squealed when he showed up to get her and she'd only recently finished her lunch. Usually, he didn't pick her up until closer to five.

Throwing her backpack on his shoulder, he scooped her up and said goodbye to the school staff. When they were close to the truck, she whispered in his ear, "Daddy, who the lady at the house? The one who look like my mama?"

After tossing the bag in the back seat, he placed her on the ground and crouched down to her eye level. "That lady is your mama."

She practically vibrated. "It is? She came back. Where she been, Daddy?"

Thinking of how pale Chelsea looked and how thin she'd felt in his arms, he answered, "She's been sick and wasn't able to be with you." He was sick thinking about all Chelsea had gone through, being told their child had died. It was unimaginable.

"Can we go see her?"

"That's why I got you early. She's still at the house."

Jordan bounced up and down squealing. "My mama came back for me! She did! Like you said, Daddy."

After getting his daughter situated in her car seat, he started the engine and steered toward home. What would he find? He hadn't asked Angie too many questions. She'd said Chelsea was okay. What that meant was anyone's guess.

The summer they'd been together, she'd been strong and loving, sad about her grandmother's passing but delighted to be on the island and outside in the beautiful, fresh air. The woman he saw this morning had been a shell of the one he'd fallen in love with. Still as enchanting yet hauntingly so. Because she thought her child was dead? Who did that to someone?

Jordan chattered away to herself on the drive back, mostly retelling herself the princess story he'd made up. Partly. The basics had been true, yet he'd never known for sure if Chelsea would ever return. Still didn't know what her plans were. Maybe he should have asked her before he let mother and daughter meet. She hadn't even realized Jordan was alive until this morning, so perhaps whatever plans she'd had would change. Could he change them, so they benefited him and their daughter?

Their daughter. He'd have to get used to that. For almost four years, the child had been his exclusively.

The car had barely stopped moving when Jordan pulled on her restraints. "Let's go see Mama."

After lifting her from her seat and placing her on the ground, he reached in for her bag. The little girl dashed up the walk and onto the porch. By the time he got up there, she'd pushed open the door and barreled into the living room.

"Angie, my mama is here. Did you see her?"

His cousin lifted her gaze to his, then looked down at Jordan. Chelsea wasn't in the living room. Had she left? No, her car was still parked outside, and she'd said she wanted to meet her daughter.

"She'll be right out."

Angie glanced at the bathroom door. The sound of water splashing came through, then the door opened. Chelsea drifted through, pale, washed out, and looking petrified.

"Mama?" Jordan stopped in the middle of the room and stared. Had excitement dimmed as reality set in?

As Chelsea dropped to her knees, the pain that pierced his heart was agony.

"Hi, baby." Tears poured down her face as she reached for the child. Jordan stepped close and lifted a hand to her mother's cheek.

"Why you crying, Mama?"

"I missed you so much." He could see the control Chelsea was trying for, but deep breaths shook her petite frame.

"Daddy said you were sick. Are you better now?"

"I'm getting there." Chelsea ran her fingers over Jordan's hair and down her cheek as she studied the little girl. "You are so beautiful."

"Daddy says I look like you."

Chelsea continued her appraisal of Jordan. "Being with you is going to help me get better a lot quicker."

"Oh, wait." Jordan froze, then ran off into the bathroom. Chelsea's hand reached out after her. A cabinet crashed open, then she came skipping back with a pink box in her hand.

"These are my princess bandages. They make me better with princess magic. Since you a princess, they make you better, too."

As Jordan babbled on about princesses, Theo moved to empty the child's backpack in the kitchen. Angie trailed after him.

"How long did she sleep?"

"Few hours. She must have been exhausted."

"I think a lot of it might be emotional exhaustion. How was she when she woke up?"

"Confused, quiet, sad. She didn't come out and say it, but she seemed upset that you weren't here."

After wiping out Jordan's lunchbox, he placed it on the counter. "I tried to get back sooner, but you know how Norma is when she gets going."

Angie's lips twitched at the corner. "She thought we were together."

"Together? Chelsea thought *we* were? Did she seem upset?"

"I couldn't tell. She said that I shouldn't worry, that she wasn't here to break us up."

What was she here for then? His gaze strayed to the doorway, so he could keep an eye on the two girls. Jordan was chatting in her typical way.

"I think I'll slip out the back and let you deal with this." Angie headed for the back door. "Call me if you need me."

"Thanks. For everything. Today and always."

His cousin left, and he lingered in the archway between the kitchen and living room. Chelsea remained on the floor, listening intently to their child.

"Your hair is long." Jordan pointed to the frame on the mantle. "I always want Daddy to cut my hair to make me look like you. Maybe I let it grow."

"Or I could cut it again to be like yours," Chelsea suggested.

Hopping up and down, Jordan squealed, "Then, we'd be the same again." Her little head whipped around, spotting him in the doorway. When she turned back, she lifted her hand. "Do you want to play in my playwoom? Can she, Daddy?"

"Sure." He could hardly take her new mom away so soon, even if what he honestly wanted to do was sit down and have a chat with his wife. God, that sounded strange to say that word again. Yet he needed to hash out a few things and find out exactly what her plans were. If she even had any. For now, he'd allow the two some time to bond. And hope it didn't backfire in his face.

———◆———

"This is my playwoom. Daddy says someday I'll get lost in the mess, and he won't be able to find me. But that's silly."

The room definitely had lots of toys. It had been a sitting room with a TV in it when she'd been living here. Now, it reminded her of the playroom she had growing up, though on a smaller scale. Was Theo compensating for something with so many play things? Like Jordan not having a mother?

But she did have a mother. And Chelsea was here now.

"What's your favorite thing to play with?" Top priority was getting to know her child. She had almost four years to make up for.

"This." Jordan toddled over to a large plastic dollhouse that was about the same height as her. Each room opened in the front, and furniture and dolls lay scattered about.

"What do you like best about it?" Her dollhouse had been one of her favorite things, too. Hers had been wooden and handcrafted especially for her. One of her nannies had always reprimanded her if she played too vigorously with it or dared to move the furniture or dolls. Obviously, Theo allowed her free rein. Knowing this made her heart lighter.

"I can make the dolls do lots of stuff." The little girl picked up a few of the dolls and began moving them about the different rooms, listing what each room was for.

Chelsea studied her child. According to Angie, Jordan looked exactly like her. There were similarities. Same dark hair and tiny ears. Upturned nose that crinkled when she laughed. Thank God her child knew how to laugh. Had she missed having a mother or not known any difference? Her excitement when she'd come in indicated having her mom show up wasn't a bad thing.

Her smile, on the other hand. That was pure Theo. The tiny dimple near the corner of her mouth, the crooked grin, and how her eyes shone bright with happiness. All Theo. It had been one of the things that had attracted him to her. His smile was addicting.

The color of Jordan's eyes wasn't what she had imagined. Neither the blue she had nor the light brown of Theo's. Jordan's were hazel with light brown specks in them. Would they change over time or stay the same? Shouldn't a mother know these things? Not a mother who had no child to show for the nine months of carrying a baby.

"And these are all a family," Jordan chattered on, showing her three dolls. "The daddy, the mama, and the little girl. She's Jordan, like me. They're a happy family, like us. Wight, Mama? Now that you're back, we can all be happy. Billy at school says I'm not happy, 'cause I only have a daddy."

"Aren't you happy with your daddy?" Fear coursed through her at the thought her precious little girl might be sad. Had she overestimated Theo?

"He's the best daddy in the whole world." Her little arms stretched as far as they could go. "I told Billy, but he didn't believe me. He don't have a daddy at home, and his mommy is always yelling about him."

"Does your daddy yell at you?"

"He don't yell, but sometimes he does this." She put her hands on her hips and made a face. "'Jordan Marie Lapierre, get your cute little bottom over here and clean up this mess.'"

Laughter slipped from Chelsea's mouth at the deep tone of Jordan's voice as she mimicked her father.

Jordan giggled. "Then, he kisses me wight here." The girl pointed to the heart-shaped birthmark on her neck. "It's so he knows where to kiss me."

"I also have one." Chelsea pushed her hair aside so her daughter could see. "That's what your daddy always said about mine, too."

The tiny squeal of delight that came from Jordan's mouth sent shivers of love and excitement through Chelsea. Anger at having this stolen from her followed behind. *Deep breath. Stay focused on Jordan. Don't dwell on the past.*

"Can I kiss yours, Mama?" Before she could say anything, Jordan stepped closer and pressed her lips to Chelsea's neck. The sweet touch filled her with longing and an emotion so deep she couldn't describe it.

"Now, you kiss mine."

Her daughter tilted her head and Chelsea leaned in, inhaling the sweet scent of her child. Something inside her roared to life. Primal and territorial. She'd die to protect this little girl. Her arms wrapped around Jordan and tugged her close, then she touched her lips to the satiny skin.

Tears welled and her lips trembled at the touch as she held tighter to this precious baby. She didn't want to let go. Perhaps her daughter didn't want to either as her hands tightened in Chelsea's hair, and she practically sat in her lap.

"Why did you call me a princess earlier?"

Looking up, Jordan grinned. "Because Daddy said you were."

Doubtful he'd meant it in a good way, but she wouldn't tell her daughter that.

"At bedtime, Daddy sometimes tells me the Mama story."

"The Mama story?"

"Uh huh." Jordan eased back so Chelsea could see her face. "A long time ago, a handsome park wanger met a princess at Jordan Pond, and she was the most beauuuuuutiful he had ever seen. Even more beautiful than the lake." The child's eyes almost bugged out of her head when she stated this.

"And when he saw her, he knew she was missing from his life. And he gave his heart to her."

Oh, God, had Theo really told this story to their child? Biting her lip to keep it from trembling, she listened as Jordan continued.

"And they did lots of stuff together, and her favorite ice cream was Moose Tracks, like mine. And they got married on the little wooden bridge at Jordan Pond and said they would love each other *forever*." Her little voice grew strong at the last word.

When Jordan's face fell, she knew what was coming next. Didn't want the story to go on.

"But the princess had to go away. The park wanger didn't want her to go, but she had to. She said she would come back, but until she did, she sent him a special gift so he wouldn't be lonely. It was a piece of her heart, and it was a little baby named Jordan Marie."

Leaning in closer, the girl whispered, "That was me. Daddy always said you would come back, and now you did."

Jordan threw herself into Chelsea's arms again and hugged her like she wouldn't let go. The embrace was returned enthusiastically. Holding her child seemed to make everything right.

Easing back, Jordan squinted. "Do you still love Daddy? Forever?"

Glancing at the door to see if Theo was nearby, she answered, "Yes, I do. Forever." It was the truth. No matter what had happened, Theo had her heart.

"He loves you, too. Forever."

Unlikely. He'd probably said it to enhance the story. How she wished it were true. With all he'd thought she'd done, there was no way he could possibly still have feelings for her, and emotions weren't something you had much control over. She should know. She'd never had any control over hers.

"Do you like games? I have Candyland, and Daddy says I'm a wiz. That means I'm good. Do you want to play?"

Her ping ponging from clingy to playful took Chelsea aback, but she simply smiled and nodded. "I'd love to." There wasn't much she wouldn't do to spend time with her baby.

Jordan set up the game and handed her a little gingerbread player, then started explaining what to do. It wasn't something Chelsea had done much as a child, since she'd mostly had nannies who didn't feel that sitting on the floor playing board games was in their job description.

After Jordan beat her three times, they switched to Chutes and Ladders. When her phone vibrated, she hated to take her attention away for even a second. Not many people had this new number. Sure enough, it was Frank Haggar, her father's business manager. He'd taken over the company when her father had died.

—*Where are you? I've been trying to get in touch with you, but you haven't been at the house all week.*—

Her fingers flew over the screen.

—*I'm at my grandmother's place in Maine. Not sure when I'll be back.*— Frank didn't need to know all the details of what was happening in her life. His job was to keep the pharmaceutical company her father had owned running.

—*I need you back here for some major decisions.*—

What did she know about running a multi-billion-dollar drug company? Nothing. Maybe if Frank knew a little bit, he'd understand she needed to stay here.

—*My husband is still here, and he has my daughter—the one dad said died. I can't believe he did that. Did you know?*—

—*Husband and child? What are you talking about?*—

Frank had been at the company for years, but it had only been in the last three or more that he'd moved into her father's inner circle.

—*Never mind. I'll tell you later.*—

—*When are you coming back? There are decisions that need to be made about your father's company—your company.*—

The company wasn't her top priority now. It never had been. And with her daughter gazing up at her with admiring eyes, it never would be.

—*I trust you, Frank. You make the decisions, and it will all be good.*—

It would be, now that she had her daughter back in her life. Did she dare dream of having Theo, too? For that happy family thing Jordan talked about? Shutting off her phone, she settled back as Jordan brought her a book and nestled snuggly in her lap.

CHAPTER FIVE

Theo stirred the pot of spaghetti sauce, then replaced the lid. It had been hours since Chelsea and Jordan had gone into her playroom together. A few times he'd peeked in but hadn't wanted to intrude. There was paperwork he'd needed to do. Technically, he'd taken the afternoon off, but he figured he could get it done while Jordan was occupied.

Quietly padding toward the playroom, he listened for joyful noises. A few times this afternoon he'd heard Jordan squealing in excitement, and the sound had played havoc on his system. What exactly did he want to come from this situation? For his daughter to have a constant mother figure in her life, yes. Did *he* want something too?

Honestly, he wasn't sure. He'd never gotten over Chelsea. He couldn't deny it. Once he'd fallen, he'd fallen hard. And permanently. However, this Chelsea was different from the one he'd fallen for. Weak, fragile, unsure. What had happened to make her this way?

Peering in the doorway, his heart skipped a beat. The two of them sat in the rocking chair in the corner, Jordan on her mother's lap. The sweet voice he remembered so clearly, the one that haunted his dreams even now, floated through the room as Chelsea read a book. Her gaze wandered from the pages to the child as she spoke, her fingers sifting through the girl's silky brown tresses. Her pert little nose nuzzled into the child's neck to inhale the sweet fragrance that was Jordan. He knew it all too well.

Chelsea looked up and blinked a few times, though not before he'd seen the tears lingering in her eyes. Had she been crying all afternoon?

"It's almost time for supper."

Jordan bounced in her mother's lap. "Is Mama eating with us?"

Again, Chelsea seemed unsure. It wasn't a look he liked on her.

"There's plenty. You look like you could use a good meal."

Pain crossed her face, and he wondered if he had caused it.

"Please, Mama, please," Jordan begged as she held her mother's face in her hands and rained kisses on her cheeks. The elation that grew on Chelsea's face had him staggering back. God, she was lethal.

"Okay, I'll stay." When she looked up at him, her smile dimmed. "If you're sure you don't mind."

"I wouldn't have asked if I did." It was amazing how he could keep his voice so neutral when every cell in his body screamed that Chelsea was finally back. "About five minutes. Jordan, you need to get cleaned up first."

"Come on, Mama," the girl said, yanking Chelsea out of the chair. "We needa wash our hands."

Theo went to give the spaghetti a last stir. As he was draining it, they entered the kitchen, Jordan still holding her mother's hand.

"Hey, peanut, how about you get silverware for all of us?"

"Yup." She skipped to the drawer and pulled it open. "See, Mama? I have a special fork for me. It just the wight size."

"Can I help with anything?" Chelsea hadn't moved from the doorway. "Set the table, maybe?"

"Sure. Dishes are in the cabinet." He tilted his head in the right direction, his hands busy spooning sauce and meatballs into a bowl.

When Chelsea stood on her toes, he couldn't help but peek at her petite figure and how her top rode up, exposing a tiny sliver of skin at her waist. *Down boy. You have no idea how long she's staying or even* if *she's staying.*

"Okay, everyone sit and let's eat."

"You sit next to me, Mama." Jordan pointed to the chair on her left. He sat on her right at the head of the table, farther away from Chelsea. Did he want her closer? His stomach was already in knots.

Using the spaghetti spoon, he dished up the pasta and placed it on his daughter's plate.

"How many meatballs do you want, peanut?"

"Two." Her small body bounced up and down on the chair.

"Two what?"

"Two meatballs, please." Looking at Chelsea, Jordan explained, "Sometimes I forget to use manners. But I'm weally a good girl. I won't forget again."

The child's eyes looked anxious for a moment. Was she afraid her mother would leave if she wasn't a perfect little angel? Would Chelsea leave? God, he wished he knew.

"We all forget things sometimes," Chelsea assured her, smiling that killer smile that had his knees buckling. Good thing he was sitting down.

When he scooped two meatballs onto Jordan's plate and began to cut them, she grabbed his hand.

"Daddy, I want Mama to cut my food, please."

"Okay, peanut."

His gaze searched Chelsea's face, but she simply picked up her silverware and cut the spaghetti and meatballs into smaller pieces.

"Is this good?" Now, Chelsea was the one who seemed anxious.

Jordan responded by gobbling up a forkful. Halfway to her mouth, she paused and mumbled, "Thank you, Mama."

"You're very welcome, baby."

Their little girl's face twisted. "I not a baby. I almost four."

"I know, but you're still my baby." Pain flashed across her face showing how much the deception had hurt.

After a few more bites, Jordan paused again, a strand of pasta hanging from the corner of her mouth. "See, Daddy? You don't needa worry about your heart anymore—cause Mama's here with it."

Heat rushed across his face as he sought Chelsea's reaction. Luckily, she was concentrating on her meal. Was she trying to save his pride or embarrassed, because she no longer felt that way about him?

Jordan kept the meal from being totally awkward with her incessant chatter. Usually, he joined in, asking questions about her day, but it seemed today she was on a mission to fill her mother in on everything she ever remembered doing. Chelsea was absorbing every piece of information and almost salivating for more.

It wasn't right to be jealous. He'd had his daughter's, *their* daughter's, attention exclusively for years and now someone else was her hero. It was hard standing down from what he considered his job.

Once finished, he grabbed his plate and Jordan's. Chelsea jumped to her feet and picked up hers.

"Let me help."

"I'll get the dishes. You're a guest." Her stricken expression dug into his chest, but the fact was she didn't live here anymore and hadn't in a long time. And it had been her choice. Hadn't it?

"Jordan, you need to clean up your playroom if you want a show before bed. Wash your face first. You're covered in spaghetti sauce." What would Chelsea do? Go with the little girl or stay here and talk to him? Was it pathetic to want her to stay with him?

"I'll help her." Before he could argue, she'd trotted off with Jordan toward the bathroom. The water sounded and some giggling, then more footsteps toward the front of the house.

The dishes and clean up didn't take that long. However, he moved slowly to allow the girls time together. Every now and then, some squeals and laughing floated out, and he couldn't help but grin. Jordan's laugh was infectious. There was no way her mother could resist it.

After wiping his hands and checking that everything was tidy, he wandered to the playroom and froze. It hadn't been this clean in…forever. Every little toy piece had been picked up, and all the games and books were sorted onto shelves.

"Daddy, look! It all clean," Jordan yelled when she saw him hovering in the doorway.

"I can see that. Did you do this all by yourself?" His gaze took in Chelsea as she tucked some of the dollhouse furniture back inside the large structure.

His daughter's impish grin split her face. "Mama helped me. We had a wace, but we had to make a plan first. And we did it all." Her arms spread wide as she twirled around.

"Thank you," he said to Chelsea, who stood wringing her hands, her face unsure. "And you, peanut, should say thank you to your mom, too."

"Thank you, Mama," Jordan yelled as she hopped over to her mother and jumped into her arms. Immediately, Chelsea wrapped their daughter in a hug and buried her face in the girl's hair. Any doubts he had regarding Chelsea's feelings toward their child were dispelled.

Giving them a minute, he peeked around the room. Maybe it wasn't quite as pristine as he'd first thought. Many things were hastily shoved on shelves or in the toy box. Still, it was a better sight than usual.

"Are you ready for a show? There's enough time for a short one before it's time to get ready for bed."

"Mama, you staying for the show?"

Again, Chelsea's hesitant gaze rose to his before dropping to Jordan's wishful ones.

"You're more than welcome to stay."

Chelsea took the hand that Jordan held out for her and allowed herself to be dragged into the living room and deposited on the couch.

"You sit there, and I'll pick a show." Jordan skipped to the cabinet and pressed buttons on the remote.

"Okay, we do this one. Daddy, you get it ready for us?"

After selecting the correct episode and making sure the volume wasn't too loud, he walked back to the couch, then paused. Normally, he sat with Jordan on his lap or at least squished up next to him, but she was already hugging her mother's side.

About to go sit in the chair, Jordan grabbed his arm and pulled him down onto the couch next to Chelsea, then stood looking at them both like she was trying to figure out where she should sit.

"Daddy, move closer to Mama, so I can sit on both your laps." The child waved in the air, showing him which direction to go. Bossy little thing. Could he be that close to Chelsea and still breathe?

Jordan wiggled into his lap, scooted half onto Chelsea's, then squirmed some more. Had she realized it wasn't comfortable?

Maybe she'd let him move away.

"Daddy, your arm. You needa move it. Put it up there." She motioned to the top of the couch, right behind Chelsea's shoulder.

Following orders, he slid his hand along the back of the couch and felt Chelsea stiffen. Was she that uncomfortable so close? They used to sit like this all the time, snuggled up together on this same couch, watching TV.

As Jordan bopped along to the music the cartoon characters were singing, Chelsea watched her, studied her like there would be a test later. Meanwhile, his eyes were glued to the woman he'd spent the last five years dreaming about, imagining she'd finally come home to them. And now that she had, he didn't know what in the world to do.

Crap. He was in a bigger mess than he thought.

A fidgeting Jordan told him when the show was over. "Time for bed, kiddo."

Jordan raised pleading eyes to him. "Mama help put me to bed?"

Did the little girl think Chelsea was here to stay? In this house with them? Or was she afraid Chelsea would vanish at the stroke of midnight? Would she? It was something he wanted to know, too.

"Do you mind?" he asked the mesmerizing woman next to him. "I have a feeling she'll get worked up if you don't." She was wired any way you looked at it, but this way maybe they could at least get her settled in her room.

"Of course not. Delighted to." That smile again, it stopped his heart. He only wished there wasn't so much sorrow tinged in.

As he herded Jordan up the stairs, he tried not to focus on the woman who followed slowly behind him. Jordan didn't need much in the way of directions tonight. Bouncing around from place to place, she showed her mom the bedtime routine, from pajamas to teeth brushing to the nightly story.

"Sometimes Daddy tells me a story, like the Mama one I told you."

Jordan had told Chelsea the mama story? What would she possibly make of that? Grabbing a book, he pushed it into Chelsea's hands.

"Read her this one. It's a favorite."

Normally, he'd be hurt if Jordan wanted someone else to read her to sleep. It was their routine, after all. But with all that had happened today, it was a relief.

Chelsea's soft tones floated on the air and wove a magic around both him and Jordan. The child relaxed, and her eyes drifted closed. It had been a busy, exciting, emotional day for her, too. Meeting her mother for the first time wasn't exactly a common thing.

Even with Jordan's eyes closed and her breathing deep, Chelsea continued to read the book as if she didn't want to break a spell. He was under that spell, too. When the last page was done, Chelsea sat watching their child for a few minutes.

He leaned down and kissed Jordan on the forehead, then smoothed back a stray lock of hair from her cheek. "Night, peanut. I love you."

As he moved back, Chelsea pressed her lips to their daughter's cheek, whispering her own words of endearment. When she stood, her eyes were filled with tears again.

He couldn't help himself. Cradling her close, he stroked her hair. What he wanted to do was kiss her. Kiss those sweet lips that had taunted him all day, heck all week, and never let her go. But he knew that would open flood gates he'd been trying to keep closed for four years.

Theo's embrace stirred up a myriad of feelings Chelsea hadn't had in years. Her instinct was to curl in closer, but most likely he was simply comforting her.

Reluctantly, she pulled away. Pressing her fingers to her mouth, she blew her daughter a kiss, then turned toward the door. Theo followed.

What was she supposed to do now? Was this the moment Theo politely booted her out of his home? The last thing she wanted to do was return to her cold, musty house. She had great memories of being there with her grandmother, however her grandmother wasn't there now. It was more of the same loneliness she'd had most of her life.

Once they reached the bottom of the stairs in the living room, she tried to think of something to say to prolong her time here.

"So, you never joined the FBI. Was it because of Jordan?"

Theo took a deep breath. "Yeah. I wanted a safer, more stable job, one where I wasn't traveling all over the place on different cases. Angie had applied for the position here, too, so I had family to help me with Jordan."

What else was there to say? Her eyes drooped, and a yawn made its way to the surface. It was time to go, but she didn't want to. Wasn't sure she could come back.

"Can I see her again?" Why couldn't her voice be stronger? Demanding. This was her daughter after all. She had a right to see her. Be with her. Didn't she? These crippling doubts that circled her constantly were a plague on her very existence.

The expression on Theo's face showed his horror. Was that it then? Would she need to get her father's lawyers involved to see her child? God, she hated using money as power like he'd done.

"Did you think you'd get one day, then I'd shove you out the door?"

Her breath whooshed back in her lungs, and her heart started beating again. He wasn't keeping their child from her.

Her eyes watered yet again, and she turned away. What must Theo think of the mess she'd become?

A soft touch on her shoulder turned her around, and soft emotion in Theo's eyes eased her anxiety.

"Of course, you can see her again. Do you think I'd get any peace if today was all she got of the mother she's been waiting for her whole life?"

Jordan. That was the reason he was allowing her access. Good, he should be thinking of their child. It was something she'd have to start putting as a priority, too.

"Let's sit for a minute, okay?"

After taking a place on the couch, Theo ran his hands through his hair and sighed. "I need to know what your plans are."

"My plans? What do you mean?"

"Are you planning to stick around, or are you going back to your fancy, rich New York world when you get tired of playing mom?"

Strength flowed into her and straightened her backbone. "You said you wouldn't keep me away from her and so I won't. Stay away, that is."

"Good." His expression was unreadable. What was he thinking?

"I've never been comfortable in the Westchester estate. I hadn't thought much past coming here and fixing up Gran's old house. Of course, I didn't know my baby would be here." Her stupid voice cracked.

Theo's eyes lowered, and his mouth tightened.

"Now that I do know, there's no way I'm leaving. I missed almost four years of her life. I won't miss any more. I'm more determined than ever to get the house livable and stay on the island near her."

"Is it unlivable now?" Did he honestly care or was this simple curiosity?

"It's okay, a little run down and musty. It needs new paint and an exterminator. I've been trying to clean all the rodent poop out of the cabinets, but it gets dark shortly after I get back from the pond cleanup, and I only got electricity turned on a few days ago."

"Maybe you should cut back on cleaning up the pond. Spend more time on the house."

So he didn't have to see her? Did he hate her so much?

"I can do both. And I'm not so high and mighty that I can't rough it a little. It'll be in better shape soon enough."

"If you need help—" He shrugged.

Was he going to help her? Did he want to spend more time with her?

"I know plenty of people on the island looking for handyman work, especially now before the tourists show up."

Oh. He'd find someone to help. Still, he hadn't booted her out.

"When can I see Jordan again?" Please, let it be soon.

"I'm at work tomorrow, and she's at school. You're welcome for supper again. I mean, you need to eat and probably don't have much in your house if you're only now getting settled in."

"Thank you. I'd love to. Can I bring anything? I don't want you to always have to feed me. I am capable of making food." Barely, but she'd muddle through if need be.

Theo fished his phone from his pocket and swiped across the screen. "Do you still have the same phone number?" His face hardened at that question. Why?

"No, there was something wrong with my phone after my dad died, so I got a new one." Pulling it from her pocket, she rattled off the new number. A second later, her phone sounded. It was a text from Theo. *My number is still the same,* it said.

"This way, if something comes up and you can't make it, you can let me know. I don't want to get Jordan all excited, then have her be let down."

"I'll be here. Nothing short of a natural disaster will keep me from seeing my baby girl. Even then, I'd fight my way here."

Theo got to his feet, so she followed suit. Guess it was time. Time to go back to her lonely, empty house.

"Can I borrow the photo album? Just for tonight?"

At Theo's dubious expression, she continued, "I'll bring it back tomorrow. I promise. I need something to prove to me that she's real. I was so freaked out today that I never even took any pictures. If it's okay, I'll do that tomorrow."

"It's fine." Moving to the mantle, Theo stared at their wedding picture, then picked up the baby book and handed it to her. "Will you be okay getting…home? I can try and find someone to take you if you aren't. I can't leave Jordan here by herself. It's one of the trials of being a parent. You're chained to the house once your child is asleep."

Was he trying to convince her parenting was hard? Yeah, she knew. Her own parents had failed miserably. Would she be any better?

"I'll be fine. Thanks."

Clutching the photo album to her chest, she eased toward the door. As she turned the knob, she said, "I'll see you tomorrow night." Or perhaps sooner, since she would probably do more pond cleanup tomorrow.

As she drove down Route 3 to Seal Harbor, she replayed the day in her head. Her baby was alive. It was still so hard to fathom. Her father had known and planned the whole thing. What had he been thinking?

Early in her pregnancy, he'd insisted she get an abortion. It was the one thing she'd stood up to him about. She wasn't killing her child. After that, he'd tried to convince her to give the child up for adoption. Since she continued to refuse, he'd apparently taken the decision out of her hands. At least, he'd given the baby to Theo and not some strangers. Did that show a tiny sliver of decency? Not particularly. How do you justify telling a new mother that her baby had died?

Parked in her grandmother's driveway, she fumbled in her purse for the keys. When she'd left the house this morning, she'd never imagined what her day would hold. The place was now pitch dark. Like her life had been after her father had lied about her child.

After flipping on lights, she threw her purse on the table and slumped in a kitchen chair. Her hands shook, and she lowered her head into them. Her whole life had changed in a matter of hours. Emotions raged through her, from ecstatic and relieved to angry and betrayed. But her daughter was alive and that would make everything better. Right?

It would, wouldn't it? Then again, her mother had never seemed happy, and she'd had a loving daughter who wanted nothing more than to spend time with her. In the end, it hadn't mattered. The stupor she'd been in so often consumed her and finally took her life. It was a feeling Chelsea understood.

Would it consume her, too? No, she wouldn't let it. Reaching for her purse, she took out the bottle of pills that were always nearby. It had been a few weeks since she'd last taken one, and she felt great. Would it last? Or would she fall victim to the depression and anxiety that had claimed her mother? She pushed the pills back in her bag and took a deep breath.

What if Theo found out about her mental illness? God, she hated that term. Hated that she had no control over things that others found easy. Would he insist she stay away from Jordan? Have her committed? Her father had kept her and her mother at home, never wanting them exposed to anyone who could hurt them. What had it mattered? Her mother had hurt herself. Permanently.

The light on her phone blinked, and she swiped the screen to check it. Frank had called a few times and texted another dozen.

It was only nine o'clock. She supposed she should call him back. After all, he had taken on the responsibility of a huge pharmaceutical corporation when it should have been on her shoulders.

He picked up on the first ring.

"Chelsea, where in the world have you been? I've been trying to get in touch with you for hours."

"I told you in the text that I found my daughter. She's here on Mt. Desert Island."

"What in the world are you talking about? When did you have a child? And you mentioned a husband? Are you having an episode, Chelsea? Maybe I should come get you and bring you home."

"No, Frank. I'm fine. I need to start standing on my own. My father took care of everything my whole life. It's time I did things for myself."

"You don't sound like yourself."

"I sound more like myself now than I ever have." Except when she'd met and married Theo. That time in her life had been perfect.

"You need to take care of your health. Remember what happened to your mother. You don't want to end up like her."

No, she didn't, but she felt like if she'd stayed at the estate, continuing on the way she had, she might have ended up that way. But why would she ever want to end her life now that she'd found her daughter? *Your mother had you and still committed suicide. Will you end up that way, too? Leaving your daughter alone and distressed*?

"I won't, Frank." Her voice was stronger now. This was something she could do. "I've got my daughter now and I feel so much better with her."

"Who's this husband? Your father never mentioned anything about you being married. I think he would have told me."

Had she told her father? That part of her life was so disjointed and blurry.

"He knew about Theo. Theodore Lapierre. He's a park ranger here in Acadia National Park. Maybe he didn't know I got married. That time was stressful, and I may not have told him."

"And what does this husband think of you showing up all of a sudden?"

"He has his own life now, but he's willing to let me be a part of Jordan's. That's my daughter." God, just saying her name out loud was so freeing. Her heart pounded louder and stronger. "Don't worry about me, Frank. I trust you to make any decisions about the company. If you need me to sign anything and give you the right to make all decisions, I'll gladly do it."

"I still don't like this, Chelsea. I'm not sure you're making intelligent decisions at the moment. You're still mourning your father's death and now you find out you have a daughter."

She wasn't in mourning, not over her father. Especially now she'd found out what he'd done to her. The thing she was mourning were her lost years with her child.

"I don't even know what to say about this husband. Maybe I need to run a check on him."

"Please don't. I know everything I need to know about Theo. Send me anything you want signed by messenger. I'll be fine."

"Chelsea."

Before he could say anything further, she disconnected the call. Frank had been a rock for her, but he was wrong about this.

Reaching across the table, she fingered the bottle of pills. No, her daughter was the best medicine anyone could give her. She didn't need these.

Your own mother took her life.

Doubt niggled its way inside as she clutched the medication. But, no, she didn't need them. Right?

CHAPTER SIX

"What are you doing here, Chelsea?" Theo asked, coming up behind her at the boat ramp on Jordan Pond.

"I'm helping with the trail." Her eyebrows slid together.

"I thought you were going to work on getting your house cleaned up and more habitable."

She shrugged. "I can do that anytime. The tourists will be here soon, and the pond won't be so quiet and peaceful."

"The pond's always quiet and peaceful, regardless of the tourists. I remember you telling me that when we first met."

Her little smile and mischievous eyes warmed his heart. God, it felt good to see her like this. Had one day with their daughter caused this change in her? If so, they'd need to spend lots of time together. Wasn't that a weird thing to say about a mother and child? It was so strange to think of sharing Jordan.

"Well, don't overdo it today. I don't want to be picking you up off the floor tonight at dinner."

Her eyes twinkled again. "I'll be good. Whose group am I in today?"

"Mine." Like he'd ever let her be in any group but his. After all, she was his wife and the mother of his child. No one else could say that.

"Lead the way."

Picking up his backpack, he slung it over his shoulders and grabbed the chainsaw. As they hiked, he explained that they'd gotten to the point where the trail was almost complete. This meant they would be working on pretty much the same area, so he and Rico had decided not to split the volunteers today. He also kept an eye on her to make sure she was all right.

"What were you thinking of doing with your grandmother's house? Anything other than painting?"

"I haven't thought much about it. I know it needs new appliances, and the porch railing looks a bit rotted. I probably should get an inspector to come out and tell me what else has to be done."

"Not a bad idea. Sometimes, you have dry rot or bug infestations that aren't apparent. I know a local guy if you want his name. He's fair and I trust him. You don't want to end up with someone who'll tell you the house is falling apart and then hook you up with friends for a kickback."

"Thanks, Theo. I appreciate it. Maybe you can give me his name and number tonight at dinner."

"Sure. Anything special you have a hankering for? I was planning to stop at the grocery store on my way home."

"I don't want to put you out. Whatever you and Jordan like."

"Tacos?" Geesh, why had he said that? The memory of the two of them making tacos and creating a mess rolled past his vision. Then, how they'd licked each other clean afterward. Stupid, stupid. Not the right time to be having those thoughts.

Her cheeks turned a lovely shade of pink, and her gaze flicked away. She remembered, too.

"I like tacos." Her eyes still couldn't meet his.

Grinning, he said, "We'll try and be a little neater tonight." Oh, God, what in the world had come over him? And why was it they were more comfortable with each other now than last week, when every second had been the epitome of awkward?

When they got to the spot they'd be working on today, he slid the chainsaw to the ground, then helped her remove her backpack. Tammi and Kelly came over and started chatting with Chelsea, so he moved away. He needed to kick his brain into gear for what had to be accomplished today. Starting up the chainsaw, he let the loud sound distract him.

All day he couldn't stop looking to see where she was, couldn't stop from reaching out to steady her as she moved over some fallen logs, couldn't stop thinking about tonight when she came over for dinner…and then later after Jordan went to sleep. Would they be able to talk a while, or would she want to skip out once their daughter was down? What did *he* want? He still didn't know. There were too many unanswered questions, ones he wasn't sure Chelsea was strong enough to answer yet. Today, she certainly seemed better.

As she rested against a tree, he approached and leaned in, taking her hand. "You'll need a manicure after this week, even with the gloves on."

Her answering smile did him in again. After stroking the etching on her wedding ring, he lowered her hand yet hated to stop touching it. This connection was making him stronger, too. Giving him back something he'd long forgotten.

When Tammi strolled by dragging a large branch, he took the cumbersome piece of wood, then started up the chainsaw. Tammi edged closer to Chelsea, as did Kelly. He wasn't usually a snoop, but since the two women kept glancing his way, he had to assume they were talking about him.

Once the roar of the machine died down, he angled himself closer to eavesdrop.

"Theo's a great guy, but don't set your sights on him, honey," Kelly said. "He hasn't gotten over his wife, though she hasn't been around in years."

"Yeah," Tammi joined in. "We don't want to see you hurt."

Chelsea's eyes sought his, and he quickly stepped toward them. "Now, listen, ladies. This isn't—"

"Any of our business. Yes, we know," Tammi replied. "But we don't want Chelsea to get hurt. If you were to finally cut ties with that no-good wife who abandoned her own child—"

"Excuse me," Chelsea said and stumbled past them. He started after her, but she shook him off, picked up a rake, and went to work on a section a few hundred yards down.

"Theo, we're sorry," Kelly said, patting his arm. "We like Chelsea, but be honest. You're still hung up on that wife of yours. It wouldn't be fair to any other woman for you to lead them on."

"I'm not leading her on." Heck, maybe he was. And it was time some people knew the truth. Chelsea claimed she wasn't going anywhere. They'd eventually find out who she was.

Rubbing his eyes with his fingers, he sighed deeply and looked to where she had gone. "Chelsea is my wife. Jordan's mother."

"She's what?" Tammi asked. "Holy cow. Now that you say it, she does look exactly like that little girl."

The surprise in their expression was expected but not the disdain. These two ladies were some of the nicest he'd met in the past four years, and they'd been amazing to him. But now their glares moved to the woman who had given him Jordan.

Following Chelsea's movements with his eyes, he said to them, "Don't judge. Not when you don't know the whole story."

He didn't even know the whole story. Soon. Soon, they'd have to hash things out. Get to the bottom of what had gone down. His gut told him her father had been involved with more than simply lying about the baby. Too bad his gut hadn't protested more years ago. His pride had taken over then.

When Chelsea picked up her backpack and slipped it on her shoulder, his stomach fell. Where was she going? Hotfooting it, he caught up with her.

"Listen, Chel. They don't know—"

"No, it's fine." Her quivering bottom lip told him it wasn't fine. "I think I overdid it a bit this morning. I'm not feeling well. Maybe if I take a short nap, I'll feel better. I still want to see Jordan tonight, if that's okay."

"Of course, it is. Go home and get some rest. We'll see you tonight. Is six okay?"

Her nod was weak. God, he hated to see her strength dwindle and disappear.

After he'd followed her down the path for a few minutes, she finally turned and said, "I'm okay, Theo. You don't need to worry about me."

Easy for her to say. But he let her go and marched back to the group. Rico waylaid him before he reached the ladies.

"Everything okay?"

It was all he could do not to roll his eyes. *Okay* didn't really touch this situation.

"Yeah, she's just tired."

"I know it's none of my business, and feel free to tell me to back off, but I noticed some of the hand-holding and you helping her with her pack. All that touchy feely crap. You were burned by her before, man, and suddenly she shows up, and you're back to playing with fire."

"It's not what you think."

Rico lifted one eyebrow. "I know what I see."

Gritting his teeth, Theo shook his head. "It's complicated."

"Whatever you say, man."

The desire to tell Rico what he could do with his concern bubbled up and almost spilled over. Besides Angie, the man was the closest friend he had in town, and there were some things he didn't talk to his female cousin about.

Tammi and Kelly weren't far off. Their faces still held concerned looks, mostly aimed at him. However, he didn't miss that their eyes followed Chelsea as she slowly trudged back to the trailhead. Waving them over, he figured he'd kill two birds with one stone.

"Chelsea, she uh…"

"It's none of our business, man." Rico meant it, too. If Theo said the word, his friend wouldn't mention it again.

"Her low life of a father told her the baby died. Then, he had Jordan delivered to me."

Their expressions all turned horrified. Rico was the first to blow.

"Who does that to their own daughter?"

"An extremely controlling man who doesn't want his daughter associating with riff raff like me."

Shaking his head, Rico actually growled. "I can't even wrap my head around that. It's too screwed up."

"No wonder she looked like a strong wind would break her this past week." Kelly frowned, her attitude taking a distinct U-turn.

Tammi looked skyward. "But I swear she seemed stronger this morning, more certain of herself. Happier."

"She spent yesterday with Jordan. She didn't even know about her until she showed up at my door. It was a pretty big shock to say the least."

"How did Jordan react to meeting her mom?" Rico was a tough guy who'd surprisingly developed a soft spot for his little girl.

"Bounced around like it was Christmas, Easter, and her birthday all rolled into one. They spent the whole day playing and reading books. Then, Chelsea stayed for supper and helped put Jordan to bed."

There was a question in everyone's eyes, but all lips stayed quiet. This was why he loved his friends.

Looking back where she'd disappeared to, Theo tilted his head and tried to get a last peek. "She's coming over for supper again tonight."

Kelly patted Theo's arm. "Will you tell her we're sorry? We didn't know. Didn't mean to hurt her feelings."

"I'll tell her."

Could he mention how sorry he was, too? For not believing in her? For thinking for one second that she didn't want her child? Their child? And would her forgiveness, if she gave it, ever be enough to get them back to where they were five years ago?

———◆———

Theo's SUV pulled into her driveway, so Chelsea skipped down her stairs and waved. She'd had supper with Theo and Jordan the last few nights, but today was Saturday. That meant he had the whole day off, and Jordan didn't have school. The suggestion they spend it together had surprised her.

At their house, she'd spent time with Jordan chattering on and playing games, then after she was in bed, Chelsea would thank Theo and head back to her grandmother's house. All alone. And not alone like she'd been in the huge house they had in Westchester, where there were a dozen people who worked for her father bustling about. None of them had ever interacted with her more than they needed to. Probably so she didn't learn of her father's betrayal. How many of them had known he'd given away his grandchild and caused his own flesh and blood to have a nervous breakdown?

"Hi, Mama," Jordan greeted her as she climbed in the front beside Theo.

"Hey, sweetheart. I missed you." Calling her *baby* had caused a wrinkled nose and pout, so Chelsea had moved to *sweetheart*. It seemed to sit better with Jordan.

"I saw you last night, Mama."

"I know, but I miss you every second I'm not with you."

"Like you missed me all the time you were away?"

"Exactly." Missed a child she'd thought was dead. Now, it was time to make up for that.

"Well, we're going to spend all day together, so hopefully that'll help with the missing stuff." Theo's jaw clenched, and his hands gripped the wheel. Was he regretting his offer of the day?

"We…we don't have to spend all day together. I mean…if you have other things to do." Her stupid voice couldn't even muster up any volume.

Clasping her hand, Theo looked her straight in the eye. A smile softened his expression. "Listen, pixie girl. We want to spend time with you."

Pixie. The nickname sent memories rushing through her and flipped her stomach around. Good thing they hadn't eaten yet.

Lowering his eyes, Theo took a deep breath, then gazed up again. "I want you to have as much time as you can with Jordan. I know how much you missed, and I still can't…can't wrap my head around what happened."

Guilt. Was that what this was all about? Theo wasn't to blame that her father had been a ruthless jerk.

"It's not your fault. You didn't know."

The guilt in Theo's eyes said he still felt responsible. Why? Because of the text he'd sent.

Her eyes crinkled with a smile, and his shoulders relaxed.

"Are we having bweakfast, Daddy?"

Pulling her hand back, she buckled her seatbelt and looked at Theo. His face colored as he gulped down a steadying breath.

"We sure are, peanut. Where do you want to go?"

"We go to Nellie's?"

Chelsea's curious stare had him saying, "It's a new place that opened up last year. It's in downtown Bar Harbor. Great home cooking."

"Sounds perfect."

The drive was filled with Jordan's little girl chatter, which only slowed down when Theo pulled in a parking space behind the information center at the Village Green.

"Can I get pancakes, Daddy?" Jordan asked as she grabbed Theo and Chelsea's hands and swung between them every few steps.

"Watch out, peanut. You'll knock your mother over, jumping like that."

"I don't mind," Chelsea answered, holding tighter to the child's hand. "As long as I know you're about to swing." And for the next few minutes Jordan kept letting her know she was going to swing. Every four steps.

The restaurant, Nellie's Kitchen, was only a block down on Main Street—cute, homey decor, and a dozen customers at a few tables. A woman with curly red hair pulled back into a ponytail stood at the counter. After tipping his chin to her, Theo guided them to a booth in the corner.

"Mama, you gonna get a pancake, too? They got real Maine maple syrup." Chelsea had to laugh. Her daughter sounded like an advertisement for the tourist board.

"Pancakes do sound good."

"Are we doing pancakes for everyone?" the redhead asked, strolling to the table with a pad and pencil.

"Hey, Katie," Theo greeted. "I think they might get pancakes, but I'll get the Lumberjack special. Chelsea, get whatever you want. Don't let the little pancake queen talk you into anything."

"I like pancakes."

"Me, too," Jordan chirped, bouncing up and down on the seat beside her. Was it good Theo was across from her? Less chance of him touching her, but there he was with his handsome face and the dimple at the corner of his mouth.

"Anything else?" Katie asked, scribbling on the paper.

"Bacon!" Jordan yelled. A few heads turned, and some chuckles floated their way.

"That's the way to go. You can never have too much bacon." A dark-haired man in a police uniform came up behind Katie and nuzzled her neck.

"Hey, I'm working here. Don't you have people to arrest or at least haul in for questioning?" Katie snarked back

"Aiden, how are you?" Theo said, reaching out and shaking the man's hand.

"Was hoping to get my wife for a few private moments in the kitchen, but she insists the customers come first."

Katie rolled her eyes. "Like he didn't already get a few private moments this morning."

Aiden patted Jordan on the head. "Who's your friend here?"

"This is my mama." Jordan's excitement echoed through the room. More than a few heads turned this time. What had these people heard about Jordan's mother? Her?

Both Katie and Aiden stared down at the wedding ring on her finger, then looked at Theo's. Yup, a matching set.

"This is Chelsea," Theo said by way of introduction. "These two clowns are Chief Aiden Cavanaugh and his wife, Katie. She owns the place. Best cook around."

"It's nice to meet you, Chelsea." Katie jabbed her elbow into her husband's side, most likely to stop him from gaping at her. Which he was. As were all the people in the restaurant. At this time of year, they'd mostly be locals, which meant they knew Theo and Jordan and the fact she hadn't been around since before her daughter had arrived.

Swallowing hard, a smile shadowed her mouth. "Nice to meet you, too, Katie. Aiden."

"We'll give you some peace, and I'll get your order in. How about some coffee while you wait?"

Picking up his cup, Theo said, "I'd love some coffee. Chelsea, did you want a cup of tea?"

He remembered she preferred tea over coffee? Did that even mean anything?

"A cup of tea would be great, if it's no trouble."

Aiden put his arm around his wife. "It's her job. It's no trouble."

"You're going to find some trouble if you don't go away and let me work."

As Katie sashayed away, Aiden smirked. "She loves me. What can I say? Guess I better get some work done, too. See you around, Theo. Chelsea, nice to see you again."

"See me again?" Her gaze met Theo's as the chief strutted away.

"Aiden's lived here his whole life. We probably crossed paths a few times the summer you were here."

She picked up her napkin and unrolled the cutlery inside. Jordan was busy coloring on the placemat with the three crayons Katie had placed on the table when she'd first come over.

Where did she even put her eyes? The people in here had gone back to their meals, but every now and then, some of them would peek over to check out what was happening. What did they all think of her? Looking at Theo was a big mistake. Every special moment they'd had five summers ago flitted through her mind, making her crazy that it had all been ripped from her.

"Pixie."

The name caught her attention as Theo's hand snaked across the table to rest on hers. The one still fiddling with her silverware.

"Don't worry about what else is going on. You're here with us, and we planned to enjoy the day together."

After a quick scan of the room, she voiced what had been on her mind. "What do they all think of me?"

His grip on hers tightened. A few more eyes roamed their way. Darn small-town folks.

"I've never bad-mouthed you to anyone. I want you to know that. I'm also not one for gossip."

"Thank you." Again with the meek voice. *Grow a set, girl.*

"When they see how much you love Jordan and how wonderful you are with her, the past won't matter."

"How do you know I'll be wonderful with Jordan?" Doubt crept in again.

His lips curled up on one side. "I've seen you with her the last few days."

"Mama, you draw me a elephant," Jordan piped up, unaware of what the grownups had been talking about. "They got a tiger, but I think we need a elephant."

"Hmm. I'll try, but I'm not sure how good it'll be." Concentrating on the picture was better than fixating on the way Theo looked at her, although she honestly had no idea what it meant. Sometimes, he seemed exasperated with her being there. Other times...it was like how he used to look at her that first summer together.

A teenager brought over their coffee and tea, with a juice for Jordan. Chelsea figured she should try some small talk with Theo but had no clue what to even say. The eavesdroppers weren't being discreet. Concentrating on Jordan seemed the best solution, but every time the child called her Mama, some head snapped up and checked them out. She felt like she was under a microscope.

When their order showed up, Katie asked if they needed anything else.

"We're good. Thanks," Theo said.

Leaning down, Katie whispered, "Sorry about my stupid husband. He's a work in progress. I'm glad Jordan's got her mom here now."

The pancakes, with their real Maine maple syrup, were excellent, but Chelsea wasn't sure she could finish them all. Not with the bacon and home fries that came with them.

"With the way you keep feeding me, I'll be fat in a month."

The look Theo gave her said otherwise. "And you'll still be the most beautiful woman around."

"More beauuuutiful than Jordan Pond," their daughter recited in a singsong voice from the bedtime story she'd been told. Both Chelsea and Theo laughed, and it felt good. Screw the others who lingered on their meals to see what would happen.

"So, what do we want to do today?" Theo directed the question to her, but Jordan was the one who answered.

"Pirate's Cove. Can we, Daddy? Please?"

"Is the mini golf place even open this early in the season?" she asked.

"Just last week and only on weekends for now. Are you game? This little peanut has gotten quite good with a club. She gives me a run for my money."

"Daddy's silly. He hits the ball all over the place."

When she'd played with Theo before, he'd been competitive. Obviously, fatherhood had mellowed that.

"Does he? Well, maybe we'll have to give him some lessons."

"I think I'd like some lessons."

The twinkle in his eye and the teasing tone to his voice set her nerves fluttering. This was definitely the Theo she'd fallen in love with and married.

On the way, Chelsea kept Jordan busy with questions about school and her friends. She wanted to know everything there was to know about her child. Then, as Theo paid the fee and Jordan helped her choose the right size club, a few people stopped to greet them. Theo was well known around the island and obviously well liked. The curiosity surrounding her was thick.

Navigating through the course, Theo acted like a kid, and Chelsea fell in love with him all over again. To hear her daughter squeal with delight and jump around so excited started piecing her broken heart back together again.

"I told you Daddy hit the ball all over the place," Jordan stated after Theo took fifteen tries to get the ball into the little hole. Luckily, there was no one behind them.

"What?" His innocent expression didn't fool her, not with the mischief gleaming from his eyes. "Maybe I need those lessons now, huh? Your mom seems to be doing okay. Maybe she should teach me."

"Fine," she said, narrowing her eyes at the gorgeous man flirting with her. It had been so long she wasn't sure she knew how to do it. "Stand like this and hold the club firmly. You're holding it too loose."

"Firm, you say?" Inching up behind her, he circled his arms around her body and positioned his hands over hers. "Like this?"

The warmth his arms provided was heavenly. "On your own club, you fool."

"This way I can feel how you're holding it. Much better, I think. Now, how do I swing?"

"Take it slow. Don't move too fast."

"Not too fast," he said with his mouth next to her ear. "Gotcha. Nice and slow. That'll help me win?"

Shivers coursed through her at the breathy quality of his voice and the feel of his cheek pressed against hers. His arm muscles contracted, tightening around her, ensnaring her inside the strength of him. God, she needed some of that strength.

"Yeah, win." Her own voice rushed out on an exhale.

"Swing it, Daddy. Hit the ball. But not too hard or it go too far again."

She stiffened at Jordan's orders, but Theo merely laughed, the sound tickling her ear. And her heart.

"Yes, ma'am." He adjusted the club slightly and sent the ball down to the end of the course. Before he chased after it, he pushed her hair aside and said, "You still smell like a garden."

What? He couldn't say that and walk away. Her mind was already a mess with the whole the-daughter-you-thought-was-dead-is-still-alive thing. Now, he was giving her compliments.

CHAPTER SEVEN

This game of mini golf was getting interesting. It had been five years since he'd done any flirting, not since Chelsea the summer they met, and he shouldn't be doing it now. Not when he didn't have all the answers he needed.

But it was fun. Her reactions were priceless, and the little shiver that had gone down her spine when he'd whispered in her ear hadn't gone unnoticed. Or how she'd leaned back in his arms when he'd put them around her. Her mouth may have told him to use his own club, but her body had said to stay close. He was listening to her body for the moment.

Seeing Jordan so excited was what made this all right. He and Chelsea would find some time to talk, but for the time being it was important for Jordan to be with her mother.

Unfortunately, the looks some of the people from town had been shooting their way were bursting Chelsea's bubble of happiness at being with their daughter. Why couldn't folks simply mind their own business?

Although, to be fair, many of them knew his situation and how much he'd struggled raising Jordan by himself over the years. Their concern was warranted. But unless he wanted to walk around shouting out Chelsea's personal tragedy, things wouldn't change.

"I did it. I did it," Jordan crowed as her ball fell into the last hole and disappeared.

"Great job, sweetheart." Chelsea's face beamed with pride and brought her back to life. Or maybe Jordan was the reason for it, along with some solid meals the last few days.

"You go next, Mama. Daddy will take all day."

After grinning at him, Chelsea gave her ball a tiny whack. The tilt of the course sent the ball straight into the hole.

"Can we go get a toy while Daddy is playing?" Jordan asked, her eyes twinkling. Little imp.

"It won't take me that long, peanut. Watch." A miniscule tap. Right into the hole. They didn't even pretend to make this one challenging.

They returned their clubs to the window and spun the ship's wheel, Jordan jumping up and down like a pogo stick when she won a token for a free game.

"Now, we hafta come back. Next time, you can win, Mama."

Jeremy inside did a double take at the word *Mama,* and Theo wanted to tell him to jump in a lake.

When they headed through the parking lot to the SUV, Jordan glanced over at the large building next door.

"Daddy, can we go to the Log Cabin?"

Shaking his head, he laughed. "We only finished breakfast a few hours ago. You can't be hungry again."

"Just some bacon, Daddy, please?"

"Warning," he said to Chelsea. "This one is always hungry. How about you?"

She touched her stomach. "Not really. I'm not used to eating this much."

"I can tell."

Her gaze flittered away, and her mouth tightened. Crap, he'd done it again.

Seizing her elbow, he tugged until she stepped closer. "I'm sorry. I didn't mean to hurt your feelings. You're thinner than you were when we were…together."

A smirk crossed her face as she placed her hands on her hips. "You mean I was fat back then?"

He couldn't stop the chuckle that erupted. "Hardly, little pixie girl."

As he tugged her along beside him and Jordan skipped on her other side, a few townies waved to them. Curiosity wafted in their direction.

"What should we do now?"

Lowering her eyes, she started to pull away. He clutched her hand tighter. No way he was letting others spoil their day.

"Maybe we should go home." Her head whipped up. "I mean, your house."

"Why? It's a gorgeous day, and the weather is perfect." He knew why, but would she admit it?

"These people…they're all walking around judging me."

As they neared the vehicle, he stopped right in front of her. "Their opinions don't matter. Jordan and me. Those are the ones that do."

He stroked her cheek. "Is there any place you'd like to go?"

One slender shoulder lifted and lowered. "Some of the shops downtown. I know we were just there, but…"

"We have all day. We can go anywhere."

God, he wanted to hold her, kiss her, and take away all the negative she'd experienced today. Once they got back to town and were strolling past the shops, she seemed to relax.

On Cottage Street, Chelsea stopped in front of a salon and tilted her head. After looking around, she shrugged and walked on.

"Did you need something in there?"

That uncertain expression crossed her face, the one he never wanted to see again.

"Not really."

"Chelsea?"

"Mama need her hair cut like mine," Jordan piped in.

"Hmm. Actually, you, little bug, could use a trim, also. It's been a while since your last cut."

"Can we get the same hair cut?" The girl jumped up and down at the thought.

"You might need an appointment." Chelsea chewed on her lip.

Theo peeked inside. "Only one other customer in there. Might as well do it now. They close in a couple hours. Let's check."

As he took a step through the doorway, he shouted, "Hey, Rhonda. You got time for a few girly haircuts? It's a twofer deal."

"Always time for Jordan and any friend of hers," the perky blonde replied. "Come on in."

Jordan dragged Chelsea inside and over to the chairs. As he reached in his pocket for his wallet, Chelsea stopped him.

"I have plenty of money. I can afford to pay for my haircut and my daughter's."

Rhonda's eyes got wide, but she didn't say a word. Working here, she heard a lot of gossip. Luckily, she wasn't the type to pass it around.

"I'll take care of them, Theo. You come back in an hour, and they'll be ready."

"Thanks, Rhonda. When I return, perhaps you'll both have your appetite back, and I can take my two pretty girls to lunch."

As he exited, he heard Jordan say, "This is my Mama, and we want the same haircut, so we look 'zactly alike." That would get tongues wagging. Especially since the other customer was Mrs. Narlee, who had to be the first person to know anything in this town and the first to tell everyone.

Even without similar hair, the two could hardly be thought of as anything but mother and child. It was why they'd gotten so many stares today. Chelsea had only been around for four months the summer they got married. And he'd kept her to himself, not wanting to share. Most people hadn't met her.

Heading back toward the Village Green, he decided he would check in at the information center there. A new volunteer had started, and he wanted to make sure she was working out okay.

It only took a few minutes to walk there, make sure she had everything she needed, chat with some locals, and leave. He had time to kill, so he headed toward the harbor and took a seat on a bench in Agamont Park. Typically, bench space was at a premium, but since it was only the end of April, he found a few open.

The harbor was beautiful, and the view of Bar Island and the other small islands spectacular. There were a few dozen small fishing boats scattered throughout the harbor. The luxury boats and summer charters hadn't arrived yet.

It gave him time to think, although maybe he shouldn't. If he did, he might get too upset over the years where Chelsea wasn't here. Jordan had been deprived of a mother. He'd been deprived of a wife and partner and someone to help him raise their child. But, God, Chelsea had been deprived of her baby. At least, he'd always had Jordan. It didn't matter what he did now, Chelsea and Jordan would never get that time back. It made him want to punch a hole in something…or someone. But that someone was already dead.

Inhaling the fresh ocean air, he relaxed his tight muscles and tried to clear his head. Memories of when he and Chelsea had first met and fallen in love still surfaced and washed over him like a huge wave. So much for relaxing. But it had been nearly an hour, so he took one last look at the peaceful scene and headed back to Cottage Street.

A familiar red sports car pulled up to the curb and parked as he approached. Dina. Seriously? Could there be worse timing? Maybe if he stayed back, she wouldn't notice him. Right, and a cat wouldn't notice a newly opened can of tuna.

"Theo. How wonderful to see you out and about and in your civvies." The look she gave his jeans and Henley was like a lion checking out his next meal. "Does someone else have the darling girl today? If so, maybe we could do lunch. I've got a quick appointment in here first."

Glancing at her hair, all poofed and sprayed, he wondered what she could possibly be getting done. His curiosity must have crossed his face.

"Need my nails filled in," she said, holding out her red claws. It was still a mystery how she managed to type with them.

"I've got plans for lunch, sorry. Jordan's in here getting her hair cut." Maybe he could extract them quickly while Dina was busy with the nail thing.

When Dina latched onto his arm and pulled him inside the shop, he knew he had said the wrong thing.

"Let's go see the precious girl and what Rhonda has done for her."

"Perfect timing," the salon owner announced as they wandered inside. "Two beautiful girls exactly as ordered."

Dina's red claws tightened on his arm at Rhonda's words. Extracting himself, he strolled toward the chairs where Jordan was having her cape removed. Chelsea picked the little girl up, so she could look in the mirror.

When they turned toward him, Chelsea holding Jordan, their faces so close together, air froze in his lungs. Good God, they looked alike. Jordan's hair was mostly trimmed up, but Chelsea now sported long bangs that fringed the top of her eyebrows and shorter hair bobbed under, barely brushing her collar. Like the day they'd met. The day he'd fallen in love with her.

Color rushed to her cheeks, and she tucked a strand behind the shell of her ear. She'd blushed often when they'd first met. It had been apparent she hadn't been all that experienced, but he'd been pleased to help her learn. Slowly. It had taken most of the summer and lots of time spent together, but he'd finally kissed her, and she'd blossomed in his arms. By the middle of August, he knew he couldn't live without her and had proposed. Especially after she'd mentioned she was going back home soon.

Proceeding closer, he knew he needed to find out exactly what happened. Having Jordan around made it harder to find time to do this, since it wasn't a kid-friendly topic.

"Aren't you going to introduce us, Theo?" Dina purred next to him, her talons somehow finding their way back to his arm.

Dina already knew who this was. She had to. Why was she playing games?

Shaking his arm loose, he stepped forward and laced his hand with Chelsea's. "Dina, this is my wife, Chelsea. Chelsea, this is Dina Bannon. She works at headquarters with me."

A little sound came from Dina's mouth, but when he glanced at her, she had smoothed her features into something fairly pleasant.

"And we're friends. Good friends." Dina's buttery smile slid their way.

"We'll let you get that nail thing done, Dina. See you Monday." Thanking Rhonda, he took Jordan from Chelsea and carried her with one arm and wrapped his other one around his wife.

His wife. It felt strange to say that but good. Maybe he needed to keep saying it.

Once on the street, he lowered their daughter to the ground and took her hand, while entwining his other into Chelsea's. They walked in silence for a few minutes, then Chelsea paused.

"Why was that woman glaring daggers at me, Theo?"

"Daggers? That's a bit dramatic, don't you think?"

Her head tilted. "If looks could kill, I'd be bleeding out all over the sidewalk right now. Who is she?"

He shrugged. "She's my boss's secretary, so I see her often."

"See her? As in dating?" Her hand disengaged from his, and the corners of her mouth pinched.

"No, not like that."

"It's okay, Theo. If you dated. I mean you thought I was gone, right? And it's been years."

Glancing around, he shook his head. The streets weren't crowded. Even so, this wasn't the place for this discussion.

"We're going to talk about this soon. Not here. But, for the record, I'm a married man and have never done anything to break my marriage vows."

As they meandered down the street toward the car, he had to wonder. It *had* been a number of years, and he'd never looked at another woman since Chelsea had left. Could she say the same?

————◆————

She's out cold."

Chelsea glanced into the back seat. Jordan's head lolled over to one side, her thumb in her mouth, eyes closed. It had been a long and busy day.

"Does she usually take a nap in the afternoon?" she asked. It was a little after four. Wasn't it sad that a mother didn't know this about her child?

"The school says she naps most days for a short while. Usually about one o'clock. At home, not so much, unless she's had a busy day like today. The car will do it, too."

"Will she still sleep tonight? You know, because it's so late in the afternoon."

Theo steered to the side of the Park Loop Road and pulled into a spot next to a bench overlooking the ocean. "She won't go down at the regular time, most likely. But it's a weekend and there's no school tomorrow, so it shouldn't be a problem."

"Do you think we should wake her up? I mean, so she'll go to bed on time." She loved putting Jordan to bed. However, since they had picked her up today, Chelsea would have to be dropped off while Jordan was still up. Why hadn't she thought of that earlier?

Theo drummed his fingers on the steering wheel. "I wanted to use this time for us to talk."

Talk. What about? Why he hadn't wanted her? This lady Dina, who obviously didn't like her but was enamored with Theo? Something worse? Better?

"I guess."

Theo opened the window near Jordan a few inches, then pressed the button to put his all the way down. "Let's go sit on the bench outside. We can catch the last of the sun before it gets too chilly."

"What if Jordan wakes up?" Or if he wanted to talk about something she couldn't handle?

"The bench is literally next to her window. We'll hear her. She'll be fine."

But would Chelsea? Opening her door, she got out and gently closed it. Maybe she should slam it, so Jordan would wake up and they could postpone their chat.

Theo was having none of it. He captured her hand and led her to the bench. As they sat down, his thumb caressed her skin.

"First of all, I want to let you know that I have never broken our wedding vows, pixie. We've been officially married all these years, and I've respected that."

"I wouldn't blame you if you had. Dina is beautiful and confident." *Unlike me.* "If you wanted to take her up on what she was offering, I'd get it."

"I won't lie and say she hasn't made a play for me, but I've never led her on. Even if I wasn't married, I'm not sure I would have dated her."

Her gaze moved over the rolling waves of the ocean. It felt like they were inside her.

"Have you?"

Waiting, she raised an eyebrow. "Have I…?"

He lifted a shoulder and looked away. "Gone out with anyone else? Like you said, it's been a long time."

"Oh, God, no. I took our marriage vows seriously, too. I barely even left the house." The fact she'd barely left her bed many times wasn't something she wanted to share. Would he be horrified at her health problems and push her away from their daughter?

"Except that trip to Europe, right?"

Her trip? "Europe? Are you talking about the trip I took in high school? That was before I met you."

"Maybe we should start at the beginning. Like the week you left to go back home."

Lifting her face to his, she waited for him to continue.

"You texted me as soon as you got home to tell me you arrived safely. I texted back that I loved you and couldn't wait to see you again."

"I got those." The ridiculous tears started again.

"Then what happened? I didn't hear from you for a while and got worried."

"I told my dad that I'd met someone, fallen in love, and wanted to move back to Bar Harbor. Needless to say, he kind of freaked out. He told me to forget it, forget you."

Theo took a deep breath in. "And so you did."

"What?" Her eyes snapped to his face. His jaw was set, and his mouth had formed a thin line. "No, I've never forgotten you. I tried to call, but I had misplaced my phone and didn't end up finding it until the next day. But as soon as I did, I called you. You never answered. I kept calling, and you never picked up."

"Chelsea, I had my phone on me almost every second at that point. If you'd called, I would have picked up. And if for some reason I wasn't able to, you should have left a message."

"It never went to voicemail." Which had left her wondering if Theo had turned that off.

"Well, yours did the few dozen times I called. I left more messages than I could count. I was frantic at not hearing from you, but I was still new at the Ranger Station. I couldn't just up and leave."

"I never got any voice messages from you, Theo. Only the text message."

"Which text? Because I must have left a few thousand of them, begging you to call or contact me somehow."

"You said it had been a fun summer, but don't bother coming back. I was a great fling, but you needed to move on." That message had left her emotionally devastated.

His expression grew thunderous. "I never sent that message, Chelsea. You were more than a summer fling. You were my wife, for God's sake. I loved you."

Loved. Past tense. A piece of her heart chipped off and fell away.

"The message was from your phone number. When I responded and asked why, you never texted back or answered any of my calls."

Standing, Theo shoved his hand through his hair as his shoulders rose and fell. "You said you'd lost your phone. Could your father have gotten it? Tampered with it? Was he that controlling?"

Until recently, she would have said no, but now she understood the true extent of what he'd done, it all made sense.

"Oh, God," she cried. "Is it even possible to manipulate a phone that way?"

Sitting back beside her, he threaded his fingers through hers. "There's a lot that can be done with technology, if you know how."

"Or have enough money to pay someone who does. I am so sorry, Theo."

His warm arms wrapped around her. He held her close to his chest, so close she could hear his heartbeat. Could she stay here forever?

"You never went to Europe then either, I'm assuming." His thumb caressed her cheek.

"No. The only time I ever went was right before graduation, although for me it was more finishing up my studies. I was homeschooled by tutors from the time I was about ten. After I begged him, my father allowed me to go on a trip with some other students to visit the museums of Europe. He sent along two of my tutors and a bodyguard. Why are we talking about that?"

"After you'd been gone almost a month, you finally sent a message asking me to stop contacting you. You had made a foolish decision to move to Bar Harbor with me. You said you were sorry and hadn't meant to hurt me, but you were too young to commit to one guy right now."

Tears fell as she shook her head, easing out of his arms. "That wasn't me."

"I get that now. At the time, I was ticked off. I took a few days and drove to Westchester, to your home."

"What? How did I not know?" The answer was obvious. Her father.

"I tried to get inside to see you, but the guy at the gate said you weren't home. When I got kind of loud and insisted on coming in, your father came over. He apologized for you and said you had done this a few times."

Theo twisted the ring on his finger, then continued. "I wondered if he meant gotten married, but then he showed me a picture of you on his phone. You were with some other young people in front of the Eiffel Tower, and you were all laughing. There was a blond guy with his arm around your shoulder, smiling at you. Your father told me that young love was fickle."

Finally, she reached over and touched him. Aside from trying to hit him when she'd first found out about Jordan, it was the first time she'd initiated contact since she'd been back.

"That was two years before I met you, Theo. That guy was nice, but we never did anything."

For a moment, Theo stared at his lap. Then, a hesitant, almost coy grin crept onto his face. "Well, that I know. You were quite innocent when we first got together."

Her heart soared at his playful manner, then plummeted again. He'd said he loved her. Was it too late to get that back? If they did, would it only end again when he found out about her condition? Was it selfish of her to want to get to know her daughter better? Spend time with her? They'd been having fun, but would it last? Could she continue to fool them into thinking she was fine?

Too many questions plagued her. The worst was knowing her own mother had still succumbed to the disease, even with a daughter who loved her so much. Did she want Jordan to get attached and then lose her the way Chelsea had lost her mom? If she went away right now, maybe it would be better. It would be easier to lose something you never knew you had, right? How did she know what was best?

CHAPTER EIGHT

"We going a your house, Mama?" Jordan called out from her seat in the back of the SUV.

After their talk, Jordan had woken up and insisted they walk along the ocean. Theo had wanted to continue the conversation, but it wasn't for little ears. Their daughter didn't need to know all the deception and lies that had transpired years ago. It was hard enough for him to understand it.

"It was my grandmother's house," Chelsea replied. "But she died a few years ago, so now it's mine."

"Can I see it? Daddy, can we go inside?"

As he pulled in the driveway, he peeked at Chelsea and raised his eyebrow in question. Her nod told him it was okay.

"Sure, peanut, but we aren't staying long. Your mother probably has lots of things to do since we kept her out all day, and it's getting late." They'd stopped for a quick bite of supper before dropping Chelsea off, since he wasn't sure how much food she had in her house.

They trotted up the porch steps and Jordan twirled around, her eyes wide. "Mama, you get to look at the ocean all the time."

"I do, sweetheart. It's very healing."

God, he hoped it healed her. Seeing her so meek and pale stabbed him in the heart. Time with her daughter should help, as well. And perhaps being with him?

After unlocking the front door, Chelsea led them in. "It needs lots of work. Still smells musty. I've opened the windows a few times, but it's too chilly at night to leave them that way."

"It is kind of cold," he said, noting the stale odor. It was April in northern Maine. The mercury often dipped low at night. "Have you set the thermostat to a certain temperature?"

Chelsea's gaze lowered to the floor. "The heat isn't on. I'm not sure how to do that. I think the control is in the basement."

"I can look for you before we leave. Why don't you give Jordan a tour?" He'd seen the house plenty when they'd been together, had helped her pack up her grandmother's clothes and things that she didn't need. They hadn't realized Chelsea wouldn't be coming back right away.

Taking Jordan's hand, Chelsea roamed from the spacious entry hall through the living room. It still had all the old Victorian furniture in it with the dated wallpaper and pictures.

"Are you leaving it like this?" he asked.

"I hadn't thought that far yet. This is all Gram's stuff, and I loved her, but it's not family friendly. I wouldn't mind getting some furniture that was a bit cozier."

"You could always keep one of the rooms in the old time period and update the others."

Her head tipped. "That might be nice. Pick out my favorite pieces of furniture and decorations, put them in that back parlor, but redo the rest of the house."

After scoping out the kitchen, dining room, office and back parlor, Chelsea led them upstairs.

"This a weally big house, Mama. Who are all these wooms for?"

"This one was my grandmother's." She pointed to the one to the right of the stairs, then moved to the other front room. "This one was mine anytime I came to visit."

As they filed inside, Theo was transported back in time. Chelsea had been here for a few months, and they'd spent lots of time together. It had been a hot July day, and they'd finished packing up most of her grandmother's things. Giving them away had been hard for her. At one point, the pain of losing her grandmother had overwhelmed her and he'd held her close, trying to comfort her. One thing had led to another, and soon they'd found themselves on her old bed, kissing, touching, caressing, and so aroused with passion they couldn't stop. That day, he knew he never wanted her to leave.

Glancing at her now, he felt the old longing and desire pulse through him, stronger than ever. Her cheeks blushed a pretty pink as she stared back. Her mind must be on the same memory.

"Can I have a woom when I visit?" Jordan asked, jumping up and down, oblivious to the charge of electricity coursing through the space.

Chelsea eyed him cautiously. Was he ready to do a split custody thing? It wasn't anything he'd ever thought he'd need to worry about.

"Maybe once your mom has the house in better shape." Right now, there was evidence of rodents and disrepair. Nothing too bad, but he'd never want Jordan exposed to any kind of danger.

"Yippee!" The jumping got more enthusiastic. "Can I pick out my color to paint it?"

"Of course, you can," Chelsea said. "What color would you like?"

Theo already knew what the answer would be.

"Pink."

"A nice pale pink would look pretty."

"You might want to choose the shade. Last time she picked out the color for her room, it was neon pink. I had to veto that."

"I'm not sure when I'll get around to hiring a painter. The inspector you recommended is coming Monday. Since the

Jordan Pond cleanup is close to done, I figured that would be okay."

When he touched her arm, she inhaled swiftly at the contact. "Concentrate on what you need to do here, Chelsea. The house needs lots of work."

"Mama, what is this?" Jordan held a small frame with some stitching on it.

Chelsea stepped closer and took the frame. "Where'd you find this, sweetheart?"

"In the drawer in there." She pointed to a back bedroom.

"Jordan Marie, you shouldn't go snooping in other people's things." He'd taught her better than this.

"It's okay. I don't mind." Chelsea said softly, quelling the anxiety on their daughter's face. "I need to go through everything in the house, anyway. I never quite got around to that when I…left."

Her gaze landed on the frame again, and her brows knit together. Then, she reached under her top and pulled out a small locket.

"The saying on this embroidery sampler…it's the same as the locket my grandmother gave me years ago. 'A joyful heart is good medicine.' I never knew where the saying came from." She held up the frame. "This says it's from Proverbs 17:22."

"Can I see, Mama?" Jordan stood on tiptoe to see the locket.

Chelsea slipped it over her head and put it around the little girl's. "You can have it. My grandmother gave it to me, and now I'll give it to you."

Jordan beamed. "See what Mama gave me, Daddy? It's a locket from her grandmother. And it says stuff on it."

Theo admired the locket and the enthusiasm in his daughter. Their daughter. *Get used to saying that.*

"A joyful heart is good medicine," Chelsea said. "You fill my heart with so much joy, Jordan, that I'll have to get better. Won't

I?"

Their daughter's eyes grew wide. "Are you still sick, Mama?"

"I don't think I am anymore. You're my good medicine."

Chelsea's expression said she still wasn't sure. There was more to her story than she was telling. What exactly did she mean when she said she'd been sick? Holy cow. Did she have something fatal, like cancer or...? God, he couldn't even think. Another conversation had to happen and soon. Again, not in front of Jordan.

"We should probably get going, peanut. Let your mom have some time to herself. It's been a long day together."

"It's been a wonderful day," Chelsea said as they trooped down the stairs.

"We should—oh, wait. I said I'd check the heat for you, didn't I?" Shuffling toward the basement door, he glanced back at Chelsea. "Do you want me to show you what to do in case you need to adjust it later?"

Her eyes got wide, and she twisted her hands together. "No, I trust you."

"Have you been in the cellar yet?'

Her head shook back and forth. "I heard noise down there. I didn't know what it was. I don't honestly want to know what it is."

"I'll check it out. Jordan, stay with your mom and keep her safe, okay?"

The little girl hugged her mother's leg and nodded.

In the basement, he found several large piles of rags and leaves. Definitely a nest of some sort. As he approached, something rustled and skittered up the side of the wall and out an open window. Squirrels. They'd had a nice dry place for the winter, but it was time for an eviction notice. He kicked at the piles and found nothing else there, so he closed the window and shoved a piece of wood in front of it to keep it from opening again. Another thing for the list of repairs to this place.

After turning the heat on, he checked the water pump and heater. The water heater had been turned off. Chelsea had been here without hot water for a week. Why hadn't she said anything? He'd have to check in with Mike Gomez, the inspector he'd recommended to Chelsea, and make sure she got the right help to get this place in better shape.

"You're all set," he said, closing the cellar door after him and locking it. "I found a few little friends down there, but they're gone now. The window needs to be replaced. I put a temporary fix on it for the moment."

"Thank you." Her expression still seemed anxious.

"The heat's on and the hot water. You didn't tell me you didn't have hot water."

Her shoulders lifted and lowered. "I didn't want to bother you too much."

Shaking his head, he said, "Jordan, give your mom a hug and a kiss before we go."

The child's eyes narrowed. "She's not coming to put me to bed tonight?"

"Not tonight, but we were together all day today, right? We'll see her again soon."

Chelsea gathered her up and clung to her. More reminders that they'd been kept from each other for too long. How would he have coped had the situation been reversed?

When Chelsea eased back, Jordan whirled around. "Daddy, it's your turn for a hug and kiss."

He laughed. "I can give you those when we get home, peanut."

"No, Daddy." Her hands plopped on her hips. "You needa give Mama a hug and kiss."

Would Chelsea allow that? He'd held her earlier but mostly in comfort. Taking a step forward, he checked her expression. Was it hopeful?

"Thanks for coming with us today," he whispered as he reeled her in. Her body trembled when he held her. Was that good or was she afraid of him?

"And a kiss, Daddy. Mama got a kissing heart like me. Kiss her there."

Pushing back Chelsea's hair, he said, "I know, peanut. You're very much like your mom." He lowered his lips and pressed a soft kiss to the birthmark on Chelsea's neck. A shiver ran through her, but when he eased away her face was still anxious.

"Will you be all right alone, pixie?" God, he wanted to hold her close and never let her go. Protect her, comfort her, love her. Did she want anything similar?

Her lips quirked up. "I've been alone for the past week. I think I'll be okay."

Still, there was something in her expression that made him think she wasn't being entirely truthful. The way her eyes darted around the room, toward the windows and the cellar door. What if something happened to her during the night? Her closest neighbors were in their sixties. Yes, he'd kept track. Aside from having her move back in—and yeah, he liked that idea—how could he help her feel safe?

"You should get a dog." Where the heck had that come from? It wasn't a bad idea.

"Yes, Daddy! I want a dog!" Jordan bounced on her feet, her face alight.

"I was speaking to your mother."

"But if Mama have a dog, it's my dog too, wight?"

"I don't even know if she wants a dog." He scanned Chelsea's face.

"When I was a little girl, I used to ask my father for one all the time. He always said no."

Jordan's head tipped to one side. "Daddy always say that, too."

"Because I work all day and don't have time to take care of a dog. Your mom doesn't work and would have the time."

Chelsea stared at him, happiness radiating off her. "You really think I should get a dog?"

He shrugged. "Sure. It would keep you from being alone when you're not with us and scare off any other critters who want to exercise squatter's rights." If they got the right kind, it could protect her. That would make him feel better.

"Okay, but where do I get one? I mean, is there a pet store nearby?"

"No, not a pet store. There's an SPCA in Trenton. We'll get you a rescue dog. Usually, they have a dozen or so to choose from. Different breeds and ages. What's more, they'll have made sure they're up to date on shots and stuff."

"Trenton. That's not far. What do I have to do?"

Dates flashed through his mind. "I have to work next weekend, which means I get the Wednesday before and after off. We could go this Wednesday."

Her face beamed. "You'll take me? Seriously?"

"Sure. We'll take the SUV, since it has more room in the back for a carrier. Wouldn't want to mess up your Volvo."

"Can I come, too? I want to come." Jordan tugged on his hand.

Grinning at her, he teased, "But don't you have school?"

"Sometime you let me stay home when you don't work." Her pout was extremely potent.

"Think we should let her come, Mama?" he asked Chelsea. Her laugh filled him with an emotion so powerful, he couldn't name it.

"Are you good at picking out dogs, sweetheart?"

"Yes, yes, yes. I can be weally good. Please, let me come."

Theo winked at Chelsea. "All right. I guess we'll let you help."

The child danced around the room, singing a little dog song. He edged nearer to Chelsea and touched her arm. "You'll be okay until we get the dog, right?"

Her head bobbed up and down.

As his fingers tightened on her elbow, he said, "If you need anything, call me. I know I've got Jordan, but I can figure something out."

"Thank you, Theo."

Scooping up his prancing daughter, he headed for the door. Chelsea stood there, looking so forlorn he almost couldn't move any farther. But he had to. For now, anyway. If he had his way, they'd get back to where they were five years ago. And soon.

———◆———

The sun reflected off the calm water of Jordan Pond, making the lake look like it was filled with diamonds. The peaceful scene did nothing to calm Theo's mind. Even looking down on it from over eight hundred feet couldn't distract him from his thoughts, the ones that centered around Chelsea.

Saturday had been a fun-filled day with the three of them. They'd had breakfast, lunch, and dinner together and spent all the in between time doing fun activities. Except for the conversation he and Chelsea'd had while Jordan had napped.

At least they'd gotten to the truth. Part of it, anyway. Chelsea's father had manipulated and lied to keep them apart. It still didn't excuse Theo's part in this.

"Hey, you all right?"

Theo turned to see Rico staring at him, his expression one of concern.

"Um, yeah. Why?" The terrain at the top of North Bubble was stable, so why was Rico worried?

"I called your name three times."

"Oh. Sorry, got a lot on my mind. I'll get back in the game."

Rico tilted his head. "I'm here if you need to talk—or get drunk."

Theo laughed. "Which always loosens my tongue."

"I don't know about you, but I'm ready for some lunch." Shrugging off his backpack, Rico wandered to a few low boulders. "Pull up a rock and join me."

Checking his watch, he saw it was past noon, and he was definitely hungry. Jordan had been slow getting ready this morning, and he hadn't had time for more than a few sips of coffee.

"Thanks. Think I will." Once he got his sandwich and took a few bites, he felt a little better. "We spent the day with Chelsea Saturday."

"You mentioned she's been over for supper every night since Wednesday, too. Everything going okay there?"

"Jordan is out of her mind thrilled."

"And you?" Rico took a huge swig from his water bottle, trying for nonchalant.

"I don't know. I don't even know what to think about all that's happened." Taking another bite, he chewed, then continued. "We finally had an opportunity to talk a bit."

His friend finished up his sandwich and remained silent. If Theo never said another word, Rico wouldn't push.

"Seems like her father had a huge hand in tearing us apart."

"Good thing he's dead," Rico replied, his mouth tight.

Theo nodded. "Yeah, he most likely tampered with her phone, so I never got any of the calls or texts she sent. And she never got any of mine, except the one *he* sent telling her it had been fun but only a summer fling and not to come back."

"The worm."

"That's kind, considering what I think of him."

"I'll bet. So what happens now?"

Theo wished he knew. "I'm not sure what I expected once we had a chance to talk. That everything would magically go back to the way it was when we got married? That the hurt and pain of almost five years would suddenly disappear? After we had our conversation, she seemed distant and sad. The rest of the day she was quiet, except when Jordan needed her."

Stuffing his trash in his bag, Rico leaned forward, his forearms on his knees. "How would you feel if you discovered your dad manipulated you, cost you the man you loved, and made you think your baby was dead?"

"Point taken. I'll give her some time to adjust, to get used to being with Jordan—and me—again. Thanks."

"Didn't do anything."

"You listened. I appreciate it."

"Any time." Standing, Rico swung his bag onto his back and checked his watch. "Let's head to the Overlook before descending."

"Sounds good."

As they hiked, Rico asked what they'd done Saturday, and Theo filled him in on the activities, as well as the curious stares they'd gotten from a number of residents.

"Nosy people. Did you end up staying in Sunday to avoid that?"

"Jordan had a birthday party yesterday for one of her school friends, so we didn't see her mom. But I got more of the same while I was there. That divorced mother I told you about? She had lots of questions about Chelsea."

Rico smirked. "The one you said is always inviting Jordan over to play but insists you stick around while the kids have fun?"

"Yeah, that's the one. Good thing Jordan isn't best friends with that kid, or I'd be in trouble."

They spent the next few hours hiking the trails, stopping every now and then to clean off or reset the trail markers. Clouds rolled in, and the day grew chilly. Hopefully, Chelsea's heat was working.

"You know, when I first met Chelsea, she was so filled with life, so happy to be here and with me." The words escaped his mouth before he realized. Pausing, Rico looked his way and smiled, so he went on. Maybe he needed to talk it out.

"Everything was new to her. She devoured life. I know she grew up sheltered, and now I know exactly how much so, but she blossomed when she was here, even with the sadness of losing her grandmother. Now…" He stared at the gray sky and felt darkness invade his soul. "She's this shell of a woman I don't even know. When we went out Saturday, I'd see parts of her emerge, but then she'd revert to this meek, scared stranger."

"What do you want to happen, Theo?"

Shaking his head, he mulled over that thought. "I want to go back in time and keep her from leaving. I thought she'd only be gone for a short visit. It's what she thought, too, but neither one of us could ever have imagined what her father was capable of."

The wind picked up, and he zipped his jacket higher. "I should have trusted her. Trusted that she loved me. Things didn't feel right, but I let my stupid pride get in the way. She was only twenty and innocent. I allowed myself to believe that it had all been a fun adventure for her, that once she realized she'd have to live in my tiny house and on my meager salary, she'd had second thoughts. Why the heck didn't I trust her?"

His heart beat in his chest rapidly, like he'd been running at full tilt. His friend merely stood, listening to him rant.

"The least I should have done was see her face to face. Make her tell me in person that she didn't love me, didn't want to be married to me. I should have pushed harder to see her."

Except he hadn't, and now he wondered if she would forgive him. Not only had she lost him, she'd been made to think her child had died. She'd lost four years of her daughter's life. Why hadn't he fought harder?

Rico gripped his shoulder. "You can't change any of that. You need to look forward. What do you want now? Ideally?"

"I want her back, Rico. In my life and in Jordan's life. I want her to move in and be my wife in every sense of the word."

"She doesn't want that?"

"I haven't asked her."

Throwing his hands in the air, Rico growled, "Why not? Maybe it's what she wants, too."

What the heck was he doing? "We were only married for two weeks. Had only known each other for four months. I keep asking myself if I imagined how we felt for each other, if I haven't built it up bigger than it actually was. I guess I'm afraid to get my heart ripped apart again. The few times I've pushed forward, she seems to back away, like she's scared."

"Her heart's been ripped apart, too. You weren't the only one hurt."

"I know. I have to wonder if she blames me. Maybe she can't forgive me. I didn't trust her, and I let her down. The result was Jordan spending the first four years of her life without a mother, a mother who obviously loved her. My baby girl suffered because of me."

"Jordan loves you, man."

"I know." Taking a deep breath in, Theo stared at his feet. "Sorry for dumping all this on you."

"What are friends for? Sometimes you gotta vent or you'll blow."

He shook his head and closed his eyes. Now that he'd talked it out, he did feel a bit better. However, he was still unsure about what he should do.

Rico clapped him on the back and started down the trail again. "Hey, maybe someday I'll need pay back."

Aside from the one time they'd both been toasted, Rico was as closemouthed as a clam.

"Sure, pal. Sure."

CHAPTER NINE

Chelsea glanced down at her phone.

—Sorry. Car problems. Be there soon.—

She sighed as she shuffled outside. Her first thought when she saw the text from Theo was that he was canceling. It had been his suggestion to get the dog, but now she was more excited than she'd been in a long time. No matter how many times she'd asked her father growing up, he'd always said no. With all their money and the amount of land they owned, it would have been easy enough to hire people to make sure the dog was clean and walked and didn't bother her father. Another way he had controlled her.

Tossing the trash bag in the barrel out back, she turned and grabbed the railing to go back up the steps, still looking at her phone. The wood swayed and cracked. She tried to catch herself but ended up falling over the side, her leg scraping on the concrete landing.

Ow, that hurt. The broken railing post had dug into her side, and she'd landed hard on her butt. That would leave a bruise. Not that anyone would see it. Reaching for her phone, she checked that it hadn't cracked in the fall. Nope, all good. The heavy-duty cover she'd gotten had protected it. Too bad she didn't have a heavy-duty cover, too. When she lifted her top, she saw a jagged scratch down her side with several spots seeping blood. At least Theo being late would give her time to clean it up.

Getting to her feet was a bit harder, as her side hurt and her shin throbbed. She limped to the downstairs bathroom. Did she even have any medical supplies? It hadn't been something she'd ever had to think about. The estate had been filled with anything you'd ever need. Well, except love. And comfort. Some of the staff had been kind to her, but mostly her father hired people with little emotion, who could do their job without getting involved with the occupants.

There were a few bandages in the cabinet over the sink, so Chelsea took a facecloth, wet it with warm water, and began patting the scrapes on her side. After taping up the worst of the injury, she attempted to pull up her pant leg, but the jeans were too snug. The scrape stung. She removed the pants and scanned the damage. Yuck. Most of her shin was scraped. Where the edge of the step had gouged into her was already beginning to turn colors.

Okay, jeans wouldn't work today. Once she'd cleaned off the wound and wrapped some gauze around her leg, she went upstairs and changed into a pair of loose linen pants. A quick brush of her hair and some makeup and she was ready to go. Plus, some painkillers to dull the ache in her side and leg.

As she got the ibuprofen from her purse, her hand encountered her medication. The stuff she hadn't taken in a while. Should she? Would it help quell the anxiety pouring into her at the thought of being with Theo again?

Not that Saturday hadn't been amazing. It had been. But too many people had stared at her like she'd either had six heads or had murdered her entire family in their sleep. Would that happen again today? They were heading off island to Trenton, so hopefully no one would know the history between her and Theo.

The sound of a car pulling into the driveway cut her thoughts off quickly. After downing the pain pills and slipping the others back in her bag, she grabbed a gray hoodie and trotted out to the front porch. The back stairs would be another thing to add to her list of what had to be fixed.

"All ready?" Theo asked, emerging from the driver's side.

"I am. Thanks for taking me." Getting into the car caused a few twinges, so she gritted her teeth and dragged a smile onto her face. Not hard when she glanced in the back and saw the beaming face of her daughter. Her daughter. She'd never get tired of that.

"Hey, sweetie. Ready to help me pick out a dog?"

Jordan's eyes widened. "Yep, Mama, I'm so excited. But Daddy said the doggy has to stay at your place, since he's not home much."

Theo put the car in gear and pulled onto the road. "I wanted her to understand we aren't keeping the dog. That doesn't mean you can't bring it over when you visit."

"I appreciate that." Especially since she planned to visit as often as Theo would allow. She wished she was brave enough to ask if she could take Jordan during the day sometimes. Was she ready for that? Having her daughter all to herself? Maybe taking care of the dog would show Theo she could be trusted. Right? Because dogs and children were so similar.

As they drove, Jordan chattered away in the back seat about some of her friends who had pets. Theo chuckled, asking, "What did Mike have to say about your house? He came on Monday, right?"

Mike Gomez had been great. Chelsea was glad Theo had suggested him. "He said the house was structurally in good shape, but there are some things that should be replaced or updated."

"Good. Did he give you any idea of people who could do this?"

"He gave me lots of names. Said I should check them out myself, but he's worked with all of them and highly recommended most of them. I think I'll start with updating the bathrooms. At least the upstairs one first. The carpets also all need to be ripped out because of rodents and general wear and tear. He suggested I don't put in the new carpets until all the walls have been repainted. You don't have to worry about spills and stuff that way. But I'll be without carpets for a while."

"There's a place in Ellsworth that has carpet remnants real cheap. I'd be glad to pick up a few for you to use until you can get the new ones installed."

"Really? You'd do that for me? Thank you."

"I want you to be comfortable, Chelsea. What else needs to be done?"

"The front porch has a few railings that have rotted out and need to be replaced. The back steps, too." She touched her side where the throb had only slightly lessened.

They chatted for the whole drive about her house repairs and the new appliances she wanted to get.

"I want a refrigerator like yours. That's the exact one I wanted when we were…you know…back then." Talking about when they were married, all two weeks of it, was difficult. How did you go back there after so many years apart?

"I know." The look he gave her said plenty. Was she brave enough to think he'd gotten it because of her?

When they arrived at the SPCA, her stomach was in knots. Luckily, Jordan's enthusiasm helped distract her from her anxiety. What did she have to be nervous about, anyway? She was only getting a dog. One she'd be responsible for. Have to take care of. Who would rely on her to be fed and walked and… Oh, God. Maybe she wasn't ready for this.

"It'll be fine," Theo said. He took possession of her hand as Jordan took her other and dragged her along. It's like he could read her mind. Or was she that transparent? If so, what else could he read from her? That she wanted so badly to be back with him the way they'd been before.

Theo took care of the introductions, having called ahead to make sure they had a few dogs to choose from that were appropriate for her.

"You're fairly petite, Chelsea," he'd said, "so something too huge might not be the best choice. And nothing too small, since part of the reason I suggested a dog was for protection."

She had to trust Theo on that, seeing as she had no experience whatsoever with dogs.

The man at the pound, Hank, showed them down a long hallway with cages on each side. Her heart broke seeing the dogs inside, some old, some still puppies. How was it so many dogs ended up here? Although counting the cages, she realized there were only about ten.

Hank stopped at each space and told them the story of each dog. How old they were, why they were here, and any medical information they knew about. This was hard. She wanted to take them all home.

At the last kennel, Chelsea inhaled deeply. The poor thing cowered in the corner, his eyes sadder than any she'd seen so far.

"This is Bandit. He's a German Shepherd/Sheltie mix, and he's almost a year old, which means he probably won't get a whole lot bigger than this. He's been neutered already and is up to date with all his shots."

"What's his story?" she asked, needing to know why the poor thing was huddled in the corner. There had been times she'd been known to do that, especially after Jordan's birth.

"He was given as a gift to a family who really didn't want a dog. They took care of him for a while, but a few weeks ago they brought him here and said they couldn't take care of him any longer. With his anxious behavior, we suspect he wasn't treated all that well." Just like her.

Tears formed in her eyes, and she bit her lip. How could anyone do that to a poor, adorable creature? The other dogs half forgotten, she crouched down and spoke softly to this one.

"Hey, sweetie. You're a handsome boy, aren't you?" At her hushed words, his ears perked up and his tail swished, but he still remained planted in the far corner.

Looking up, she asked, "Can I get closer?"

"Sure." Hank pushed a key into the lock. "Let me get him adjusted to someone in with him. He's a nervous thing but hasn't shown any violent tendencies yet."

After a few minutes of Hank chattering away and rubbing Bandit's fur, he looked at her and nodded. "Come in slowly and stop in the middle. The lower you get, the more comfortable he'll be."

"Do you want me to go in, Chelsea?" Theo asked, his eyes filled with concern.

"No," she answered automatically. "If this dog will be mine, then I need to get him used to me first. But thank you."

Jordan bounced around near the door of the cage, until Theo picked her up and whispered something in her ear that made her calm down.

Slowly creeping in, she claimed a spot on the floor a few feet from where the dog sat. When Bandit checked her out, she murmured little words of welcome. Finally, after a few minutes of looking all around, he scooted forward until he was right in front of her. Reaching out, she allowed him to sniff her hand and when he licked it, she chuckled. That was a good sign, right?

"You're such a good boy, aren't you, Bandit? Aren't you? Yes, you are."

The dog wiggled closer and within seconds had climbed in her lap. Immediately, she rubbed his fur and scratched behind his ears, sending his tail thumping so hard it sounded like a heartbeat.

"I think he likes you," Hank said, still seated in the corner where Bandit had been.

"I like him, too." She allowed the dog to lick her face. Why had her father made this seem like such a nasty thing? "What do you think, Bandit? Want to come live with me?"

Her gaze automatically moved to Theo. Looking for approval? His opinion? Or simply to see the handsome man he was and assure herself he, and their daughter, were real?

Jordan was bopping up and down in Theo's arms, and *his* smile was huge. Guess that was a good sign.

"What do we need to do to adopt this guy?"

Hank's grin swallowed his face. It must be nice to see one of their dogs get a new home. "There's some paperwork to do first, and we'll need to get him ready to go. Mostly cleaning him up. Do you have everything you'll need for a dog?"

Yikes. "No, I didn't even think of that. What will I need?"

Hank rose, took a leash from the wall, and hooked it to Bandit's collar. "I've got a list of the typical stuff, plus the kind of food you should give him for a while."

The dog appeared confused when they led him from the cage, but his tail never stopped wagging. Chelsea stayed close and kept leaning down to rub his head and back. In the hallway, Theo finally put Jordan down.

"You may pat him gently, peanut. Let him get used to your smell first."

When Bandit sniffed then licked the little girl's hand, she giggled. "It tickles."

"He's learning who you are, so he'll know you're a friend."

At the front, Hank handed the dog over to a young woman as Chelsea called out, "We'll be back soon, Bandit."

From behind the desk, Hank handed Theo the forms. "We don't charge for adoptions, but if you can make a donation, we'd appreciate it."

How much should she give? Glancing at Theo, he shrugged and asked, "How much would this breed run if you bought it?"

Hank looked up from the computer. "Four hundred to six hundred probably. We don't expect that big of a donation. It is nice to get something back for what we've put in."

Chelsea scanned the room as they waited for Hank to pull out the list of stuff they'd need for the dog. Behind a glass window sat a box of three little kittens. All black.

"Have they lost their mittens?" she asked, wanting desperately to pick them up and snuggle. Her father had said no to a cat, too. They shed too much. Of course, there was something wrong with every animal she'd ever wanted. Bird, hamster, goldfish. It didn't matter. She'd had to make do with the squirrels and chipmunks who ran through the gardens in the back yard.

"What?" Hank said, his gaze moving to where she stood. "Oh, those little cuties. No, no mittens. Probably not many takers either, unfortunately." He looked back down at the screen as he typed.

"Why not? They're adorable."

After printing out a list for them, he walked over and stared at the felines. "They're black. Not too many people want black cats. Bad luck, you know."

Jordan ambled over and lifted her arms to be picked up. Chelsea scooped her up, and the child squealed at the site of the tiny kittens snuggled together. How could anyone think these darlings were bad luck?

"So, if no one adopts them, what happens to them? They live here in a cage forever?" That sounded horrible.

Hank only shrugged. "Most likely. They also take up space we could use to help another animal that needs it."

"I could take them." The words jumped out of her mouth before she could sensor them. Seriously? Did she think she was capable? Her eyes zoomed to Theo's. "Couldn't I?"

A grin split his face. What did that mean? Either he thought she was a lunatic, or he was okay with it. Was she up for the job?

"It's your house, Chelsea. You can do whatever you want."

It was her house. Yes, it was her decision. Not her father's. Not Theo's or even Jordan's. Hers. For a second, she felt totally empowered. It didn't last that long as doubt crept in again. Theo's smiling face helped her decide.

Pushing her shoulders back, she announced, "I'll take the kittens, too. I assume they're siblings."

Hank nodded. "There were six of them, but the others were multi-colored and got adopted quickly."

And these poor babies were left behind.

"Well, I can't separate them, so I'll take all three. Do they have names already?"

"Nope. They're also not fixed, so unless you want more kittens, you'd best take care of that. It can be pricey."

Was he trying to talk her out of it? "Are they old enough to be fixed?"

"They're right about the age it should be done."

Theo nodded at her. "There's a vet clinic on Federal Street downtown. You can get it done there."

"Okay, I'll get the kittens cleaned up and ready to go, too." Hank dug around in a drawer and pulled out another sheet of paper. "Cats don't need quite as much, but here's a list of things that help, especially when they're so young. Luckily, they have each other, so it shouldn't be as bad."

"We getting the kitties, too," Jordan squealed, her heart hammering in her chest so loudly Chelsea could hear it.

"Yes, and you can help pick out some toys for them. How long will it take to get them ready for us?"

Hank checked his watch. "Give us about an hour."

Theo pursed his lips and stared at her. "Are you sure about all this, pixie?"

The nickname sent a shiver through her. Standing tall and confident, she nodded. "Yes. I have plenty of room and plenty of love to give them."

The smile on Theo's face highlighted those amazing dimples at the corners of his mouth. She'd done the right thing.

―――――◄○►――――――

The change in Chelsea once she'd decided to get both the dog and the kittens was astounding. At first, she'd seemed unsure, constantly looking to him as if asking for permission. His instinct had been to step in and take over and do everything for her, but that wasn't going to help her get back on her feet and regain that optimistic personality he knew was inside her. The one he was getting a peek at now.

As they pulled into the pet store parking lot, he could feel her excitement rising. Hers and Jordan's. "You've got the lists, right?" At her nod, he added, "Do you have enough money on you? I can take care of it, if you don't."

Chelsea rolled her eyes at him. "You're asking if I have enough money. I could buy all new appliances with the cash I have on me."

"Don't say that too loud," he warned.

As they went up and down the aisles, considering which dog bed or kitty climber to get, he marveled at how normal this all seemed. To the casual onlooker, you'd never know that his stomach was in knots and his mind was a jumble of emotions and confusion. They looked like a regular family out for a weekday shop.

"I think the kitties need this." Jordan showed them yet another small toy.

"Why don't we concentrate on the basics for now?" he said, pushing one of two carriages down the aisle, since the dog crate they got for Bandit filled an entire one by itself. He'd been stuffing things inside to conserve space.

Once the crates, beds, food, water dishes, litter boxes, leash, collars, and various other supplies were loaded up and paid for, they filled the back of the SUV and headed out.

"How about we stop and pick up some food? We could have a little picnic once we get the animals."

"You want to have a picnic?" Chelsea's expression showed confusion.

"I'm sure Bandit and the three little kittens might like to run around a bit before being stuck inside your house. You'll want to adapt them to your yard slowly. I know a great place we can go."

Chelsea nodded, so they grabbed some takeout and made it back right as the dog and kittens were being brought out to the front.

"Hey there, Bandit," Chelsea greeted the animal, and the dog responded like he hadn't seen her in years. He understood the feeling.

"You know he's still young enough," Hank said, "that you could probably get away with changing his name. There are some tips to doing that."

Leaning down, she scratched the dog's head. "No, the name fits him. He stole my heart."

As Chelsea wrote a check out for the organization, one that was much more than any of the animals were worth, he picked up the box of black furballs. Like she'd said, she had the money. After she'd left him years ago, he'd done some web surfing and knew in the vicinity how much her father's company was worth. Who knew how much money he had beside that?

"Can I hold one of the kitties, please?" Jordan begged as she climbed into her car seat. He tucked the cats into their carrier, strapped next to her seat.

"Not right now, peanut. We'll be stopping in a few minutes. You can do it then."

After making sure the kittens were safe, he opened the back and assisted Chelsea in getting the dog into the larger carrier. The animal balked a bit, but when Chelsea climbed into the back next to the carrier, he settled down.

"I'll stay here, so he's okay."

"There's barely enough room for the crate."

"I'm small." She shrugged, grimacing as she adjusted her legs. No way he'd argue with her. These animals were better than any therapy he could think of.

The drive to the Thompson Island picnic area took no time, and soon Bandit was back on his leash and Theo had placed the kitty carrier on the grass next to a picnic table.

"Let's eat first while they get used to being outside." He tucked Bandit's leash under the leg of the table and started retrieving food from the bags. Jordan, as usual since her mother had arrived, sat next to Chelsea. The child's eyes held such hero worship and love.

That was a good thing, right? No reason to be jealous of his daughter wanting to be with her mother. Little girls needed their moms, and his had been without for too long. Maybe he was simply jealous that Chelsea chose Jordan over him. At one time, she'd said he was her world. Now, her world had grown. Looking down at the pets, he would say it had grown a lot.

Jordan gulped down her meal in record time and asked to play with the kittens. She was excited about the dog but didn't seem ready to get too close without someone else nearby.

"You can sit next to their carrier and talk to them, but don't take them out until either your mother or I are with you.

Understand?"

"Yes, Daddy," she chirped, flopping on the ground next to the kittens.

Chelsea peeked down at the animals, then glanced back at him. "Do you think I did the right thing? Or do you think I'm crazy for taking them all?"

He laughed. "You might very well be crazy, but I also think you did the right thing. The look on your face when you made that decision, you were happier than I've seen you since…since before you left me."

Pain filled her eyes, and he wanted to take the words back. He squeezed her hand and whispered, "I'm sorry. I shouldn't have said that."

"No, it's the truth. I left you, and I've regretted it every day since. Even more now that I know what my father did. He didn't deserve the courtesy of me telling him I'd gotten married. At the time, I thought he did." Her sad face looked off toward the ocean.

"Are you done? I'll take care of the trash while you go run with Bandit. He looks like he's ready."

"Thanks." Her eyes said thanks for more than simply letting her run with the dog. Changing the subject maybe, or not dwelling on the fact that she'd left him, which had started this whole nightmare.

As he cleaned up the trash, Jordan and her mom took Bandit and trotted around the large grassy area. Situating himself near the kittens, he opened the carrier and pulled them out to romp in the grass. They were so tiny it was doubtful they'd get far. Regardless, he kept his eyes glued to them, when he wasn't sneaking glances at Chelsea and Jordan as they played with the dog.

Scooping one ball of fluff into his lap, he petted it. This one had a pink ribbon on her collar, so it was one of the females.

There were two females and a male, and they still needed names.

Eeeny, Meeny, and Miny? No, there wasn't a fourth to be Moe.

Of course, you could do the Three Stooges, Moe, Larry, and Curly. But what about Shemp? That didn't seem quite fair.

Huey, Dewey, and Louie? Bibbity, Bobbity, and Boo. Peanut, Butter, and Jelly. Flopsy, Mopsy, and Cottontail. No, they were rabbits. Better let Chelsea make the decision.

As she romped around the picnic area, he noticed her gait. Something was off. Was she favoring her right leg? Just then, she glanced up, and the light in her eyes almost blinded him. This was how she was meant to be. Always.

He waved her over, and she and Jordan loped back, the dog happily at their sides.

"Are you okay?"

Dropping down next to him, she nodded. "I'm perfect. This is so much fun." The dog rested next to her, probably not used to so much physical activity.

"You seem to be limping…or something."

Guilt flashed across her face, and she turned away. "I'm fine."

But her hand moved on her leg, the one she'd been favoring.

"Did you twist your ankle or something?" he asked as his hand covered hers on her shin. When she winced, he knew something was wrong. "Don't lie to me, Chelsea."

She shrugged. "It's nothing. The railing on the back stairs broke when I was walking up, and I scraped my leg."

He didn't wait for her to show him; he simply lifted the leg of her pants. She didn't stop him. There was a large bandage wrapped around her shin and a few spots looked like they had been bleeding.

"Did you get injured any place else?"

When he cocked his head, she pursed her lips. Apparently, she did.

"I got a little scratch on my side." She tugged her shirt down further.

"From what?"

"The broken part of the railing."

"Someone should probably look at that."

"I cleaned it up," she said quickly, her anxious expression making him sad. The exuberance she'd had for the past hour was what he wanted to see.

"Okay, but how about you let me change the bandages when we drop you off? I've got Advanced First Aid and First Responder training. I only want to make sure it isn't infected."

She rolled her eyes. "Fine."

Jordan had been playing with the kittens and giggling at their antics. One of them, the one with the purple ribbon, started jumping up and down like a piece of popcorn.

Snapping his fingers, he tried to get the little male to come closer. Instead, the cat pounced on the snapping fingers, backed away, and waited for another snap.

"Daddy, you snap for him, and this one pop at me," Jordan said as Chelsea picked up the one with the pink ribbon.

"Then, I guess you, little lady, must be Crackle." The kitten purred loud enough for them all to hear.

"Why, Mama?"

Chelsea pointed at the kitten attacking his snapping fingers. "Snap. Crackle," she said holding her kitten up, then eyed the last one, who jumped up on cue.

"Pop!" Jordan fell on her back, laughing. Chelsea followed suit and soon all of them were giggling, little kittens wriggling everywhere.

Gasping for breath, Theo agreed with what Chelsea had said earlier. It was all perfect.

CHAPTER TEN

"The carpet's all pulled out in that back office, Ms. Woodridge."

Chelsea swiveled to look at Brett Sheehan, the man she'd hired to peel wallpaper, remove the carpets, and help her move furniture around. He'd taken everything out of the back office, so she could have a spot exclusively for the animals while they adjusted to living here.

"Please, I asked you to call me Chelsea." And it should be Lapierre.

"I made sure to get all the Tackless, those strips with the nails that hold the carpet in. I know you said you were putting your pets in there, and I didn't want them getting hurt."

"That's so thoughtful, Brett. I appreciate it."

The man nodded, surveying the kitchen where she'd kept Bandit and the kittens while he'd been working. "Is there anything else you need me to do while I'm here?"

She glanced at the clock above the stove. "I'm all set for now. It's already after five, and it's Friday night. You'll be back Monday, right?"

"Yes, ma'am," he replied, his voice scratchy like he'd swallowed some sand, possibly rolled around in it, if his attire was anything to go by. He couldn't be more than mid-thirties, but his clothes were old and worn and ripped in a few spots. His blond hair was longish, and his face hadn't seen a razor in a few weeks. Underneath it all was a handsome man, yet he was broken in some way. The broken part of her could sense it and relate.

Approaching the counter where her purse rested, she took out her wallet and counted out some twenties. He'd been here all day yesterday and today, and she wanted to make sure to pay him for the time. It looked like he could use the cash.

After taking the money, he moved toward the door. "I'll be back first thing Monday and start shifting the furniture, so I can peel the wallpaper off in the living room."

Once he'd left, she puttered around the kitchen, made sure Bandit had enough food, scratched his belly a few times, then checked on Snap, Crackle, and Pop. They were still so young they napped a good deal of the day. She'd put them in a large plastic container. It was high enough they couldn't get out but had plenty of room to scamper around in. An old blanket and some toys Jordan had picked out were in there, too.

Grabbing the old hammer she'd located in her grandmother's broom closet, she took the step stool she'd also found and proceeded to the living room. If Brett was going to start on the wallpaper on Monday, she needed to take all the pictures off the walls and remove the nails.

"Lay down, Bandit. I'll be right back," she called to the dog. Having him underfoot while she tried to work would be a recipe for disaster. She'd spent a good portion of the day with him outside playing, so she didn't feel too guilty.

As she reached up to remove one large picture from the wall, the injury on her side ached. Two days ago, when they'd gotten the animals from the SPCA, Theo had insisted he look at her side and shin and change the bandages. Why she'd been embarrassed she didn't know. They were married and had been intimate for Pete's sake. They had a child together. Yet that had been years ago, and as much as she wanted that back, she knew it would take time for both of them to adjust to being together again.

God, she hoped they'd eventually be together again. At least he'd allowed her to see their daughter almost every day. Supposedly, he was stopping by with Jordan, and food, tonight. Why did she doubt him when he'd kept every promise he'd made since she'd returned? Because of what had happened in the past? There was still a tiny part of her that couldn't trust him, though she knew it was her father who had caused them to be apart.

After moving all the pictures and knickknacks into the back parlor, she positioned the step stool under the nails, picked up the hammer, and cautiously climbed on. Oh, how she hated heights. Silly, since she couldn't be more than two feet in the air. But still, her body tensed.

As she was pulling out the last nail, her front door opened and a blast of cool air swept in, along with her whirlwind of a daughter. She sure didn't get that high energy, chatterbox thing from her.

"Hey, Mama! We got pizza for you!" Jordan yelled.

The step stool swayed as she turned around. She twisted in attempt to right herself, but it tipped, her body over-balanced, and she fell.

Instead of hitting the floor, she found herself in Theo's arms. His heart beat as rapidly as hers.

"Don't scare me like that, pixie," he growled in her ear, his arms crushing her close to his solid chest. "You'll take ten years off my life."

"Sorry," she muttered, her nose squished into the great-smelling fabric of his shirt. Pine and outdoors. Could she stay here forever? His embrace felt heavenly.

Gently lowering her legs to the floor, his eyes swept over her. "Are you all right? You didn't re-injure those scrapes, did you?"

The side twinged, but she wasn't about to go all dramatic on him. "I'm fine. Thanks for saving me."

"Let's see if I can save the pizza now."

The large, flat box was on the floor. Oh, no.

Theo lifted the cover and nodded. "All good."

"Are you sure? I can run out and get another one."

Picking the box up in one hand and hooking her elbow with the other, he led her into the dining room. "We need plates. Do you have those?"

"Yes, I'll get them." This week, she'd spent a lot of her time cleaning out the kitchen cabinets, washing all the dinnerware and cooking pans, as well as wiping out the mouse poop that had accumulated over the years.

When she came back in with the plates, Jordan had Bandit next to her and was patting his head gently like her father had taught her.

"Um, Theo, I was wondering…"

His smile warmed her to her toes. "What do you need, pixie?"

"Those mouse traps you put all over the place…"

His eyebrow raised.

"A bunch of them went off. I know I should be able to empty them, but I…can't."

His grin grew. "Did you want me to do something?"

"Empty them," she said, biting her lip. "Please?"

He yanked on her hand until she sat next to him. "I'll do it after we eat. What happened here?" His eyes focused on the cuts on her thumb and palm.

"The old hammer I found has a broken handle. The metal part underneath keeps jabbing me."

His fingers gently traced over the wounds, causing more trembling inside.

"I'll fix that after we eat, too."

As usual, Jordan kept the conversation going. When would she and Theo get back to the carefree way they'd been when they'd first met? Not that she didn't love hearing her daughter chatter away, but she'd love to be able to talk to Theo about things, too.

Once the pizza was gone, Chelsea dragged the kitten box into the living room and brought the dog in, too, so Jordan could play with them on the floor.

"I'll see about those traps while you two are occupied." Theo winked. "Unless you want to help me."

Her face scrunched up. "No, thanks."

Theo puttered around the house and into the basement, then she heard him going out the back door. Hopefully, disposing of the little critters. She hated killing them—they were kind of cute —but she didn't like them pooping in her cupboards or skittering across her floor as she got ready for bed.

The sound of water splashing in the sink came from the kitchen, then Theo appeared in the doorway, the hammer now sporting some gray duct tape around the handle.

"Anything else I can do for you, Your Highness?"

Heat rushed to her cheeks as she shook her head. Jordan's laughter got their attention, and they spent the next hour playing with the kittens and the dog.

"This step stool is unsafe, Chelsea," Theo said, examining the old wooden piece. "I'll get you a new one. I don't want you getting hurt again."

"I'm perfectly capable of getting a new step stool. You don't have to baby me."

His lips curled up as he shrugged. "Old habits."

"Very old." Why did she have to say that and remind him how long it had been since they'd been together? Still, the way he was staring at her got her heart thumping and sent a zing all the way down to her clenched thighs. That hadn't happened in a long time.

Clearing his throat, he tapped Jordan on the shoulder. "We need to get going soon, peanut. It's almost bedtime."

The little girl glanced up, Crackle held tight to her chest. "Is Mama coming to tuck me in tonight?"

"She's got the pets now, Jordan. It's not as easy to pack them up and go places."

That thought had occurred to her the last few nights as she took care of them and not her daughter. Had Theo suggested she get a dog to limit the time she spent with Jordan? It didn't seem like it, but perhaps he was getting sick of having her around. Which made what she wanted to ask him all the more difficult.

"Theo, you're working tomorrow, right?"

At his nod, she continued. "I was wondering what you were doing with Jordan. I mean, day care isn't open, is it?"

"Not on weekends. I usually have Angie come over."

"Oh." She couldn't keep the disappointment from slipping out. *Grow a backbone, Chelsea. Ask him.*

"Um, I was hoping to maybe see Jordan sometime this weekend. I mean, she's at school all week, and I only see her a few hours at night."

"Did you want me to bring her over after I get out of work?" His expression was curious but also wary. Did he not want her to be alone with their daughter?

"I guess I was hoping to see her during the day. Maybe spend a bit more time with her. Would that be okay?"

His pause made her nervous. What was he thinking?

"I mean, I can come over to the house with Angie if she wouldn't mind. I know you probably don't want me alone with her. But I—" Her lip began to tremble, and she bit it to keep it still. Stupid emotions.

"Hey," he said, easing toward her and touching her cheek. "I trust you with our daughter. I guess I hadn't thought along those lines. You know how I like to have everything planned out in advance."

A tiny chuckled escaped, yet her insides still felt like a swirling maelstrom. "Let me know what's okay."

He raised his eyes in thought. "How about if you meet us around noon at the Brown Bag Cafe? I'll have Angie drop Jordan off, and I'll bring her back to the house after we have lunch, and you can stay with her while I finish up the day."

"You can meet us for lunch?"

"I get an hour. Plus, I've got some things to do in the area, so I can kind of fudge my time. Does that work for you?"

Her head bobbed up and down. No way she'd object to any time with her child. "Thank you."

He got a strange look on his face. "You don't need to thank me. I appreciate your staying with Jordan, and I'm sure Angie wouldn't mind the time to herself. She only gets two days off every week, and if she's with Jordan she doesn't get to do all her errands."

"I'll stay with Jordan any time you need me."

Reaching out, he grabbed her leg and pulled her across the floor. What the heck?

"I want to check your injuries before we go home."

"They're fine, Theo. You don't have to worry about me."

"I will, anyway." Gently, his fingers bunched up her pant leg and examined the bruise, which was now a lovely shade of purple. "That must hurt."

"Only if I accidentally touch it." She wouldn't mention the few times she'd bumped it today playing with Bandit.

"Let me see the side."

Ignoring her shaking head, he lifted the hem of her shirt and leaned closer, his hand skimming over the broken skin. When he frowned, she got nervous.

"What's the matter? Is something wrong?"

"No, it's healing nicely." His eyes lifted to hers. "I hate that you got hurt is all."

The touch of his fingers on her skin caused a rush of blood to her face and many other places. How could a little touch do so much to her? And he didn't take them away quickly. It was like he was examining every inch with care.

Finally, he dropped the shirt and sat back. "Time to go, peanut. We'll see your mom tomorrow. She's going to meet us for lunch and then stay with you until I get home."

"You are?" Jordan's eyes got wide and excited. Before she could start her jolly jiggle, Theo scooped her up.

"Say a quick goodbye to her and the pets."

When he lowered her to the ground again, she jumped into Chelsea's arms and hugged her tight. This was the toughest part. Saying goodbye. Every time, she had this awful feeling like she'd never see her again. The pain of losing her the first time was still too fresh in her mind.

"Will you bring Bandit and the kitties tomorrow?" Jordan asked, her expression hopeful.

Chelsea glanced at Theo, who rolled his eyes but nodded with a grin.

"I will. They'll have to stay in the car while we have lunch."

"Actually," Theo said, scratching Bandit's ears. "They have one section of their place that dogs are allowed. Not sure how well the kittens would do in there."

"Really? Okay, I'll leave the cats in their carrier with the windows open. I'll see you both tomorrow at noon."

"Noon. Let's go, peanut. It's getting late. Good thing you don't have to get up for school tomorrow."

"Does that mean—"

"No," Theo interrupted. "You can't stay up late tonight."

"Daddy. How did you know what I was gonna say?"

Theo narrowed his eyes. "Because I know you, peanut."

Moving closer to Chelsea, he ran his hand down her arm and encircled her wrist. Drawn in, she smiled up at him. Oh, God, would he kiss her? Did she want him to? Yes.

His lips lowered but only touched forehead. "Thanks for helping out tomorrow."

As they left, Chelsea plopped onto the couch and lifted the kittens onto her lap. Bandit jumped up next to her.

Helping out.

Parents didn't help out, did they? Parents parented. Would she ever get to the point where Theo thought of her fully as Jordan's parent? It had only been two weeks since she'd come back here, but she already felt so much love for her child she'd do anything for her. But she couldn't read her thoughts and finish her words like Theo could. Would she ever be able to? Pulling the kittens closer, she hoped she would.

Theo slammed the door of his work truck and stretched his shoulders back. *Man, that hurt.* Idiot college kids. Someone had called in a disturbance along one of the steeper trails up Cadillac Mountain, and when he'd gone to check it out, there'd been no evidence of a disturbance, except the rocks that had come tumbling down around him. A large one had hit him square in the back. If he'd been a step down, it could have hit his head and knocked him out. Or worse.

Too often, the college kids from the nearby university liked to do a few pranks before they left for the summer. Classes ended next week, and some of them must have been gearing up early. Unfortunately, the hit had left him stunned for a couple moments, giving whoever had been responsible time to flee before Theo could get a look. It didn't leave him in the best mood for meeting Chelsea for lunch.

Her car was parked right in front of the Brown Bag Cafe, and as he passed, he spotted the kittens in their carrier case. They were snuggled together, sleeping. The windows in the car had been rolled down. Early May was still cool enough there wasn't a worry about the animals getting too hot.

As he strode in, Bandit gave a tiny yip only to be shushed by the beautiful brunette seated in the pet-allowed section on the right. Tammi and Kelly loved animals and hated to deny anyone service because they had one. Like many of the Bar Harbor businesses, dogs were welcome provided the owners kept them on a leash and under control. This small dining section, however, had a decorated gate around it just in case.

"No Jordan or Angie yet?" he asked as he sat across from Chelsea and reached down to pet the dog, whose nose nudged at his hand.

Glancing at her watch, Chelsea shook her head, biting her lip.

"No need to be nervous. Jordan isn't the easiest kid to get out of the house. Getting shoes on her feet can take hours. Angie's a bit of a pushover when it comes to my—our daughter." Crap, better not slip up again.

The bell over the door jingled, and their whirlwind little girl pranced her way in, Angie a few steps behind.

"Sorry, we're late. She has a dozen pair of shoes. You'd think it would be easy to find a matching set."

"You'd think," he replied. "Yet we never can." He shot a look at Chelsea that said, "*See?*"

Jordan pushed through the gate and hugged the dog, who was thrilled with the attention and licked the child's hand. Theo couldn't miss how her mother's face fell.

"Peanut, how about you say hello to your mom first," he instructed.

The cherubic little face looked up. "Hi, Mama."

Angie rolled her eyes. "She's a fickle thing. It's good to see you again, Chelsea. How are you getting along?"

He and Angie had talked a bit about the situation and how he was feeling. But since he still wasn't sure what would happen or what he wanted to happen, he'd kept some of his thoughts to himself.

"I'm better than last time you saw me."

Which didn't answer the question. Last time Angie had seen Chelsea, she'd just seen her daughter for the first time.

"Are you joining us for lunch?" Chelsea invited, pointing to the seat next to him. Of course, she'd want Jordan next to her.

"Thanks," Angie said. "But if I've got some time to myself, I'm using it. Appreciate your jumping in to stay with Jordan this afternoon." Her head tilted. "And tomorrow?"

Both women looked at him. He hadn't thought that far ahead. "If you're available, that'd be great."

Rubbing her hands together, Angie grinned, then bent down to kiss Jordan on the cheek. "See you later, squirt. Your mom has you the rest of the weekend."

"Bye, Auntie Angie. See my new dog? Well, my Mama's dog, but he's kind of mine too, right, Mama?"

That got a smile on Chelsea's face. Thank God. Finally.

"Yes, sweetheart. You helped me pick him out and everything."

Angie nodded patiently while Jordan gushed about the dog, then managed to slip out.

"Are we ready to eat?" Theo interrupted Jordan who was still going on about the dog. "I've only got an hour, and I think I've used up too much of it."

"I want a turkey sandwich, Daddy. I'll stay here with Bandit, okay?"

Chelsea looked at him curiously.

"Do you know what you want, Chelsea? If not, Jordan's fine here for a couple minutes."

The counter was only a few feet away, so Chelsea nodded and followed him over. After scanning the menu, which was mostly sandwiches and a few different kinds of soups, she nodded and started to pull out her wallet.

"Don't bother. I've got it. And no arguing. You've got to keep Jordan and the animals busy all afternoon. It's the least I can do."

They both ordered, and Kelly smiled at them. "It'll be only a few minutes. I'll give you a yell when it's ready."

As they turned to go back, a large man stepped inside, his denim dusty and worn. Brett Sheehan. Aw, crap. This was someone he usually tried to avoid.

Gripping Chelsea's elbow, he steered them toward their table, but she stopped and smiled.

"Brett. It's good to see you again."

Brett tipped his head. Then, he noticed Theo, and his eyes turned cold.

"Lapierre." The word was spit out with disgust. The glare from his gaze was lethal.

Chelsea froze. She looked up at him, then back at the newcomer.

"Is something wrong, Brett?" she asked.

"How do you know him?" Theo kept hold of her elbow.

"I hired him to do some of the work around the house."

Not where he wanted Brett to be. Now, he'd worry even more than before she got the dog.

Brett pushed his hands into his pockets and snarled. "I'd watch who you hang out with, Ms. Woodridge. The ranger here doesn't care all that much about anyone's safety or well-being. He might seem like the perfect professional, but he's not."

"Listen, Sheehan. Back off, okay? Go home and sober up."

He didn't smell or act like he'd been drinking, but Theo had seen the man often enough that way to be concerned.

"Theo, what…?"

"Mama, I have a drink of lemonade, please?" Jordan interrupted.

"Sure, sweetheart."

Brett's gaze veered toward their daughter, and his face hardened. "You're the missing wife. The one who walked out on this guy. Smart move."

Her eyes opened wide, then her lashes lowered, and she headed to the drink fountain. Once she'd filled a small cup, she returned to their seat, leaving him and Brett by themselves.

"I'm warning you, Sheehan. Play nice."

Whatever Brett was about to say was stopped short by Tammi saying, "Your order's ready, Brett. Thanks for calling ahead."

Theo backed toward their table, keeping his eyes on the denim-clad man at the counter. Once Brett was gone, he took his seat and relaxed.

"What was that all about?" Chelsea eyed him warily.

"He lost his sister a few years ago. He's never gotten over it."

"But what does he have against you?"

"He blames me for her death."

"Why?"

Clearing his throat, he said, "They were hiking, and she got lost and fell. Brett contacted the ranger station. He thinks we didn't get there fast enough."

"Because she died?"

He nodded. "We had to gather a bunch of information before we could send anyone out, get the exact spot of her last known location, and a team needed to be assembled with the right equipment. By the time we found her, she was already dead."

"He blames you." Sadness entered her eyes.

"I was the lead ranger on the rescue. It wouldn't have mattered. The coroner said she died on impact." If only Theo could convince himself that was the case. Having someone die on your watch was the nightmare of every ranger in the park.

"You still feel bad. I can tell."

She always could read him so easily. Could she tell how much he wanted her? Wanted things back to where they were when they'd gotten married?

"Brett was devastated and started drinking heavily. He lost his job as a mechanic because of it. He seems to blame me for all his problems since then."

Tammi called out his name, and Chelsea followed him to the counter.

"It's good to see you again, Chelsea," she said. "You and your daughter look adorable together. Throw in that pup, and you should be on the cover of a family magazine."

"Thanks, Tammi," Chelsea said, picking up the tray while Theo filled their drinks with soda. "We're getting there."

As he passed the counter, Kelly grinned at him. "Nice family."

Yeah, if only wishing it would make it so. For the moment, he had to worry about who Chelsea was letting in her house.

"I don't like the idea of that guy being in your house while you're alone, pixie."

Her startled gaze aimed his way, and her mouth tightened. "He's got nothing against me, Theo. He's been polite and respectful the last two days. And I could tell he's been through something. He has that broken look, and if working for me can help, then I want to help."

She'd know about being broken. It was what he saw most of the time when he looked at her.

"Be careful, then. If you suspect he's been drinking or he does anything out of the ordinary, call me right away. And keep Bandit by your side."

After taking a bite of her sandwich, Chelsea patted his arm. "I'm sure I'll be fine, but thank you for being concerned."

Knowing how much Brett despised him, he *was* concerned. Maybe he needed to keep Chelsea closer than ever. For some reason, he didn't hate that idea.

CHAPTER ELEVEN

Theo pulled open the front door and froze. The smell of something burning had him jumping over the blankets piled on the floor and into the kitchen.

"Is everything okay?" he shouted above the sound of the oven vent turned up high.

Chelsea waved a dish towel in the air, fanning smoke away from the stove. Something charcoal rested in one of his frying pans.

"I'm sorry," her tiny voice chirped out, her eyes like a frightened doe. "I guess I'm not used to this stove."

Rushing toward the offending appliance, Theo flipped the burner off and slid the pan to the side. He bit his lip to keep from laughing. Chelsea had done a few things like this when they'd first been married. Having grown up with tons of household help, cooking wasn't something she had much practice at.

"Hi, Daddy," Jordan greeted from the floor where she sat with the three black furballs scrambling over her lap. Bandit whimpered near the back door.

"Does the dog need to go out?" he asked. Chelsea's anxious eyes moved in that direction.

"I think so, but I had to get this under control first."

Inching closer, he took the dish towel from her and lightly pushed her toward the dog. "Take Bandit out, so he doesn't do his business on the floor. I'll see what I can salvage here."

Once the back door shut, he grabbed a sponge and started mopping up the grease around the stove.

"Peanut, what's this supposed to be?" He indicated the blackened food in the pan.

"Fried chicken."

Chicken. Maybe he'd have to start giving Chelsea some cooking lessons. The ones they'd had five summers ago had been fun. Although not a lot of food had been cooked.

It only took a few minutes to clean up the mess and cut through the black to see if the chicken had been cooked through. Luckily, it was.

"I'm really sorry, Theo." Chelsea sniffed as she pulled Bandit's leash to bring the dog back in. "I'll clean it up. I was trying to get dinner ready, so you didn't have to. You've been cooking for me most nights. I thought it was time I helped out."

"Hey, it's fine." He kneaded her shoulder. "I make dinner every night, anyway. It's no more work for an extra person."

"It is when you have to clean up my mess."

"If you want to help, why don't you pick up the blankets in the living room?"

Jordan jumped up and skipped over to him. "We made a fort, Daddy."

A smile automatically rose to his face at the image of Chelsea and Jordan draping blankets over cushions and tables.

"It sounds like a ton of fun, peanut, but now it's time for dinner, so we have to pick up. Go help your mom, please."

"Okay."

After picking up the kittens and putting them back in the large laundry basket she'd used to corral them, Chelsea followed their daughter.

It took some doing, but Theo managed to scrape off much of the blackened coating on the chicken. Luckily, Chelsea had put on a thick coat of whatever she'd used for batter. Adding some canned vegetables and tater tots to the meal, it would be salvageable.

"This got some animal fur on it." Chelsea held up the handmade quilt he usually had on the back of the couch. "I can wash it if you want."

"Put it on top of the washing machine. I'll do it later." Laundry wasn't one of Chelsea's skills either.

"It's beautiful. Where'd you get it?"

Heat rose up his neck, and he fussed about in the fridge to keep her from seeing. "My mom sent it."

"She made it?"

Placing the platter on the table, he indicated she should sit. "Yeah. She sent it as a wedding gift."

"But—" Confusion filled the air.

After cutting Jordan's chicken and instructing her to leave the dog alone, he said, "I got it a few days after you left."

Chelsea picked at her meal. Because the chicken was burnt or due to the melancholy that always seemed to linger since she'd been back?

"What do your parents think of me?" Her voice was barely more than a whisper.

"It doesn't matter."

"They hate me, don't they?"

He couldn't tell her no. They hated the situation he'd been put in with a newborn and the pain he'd gone through with Chelsea leaving. Being so far away, contact with them was sporadic, but they loved to video chat with Jordan a few times a month. They hadn't done it recently. Truthfully, he'd avoided it, since there was no way Jordan wouldn't spill the beans about her mother being back.

Except his parents didn't know the real story. He had to call and tell them soon. Angie had said she would refrain from saying anything to her father until Theo gave the word. He was hoping he could give them good news. Like he and Chelsea were back together, and all was wonderful. But it wasn't. Yet.

As always, Jordan kept the topic of conversation going with her chatter. Mostly about the dog, the kittens, and the blanket fort.

"It sounds like you had a great day, peanut." When he glanced at Chelsea, she didn't look as pleased.

After cleaning up and allowing Jordan one TV show, he lured Chelsea into the kitchen.

"Is everything all right? Was it too much for you today?"

Her eyes grew large. "No, I love being with Jordan. But I wanted to have dinner ready, and I guess I'm not good at that. Plus…" Her gaze strayed to the back porch.

He tilted his head and remained silent, waiting for her to continue. She bit her lip, strode through the door, bent down, then came back in. One of his sneakers was in her hand.

"I'm sorry. I was busy with the chicken and didn't notice until it was too late. I'll buy you a new pair. I'll buy you ten new pairs. I'm sorry."

He sighed. His shoe was mangled, and part of the leather had been torn off. That had been his most comfortable pair of running shoes. The tears in Chelsea's eyes wouldn't let him say anything negative. This fragile state was starting to be a problem.

"It's fine. Let's spend some time with Jordan before we put her to bed."

They played a few games and read too many stories before getting the cherub tucked in her bed. Chelsea spent longer tonight hugging and kissing the child than she had last week.

When Jordan finally zonked out, they headed downstairs.

"You must be exhausted," he said as she picked up some books that had been left downstairs and put them on the end table.

When she turned, Theo's heart stuttered. Her face crumpled and her lips quivered.

"Please, don't make me leave her." A sob ripped from her throat. What was she talking about? "I know I made a mess of everything today, but I'll try harder. I'll leave the animals at home. I can be responsible, I promise. I just need to get used to all this. Please. I can't live without her."

Holy crap. Is that what she'd been thinking?

"Have you been worrying about this since I got home?" No wonder she was a mess all evening. "Why didn't you say something earlier?"

"I didn't want Jordan to hear. Didn't want to make you the bad guy if she couldn't see me again." Tears rolled down her cheeks, and he lifted a finger to wipe them away. It killed him to see her this way.

"You never made me the bad guy, never put me down in front of our daughter. You could have. Could have said horrible things about me to her. I appreciate that. More than you know."

Leading her to the couch, he sat down and bundled her into his arms. Cupping her cheeks, he stroked his thumbs over the trail of tears.

"Please, let me still see her, even if it's with someone else around. I can't lose her again. I won't make it this time." Her eyes lowered, and she wrapped her arms around her middle.

"I would never keep you from our daughter." His words were gentle but firm. "She loves you and you love her. Today wasn't a test, Chelsea, to see if you could be super mom."

"So, I can come over tomorrow? Even with all the dog stuff and dinner?"

Pulling her closer, he stroked her back and nestled his nose into her silky hair. God, she smelled amazing. "Jordan wants her mother here. I want you here with her, too."

"I'll leave Bandit at home. I promise."

"So he can chew up your house and eat nails that have fallen on the floor while you're not there? I don't think so."

"But your sneaker…" She tried to pull away, but he wouldn't let her.

"It's only a sneaker, pixie. I can buy a new one. Jordan can't get a new mom."

At that, she did pull away. "I bet you could get her a new mom easily if you tried. I've seen how the women in this town look at you."

He stared into her eyes. "But I don't look at any of them that way. Jordan already has a mother. She's the only one I'm looking at right now."

Her eyes filled up again, and he kicked himself. Had he moved too fast? Scared her? *Distraction needed.* Grabbing the remote, he clicked on the TV.

"Let's watch something that doesn't have cartoon characters in it. What are you in the mood for?"

The smile she sent him made him feel like a hero. If only. The channels zipped by, and suddenly she breathed in an "oh."

It was an old black and white classic they'd seen a few times the summer they were together. She loved it, and he'd come to appreciate it, also. Didn't even want to admit how many times he'd watched it since she'd been gone, on the days he wanted to torture himself.

But not today. After shutting off all the lights in the house and transferring the kitten box and the dog into the living room, he eased beside her and focused on the screen. Her expression during the humorous parts was great, but it was the romantic scenes where he had a hard time controlling himself. Finally, he gave up and put his arm around her shoulder, gathering her against his chest. They snuggled into the corner of the couch and enjoyed the program. Like old times.

Except this wasn't old times, and they wouldn't be going upstairs to bed together in the most intimate way. Man, he wanted that. More than he could say. But this was closer than they'd been since her return, and she finally seemed relaxed against him.

When the movie ended, he continued to hold her as another old show came on. Her body grew heavier on his shoulder, so he extricated the throw pillow from under his arm and placed it on his lap, her head cushioned by it. Her silky hair spread around the fabric, and he slid his fingers under it to move it off her face. He didn't want to stop, so he kept stroking her cheek and her neck, the heart-shaped birthmark he so wanted to kiss. Eventually, her eyes closed, and her breathing grew rhythmic.

Waking her up was something he hated to do. It was obvious she was exhausted, and she had to come back here again in the early morning. Easing out from under her, he waited for a moment to see if she'd wake up. Her eyes stayed closed, her face so peaceful. Bandit rested near the fireplace, and the kittens were curled up together in the laundry basket on the old blanket inside it. If Chelsea went home, she'd have to carry the kittens and the leash for the dog. At this time of night and being tired—no, he couldn't do it to her.

Kneeling next to the couch, he gazed at her sleeping face. God, she was so beautiful. So perfect in sleep. Could they get her back to where she was before? Her figure was already filling out with the meals she'd been eating with them, and her complexion had started to glow again. The pasty, white, sick look was easing away.

"Oh, pixie, you don't know how much I've missed you." Leaning down, he kissed her cheek. When she didn't stir, he whispered, "How much I love you."

After placing another kiss to her forehead, he stood, covered her with one of the fort blankets, then set about locking up and shutting off the TV. One small light was left on in case she woke up disoriented, but after a full day with an almost four-year-old, she had to be tired.

It was impossible to move away, but he had to work tomorrow. His job required his full attention, or it could mean danger to many. Touching her cheek one last time, he finally crept up the stairs.

Chelsea opened her eyes as the creek of the front door sounded. Disoriented, she glanced around. Theo's house. His couch. They'd been watching a movie, and she must have fallen asleep. And he'd left her here?

As Theo zipped in, she pulled herself to sitting and shrugged off the blanket he must have thrown over her. God, he looked good. Sweaty t-shirt clinging to his lean muscles and shorts showcasing his strong calves and thighs

"Hey, good morning. Did you sleep all right?"

Pushing her hair out of her eyes, she nodded, still groggy.

Bandit came in behind him on a leash and trotted over for a scratch.

"It was late, and you fell asleep. I didn't have the heart to wake you, especially since you were coming right back here this morning. Hope that's all right."

"Yeah. You went for a run?" He'd done that almost every morning when they were together.

Moving toward the kitchen, he smiled at her. "I figured, since you were here with Jordan, it would be fine. I took the dog. Thought he could use the exercise. Good thing, too, since a car almost ran me off the road. Bandit jumped up and pushed me to the side. Someone who hadn't had enough coffee yet, apparently. Normally, I don't get a chance to go in the mornings. I'll sometimes do a run on my lunch or after work if Jordan goes with Angie or to a friend's."

He'd given up so much for Jordan. She should have been here to help. If only she'd been stronger. Stood up to her father better. Stood up to him at all.

A few moments later, he popped back through the kitchen doorway. "I put coffee on and am heading up to take a shower. Do you need anything?"

She glanced down at her rumpled clothes and frowned.

Theo stepped closer and her nerves tingled. "Some of your clothes are still upstairs in that little dresser in the corner."

He'd kept her clothes? Why would he have done that?

When she heard the shower start, she dashed upstairs into his room and over to the corner dresser. Opening the drawers, her heart leaped. It was everything she'd left here. Including her underwear and a few bras. Like it hadn't even been touched. Well, except the silky nightgown she'd worn after they got married. That was in disarray as if it had been shoved in hastily.

Reaching inside, she picked out a pair of capris and a short sleeve top. The weather was supposed to be fairly warm today. The lacy bra and panties she chose were so unlike what she'd worn at the estate in Westchester. There had been no need for anything sexy there. Was there a need for it now? Doubtful. It would perhaps give her some confidence. Something she'd been sorely lacking in lately.

As she dropped the clothes on the large double bed, the bathroom door opened, and Theo appeared with a beige towel wrapped around his waist. Holy cow. The man had always been gorgeous, but the five years apart had definitely matured him. She turned away, not wanting to stare. Well, she did want to stare, wanted to study him like an art student studies museum paintings, but things were still too awkward.

"You found the clothes. Good. Let me throw on my uniform, and you can use the room to change."

When the closet door opened, she turned around to sneak a peek. The sight stopped her cold. Beside his pressed olive green pants and gray shirts hung her wedding dress.

"You kept it." Her voice was barely above a whisper. What did this mean?

When she'd turned away, he had slipped on a pair of boxer briefs, and he now pulled on his uniform pants.

"I couldn't very well throw your wedding dress away, pixie." The torment in his eyes slashed through her, uniting with her pain to intensify it.

"You had every right to hate me after what you thought I did, abandoning our daughter."

Snapping his pants and buckling his belt, he advanced. "I won't lie and say it never bothered me, but even when I was walking all night around the house when Jordan was colicky, I never hated you."

A few of her sundresses hung behind the lacy peach one. "You kept all my clothes." Confusion drifted through her mind, making things foggy.

She startled when his fingers touched her cheek. They felt wonderful as they caressed from her forehead to her chin.

"I always hoped you'd come back." His voice cracked, and she looked up to see his gaze boring into her. Automatically, her body swayed toward him, and he cradled her in his arms. Bringing her home.

Lowering his head, he pressed his lips gently to hers. The touch was soft and questioning. Her answer was yes.

Those strong arms held her tighter, and he crept his fingers up her back, stroking soothingly as if she might be frightened by his actions. Nothing had ever scared her less.

His rugged chest pressed against her own felt amazing, so she slid her hands up and explored before she circled her arms around his neck. When his tongue teased her lips, she gasped and opened her mouth.

"Daddy?" Jordan's door banged open, and her little footsteps pounded across the hall. They broke apart yet not before the child pushed her way into the room.

"Why you kissing Mama?"

The air barely had time to rush back into her lungs. Still, she managed to say, "It's only a good morning kiss. Don't I get one, too?"

Jordan rushed into her embrace, and she scooped the child close. As the girl's arms wrapped around her and held her tight, Chelsea sighed with the warm emotion. Was it possible for some of her broken parts to start squeezing back together with this child's hugs?

"Why don't you get dressed, peanut, and I'll be down in a minute to make breakfast?"

Jordan snickered in her arms. "You needa get dressed too, Daddy. You forgot your shirt and shoes."

"Yes, ma'am."

Theo reached into the closet for his shirt. Meanwhile, Chelsea held out her hand for her daughter.

"I'll help you get dressed, sweetheart, and we'll let Daddy finish." When they walked out Theo was reaching down for his hiking boots. Ooh, those uniform pants fit nicely.

Once Jordan was in her clothes, Chelsea sent her downstairs, and she managed to clean up and get herself ready. The clothes were slightly loose but not drastically so. The meals Theo had been making had helped get her weight back up.

The kitchen was bustling when she got down there. The kittens were scampering around on an old towel with Jordan hovering over them, and Bandit munched away on some kibble she'd brought over yesterday. Could she do this again today? Theo had been so sweet about yesterday's mishaps, but would his patience run out if more trouble occurred?

"Chelsea, have a seat. I'm scrambling up some eggs and throwing in a bit of ham for breakfast."

"Can I help in any way?" After all he'd been doing for her, she hated to be more of a burden.

His head swiveled. "Um…Yeah, you could get dishes and silverware. And pour Jordan some milk and whatever you want to drink."

Once the table was set, she got out two cups and poured milk in one and juice in the other. Theo already had a steaming mug next to him as he stirred the eggs. His cotton shirt stretched across his shoulders as he did. The uniform fit him well and emphasized how handsome he was. Looking at him in it did things to her insides that hadn't happened since she'd left.

"Is there anything you want me to do around here today?" she asked, taking a bite of the well-cooked meal.

Theo shook his head. "Hang out and have fun with Jordan. It's only a mile to Pepper's Pizza if you want to take a walk and get lunch there. I'll leave you some money."

"I have plenty of money, Theo," she interrupted. Did he not remember who her father was?

"Sorry. Habit. I'll bet Bandit would love to explore Hull's Cove."

"And we could find some pretty shells, Mama," Jordan piped in.

"Sounds like a plan." And maybe if they stayed out of the house most of the time, she couldn't ruin anything else in it.

After helping Theo clean up the dishes, she followed him and Jordan into the living room. He stopped short and dashed into his office. When he came out, he carried a small photo album.

"I wanted to show you this. Jordan loves looking at it, too."

"More pictures when she was little?"

The cover of the book held a photo similar to the one on Theo's mantle—the two of them as they'd gotten married on the little wooden bridge at Jordan Pond. When she opened it, more pictures of their wedding day were there.

"How did you get this?"

"Remember my friend, Kim, the paramedic? She took a ton of pictures that day."

She remembered. Vaguely. Her mind had been too busy imagining her new life with Theo, the man she loved.

Jordan reached up, finagled the book from her hands, and looked through it.

"Kim gave that to me about a week after you left. At that point, I didn't realize you weren't coming back."

Another dagger sliced through her heart at the memory of the pain both of them had gone through.

"Look at Daddy." Jordan held up the book.

"Yes, he's so handsome. Isn't he?" Her gaze automatically moved to the man in question.

"Yep," Jordan chirped. "The handsome wanger, like in the story. And you are the beautiful princess. See, Mama?" The girl pointed to her in her lacy peach dress.

Theo took the album and placed it on the coffee table. "You can look at that later, once I'm gone. Right now, I need a kiss or I'll be late for work."

Their daughter jumped up and down, until Theo scooped her up and planted a kiss on her neck. Her birthmark. The kiss turned into a raspberry, and Jordan squealed loudly, wiggling in his arms.

When he placed her back on the floor, she tugged on his hand. "Mama's turn. She has the heart, too."

Chelsea's breath stopped as Theo prowled toward her. "Have a good day, pixie. Don't worry about anything other than spending time with Jordan. Okay?"

At her nod, he lowered his head and placed his lips on the mark on her neck. Instead of the blowing he'd done to Jordan, his lips were soft and gentle. When his tongue slipped out and licked along her skin and his teeth took a little nip, she groaned. This man could make her lose all ability to think.

"Don't worry about supper," he said as his hand curled around her neck, under her hair. "I'll bring something home."

Home. Did he mean that? For her? She couldn't dwell on that as his lips covered hers. Only briefly, but there was strength in the kiss.

"Don't cry when you go through that," he said, indicating the photo album. "It's going to be all right. We'll get back there. It's just going to take some time to adjust."

Before he backed away, he joined his lips to hers again.

As he left, she considered his words. They'd get back there. She wanted to believe him so much.

CHAPTER TWELVE

H ours later, Chelsea tugged on Bandit's leash as she juggled the cat carrier onto the porch and set it down to retrieve her keys. As she opened the door and turned on the inside light, headlights came up the driveway. Who the heck? It couldn't be Theo. They'd put Jordan to bed right before she'd left, and he'd given her the sweetest kiss goodbye. Nothing too sensual or passionate, but it had given her hope.

The black BMW slowed down and stopped behind her car. Should she slam and lock the door or see who it was? Keeping Bandit by her side, she readied her phone in case she needed to call Theo for help. What he could do for her, she didn't know. He was over twenty minutes away and had a sleeping child at home.

"Chelsea?"

Frank. Her father's business partner and protege. Opening the door wider, she invited the mature blonde man in.

"What are you doing here, Frank?"

"I drive all this way to see you and that's the reception I get?" His expression was one of disapproval. Kind of reminded her of her father. Then again, Frank had been helpful and comforting when Edward Woodridge had died. Before she'd known how horrible of a man he'd been.

"I'm sorry, Frank. It's good to see you." She hugged him, and Bandit growled. "Down, boy. Be good."

"You got a dog?" Frank scowled at the canine, then cocked an eyebrow at the carrier case on the floor behind her.

"And three little kittens. They were at the shelter, and no one else would take them."

"What are you doing, Chelsea? You need to come home. It isn't good for you to be here all by yourself."

"You mean I'm better off at the estate in Westchester? Where the staff walk on eggshells around me. No one tries to interact or get to know me or give me any support when I need it. At least here I can get out of the house and go shopping. Talk to people on the street." When they weren't looking at her like she was gum on the sidewalk.

"I'd be willing to take you out more, Chelsea. You know I've said that before. Unfortunately, when your father died, it left me with a great deal to do. I'm sorry I wasn't around more."

"You were great, Frank, and I appreciate how supportive you were. But that place doesn't hold good memories for me anymore. I'm not sure it ever did."

When his arm went around her shoulder, Chelsea couldn't help but compare it to Theo's touch.

"You're welcome to come live at my place. I have a number of guest rooms and a smaller staff. I'm also closer to town, so you can get out more."

The hand rubbing up and down her back should have felt good, but Frank had never been a romantic option. For some reason, his words and actions felt that way now. Had she mistaken all his comfort and support a month ago? No. He was almost forty years old. Even if she hadn't been ruined by Theo, she never would have considered him. Theo was five years older than her, and it seemed like a huge gap. At least it had when she was twenty.

"Thanks for the offer," she said, escaping from under his arm and opening the carrier to scoop the kittens out. She carried the squirming bundles of fur to the kitchen where she fed them. Frank followed and Bandit followed after him. The dog's fur stood on end. Guess he didn't feel comfortable around Frank either. "Honestly, I don't want to even think about the estate anymore. I'm getting this house in better shape."

"Are you going to sell it then? I can get people to do the work for you, so you don't have to stay here. You can make some excellent money."

Staring at him, she tilted her head. "What on earth would I need more money for? I don't want to sell this place. I want to live here. I'd like to sell the estate and the business and forget it ever existed. I want to be here where my daughter is."

"Sell the business?" Frank's expression grew hard.

She shrugged. "Or I suppose I can keep it, but I don't want to be part of running it. You can continue being in charge if you want. Or choose whatever position you desire, and I'll approve it. I don't want any part of it. Can you understand? I need to be with my daughter."

"I still don't understand this whole situation. Husband? Daughter? None of it makes sense. Your father never mentioned anything."

"I'm sure he didn't. Who would ever admit to something as heinous as telling his own daughter her child had died and then stealing it from her? I can't believe what a horrid person he was."

"I'm sure he was doing what he thought best for you and your condition."

"Forget about my *condition*." She slapped her hands on the counter, and Bandit growled again. At Frank. "Most of my emotional state was brought on by thinking my child was dead. Now that I know she isn't, I'm feeling better than I ever have."

"What of this husband of yours? Does he want you back?"

Did he? His kisses today certainly hadn't said *go away*.

"For now, we're focusing on Jordan and what she needs. I'm also helping do some cleanup around Jordan Pond. I know I've mentioned how much I love that place. It's why our daughter is named Jordan."

"You're doing cleanup? What can that possibly do for you?"

"Believe it or not, Frank, doing physical work feels good and doing it outside is therapeutic. Tomorrow, Theo is going to show me how to run a chainsaw. There are a few trees that have started to tip because of loose roots on some paths near the lake. If they aren't cut down, they could be dangerous to anyone hiking nearby."

"Working a chainsaw, Chelsea? Your father would be mortified."

"Like I care what he would have thought. He certainly didn't think about me when he kidnapped my daughter and told me she was dead."

"Okay, calm down." Frank ran his hand down her arm. "I'm only thinking of your safety. Regardless of what your father did, I would never want to see you hurt in any way. I hope you know that. I care for you deeply."

"I know, Frank. Thank you. You've been so good to me, and I appreciate your taking on all the responsibility of the business and the estate and everything else my father owned. I don't know what I would have done without you." And she meant this. He'd been wonderful to her.

"I only want to do what's best for you. It's been a difficult few years."

"Yes, it has been. Where are you planning to stay tonight?" Should she offer him a room? None of them were in any shape to be slept in, except hers, and even that was still musty.

"I had the staff get a few rooms at the West Street house in shape. I had wondered if you preferred that place to this one. It's right in town."

The West Street house had been where her father had summered for years, where he'd lived when he met her mother. But it was massive and sterile, and she'd never felt comfortable in it. The caretakers were old crotchety people who didn't like anyone messing things up. Her grandmother's place here in Seal Harbor was always more inviting. True, it was big, but it was comfortable and homey.

"Do whatever you want with that place. I'd even give it to you if you wanted. I have no interest in it."

"Well, I'll only be there for a day or two before heading back. I was hoping to bring you back with me. I flew into the small Trenton airport and rented a car. I can arrange for someone to drive your vehicle back."

"That's sweet of you, Frank, but like I said, I can't leave my daughter."

"It's easy enough to bring her back with us."

Her heart pounded roughly in her chest. "Theo would never allow that." Nor would she ever take her daughter away from her father.

"We have the best lawyers money can buy, Chelsea. It would be simple enough to get exclusive custody of your child. Dig up a little dirt on your ex, and he won't stand a chance. And if there's no dirt, we invent some. You get your daughter back full time."

Could she have been so wrong about Frank? Was he as evil as her father? Or is that how all people with money solved their problems?

"My daughter needs two parents. Theo's an excellent father, and I would never take her away from him."

"Even though he's had her all this time, away from you?"

"He didn't know the situation. It's not the same."

Frank let out a deep sigh and bent to kiss her cheek. No warm fuzzy feeling like when Theo pressed his lips to her skin.

"Call me if you need anything. I'm here for you, even if I'm in Westchester."

"I appreciate it. Thanks. I'll be fine."

As Frank left in his expensive rental car, she knew she would be fine. Her daughter was here, and Theo had kissed her. Things were looking up.

"Ready to cut down some trees, my little lumberjack?"

Chelsea grinned up at him, and Theo's heart exploded. How did she do that with only a smile?

"You want to carry the chainsaw?"

She nodded, nibbling on her lip. "If you want me to."

Leaning down, she grabbed the handle and lifted. The machine went up a few inches as her face tightened. "On second thought, I may need to work up to this."

He laughed, moving toward her. "I was only kidding, pixie. I can get it."

Her nose wrinkled as she made a face at him. God, he wanted to pull her close and kiss the living daylights out of her. A shame Rico was only a few feet away.

"You sure you don't want to switch helpers today?" Rico asked, eyeing Chelsea and then the fifty-something man who had also volunteered for tree duty.

"Not on your life, chump. I'm sticking with mine."

Narrowing his eyes, Rico smirked. "Maybe you two should have a chaperone."

Theo shrugged his backpack on, then hefted the chainsaw. "Seeing as we're married, I don't think that will be necessary. Catch you later."

Laughter echoed behind him as they started along the path. The tiny smile that found its way to Chelsea's face when he said the marriage comment made him feel like a hero.

"You okay carrying those clippers and the shovel?"

"I think I can manage. You've got the chainsaw, after all."

The morning silence surrounded them as they hiked. Chelsea kept breathing in the cool air deeply, and her shoulders relaxed with the peaceful atmosphere. It was nice, seeing her this way after a few weeks of being practically shattered. It gave him hope. That and the way she responded to his kisses.

There had only been a few, but it was like leaping into the past. The way they'd kissed and melted into one another when they'd first met. The feeling was still present. For him at least, and he'd bet anything, from Chelsea's response, for her, too.

It would take them about ten minutes to get to the first tree that he'd tagged. That gave him time to think about yesterday's chat with his parents. Typically, they had a video call a few times a month, but he'd put it off once Chelsea arrived. Finally, yesterday, when Chelsea had taken Jordan and Bandit for a walk, he'd texted his parents and met them online for a face-to-face chat.

The conversation was uncomfortable at first when he'd told them Chelsea had returned. They were concerned that she suddenly wanted Jordan and would take the child away from him. Would she bring trouble? They knew how devastated he'd been when she hadn't returned. Fortunately, his parents were good, kindhearted people, and once they'd heard what her father had done, they'd backed down. He wanted them to meet her but knew she wasn't ready for that yet.

Once Jordan had returned and started to chat with them, nothing else could be said. All the little girl could talk about was the dog, the kittens, and her mom coming back. Her enthusiasm was obvious, especially when she showed them one of the kittens. Chelsea had stayed far in the background, her anxiety at what his parents would think apparent.

After they'd put Jordan to bed at night, he kissed her a few more times. Nothing too passionate, but he'd felt shattered, and he wanted her to know he was interested in rekindling what they'd had. Did she want that, too?

"This is the first tree we've got to deal with." They approached the leaning tree with the bright red ribbon attached.

Tilting her head, she eyed the half-exposed roots. "What do I do?"

After putting down the chainsaw and shrugging off his backpack, he closed the distance and cradled the back of her neck. "You kiss me."

That smile flickered again as she rolled her eyes. "I don't know how that'll take care of the tree."

"It'll take care of me and give me the strength to cut up the tree." Lowering his lips, he pressed them against hers, softly, slowly, sensuously.

The tiny sound that erupted from her throat drove him wild, and he bundled her closer, his other hand curling around her back. Before he plundered again, he took a quick peek to make sure they couldn't be seen by anyone across the lake. Nope. Deep enough in. The last thing he needed was Rico teasing the crap out of him. Not that he couldn't handle the ribbing, but he wasn't sure how Chelsea would handle it if she heard. He didn't want to do anything that would hamper the repair of their relationship.

The crackling of his radio had him reluctantly backing away. As Chelsea's face colored a deep pink, he pressed the button and answered.

"Lapierre."

"Theo," Dina's voice came through. Seriously? The woman had bad timing. "I was wondering your location."

"Rico and I are taking care of the questionable trees at Jordan Pond. Already talked to Norma about this. Is there something you need?"

"Simply filling in my records. Norma's in a meeting, and I didn't want to disturb her."

"Okay, we'll check in later if anything is out of the ordinary." The woman needed to back off. She hadn't radioed Rico.

Before he clipped his radio back to his belt, he held it out. "Let me show you how to use this, just in case."

Her eyes got wide. "Why would I need to use it?"

"Doubtful you will, but it's not a bad idea to know how if anything happens."

"I don't like that thought."

"Here." Handing her the device, he positioned himself beside her and showed her which buttons to press. One arm ran up her shoulder, under her hair to caress her neck.

A chuckle sounded as she tipped her head to stare at him. "Ulterior motives for showing me, maybe?"

"Maybe." He dipped his head to kiss her birthmark. The silky skin of her neck tasted sweeter than any candy.

Her voice quivered. "We won't get many trees done this way."

"Are you complaining?" he asked, his lips wandering up the side of her neck to right below her ear.

A shiver ran through her, and he nipped her lobe.

"Oh, God. No complaints." Her breathy whisper nearly did him in, but she was correct. They'd never get the work done if he spent all day kissing her. Perhaps he could spend all night doing it instead. That thought got him motivated to finish up.

After a last nip to her neck, he reluctantly set about his job and prowled around the tree, assessing how best to tackle it. He got Chelsea to work on clipping some of the smaller exposed roots, warning her to stay on one side of the tree. Last thing he needed was it falling on her, or him. A few of the branches dragged on the ground, so he started up the chainsaw and took care of those.

Once they'd cleared away as much as they could, he pointed Chelsea to a spot a few hundred feet away. "Stay over there while I try and get the trunk down. You never know how it's going to fall."

It took a good half hour to get all the way through the trunk, but it finally settled on the ground. He'd come back another day to cut it all up. Today was simply for making sure the few leaning trees didn't come down on anyone.

When they moved to the second tree, he showed Chelsea how to use the chainsaw. She was nervous but managed to cut a few small limbs off the trunk while he stood behind her, supporting her.

"Do you have anyone working on your house today?" Theo asked as they marched toward the last tagged tree. "You said you wanted bathrooms done first, right?"

"I do, but the plumber can't come for another week. Brett showed up before I left. He'll be peeling all the old wallpaper off in the downstairs rooms."

"I don't like the idea of him being in your house with you."

"He's not in the house with me now, since I'm obviously with you." Her eyes narrowed. "He's been super nice. He even offered to keep an eye on the animals today and take Bandit for a short walk."

"Did he smell like alcohol or act funny at all?"

"Aside from looking like he needs some new, clean clothes, he hasn't done anything strange. You don't need to worry, Theo."

Stopping on the path, he pulled her close. "I do worry about you, pixie. He doesn't like me, and I don't want him taking it out on you."

When he kissed her hair, he could smell the floral scented shampoo she loved so much.

She reached up and stroked his cheek. God, it was heavenly.

"I promise if he does anything that makes me uncomfortable, I'll call you right away."

Which didn't thrill him, since the man could do all sorts of things to her while he was trying to get there.

"Let's get this last tree done, then we can break for lunch. You've been a great helper today."

"I haven't done all that much. Just clipped a few roots and stood here while you did all the hard work."

"You kept me company and are much better looking than some of the volunteers I've had. This is one of those projects we need to have a second person in case of accidents. I appreciate your coming along."

"Happy to."

Setting his backpack and the chainsaw aside, he started around the perimeter of this last tree. It was huge and leaning heavily on its side with tons of roots exposed. It might not take much to get it all the way down. Chelsea stood about halfway down the trunk, kicking at the dirt where one of the larger branches rested, waiting for his assessment.

As he rounded the back, he realized that some of the roots had already been cut. Who the heck would have done this? Rico was on the other side of the lake, and he never would have severed these specific roots as the tree would tip in a dangerous direction.

Whipping around, he trotted back toward Chelsea. She was most likely out of the way, but he didn't want to take any chances.

"Chel, why don't you move back a few more steps? These roots are kind of wonky."

A noise behind him grabbed his attention, but when he took a few steps around the large tree, nothing was there except some swaying leaves in the undergrowth. Had someone been there? Or only an animal?

As he carefully picked his way back around, the tree started to creak. Another loud sound cracked behind him, but the tree started listing to one side, so he ignored it and ran. The trunk started to fall. Then, one of the large branches hit the ground, and it altered course. Straight for Chelsea.

"Pixie, move!" Tearing off in her direction, he thrust her out of the way, but his foot caught on something, and he tripped. The ground rushed up to meet him, scraping his hands and knees. The tree continued to fall. He rolled over, unable to scramble out of the way fast enough. Too soon, a hundred and fifty feet of white pine descended, pinning him to the dirt.

CHAPTER THIRTEEN

"Theo!" Chelsea cried.

As she crouched near him, tears leaked out. Had this been her fault? She'd been kicking around near one of the branches holding it up. If Theo died because of her...

"Theo?" she screamed again, praying he'd be okay. A few of the smaller branches had kept the tree from totally crushing him.

"I'm okay, pixie. I'm okay. Just pinned a bit. I can't seem to get my leg loose. Luckily, the whole weight of the tree didn't land on me."

"Are you hurt anywhere?" God, why did these things happen when she was around?

"The leg's...stuck. Can't really move it, and it's feeling a bit of a pinch. Nothing too bad right now. We need to get this stupid tree off. Can you call Rico?"

"Oh, God, oh, God, oh, God," she chanted, her heart racing like a rabbit being chased by a fox.

"Chel!" Theo snapped at her. "Get the radio off my belt and call Rico."

"Yeah, yeah, I can do that." *I can do this.* Moving closer, she reached under and tried unhooking the radio. It was stuck. *Why can't anything go right?* Finally, she managed to get it and pressed the button like Theo had taught her.

"Rico? Rico," she cried. Were there special code words she needed to get his attention? She looked at Theo's stern face. "He's not answering. What do I do?"

"He will. Just say his name again. He could be in the middle of using the chainsaw."

Before she could press the button, the device squawked at her.

"This is Montenegro. Who is this?"

"Rico, it's Chelsea. We need help. A tree came down, and Theo's pinned beneath it."

"Where are you?" His voice was gruff but calm.

"I don't know." What kind of help was she?

"Tell him we're at the third marked tree," Theo called out. She didn't like his breathless tone.

She relayed the information and waited. Theo's face had paled. His eyes were closed tight, his jaw clenched.

"Crap. It'll take me a half hour to get there from my position. Is he conscious?"

"Yes."

"Bring the radio closer to me." Theo lifted his hand slightly to wave her over.

Holding it to his mouth, she pressed the button to talk.

"Rico, I'm okay for now, but the pressure on my leg is increasing. I think the branch that's keeping the tree from totally crushing me is sinking into the dirt with the weight of the pine. Quicker would be better."

"On my way and double timing it."

Chelsea's gaze moved to the branch that was giving Theo a few added inches. It didn't look all that sturdy.

"Pixie, you need to help me."

"What can I do?" Her eyes stung. How could she get so close to having Theo again only to lose him?

"See if you can find a thick stick or something to use as a lever. If we can buy me a few extra inches, maybe I can slide out from under here."

A stick. Lever. Okay. Glancing around, all of the sticks she saw were still attached to the tree.

"You might need to check farther away from here."

"No, I can't leave you," she whimpered. "This is all my fault."

"Chelsea, listen to me. It's not your fault, but you do need to see if you can find something to keep this tree from turning me into one of those pancakes that Jordan likes so much."

"Pancakes, okay." Getting up, she ran a few yards in one direction, then pivoted and went the other way. Stick. Stick. Too small. Too thick. Rotten and would fall apart in a second. Finally, she found one that might work.

Theo lay too still as she returned, his face tight and his hands pushing against the trunk.

"Where do I put this? I'm so sorry. I didn't get outside much as a kid so never played with sticks."

"Right here next to my hip. See if you can get it under the tree a little and then push that rock under it. You should be able to press it down, and it might lift the trunk off and relieve some of the pressure."

"I'll try."

"Do or do not. There is no try."

Chelsea chuckled. God, he was quoting Yoda when he had a huge pine tree crushing him. She set up the stick and rock and started leaning on it, remembering the summer they'd met. When he'd discovered she'd never seen the original science fiction saga, he'd insisted on watching them. All three in a row.

As she pressed down on the stick, the trunk didn't move.

"Keep going, pixie," Theo encouraged.

"I'm not heavy enough."

"I'll need to feed you more to fatten you up. I promise to make your favorites if you get this stupid tree off me."

Pressing again, the tree lifted slightly. Could he slide out?

The crack of the wood made her blood run cold. "It's breaking. What do I do?"

"Shove it under the trunk as far as you can. It will keep the tree from pressing all the way down."

She did as told, but she could tell it wasn't giving Theo much relief. When would Rico get here?

"You need to use the chainsaw. You're going to have to start getting some of this off me."

"What? I don't know how to operate the chainsaw."

"Listen, pixie." His voice sounded like gravel. "My leg is going numb, and I really don't want to lose it."

"But what if I cut your leg off instead of the tree?" With the way her life was going, she didn't doubt it might happen.

"You don't need to cut anywhere near me. But this tree is over a hundred and fifty feet long and most of that is currently pressing down on me. Start on the smaller part to the left of me, and it should help."

Could she do it? She'd have to if she didn't want Theo to lose his leg. Or possibly die. Grabbing the chainsaw, she hefted it and moved it closer to the pine.

"Pull the starter like I showed you. Remember to yank it forcefully."

"Okay." Her tiny word sounded pathetic to her own ears. Did she have the strength? The cord didn't want her to succeed, but as she watched Theo's eyes squeeze shut and his jaw tighten, she knew she had to find the strength.

After a few tries, the machine roared to life.

"Don't try and cut through the whole thing all at once, pixie," Theo said. "Cut out some smaller V-shaped pieces until you get through."

How the heck was she supposed to do this? She wasn't a lumberjack, for Pete's sake. Nevertheless, seeing Theo in pain helped her along. The chainsaw jolted her arms as it sliced through the pine. One small cut, then another. This was taking forever. Could she do it before it was too late?

His complexion grew paler, and his lips compressed together as the tree shook from the effects of the saw. The ridiculous machine kept getting stuck in the wood of the tree, and she had to yank forcefully on it to get it out. Surprisingly, she hadn't sliced her head open yet.

"You can do it," Theo encouraged again, however his voice wasn't as strong as it had been. Being a hero had not been in the job description when she signed up for this work. Still, she kept going, sawing away at the wood inch by slow inch.

"Only a little more, pixie. You're doing great."

As Theo spoke, the chainsaw sputtered and stopped.

"What? No!" She wiggled it out of the wood and tried tugging on the pull cord again. Nothing.

Theo's sigh could be heard in the now silent forest. "You ran out of gas. I was afraid there wouldn't be enough."

The emptiness in her stomach threatened to swallow her up. "What do I do now?"

The pain lines around Theo's eyes were deep. Lifting one hand, he held it out. "Come over here and talk to me."

"You've got a huge tree flattening you into the ground, and you want to chat?"

He wiggled his fingers, coaxing her near. When she knelt down beside him, he grabbed her hand and squeezed. "You got most of the way through. Rico should be here soon, and he can take care of the rest."

The tears she'd pushed aside as she cut through the tree returned. "I should have done more. I should…"

"Kiss me."

Did he seriously say that? "Kiss you? You're stuck under a tree."

"I can't think of a better distraction than having your lips on mine."

God, the man was crazy. Leaning closer, she pressed her mouth to his. If she wasn't so scared that he was going to die on her, she would have enjoyed this.

His fingers closed around her neck and drew her near. Bracing her hands on either side of his head, she put her all into the kiss. He needed a distraction; she'd give him one. Theo's lips against hers made everything disappear. Memories of the years of loneliness, losing her child, her father's betrayal, they all took a back seat now that she connected to the man she loved. He kissed her as if his life depended on it. Maybe it did.

"Sheesh. Can't leave you two alone for a minute."

Chelsea yanked away. Rico. Thank God.

"About time you got here," Theo groaned, his face strained.

As Rico paced around, assessing the tree, he said, "I told you a chaperone was required."

"Just cut the flippin' tree and get it off me."

"You do this, Chelsea?" Rico indicated the deep V-cut in the trunk as he started up his chainsaw.

Stepping back to allow him to work, she nodded. She positioned herself by Theo's head and clasped his hand as the tree shook with the vibration of the machine. It took Rico only a few minutes to cut through the rest of the wood. As the last part cracked and broke apart, Theo let out a pain-filled groan.

"It's almost done," she whispered in his ear, stroking the hair back from his sweaty brow.

"Okay, Chelsea, I'm going to lift this up if I can. I need you to help pull him out. Can you do that?"

She positioned her hands under Theo's arms and waited for Rico to push up on the remaining wood. It moved an inch and then two, and she pulled with all her might. Theo's non-trapped leg dug into the dirt and stretched, and soon he was free.

As Rico lowered the trunk again, Chelsea dropped into the dirt, cradled Theo's head, and kissed his face.

"Let me take a look at that leg. See if there's a fracture."

Theo didn't do much except nod and close his eyes as Rico ran his hands over his leg. Once he'd finished, Rico reached for his radio. "I've got him out. What's your ETA?"

The device crackled and a female voice came through. "Almost there. We heard the chainsaw."

"What's the damage?" Theo opened his eyes a narrow slit, his mouth still in a straight line.

"I don't feel any obvious fractures, but Kim will be able to tell better. She's almost here."

"Kim?" she asked. Why did that name sound familiar?

"She was at our wedding," Theo said. "The paramedic friend who took the pictures."

That's where she'd heard the name. And when the pretty blonde trotted into the clearing, Chelsea remembered. Behind Kim was a forty-something man who carried a metal stretcher of sorts. Two other rangers followed behind.

"Getting in trouble again, I see, Lapierre," the female paramedic teased, yet her eyes held concern.

"I haven't seen you in a while and thought this might be the only way to get you to come hang out." Theo might joke, but the clenched way he spoke told the true story of his discomfort.

Chelsea sat back while Kim and the other man, whose name was Pete, worked on Theo. When they helped him to stand and he placed his foot on the ground, he swayed and his face tightened. Kim glared at him.

"We're using the litter and no arguments."

In minutes, they had Theo loaded and strapped in, grumbling as they picked him up.

"Stop your belly aching," Rico said, hefting a chainsaw in each hand while the other rangers took a hold of the back of the stretcher, and Kim and Pete took a handle on each side of the front.

"What can I do?" Chelsea felt completely useless.

"If you could grab the backpacks and shovel, it would be great."

Quickly, she retrieved them, strapped one on her back and one on the front, then hefted the shovel. In a second, she caught up to Rico.

"I'm sorry I couldn't get the tree off him." Her stupid voice wobbled. Why couldn't she be as strong and steady as these rescue workers?

Pausing for a step, Rico looked at her strangely. "What are you talking about? You did most of the work for me. If it hadn't been for you, I'd still be ripping that tree apart, and Theo's injury might be worse."

"Do you think he'll be all right?"

"Theo's built of sturdy stuff. He'll be fine." Rico's eyes grew mischievous. "But I'm sure he could use some extra pampering for a few days. You up for that?"

"Of course." She'd do anything for Theo.

"Some of what you were giving him earlier might go a long way in helping him heal."

Heat rushed through her face, and she glanced toward the water. With the overcast day, the lake didn't sparkle like it usually did, but the stillness soothed her, anyway.

The hike back to the boat ramp was solemn. Rico tried to make small talk. She got the feeling it wasn't something he did often, but she appreciated the effort. It didn't make her feel any better about Theo being injured. He'd pushed her out of the way. It should have been her under that tree.

Would anyone miss her if she was gone? She used to think her father would, but now he was dead, and she knew he'd never truly loved her. Not in any real way. If he had, he never would have stolen her child from her and told her she died.

Jordan might miss her. They'd grown closer since she'd been here, and her little girl told her she loved her every night. Those words helped piece her broken heart back together, bit by bit. And what of Theo? His kisses made her heart sing but what did they mean? And would they remain if he knew how completely messed up she was?

"Well, Mr. Lapierre, looks like nothing's broken," the doctor who'd been poking and prodding Theo said as he waltzed back into the room he was being treated in.

"So I'm free to go?" Theo crept toward the edge of the bed. Not that he minded the two-hour rest. His leg felt like it'd been through the ringer. Still, there were things he needed to do, like getting Chelsea to stop feeling guilty and looking like a sad puppy.

"Not so fast." The doctor rifled through a stack of papers. "You've got some severe bruising, no doubt. I want you to stay off that leg for a few days, keep it elevated, and ice it at regular intervals. I'll have the nurse bring you in a pair of crutches. If you have any problems, we want to see you back here immediately."

The doc rattled off a list of things he should look for and be cautious of. Chelsea sat in the corner, taking in every word. When he left, Theo held his hand up to her.

"Come here."

Moving quickly, she entwined her hand with his.

"I'm so sorry, Theo. I should have moved out of the way, so you didn't have to jump in and save me."

"Pixie, stop. The tree shifted directions at the last second. You couldn't have foreseen that."

Her eyes filled with tears as she bit her lip.

"The more immediate question is do we have a ride home? You came in the ambulance with me. Do I have anything to wear, since they cut my pants off?"

An eruption of pink stained her cheeks.

"Rico came by while you were having your x-ray and dropped off your SUV." Her head cocked to the side of the room. "You had a bag in there with spare clothes."

Thank God for Rico. The man always came through.

"Can you bring that over here and help me get the pants on? Not sure I can bend the leg at the moment."

"Sure."

As Chelsea slid the pants over his feet and pulled them up, he cupped her shoulders in support. Mostly so she'd have to get the pants all the way around his waist. Her cheeks were on fire by the time he adjusted the zipper and button.

He'd managed to get his boots back on when the nurse arrived with a pair of crutches. She handed some papers to Chelsea.

"These are the instructions and number to call if you have any questions or concerns. We had the hospital pharmacy fill a prescription for an anti-inflammatory and painkillers. They're in the bag with his clothes." Yeah, his totally cut up clothes.

"I'll make sure he takes them." Her voice was firm.

Grabbing the crutches, he balanced on one leg and hobbled toward the door, Chelsea hovering by his side.

"Do you have the car keys?" he asked when they crossed the parking lot.

"Yes, and I'll keep them. They gave you a shot for pain. You shouldn't be driving."

Except he felt fine, but he wouldn't argue because she was right. Especially since they needed to go get Jordan. He directed her to the school their daughter attended, then started getting out of the vehicle.

"I can get her, so you don't have to walk," she said.

"You aren't on the approved pick-up list." At her crestfallen face, he added, "But we'll get you on there when we go in."

The director, Tracy, hopped up from her desk when she saw him with the crutches.

"What did you do to yourself, Theo?"

Shaking his head, he frowned. "A little accident. It's not even broken, so no need to worry."

"Well, that's good. Obviously, why you're so early. There might still be a few napping in the preschool room. Do you want me to get Jordan for you, so you don't have to walk up the stairs?"

"Actually, I want to get someone added to Jordan's pick-up list. This is my wife, Chelsea. Jordan's mother."

Tracy got credit for keeping a neutral face when he called Chelsea his wife. So many others had looked at him like he'd said she was from Mars.

It took a few minutes to get the formality done, then he showed Chelsea the way to Jordan's classroom. It was only a short flight of stairs, but he hadn't realized using the crutches would be so difficult on them. If he tried to put any weight on his leg, the pain was intense.

"It's almost two. Most of the kids should be awake, but they do have a few who like to nap longer, so we should be on the quiet side."

A grin lit up her face. "I'm going to assume our daughter is not one of the long sleepers."

Laughing, he replied, "No. She will fall asleep, but an hour is usually all they get. When she was younger, she could nap all day."

The light drained from her face. God, he hated that she hadn't been around to see all the milestones Jordan had mastered. As expected, Jordan was sitting up on her mat, looking at a book.

When she saw them, her face beamed, then fell as she took in the crutches.

Her teacher, Miss Ashley, nodded for her to get up, and she zoomed to the door.

"What happened, Daddy?"

"Got a little banged up at work. Nothing to worry about, peanut." He kept his voice low, even though most of the children were sitting up on their mats. "While you put your mat away, I'll get your stuff."

"Hey, Mama. You come to get me today." The little girl bounced up and down in her usual exuberant manner, then jumped into Chelsea's outstretched arms.

"Hi, you must be the mom Jordan has been telling us about for the past few weeks," Ashley said, walking over with Jordan's bag and sweater.

Taking the stuff, Theo made the introductions. "This is my wife, Chelsea. She's on the list now to pick up Jordan."

"It's nice to finally meet you." Ashley extended her hand to shake Chelsea's. "Jordan has been so excited and has been talking non-stop about having you around."

It was nice to see Chelsea finally look cheery, but once they got in the SUV, she looked nervous again.

"Do you mind if we take a slight detour? You said you felt okay, right?"

"Where do you need to go?"

"I want to check on the animals. Brett said he'd watch them, but I don't know what time he was leaving."

Brett. It wouldn't be a bad idea to see what the man had done to Chelsea's house. Make sure he hadn't made it worse instead of better. Or left her any surprises.

He was glad Chelsea was driving. The pain pills had made him groggy, but he roused himself once they got to her house. Brett's car was nowhere in sight.

"I'll only be a minute. I need to make sure they can't get out of the back office for the night."

"Are you not planning on coming back here tonight?" There'd only been the one night she'd stayed. Was she going to repeat that?

"I need to take care of you."

"I'll be fine, but if you feel the need to play nursemaid, we should probably bring the animals to our place for the night. Who knows what kind of trouble they'll get into alone?"

Our place. How would she interpret that? His and Jordan's? Or all three of them? Yeah, he liked that thought.

As soon as they got inside, Bandit started barking. Jordan rushed over and patted the dog over the baby gate. Chelsea got food ready for them in the kitchen.

"I might as well feed them all now. That way, I won't have to bring as much with me."

"Good idea." It might not be a bad idea for him to get some dog and cat food for his house, since they seemed to spend almost as much time there as here.

Once the animals had been taken care of, Chelsea rushed up the stairs, calling back, "I'm going to get some clothes to change into. Be down in a sec."

This would be a good time to look around and make sure Brett hadn't done any damage. Mostly, it looked like he'd stripped the wallpaper off. He'd also left a note on the kitchen counter, anchored by the broken hammer, saying he'd run to the store to get more wallpaper stripper. Chelsea had scribbled a note underneath his, saying she had the animals, not to worry, and to lock up when he left.

"I'm all ready," Chelsea said a few minutes later as she ran down the stairs. It was good to see color in her cheeks again. "Jordan, we need to put the kitties in their carrier."

The drive back was normal with Jordan chattering on, this time to the dog and kittens. When they finally managed to get them all in the house, Theo was exhausted. The trauma with the tree had wiped him out. Or maybe it was the pain medicine. Either way, he needed to get horizontal.

"If you don't mind, pixie, I'm going to rest my leg for a bit. If you're hungry, there are some leftovers in the fridge you can nuke in the microwave."

"Aren't you hungry? You didn't have any lunch either."

Slumping onto the couch, he shook his head. "Not sure I have the energy to eat anything right now."

Chelsea set down the cat carrier and rushed next to him. "Can I get you anything?"

Reaching for her head, he pulled her down for a kiss. "That's always nice. Maybe keep Jordan and the menagerie in the playroom for a bit, if you don't mind."

"Of course. Of course. You get some rest. I'll be here if you need me."

They all scurried off into Jordan's playroom, then as his eyes were sealing shut, she rushed back in and deposited a bag of ice wrapped in a towel onto his leg.

"The doctor said you need to ice it. Hopefully, that will help."

Drawing her close again, he gave her another kiss. This one longer and deeper. "That will help."

Before she stood, she returned the kiss with even more passion. Now, she was getting the picture.

CHAPTER FOURTEEN

Chelsea tiptoed downstairs after she'd put Jordan in bed, not wanting to disturb Theo if he was asleep. During the afternoon and early evening, he'd dozed off and on, mostly due to the painkillers. He was trying to be stoic, but a fully grown pine tree had fallen on his leg.

As she crept toward the kitchen, she glanced his way. A crooked grin spread lazily across his face.

"Thanks for putting her down. Don't know if I could climb those stairs. The leg's throbbing now."

"Let me get you some more ice." She scurried into the kitchen, filled the bag she'd been using with ice, and rewrapped it in the towel. Once it was on his leg, she said, "I'm going to tidy up the kitchen. Do you need anything else?"

"Don't worry about the mess. We can clean it up later."

"I'll clean it up now, unless you need me to get you something."

A frown darkened his face, then a sly smile took its place. "I would like to get more comfortable for the night. Can you help me with that?"

"Help you upstairs? Sure." *Could* she get him up the stairs? He towered over her.

"No, I think I'll sleep down here tonight. Hopefully, by tomorrow the swelling will have gone down, and I'll be able to move the leg a bit more. I don't want to take any chances trying to get up there tonight."

"Will the couch be comfortable for you?"

"Yeah, if I can get out of these clothes."

His boots had been removed several hours ago, but he still wore his work shirt and pants. Not exactly sportswear.

"I can run up and get you some pajamas."

His chuckle was deep. "Do you ever remember me wearing pajamas, pixie?"

Heat rushed to her cheeks. If her memory was correct, he rarely wore anything to bed.

"Help me take off the pants. I'm pretty sure I can do the shirt, but the leg's a bit touchy right now."

Sitting up, he unbuttoned his shirt and shrugged it off, then undid his belt buckle.

"I'll slide the waist off. If you tug from the bottom, I won't have to move too much."

Sure. She'd just help him take his pants off. Why was the room a million degrees all of a sudden?

"You won't hurt me, Chel, but I can't do it on my own without bending my leg."

Gently, she pulled on the hem of his pants until they slid off. Keeping her eyes on the fabric, she folded and placed them on the chair, then picked up his shirt and did the same thing. Anything to keep from staring at him in his underwear.

"Okay, I'm going to clean up the kitchen now. I made a huge mess." She had, though it wasn't the real reason she hurried out of the room. Theo, in nothing but a pair of boxer briefs, was bringing back too many memories. Ones she couldn't do anything about at the moment.

The kitchen was cleaned far too quickly, and she took her time heading back into the living room. Thankfully, Theo had draped a quilt over his legs, but not his gorgeous torso.

"How about a movie or show? It's still early."

Looking around, she grabbed the remote and flicked on the tv. Handing the device to Theo, she moved toward one of the chairs.

"Nope, I need you over here."

Tilting her head, she said, "There isn't any room on the couch. I don't want to hurt you."

"It'll hurt more if you aren't next to me. Bring that ottoman over, and I can put my leg on it."

Doing as he asked, she helped lift his injured leg onto the cushioned stool. The quilt slipped off his lap. His long legs were toned and sprinkled with hair. She remembered how they felt when they mingled with hers in bed.

"Get comfortable, too, Chelsea, then join me. I'll try and find something good to watch."

Putting her pajamas on wasn't going to be comfortable, not since she'd only brought a loose pair of shorts and a tank top. Even so, she trotted up the stairs, brushed her teeth and got ready. Borrowing his comb, she brushed out her hair, then chastised herself for her vanity. Theo was hurt. It wasn't the time to seduce him. Assuming she even knew how.

The tv was on a sitcom, and Theo had tossed the quilt over his lap. His bare feet rested on the ottoman. When she drifted into the room, he patted the seat beside him in invitation.

As she came to rest a few feet from him, he coiled his arm around her waist and pulled until she was flush against his muscled chest.

"I like you here. Hope that's okay." His mischievous grin warmed her inside and out.

"Of course. Whatever makes you happy."

"You make me happy, pixie."

Her insides quivered, and her heart raced.

"Thanks for helping me out with Jordan today. Not sure I could have managed without you. She tends to get excited about things."

So he liked that she took care of Jordan today. Was that it? God, how was she supposed to read this? But his arm around her shoulder, caressing her neck and ear kept her from dwelling on anything else. Even the show they were watching.

When a few more shows finished and she'd given Theo another dose of painkillers, she caught him nodding off.

"I'll let you get some sleep. What else can I do for you before I go upstairs?"

His strong arms tightened, and he kissed her. It wasn't the first time, and it wasn't the most passionate, but the connection between them was there. She felt it and joined in freely. Theo leaned back, and she fell against him, their lips never leaving each other. Touching his chest and feeling his strength caused her to become brave.

As she combed her fingers through his hair, his hands roamed down her back and caressed her backside. God, it felt amazing. Wiggling closer, she wanted, no needed to have him touch her more intimately.

Whump. His leg slid off the ottoman. His face scrunched up in agony, he bolted up and stifled a curse.

"Oh, my God. I'm so sorry. I'm sorry. I shouldn't have—"

He gripped her hand so she couldn't move away. "Yes, you should have. That wasn't your fault either, pixie. You seem to like blaming yourself for everything. I started it, and I sure didn't mind you joining in."

Biting her lip, she whispered, "I didn't mind joining in either."

His laugh rang through the room. "Good to know. I guess it is time to call it a night. Those pills are working their magic. Help me get this leg onto the couch again."

Once he was resting and she'd covered him with a quilt and given him a good pillow to use, she wandered around making sure the doors and windows were closed and the lights were off. As she neared the stairs, he crooked his finger at her.

"I need a goodnight kiss like Jordan gets."

An impish grin escaped as she said, "But you don't have a kissing heart."

"Then, you can put it right here." He pointed to his lips.

"This is how we got in trouble a few minutes ago. Are you sure it's a good idea?"

He reached out and reeled her in. "It's a very good idea."

———◆———

A quick rap on the door distracted Theo from his attempt at washing out the coffee pot. Grabbing one crutch, he maneuvered into the living room as the front door opened. Rico's dark head appeared, a grin on his friend's face.

"Don't get up on my account." Rico entered and closed the door behind him. "I was only checking to make sure you don't need anything."

"I was already up," Theo answered. "Nothing wrong with me, except a little bruise on my leg."

Rico's eyebrows raised. "A *little* bruise?"

"Okay, a big bruise. It's nothing I can't handle."

"Norma doesn't seem to think it's nothing. I heard she's got you on leave for a few days."

Theo gazed skyward, trying not to roll his eyes. He liked his boss but wished she hadn't put her foot down on this.

"Yeah, which is ridiculous since I'm fine. Maybe she'll let me do desk duty tomorrow, if I promise to be a good boy."

"Dina would love that," Rico said with a smirk. "You'd be right where she wants you. Can't you see her finding all sorts of things to do around your desk? Running those long fingernails along your arm, down your back, brushing against your—"

"Okay, desk duty probably isn't the best idea. Guess I could stay home and enjoy some time with my family."

Rico looked around. "Are you talking about Jordan or Jordan *and* Chelsea? Speaking of...where are they?"

"Chelsea and Jordan took Bandit for a walk. I think they were bringing back food from Pepper's. I got stuck here babysitting."

"Babysitting?" The expression on Rico's face showed his confusion.

Theo pointed to the laundry basket near the couch. "Babysitting."

Rico edged closer and eyed the black puffballs in the basket. Scooping one up, he grinned. "You got kittens?"

His leg had started to throb again as he'd placed his weight on it, so Theo hobbled to the couch and sat down under the guise of showing his friend the animals.

"Chelsea saw these when we picked out the dog. Since they're black, there wasn't a good chance they'd get adopted. She's such a softy; she couldn't leave them there."

"And you didn't try and talk her out of it?"

"You should have seen her face. She was so excited. Almost more so than Jordan, although Chelsea didn't jump up and down clapping like our daughter."

"*Our* daughter. That's rolling off the tongue a bit easier these days." Rico placed Snap back in the basket and pulled out Pop. The kitten immediately started jumping.

"I have to be real careful about saying that. The look on Chelsea's face when I make a mistake? It's awful, man. You have no idea."

"She seemed pretty upset about your accident yesterday. She obviously cares about you."

Theo glanced at the kitten he'd picked up. "How we feel isn't the problem. We were only married for two weeks before she left and that was almost five years ago. Things have changed. Our lives have gone in different directions. Not to mention, Chelsea still isn't back to where she used to be. I don't want to push anything on her that she isn't ready for."

"And maybe you still harbor some resentment that you had to raise a baby all by yourself?"

Theo's head snapped up, his tongue ready with an angry retort. But was Rico right? Did he still resent that he'd raised his…their…daughter all by himself? He couldn't blame Chelsea. She'd been as much a victim as he'd been. But the bitterness and despair at what had happened, and how much Jordan had lost because of it, was still strong in his memory.

"Maybe. Of course, the resentment has shifted all to her father. And maybe to me, too. I never forced the issue like I should have."

"Look to the future," Rico said, holding up Pop. "You have three little kittens in your life. As well as a dog, a child and, hopefully, a wife."

After plunking the kitten back in the basket, Rico stood and peered out the window. When he looked back, his face was solemn.

"What's up? You didn't come here to discuss kittens."

"I went and had a look at that tree after I got back from dropping off your things at the hospital."

Theo narrowed his eyes. Where was this going? "And?"

"The roots were cut, not broken. I asked Chelsea on our walk back, and she said neither of you had done anything to them. She seemed to think the tree might have fallen because she kicked a little dirt near the base."

"Chelsea barely went near the base of the tree. I thought the roots looked strange, but then the tree started tipping and there wasn't time for anything else."

"Is there someone who might have wanted to harm you or her?"

"Harm us? Like who?" Brett Sheehan came to mind. He hadn't been at the house when they'd gone back later.

Rico shrugged. "I don't know. Could've been teenagers fooling around, but the roots were definitely cut and quite a few of them. It wasn't an accident."

Rubbing his thigh where the bandage covered his injury, Theo thought back to the last week.

"I hate to sound paranoid, but there have been a few things lately that I kind of shrugged off."

"Like?" Rico shoved his hands in his uniform pockets and rocked back on his heels.

"Remember I told you I had those rocks tumble down on the North Ridge Trail?"

"Yeah. You had a humongous bruise on your back, if I recall."

"And Sunday, Chelsea stayed overnight…" Theo frowned when Rico smirked. "She fell asleep on the couch watching tv, and she was taking care of Jordan the next day, so I let her sleep. On the couch. I slept upstairs."

"I didn't say anything." The expression on Rico's face was anything but innocent.

"Anyway…Sunday, I went for a run and took Bandit with me. A car almost ran me off the road. If the dog hadn't jumped on me, I might have been hit. I passed it off as someone who hadn't had their coffee yet, but now I wonder."

"Did you see the license plate or make and model of the car?"

"Big, dark car. That's about it. I was too busy brushing myself off in the gutter."

Twisting away from the window, Rico stared hard at him. "Maybe it's time to have a chat with Aiden Cavanaugh."

"And tell him what? Some rocks slid down a mountain? I was running in the road? A downed tree fell? The tree would have hit Chelsea if I hadn't pushed her out of the way, but she wasn't anywhere nearby with the other two."

"Yet the tree ended up falling on you."

"Too random. There may have been some foolish pranks involved, but I don't think I need to get Aiden involved. I will keep my eyes open a bit wider in the future."

A ruckus on the front porch stopped their conversation. The front door opened, and Bandit scampered in, followed by a skipping Jordan and Chelsea, who seemed totally out of breath. In her hands was a large bag.

Theo started to lever himself up, but Rico stepped in and grabbed the bag.

"You all set there?"

Those gorgeous blue eyes focused up, and humor appeared on her face. "Thanks, Rico. Hi. Sorry, Bandit was in a running mood on the way back. Guess I'm out of shape."

Not from where Theo sat. Her long, slim legs were a vision in the conservative khaki shorts she wore, and her snug t-shirt emphasized her small but shapely chest.

"We got subs, garlic bread, and some chicken fingers. Plenty if you want to stay and share some, Rico."

Jordan got down and played with the kittens while Rico helped Chelsea organize things in the kitchen. Theo fed Bandit and put him out on the back, screened-in porch, so he wouldn't bother them while they ate. Once the food was gone and cleaned up, Chelsea and Jordan took the kittens into her playroom and Theo escorted Rico out to his vehicle.

"Let me know if you need anything."

"Chelsea's been here, so I'll be fine. She's also an expert on buying things, so I don't think I need to worry there."

"Shopaholic?"

Theo shrugged. "Not sure I'd call it that. It seems she wants to make up for all the birthdays and Christmases she's missed with Jordan."

"So she's set with money? Does she have a job?'

"A job?" Theo scoffed. "No, Chelsea comes from money. Her father left her quite well-off, I'm sure. I think that's half the problem."

"Having money?"

"Having *only* money." They'd had a few conversations after they'd gotten married, and it sounded like Chelsea had grown up pampered but lonely. Anything material she had, but someone to love her? That had been absent. Perhaps it was why she'd blossomed so quickly with him. Or was it why she'd thought she was in love?

"I know you said her dad was a piece of work. What about her mom?"

Theo shook his head. "I don't know. Her mom died when she was younger, like ten maybe. She always got quiet whenever the subject came up, so I didn't push her on it."

"You should take the next few days and see about getting back some of what you lost while she's been away."

The idea had merit. A few days with Chelsea and Jordan being a family. And all paid for, since his accident had happened during work and on National Park property.

"That might be a great idea. Plus, it would keep me away from Dina."

Rico chuckled. He got in his truck and drove away.

———— ◆ ————

"Mama, are you gonna stay here again tonight?"

Chelsea looked up, busy extracting Crackle from the third floor of the dollhouse yet again. Jordan loved the fact the kittens could fit inside. The girl didn't seem to realize the animals could get hurt if they tumbled out, no matter how many times she'd been told, and the kittens didn't quite get the message to stay inside.

"Um…I'm not sure, sweetheart. It depends on how your father is feeling. We'll see if he still needs help tonight."

Truthfully, she'd loved to spend another night in Theo's bed, although it would be far more satisfying if he was in it with her. Even without him, his lingering scent had set her senses on high alert and given her the most luscious dreams.

"Hannah's mama and daddy sleep in the same bed."

Glancing at her daughter, Chelsea wondered where she'd gotten this information.

"But Holden's daddy doesn't. He lives in a different house like you live in a different house."

"How do you know this, Jordan?"

"Hannah said she gets to sleep in her mama's bed if her daddy goes away for work. My daddy sometimes lets me if I have a bad dream."

"That's because he's a good daddy, and he loves you."

"Can I sleep in your bed if I have a bad dream?"

Chelsea sighed. How to answer this question? "If we're in the same house, of course you can. Bad dreams always go away quicker when you're with someone you love."

"But you and Daddy don't live in the same house. Like Holden's mama and daddy. Holden's daddy has a girlfriend. They gettin' married. Are you getting married to someone, too, Mama?"

"I'm already married to your father, sweetheart. I can't marry anyone else."

Jordan gathered all three kittens into her lap. "Good. I don't want another daddy."

"Yours is a pretty good one."

As Chelsea tucked furniture back into the dollhouse, Jordan turned and tilted her head, allowing all three kittens to squirm off her lap. "Mama, how come, if you and Daddy are married, you don't live in the same house?"

That was an excellent question, and she wished she knew the answer.

"We did live in the same house—this house—when we first got married. But then I got sick, and I had to live somewhere else. I didn't get better for a long time."

"But you're better now. So you can come live here, wight?"

Glancing toward the door, she made sure Theo wasn't nearby. Twenty minutes ago, he'd hobbled up the stairs to take a shower. Hopefully, he wouldn't pop back down in the middle of her explanation.

"I have to clean up and get my grandmother's house in good shape."

Jordan bounced up and down. "Can we live in that house? When it's weady?"

"Would you like to live there?"

"Yeah, 'cause you live wight by the ocean."

"The ocean is nice, but I'm not sure if your father would want to move there. He's lived in this house for a long time."

"Daddy loves the ocean. I bet he'd want to."

"Want to what?" Theo asked from the doorway. How had she not heard him come down the stairs?

"Live at Mama's house. You like the ocean, wight, Daddy? Mama gets to look at the ocean every single day."

The girl's eyes were wide, and her expression excited. Theo's was closed. Chelsea wished she could read what he was thinking.

"You want to live with your mom instead of here?" His gaze turned intense.

Jordan nodded. "But her house not weady yet, so we can stay here for now." She skipped over to Theo and stared at his leg, then up at him.

"Daddy, how your leg feel?"

A crooked smile smoothed out the scowl on Theo's face. "It's feeling pretty good, peanut. Nothing to worry about."

Jordan frowned. "I want it to not feel good."

"What?" Theo's eyebrows nearly climbed off his face. "Why would you say that?" He threw a questioning look in her direction. Did he think she was a bad influence on their daughter?

"If your leg still hurt, Daddy, then Mama can stay here again. I want Mama stay here."

"Oh, I see." The apologetic look he sent her confirmed that he did.

Limping over to them, he struggled to get on the floor. Finally down, he pulled both her and Jordan over near him. The thumb he rubbed back and forth over her skin was so distracting she had a hard time concentrating on what he was saying.

"Your mom is welcome to stay here if she wants to, but remember she also has to take care of her house. It's kind of hard to fix it up if she isn't there."

Warmth filled her at his touch. Nothing could be better than staying here with him and their child. He'd also given her an out if she wanted to take it. Did she?

Her mind whirled with confusing thoughts and emotions. The kisses Theo and she had shared recently had given her hope for the future. The blame for their split had shifted, and they were starting to grow closer again. But would that remain once Theo discovered her secret? The fact he'd looked her way when Jordan had suggested moving into the oceanfront property made her realize something. He'd looked at her with blame.

There was still a level of trust and comfort that they hadn't quite reached. Until they got there, she couldn't think about a future with all three of them together.

Chapter Fifteen

"**W**hy do people think going out in fog this thick is a good idea?" Theo asked as he switched the windshield wipers on. It was only misting, but it was enough to make visibility next to nothing.

"It's a Saturday in late May, and they've paid big bucks for their weekend hotel. They'll come out and enjoy the park whether they can see it or not," Rico replied from the passenger seat. Fog always made things more dangerous, so they'd doubled up today.

"Making our jobs of keeping them safe even harder." They'd been scanning the Park Loop Road for the last hour. Fortunately, not too many visitors had ventured out. But there were always a few.

"We might want to stop and check at Thunder Hole. Always a handful of stupid tourists who think climbing on the slippery rocks is cool."

In agreement, Theo maneuvered into the parking lot and put the truck in park. His leg had healed fairly well over the past week and a half and only stiffened occasionally. Like now. Most likely the damp weather.

As they slowly crossed the street in the thick fog, Theo thought about when he'd first gotten injured. Chelsea had decided not to stay over again the second night, and he had to admit to being disappointed. He also knew she'd been hurt when he'd aimed his silent accusation her way. He hadn't meant to indicate she'd been responsible for Jordan wanting to stay with her, but thinking his daughter had chosen her mother over him had stung. Eventually, he'd realized their child simply wanted to be around both of them more. At that point, regrettably, it had been too late to take it back.

"I don't hear a lot of chatter." Rico maneuvered carefully down the stairs toward the attraction. "Maybe no one's here."

"I can't believe how thick this pea soup is. Seriously, I can't even see my hand." Or the flashlight he held in it. The sun wasn't scheduled to set for another few hours, but the low clouds that shrouded the land made everything darker.

"Is Chelsea planning to cook dinner tonight for all of you?" Rico's teasing voice reached him, though the man himself had vanished in the mist.

"I told her not to, but she always feels like she has to earn her keep. Having her stay with Jordan during the weekends I work is a blessing and more than makes up for the food I feed her. Not that Angie minds, but I hate bothering her when it's her only time off. She's got a life, too."

The granite under Theo's feet was slick. He held tighter to the railing as he made his way toward the crashing sound of Thunder Hole. Aside from the noise, there wasn't a whole lot to see. Only another hour of his shift before he could clock out and go back home.

Would Chelsea have attempted to make dinner? The hot dogs and beans he'd gotten were easy enough. Hopefully, he could get her to at least stay. If she tried to drive in this fog, his nerves would be on edge until she got home. He'd made her text him every night after she'd left, so he knew she was all right. His way of making up for his stupidity. That and the gentle kisses he'd given her before she left. Nothing too passionate, even with his body wanting more. Enough to let her know he cared for her.

Had it been only a month ago that she'd shown up here, turning his world upside down yet again? They'd come so far yet not far enough. Not for what he ultimately wanted. But he'd be patient. If the end result was Chelsea back in his life and Jordan having her mom full time, then yeah, he could wait it out.

The roar of the crashing waves got louder, and Theo could tell he was right on top of Thunder Hole. The tide was coming in, even if he couldn't see it.

"Looks empty down here," Rico commented from beside him. Yikes, this fog was bad.

"*Looks* empty? Like you can actually see anything."

"You know what I mean." Rico bumped his shoulder and pushed past him. "How about we head back and finish the Park Loop Road?"

About to follow him, Theo decided to call out first. "Hello? Anyone here?"

Some rocks skittered nearby, and a noise that sounded like a cough echoed through the mist.

"Seriously?" Theo muttered, easing between the railings that were there to keep people safe. So many simply ignored them. It was lethal on a day like today.

"Hello? It's not safe on the rocks today, so I suggest you come back here."

No answer. Then, he heard it again. A slight cough and the sound of rocks being kicked around. The spray from the incoming waves soaked through Theo's coat as he stepped toward the noise. The rocks in this area were super slippery, and his boots slid as he made his way carefully over them. One wrong step and he could go over the side.

"If someone is there, can you call out? Make a sound. Do you need assistance?"

The wind kicked up and buffeted him as another wave crashed nearby, the spray icy cold on his already chilled body. Time to head back to the vehicle. Before he could take another step, he felt something nearby. Next thing he knew, his foot had slipped over the edge, and he felt himself falling.

Throwing his arms out, he managed to catch the edge of a rock. His body slammed into the side of the rockface, and he hung on. Was there something below to drop down onto? Crap, he couldn't tell. Reaching with his other hand, he gripped the ledge and attempted to pull himself up. Another wave crashed into his back, and the wind took that moment to blast him. It took all his strength to keep from falling further down. If only he could see through the flippin' fog. There might be some footholds nearby he could use.

"Rico!" Had his friend already gotten into the nice, warm truck? There was no way Theo could even try to reach his radio. If he let go with one hand, he'd surely drop. Forcing his boots against the rock, he tried to find something to propel him up. The granite was too smooth.

The spray from the incoming tide buffeted his back, and the cold leached into every cell in his body. His frozen hands grew weaker, and he shouted again.

"Theo?"

Thank God. The voice was fairly close.

"Over here! Hurry. I slipped over the edge. Not sure I can hang on much longer."

Footsteps approached, and Theo kept talking, directing the other ranger to his position.

"What the heck, man?" Rico's gloved hand covered his as it began to give up. "I've got you."

Together, they managed to heft Theo up the rocks and onto solid ground. His legs, his whole body, shook. The cold had permeated every pore and cell.

"Let's get you back to the truck."

Theo allowed himself to be helped back, though once he got his legs moving, they seemed to work okay. He was merely cold. As he huddled in the passenger seat, Rico climbed in and blasted the heat.

"What the heck happened? You were right behind me, then suddenly nothing."

"I heard something. I couldn't tell if it was a person, but it came from near the rocks. It sounded like a cough. I went to investigate. Called out a few times. No one answered."

"How'd you end up going over the edge? The fog get you turned around?"

"No. I can't be sure. Maybe I'm paranoid, but there must have been someone there."

"After the other things you told me about, I might be kind of paranoid, too. You think someone what? Pushed you?"

Theo shrugged. "The waves were crashing pretty close and the wind had kicked up, so I honestly couldn't say. But as one of the waves broke, I thought I felt something push against my injured leg. It gave way, and when I tried to correct, my other foot slipped over the edge of the rocks."

"You're lucky you didn't crack your skull open." Rico's eyes were intense and concerned. "Are you hurt anywhere? Should we go to the ER?"

Taking inventory, Theo cataloged his aches. Bruises, for sure, but aside from the deep chill, he felt okay. Meanwhile, fear crept along his spine, sinking into his bones.

"I'm freezing and wet. Nothing a good hot shower won't fix."

Shifting the truck into gear, Rico pulled onto the road. Once the air in the vehicle had warmed up, he shucked his jacket and shirt and grabbed his bag behind the seat to throw on an old sweatshirt. It was all he had since he hadn't replaced his extra clothes after his last injury.

"Maybe Chelsea can help warm you up," Rico said, his tone mischievous.

The thought of her alone could warm him up, but right now his blood ran cold with thoughts that someone might want to hurt him. Want him dead. That could certainly have been the end result if he'd been thrown into the ocean. No one would have found him in this weather.

What would happen to Jordan if he was seriously injured or died? Yes, Chelsea was her biological mother, but he didn't want her to have to go through any legal battle or red tape to take care of their child. First thing Monday morning, Theo planned to call his lawyer. It was time he changed his will to make Chelsea the benefactor and give her all legal rights to their child.

———●○●———

"Theodore, it's so great to see you."

"Hey, Mom," Theo answered, slipping into his mother's embrace. "It's great to see you, too."

"How's my granddaughter?" she asked, peering down at Jordan wrapped around his leg. Bangor International Airport was crowded and noisier than she was used to. Not to mention, she normally only saw his parents through the computer screen. They'd only been able to visit in person a few times since Jordan was born. You'd think the girl was shy.

"I don't know." Theo craned his head to the right and left. "She was around here somewhere, but I seem to have lost her."

A tug on his pant leg was followed by a tiny voice. "I'm wight here, Daddy."

"Hmm…I thought I heard something. Did you hear something, Mom? Dad?"

That got the child jumping up and down and finally hopping into her grandmother's arms for a hug. It always took a few minutes for her to warm up to people she hadn't seen in a while.

"I hope I'll get one of those, too," his father said as he reached for Theo. Theirs was a quick clap of the back followed by a handshake. By the time they got to baggage claim, Jordan was riding on her grandfather's back.

There were times he regretted not going back to Ohio, so Dan and Laurie Lapierre could spend more time with Jordan. Luckily, his older sister and brother had provided them with plenty of other grandchildren to spoil. Now that Chelsea had returned, he knew he'd made the right choice. With all the sabotage her father had thrown at them, she never would have sought him out, even if she'd known where to look, and Jordan would have missed out on ever seeing her mother.

"We're so excited to be here for your birthday, honey," his mom said to Jordan as they waited for their luggage.

"I'm gonna have face paint and magic and a big cake." Jordan's eyes were huge as she listed off her party activities.

"And what do you want for your birthday?" his father asked, getting down on her level.

"Daddy already got it for me."

Both his parents grinned at him, and he looked at them confused. Her present was being constructed as they spoke. He and Chelsea had gone in together and bought a big swing set and climbing structure. His budget had been set, but when he'd mentioned it to Chelsea, she'd asked if she could pitch in and get a larger model. Although he hated to accept her money, he'd agreed, since the one he'd picked out wasn't the one he'd liked the best. He wouldn't let her put any more money in than he had. But how had Jordan known?

"What did you get?" his father asked.

"I got my Mama back."

The adults all froze at her softly spoken words. The emotion in his child's voice crushed him. It was something she'd asked for many times.

"It's even better, 'cause she got a dog and kitties and they are so adorable and I can play with them."

The carousel started spinning and pushing out luggage. His dad took Jordan's hand and led her closer, inviting her to help him find the bag.

"Are you okay, honey?" Mom touched his elbow.

"Yeah. It's just that Jordan asked me when her mom was coming home a dozen times. It still doesn't seem real that's she's back. I keep expecting her to disappear in a puff of smoke like in some fairy tale."

"How are things between you and Chelsea?"

"Moving slowly, but they are moving. So I guess it's all forward, and forward is good."

"She didn't want to come today?"

Taking a deep breath in, Theo said, "First, she's at the house, because Jordan's real present is being delivered and set up. Second, she's nervous about meeting you."

His mother's face crumpled. "Why?"

"She figures you hate her for deserting me and Jordan."

"Oh, honey." She hugged his arm tighter. "We certainly hate what happened to both of you, but now that we know the whole story, we can hardly blame her."

"Thank you, Mom."

His jaw tightened simply thinking about what had happened to keep them apart.

"But you still blame yourself, don't you?"

Facing his mother, he wrestled a smile onto this face. Couldn't get anything past her. "If I had pushed to see her and not accepted what her father had said to me, Jordan wouldn't have gone almost four years without a mother."

"You have to forgive yourself."

"I wish I could. Maybe once Chelsea and I have gotten back to where we once were, I can think about it. Right now, the pain in her face every time she looks at our daughter, it's like a knife to the gut. It's hard for her to forget that she missed so much of her child's life."

Jordan squealed when the bag came around, and she helped her grandfather grab it. They chatted about the rest of the family as they trudged to the SUV and stowed the bag. His mom and Jordan kept up a running dialog in the back during the hour drive home, while his mind kept returning to Chelsea.

As they pulled onto their road, he asked his mom to blindfold Jordan. The girl got so excited it was hard to keep her contained. Chelsea worked in the side yard, picking up scraps of cardboard that were most likely left over from the delivery. The slide, swings, and little fort climbing structure looked great. Jordan would love it.

"Are you ready, peanut?"

"Yes, Daddy, yes! What is it? I want to see."

After hoisting her from her car seat, he carried her to the side yard and placed her on the ground. Chelsea and his parents were eyeballing each other, but he needed to show Jordan her birthday gift first.

"Your mom and I hope you like this." He quickly readied his phone to take a picture, then lifted the cloth off her face.

Jordan's eyes bugged out and the excited bouncing began. His gaze sought out Chelsea's, and they both smiled. They'd done something together for their child.

"Can I play on it? Please, can I?"

Laughing, he said, "I think so. Better ask your mom, since she's the one who was here when they set it up."

"Mama?" If Jordan's eyes got any bigger, they'd take over her face.

"They said it was ready, sweetheart."

In less than a second, the little girl was ducking under the doorway into the little fort then climbing up the back ladder and swishing down the slide.

He slung his arm around Chelsea's shoulder. "I have a feeling she likes it. Nicely done, pixie."

Pink settled on her cheeks, and she leaned against him. Having her close was something he never could resist. He kissed her forehead and squeezed her tight. After a few seconds, she must have remembered his parents there and stiffened, trying to ease away. Nope, not happening.

"Chelsea, I want you to meet my parents, Dan and Laurie. Mom, Dad, this is my wife, Chelsea."

His mother was the first to make a move. She drew Chelsea into a warm embrace and hugged her. For real. The tears that gathered in Chelsea's eyes had him panicked until he saw Chelsea squeeze back. Had her family ever hugged her that way? God, the thought that they hadn't broke his heart.

"I can see why Theo is so taken with you," his father said, and moved closer for a smaller hug. "It's amazing how much you and Jordan look alike."

"We're excited to get to know you better while we're here." His mother watched Jordan scamper around her new present. "I understand Theo has to work tomorrow. I was wondering if you'd be around to enjoy the day with us."

Chelsea's eyes swung to his, and Theo tried to encourage her. "If you have stuff to do, it's fine. But I know they'd love to spend time with you."

Biting her lip, she nodded her head. "Okay. I have to get the plumber set up at the house first thing, then I can come over." She lowered her voice. "Do I have to cook for them?"

His loud laugh couldn't be contained. "My mom's an excellent cook. I'm sure she'd be delighted to make the meals."

His mother smiled. "I'd love to teach you how to make some of Theo's favorite foods."

Burrowing deeper into his embrace, Chelsea chuckled. "You could certainly try."

CHAPTER SIXTEEN

A nother car pulled up, and Chelsea exhaled. Again? How many people had Theo invited for this little birthday party? There were already five other children, plus Jordan, and all their parents. One mom couldn't take her eyes, or hands, off Theo. That wasn't helping her anxiety at all.

When Rico got out, along with their paramedic friend, Kim, she sighed with relief. She didn't know Kim all that well, but Rico had been around enough that she was beginning to feel comfortable near him. Mostly because there was nothing about his actions that were in any way judgy. The same couldn't be said for some of the parents here today.

"Hey, Chelsea," Rico called and held his hand out to Kim. "You remember Kim, don't you?"

The women nodded at each other, and Kim held up a brightly wrapped box. "Where should I put this?"

"There's a table on the front porch. Help yourself to some drinks or snacks. The kids are having a ball, either using Jordan's new birthday present," she indicated the swing set, "or with Angie's friend, who's doing some magic tricks."

"That's James Yoshita," Kim said to Rico. "You've met him. He works at Paxton Labs. My guess is his 'magic' is actually science."

"He's hung out with us a few times." Rico glanced over the children scurrying about. "Did the birthday girl get any sleep last night? Theo said she was wired to the hilt."

"She has been extremely excited, especially since her grandparents are here, too."

Yesterday, Chelsea had spent most of the day with Jordan and Theo's parents. They'd tiptoed around each other, though both of them had been super sweet to her. What exactly they'd been told, she didn't know. Apparently, Theo had filled them in on her father's misdeeds, but what would they think if they found out she was a nutcase?

Then again, was she? The last month here had been amazing, and she hadn't felt this good in a long time. Since the summer she and Theo had met. It didn't mean that something wouldn't arise to push her back over the edge of insanity. It was her greatest fear. Well, behind losing her daughter again, but they both kind of went together.

"Oh, geesh. Angie is waving me over," Kim growled softly. "She roped me into helping with the face painting. I'll catch you later. Here, Rico. Put this on the porch." She shoved the present into his hands.

"At least I don't have to paint faces."

Rico swaggered away, and Chelsea looked around again. Was anyone watching her? Seeing how anxious she was and guessing that her insides were tied in triple knots?

"Everything's going as planned, pixie," Theo said as his arm snaked around her shoulder, reeling her in against his chest. How she loved being there. So warm and protected, like nothing could harm her.

"Should I be doing something?" What exactly was her job here? Theo had planned the party. His mother had done all the food and even made the cake. She'd merely helped with decorations.

"Simply stand here and look beautiful." He pressed his lips to her hair.

Heat spread along her cheeks and down her neck. "Um… We're outside, and there are tons of people here."

His grin grew cocky. "What does that have to do with anything? You're my wife. There's no reason I can't kiss you if I want, right?"

"I guess." Why was her voice so meek?

Tucking a strand of hair behind her ear, he whispered, "Do you want that? A kiss?"

"Always." Again with the breathless tone.

"That's what I like to hear." He lowered his mouth to hers. Not long. Not passionate. Definitely possessive.

"Mama, Daddy! Look what Uncle Rico made me."

Jordan's excited squeal pulled her out of her dream, the one where Theo swept her off her feet and carried her away. Away from judging eyes and gossiping tongues.

"That's awesome, peanut." Theo chuckled. "I guess he has talents we didn't know about."

Jordan held a pink balloon twisted to look like a dog. Several children stood in front of the ranger waiting their turn. The handsy mom also waited. Chelsea doubted it was a balloon she wanted.

"Is it just me or does Kim look irritated at the touchy-feely mom?"

As Jordan scampered away clutching her balloon animal, Theo glanced toward her. "The touchy what?"

Rolling her eyes, Chelsea sighed. "You know, the mom who was hanging all over you earlier? Kim looks annoyed at the way she's flirting with Rico." Better Rico than her husband.

Theo shrugged. "I don't know. Kim and Rico are only friends. But, yeah, Hailey could irritate the pope."

"Only if he was young and good looking," she mumbled. Still, Theo must have heard, because he laughed and wrapped her in a hug. No complaint there, except people were staring at them now.

Pulling her along, he asked, "Do you want a balloon animal or to get your face painted?"

Dread exploded in her stomach. What would make her stand out the least?

"Chelsea, honey," Laurie Lapierre called out from the front porch. "Could you give me a hand bringing out some of this food?"

Saved. "Of course." She tapped Theo's arm. "I have to help your mom."

Theo tapped back, then winked as she scurried away.

"What can I help with, Mrs. Lapierre?" she asked as she entered the kitchen.

Theo's mom smiled. "You're Mrs. Lapierre, too, honey. Why don't you call me Laurie? Or you can call me Mom if that isn't too hard on you. Theo told us you lost yours quite young."

"Mom?" She tried the word out on her tongue. It's what Jordan called her, but it wasn't something she'd called anyone in a long time.

"Only if you want to. Now, this tray of sandwiches needs to be put on the table on the porch. I don't want the kids bumping into it in the yard and knocking everything over. Not to mention, we can put stuff out and clean up easier if it's close. Does that sound okay?"

"Um, yeah, sounds fine." Had she wanted Chelsea's opinion or was she simply being kind? She hadn't been anything but since they'd met Thursday afternoon.

After a few trips back and forth, the table was full, and Chelsea looked around the kitchen to see if there was anything else that needed to go out. Having something to do was preferable to standing around trying to interact with the parents. Theo knew them all, but even after introducing her, she didn't feel comfortable with any of them. Would she ever?

"You okay, honey?" Laurie asked, tossing a crumpled napkin in the trash.

"Yeah. Making sure we didn't forget anything." Could she find something else to do in the house?

"Everyone's getting food. I think Theo wanted to do cake and gifts right after, in case anyone wanted to cut out early."

"Okay. I guess I should go out there then." Her feet didn't move.

As Laurie leaned her elbows on the counter, her eyes softened. "Theo's glad you're back."

Staring at the floor, she said, "I know. Jordan needed a mother."

"That's not the only reason he's happy to see you. I never could understand why he kept holding to the thought you might come back, especially after…well, after what we thought happened. Now that I see you two together, I can understand why."

"You can?"

Laurie nodded. "There's something between you. Something strong. I know you two had a lot working against you and you have to learn to trust each other again. Have faith that you'll get there. Don't give up on each other, all right?"

"I won't."

"Now, let's you and I get something to eat before it's all gone. After all that work, I'm starving." Laurie hooked her hand through Chelsea's arm, and they walked out to the porch together.

———⚫———

"Did she finally calm down?" Chelsea asked as Theo carried a limp Jordan around his office.

Slowly spinning, he let Chelsea see that Jordan had not only calmed down but fallen asleep. The little girl had been so hyped up on party, presents, and cake that she'd had a slight meltdown a few minutes ago when they hadn't allowed her to have yet another piece of her birthday cake. It had been up to him to handle it, since Chelsea had looked about to explode with fear. The last month with their daughter had been much smoother. Sure, there had been small incidents here and there, but nothing like the subatomic blast wave they'd just experienced.

"She fell asleep. That didn't take long." Chelsea's eyebrow rose.

"No nap today and honestly not a ton of sleep last night. She was too excited. The sugar from the party goods kept her going for a while, but all good things must come to an end." He hoped the good things that had been going on between him and Chelsea would continue.

"Do we put her down like that?" Chelsea's nervous gaze darted around the room. Like she was looking for an answer written on the walls or floors.

"I'll carry her upstairs. Why don't you dampen a facecloth and help me clean up the worst while we put her down?"

As they wove their way through the living room to the stairs, his parents blew kisses to the child, then went back to picking up the party leftovers.

By the time he'd managed to pull the trundle bed from under Jordan's twin size, Chelsea had reappeared with the wet cloth.

"Is this where she's sleeping?"

Theo laid her down and proceeded to peel off the girl's shoes and socks. "Yes. I gave my parents my bed, and I've been on the twin."

Chelsea wiped down their daughter's hands and face, then tugged her cake and dirt-stained shirt over her head and removed her shorts. Jordan didn't even twitch.

"Wow, she's really out, huh?"

After locating a long t-shirt, he and Chelsea worked together to wiggle it on the child. A few kisses and whispered "I love yous" and they turned off the light. Standing in the doorway, they watched the peaceful face of their daughter in the glow of the night-light.

He pressed Chelsea back against his chest, feeling her warmth. They fit so perfectly together.

"She had a great day." Chelsea's soft voice drifted toward him.

"Yup, and you are part of the reason."

"Me? I didn't do much. Hung a few balloons and carried out some food."

"There was only one thing she wanted for her birthday, and she got it."

Chelsea tilted her chin up. "That swing set did get her excited."

Spinning her around, he tucked some hair behind her ear. "The swing set was nice, but it wasn't what she'd wanted for years."

The confusion in Chelsea's expression was thick.

"She wanted her mom to come back. I've kind of had that same wish myself."

Tears filled her eyes, and she bit her lip. "You know, every year at this time, I almost couldn't make it through the day. I'd go somewhere quiet and cry until I couldn't breathe any more. This year, I thought maybe if I was here, it would be different. I could finally put it behind me and start to heal."

Holding her tighter, he rubbed her back and stroked her hair. What he wouldn't give to make all her past hurt go away.

"I'm so sorry, pixie. I wish I could change the past." His own eyes grew wet.

She straightened up and touched his cheek. "I know we can't go back to the beginning, but we can start from here and make a better ending."

"Such a wise woman."

Chelsea giggled. "It's not mine. I read it somewhere."

God, he missed this. Holding her, being with her, simply talking with her. "Then, we'll definitely go from here and make a better future."

When they went downstairs, his parents were in the kitchen, washing and drying the trays and pans that had been used today. "What can we do to help?" Theo asked. "You shouldn't be cleaning up this mess. Chelsea and I can finish it up. Why don't you two relax in front of the TV?"

"It's not even eight," his mother said. "Nothing good starts until prime time."

His dad placed a tray on the kitchen table and tilted his head toward the front of the house. "Go outside and canoodle with your girl. We've got this."

The old-fashioned term had him laughing, but he always did what his parents told him to. Most of the time. Grabbing Chelsea's hand, he picked up a light throw blanket and led her onto the porch. The tables they'd used up here for the food had been folded and returned to the cellar, thanks to Rico and James, and now only the bench swing was left.

"Right here, young lady."

A blush covered her cheeks as she sat down. The sun wouldn't set for another twenty minutes, so he had some time to focus on the beautiful woman next to him.

Throwing the light blanket over her shoulders, he scooted closer. "My father told us to canoodle."

"I have no idea what that means," she said, her face blooming with happiness. Because they were out here together or because his father seemed to approve of her?

"First, you need to be as close as possible." His arm looped around her shoulder and urged her head onto his chest. No resistance at all.

"Maybe even closer." Lifting her legs, he draped them across his lap, so she was leaning on him and only her butt rested on the bench.

"This is canoodling?"

"Well, this is the start of canoodling."

"I like it so far." Burrowing into his chest, she sighed like a contented kitten.

After shifting the blanket on her shoulders to protect her from the approaching chill, he leaned down and pressed his lips to hers.

"Is that part of canoodling, too?" she asked once he'd eased back.

"One of the best parts. But you have to do lots of it for it to actually be called canoodling."

Her smiled grew into an impish grin. "Then, by all means, proceed."

God, she was adorable. This. This mischievous side of her was what he'd missed for so long. They'd had such fun simply hanging out with each other, teasing and touching.

"As you wish, m'lady."

Her lips called out to him and he listened, pressed his to hers and absorbed all the emotion she was sending out. The tiny sounds, whimpers, and sighs emanating from her drove him crazy. As their mouths mated and danced, he couldn't help but run his fingers through her hair, along her neck and over her shoulders. The feel of her skin, her softness under his hands, had his heart beating like a disco rhythm.

"Oh, God, pixie."

"Mmm, yes." It wasn't a question, simply her response. It was the one he'd wanted to hear.

Shyly, she stroked her fingers down the side of his neck to the opening of his button-down shirt. If he recalled correctly—and his memory of this was pretty danged good—she had enjoyed running her hand over his chest. Slipping two buttons from their holes, he repositioned her hand on his heated skin.

"You've filled out a bit in the time I've been gone." Her voice was breathy and shaking.

"Are you saying I've gotten fat?" Pretty sure that wasn't what she was saying, but he wanted to hear it from her.

"Hardly." She laughed and continued with her exploration. "You've filled out nicely. There's a bit more hair for me to play with."

"Play away. I love having you touch me." As her fingers twirled his chest hair around, he decided to do some touching of his own. Nothing that would get him too heated. His parents were right inside.

Shifting slightly, he concentrated on her tiny heart-shaped birthmark, licking and sucking until she dropped her head to the side. His lips drifted lower, and he slid the strap of her shirt over until it fell off her shoulder.

"Did you seriously not have a bra on all day?" he groaned, viewing the top of her rounded breast as it peeked out at him.

Half-mast eyes gazed at him. "This tank top has a shelf bra. It's not like I need much more."

"It's a good thing I didn't realize this earlier. I wouldn't have been able to walk."

Skimming his hand down her front, he kept it on top of the fabric. No way he could touch her that way and stay in control.

"Are you sure canoodling involves this?" She didn't attempt to stop her journey inside his shirt.

"Oh, definitely. No doubt about it." His own hands continued to knead her through the cotton.

"I can't imagine your dad suggesting we do this."

"Why not?" Another kiss to her neck, her cheek, a nibble on her ear. "We are legally married after all."

"I still need to go home."

"Wish you didn't."

Her body stiffened, though she never pulled away. "I can hardly share Jordan's tiny twin bed with you, plus I need to make sure the animals are okay. Brett said he'd walk Bandit a few times and make sure they had enough food. But he's long gone by now, I'm sure."

The idea of Brett Sheehan anywhere near Chelsea boiled his blood. He wasn't about to start an argument with her now. Not when they'd come so far in the last few days. Soon enough, they'd be able to be together permanently.

His sigh was long and loud. "I guess the animals win. How about you bring them over tomorrow when you come? That way you can stay later if you want."

"You're sure your parents won't mind?"

"My parents have three dogs, much larger than Bandit, and two cats. They'll be okay."

Chelsea glanced at her watch and sighed against him. "Fifteen minutes. I'll leave in fifteen minutes."

A grin formed on his face. "If that's all I have for now, I'll take it." And he took her mouth once more with his.

CHAPTER SEVENTEEN

B andit lifted his head from his dog dish and started barking. "Your food is right there, you silly dog. What are you yipping about?"

There was a quick knock on the front door, then the sound of it opening. Chelsea scrambled toward the entryway. Before she could take more than a few steps, a singsong voice called out, "Hello. Anyone home?"

The buxom redhead who worked with Theo, Dina something, strolled through the hall and entered the kitchen like she owned the place.

"Hi, um…Dina, right?" What the heck was this lady doing here? "Is Theo all right?" It had been bad enough when he'd been trapped under the tree. If something else had happened to him, what would she do?

"Theo is perfect, as I'm sure you know." She cocked her head to one side and slid a large manila envelope onto the counter beside her.

Relief. But then what did this woman want? "Theo's not here. He's working today."

"Yes, I know. We were just *together*." Dina glanced around the kitchen and wrinkled her nose at the disarray. The wallpaper had all been stripped and the floors had been ripped up.

"Sorry, it's a mess. The painters are coming this afternoon to do most of the rooms, and the floors will be done next week." Brett had done a great job getting the walls sanded and ready. Theo still didn't trust the man, but he'd been a godsend to her.

Dina's long red nails tapped a rhythm on the counter, then played with some leftover screws and the taped-up hammer resting next to them. Bandit growled. Yeah, Chelsea didn't like her any more than the dog did.

"I didn't come over to discuss your decorating."

"Why are you here?"

A smirk twisted Dina's painted lips. "I wanted to discuss Theo."

"You said he was fine."

"And he is fine." The way Dina emphasized the word told her exactly what she meant by *fine*. "But I'm worried about his happiness."

"His happiness? What about it?" He'd seemed pretty darn happy the last two weeks. Their time on his porch canoodling had been the start of nightly make-out sessions. She wasn't quite ready to go any further. Or maybe she was afraid to. Using Jordan as an excuse, she'd always left once things heated up too much. Theo had seemed to understand and hadn't pushed. It had made her love him even more.

"I think you need to leave Theo alone. He was satisfied with his life until you came back. He may think everything will be great, and you can go back to playing house again, but really, let's face it—you left before, and you'll leave again when you realize he's not that into you."

"He discussed this with you?" The only time she'd seen Dina before, Theo had seemed uncomfortable around her. Was it because they'd had something going on?

"We've had conversations about you. He was all set to move on with his life and then you showed up, confusing him. Now, he's stalled."

Dina pushed the large envelope across the counter. "Then again, maybe not. I'm guessing divorce papers. If you know what's good for you and that little girl of yours, you'll sign them and disappear again. She doesn't need a mom who isn't there for her, one who pops in and out of her life."

"I would never leave Jordan." Would she? Self-doubt crowded in, smothering all the confidence she'd attempted to build up the last few months.

Dina didn't appear to have heard her as she peeked into the dining room. "I know a great real estate agent who could get you a few million for this house. Imagine all the places you could go with that kind of money. Better than this little island."

Theo and Dina must not have discussed all that much about her if Dina didn't know the money her family had.

"Did Theo ask you to bring that over to me?"

Dina shrugged her dainty shoulders, causing her large breasts to rise and fall. "He asked me to get a courier to deliver it today, but since I had other errands to run, I figured I'd do the honors and deliver my own little message along with it."

What should she think? Had Theo lied to her when he said he'd respected his marriage vows?

"Have you and Theo…?" How did she even word it?

A sexy pout appeared on Dina's face, and her eyes twinkled. "Been intimate? Well, not in *that* way, no. Theo is extremely loyal, but I'm guessing with this," and she pointed to the envelope, "we will be soon enough. We've always been very close, and I can see how much it frustrates him not to be with me."

As she eyed the item on the counter, Dina flipped her hair over her shoulder and flounced out. "Don't be delusional and think he'll be satisfied with a little mouse like you. Sign the papers and leave."

The front door opened and closed, and it wasn't until Bandit jumped up on her that Chelsea snapped out of her daze. She dragged the envelope toward her. Her heart raced. Dread drenched her so thoroughly her hands shook. Surely, Theo would have said something if he'd wanted a divorce. Why was she being so ridiculous? They'd spent the last few weeks kissing like hormonal teenagers on their parents' living room couch. Or was he frustrated, as Dina had said, that they hadn't taken it further?

Only one way to find out. Twisting the clasp, she opened the envelope and slid out the document. Very official. No. Was it divorce papers? She never took Theo for a coward, to ask for a divorce through the mail without ever mentioning it in person.

As she scanned the papers, her heart slowed and her breathing calmed. It was a custody document. It stated that if anything happened to Theo, she would get full custody of Jordan. Why would she even need this? She was Jordan's mother. Naturally, she would get custody of the child in case of Theo's death. Wouldn't she? Had he put something in place before she showed up to keep her from her child? She hadn't even known she had a child.

What did this mean? Maybe Theo had no desire to get back together with her. Was he simply leading her on, making her think they could be together? It didn't seem that way.

Or did he believe she'd up and leave again like Dina had said? Was he testing her to see if she'd last? Would she be better leaving if Theo didn't want her? No. Her daughter was here, and she could never be without her again, no matter how painful it would be if Theo ended up with someone else. Someone like Dina.

Another thought entered her mind. No matter what Theo and Dina had done recently, he had married her. They'd been blissful and in love once. They could do it again. She needed to stay and fight. Fight for Theo's love. They had a daughter together, and regardless of what Dina had hinted at, she had a feeling it wouldn't take all that much to stay in Theo's life.

The painters were showing up soon, then she'd run a few errands and pick up Jordan early from school. Theo had given her the use of his SUV this morning and had Rico drive him to work, so she'd have the car seat and the space in the back for the materials she needed to get.

Once back at the house, she'd have to figure out the best way to let Theo know she was serious about sticking around. Perhaps use that nightgown that was stashed in the corner dresser in his room.

<hr/>

Her cell phone rang as Chelsea was settling the kittens in the gated off room at the back of the house. It was the only room not being worked on in the next few days, so it was perfect until she could get back after dinner. Swiping her thumb over the screen, she saw it was Frank. Seriously? She didn't have time to chat with him now, but she'd ignored his last half dozen calls and texts.

"Hi, Frank. What can I do for you?"

"Where have you been, Chelsea? I've been trying to get in touch with you for a few days."

"I've been busy getting the house fixed up. I'm on my way out the door now. Can I call you back later?" Patting Bandit on the head, she threw his ball to the back of the room, and he skittered across to pick it up. Before he could return, Snap and Pop attacked his paws. It was so adorable how he loved playing with the kittens.

Frank's sigh could be heard through the phone line. "I wanted to know if you needed any help. I know you're trying to be Miss Independent, but you know you don't have to do everything by yourself. I can have the company jet fly me up and be there by tonight."

"That's so sweet, Frank, and I appreciate the offer, but I'm honestly all right." Although Dina's little message this morning had planted some seeds of doubt, there was no way was she going to give up on being with her daughter. Or Theo.

"I still don't like you being up there with no one around to help you. I wish you'd come home and forget about Maine. You're needed around here."

"I can't forget about Maine. This is where my daughter is, and I have no intention of leaving her." Had Frank forgotten this fact?

"I told you we can get custody. Wouldn't she have a better life here, with all the amenities she'd get from living on the estate? A private school, nanny, house staff. You can't tell me you like picking up after yourself."

"I feel like I'm accomplishing something, and I have plenty of people around here to help me. I've met a ton of the locals. They all go out of their way to give me a hand." Well, most of them did. There were still a few who stared at her cross-eyed. Closing the front door behind her, she headed to Theo's SUV.

"Maybe I'll drive up this weekend and check on you myself. Your father would be horrified if he knew what was going on."

"I don't give a fig what my father would think." He definitely wouldn't care for her attitude. Too bad. This was her life now. She was in control. "I need to go, Frank. I'm getting in the car, and I don't like to drive while on the phone. You can come up if you want, but don't do it for me. I've got painters coming over and flooring going in, and I'll be occupied with them."

"Put your Blue Tooth on, and we can continue while you drive."

Chelsea started the car and snapped in her seat belt. "Sorry. I've got Theo's SUV, because I need to pick up Jordan. It doesn't have Blue Tooth. Thanks for calling, Frank."

"Chelsea…"

She swiped the phone off and tossed it on the passenger seat. First, she needed to pick up some more cleaning supplies and a few fans to keep the paint smell from getting too strong. Sleeping in her room over the next couple days wouldn't be pleasant with the odor. However, if she played her cards right, perhaps she could be sleeping in Theo's bed.

With the car in drive, she steered down the street, the ocean a brilliant shade of blue. God, she loved this place. Relaxing on her porch, watching the waves roll in, and hearing the crash of the surf on the rocks was her idea of heaven.

Theo's arms were heaven, too. A different kind of heaven. If they managed to get together and stay together, and she could keep her head straight and her mind in the here and now, could they make their marriage work? Would Theo want to move into her grandmother's cottage? It was certainly big enough for all of them. Not that his cute little house didn't fit them all, but she had much more room. And the view.

Jordan had mentioned coming to stay here by the ocean. Years ago, when they'd first gotten married, it had been the plan to live in her grandmother's house once all the red tape had been cleared and they could clean and fix it up. Would Theo still want to go along with that plan, or had he gotten so comfortable living in his house that he wouldn't want to leave? Did he trust her enough to give up his house to live in hers?

As she turned onto Route 3 and headed toward Bar Harbor, the custody papers Theo sent came to mind. What if she put the deed to the house in both their names? Would that convince him she was serious about staying married to him?

Do you want him if he doesn't trust you?

Good question. She still hadn't figured out if she trusted herself. She was beginning to feel much more confident in many areas, but Jordan's breakdown at her birthday party had frazzled her more than she'd thought it would. That was stuff she could learn, wasn't it? It had barely been two months since she'd begun actively parenting. Even then, she figured Jordan had been on her best behavior, because it was still so new to have a mom in her life.

The car sped up as she passed the Otter Creek Market, and she tapped the brakes. Preoccupied, she hadn't noticed how fast the SUV was moving. She tapped again, then pushed down harder on the brake pedal. Nothing. The brakes had felt sluggish when she'd taken the last turn, but she'd put it down to Theo's car being an older model.

The gradual downward slope of the road had her picking up even more speed. Crap. How did she slow this thing down? Was she forgetting something? Did his car have some other method she didn't know about? God, she should have had Theo take her out driving for practice on this before she'd agreed to take it.

The car in front of her was too close. Swerving, she swung into the oncoming lane, but two cars approached. Their horns blared. What else could she do? She tugged the steering wheel to the right and almost smashed the rear bumper of the car in front, so she kept turning right. There was a driveway coming up. Could she glide into that?

The SUV shuddered as it careened over the grassy strip on the right, and she continued jamming her foot on the brake. Nothing. Too late. The grass dipped low, and the SUV followed right along. A large pine loomed closer as the vehicle bounced along the ground. Chelsea covered her head with her arms and screamed.

Hopefully, this meeting would be quick. Knowing Norma, and the fact so many new summer staff had just started, it wouldn't be. Theo shoved the last of the granola bar into his mouth, wondering when he'd be able to put something more substantial in it. It was well after lunch time, and he certainly didn't want to wait until he got home for dinner.

God, he couldn't wait to get Chelsea in his arms again. It usually ended up with him needing a cold shower by the end of the night, but however long she needed to feel comfortable with him again, he'd give it to her.

Dina sat like a queen at her desk outside Norma's office and watched him approach. It had been harder and harder to avoid her lately.

"Theo." Her greeting was like a cat purring, ready to pounce on its next meal.

"Hey, Dina." Glancing down at his watch, he saw it was still ten minutes until the meeting started. "Want to get a good seat."

"I made sure to get those papers over to your ex-wife this morning," she said before he could cruise past.

"Chelsea is my wife, not my ex-wife."

One slender shoulder moved up and down as Dina's bright red mouth twisted in a pout. "Your wife for now, but I assume those were divorce papers. It's about time you cleaned up your life, Theo. Got rid of the excess baggage. Now, you can start over with someone more substantial."

Divorce papers? What? Narrowing his eyes, he said, "Not that it's any business of yours, but those weren't divorce papers, Dina. I have no intention of divorcing Chelsea. I'm glad she's around."

Rising, Dina skirted her desk and rested a round hip on the side. "Theo, let's be honest. She's still staying at her own house. That can't be *satisfying* for you."

Leaning closer, she placed her hand on his arm. "I could make sure you're completely satisfied."

"Appreciate the offer, but it's unnecessary." When several other rangers arrived, he seized the chance to escape. "Can't be late for the meeting." He scooted down the hall to the conference room and claimed a seat by the door. A minute later, Rico dropped into the chair next to him.

When Norma marched in, all business and professional, everyone sat up and paid attention. The woman was petite but solid and wore her uniform like a badge of honor. She'd been a ranger at least fifteen years longer than Theo and had worked in a number of the National Parks throughout the country. Pushing a dark curl off the light brown skin of her forehead, she got down to business. It was the middle of June, and school was letting out soon. That meant the tourists wouldn't only be showing up on weekends anymore. The busy season had started.

Twenty minutes into the meeting, Theo's phone vibrated in his pocket. Luckily, he'd remembered to silence it before coming in here. If it weren't for Jordan, he wouldn't even look, but if it was the school and something had happened, he needed to know. Slyly sliding the device from his pocket, he glanced down and swiped the screen.

Aiden Cavanaugh?

Why would the police chief be calling him? No way he wanted to answer if the man was merely asking to get a beer after work. In the few seconds it took to decide, the call went to voice mail. A second later, a text popped up. From Aiden.

—*URGENT. Call me.*—

Crap. Pushing his chair back, he swallowed and held up his phone in apology to Norma. "The Police Chief. I'll be quick."

Once he was out in the hall, he pressed the button to call back his friend.

"Cavanaugh."

"Aiden, it's Theo. What's so urgent? It better be good. I was in a meeting with Norma."

"Sorry, but I thought you'd want to know. Your SUV was in an accident about twenty-five minutes ago."

His heart stopped. "Chelsea? She had my car today."

"Yeah, I figured you'd let her use it."

"What happened? How is she? Was Jordan with her?" The thought of losing either of them was like ice in his veins.

"She was alone, and I'm not sure exactly what caused the accident. She went off the road on Route 3 this side of Otter Creek. One of the witnesses said the car swerved a bit before it left the road. Theo, she hit a tree."

Oh, God. Please, let her be alive. "What's her condition?" Please, please, please, say *alive*.

"The paramedics are loading her in the ambulance now."

Alive. But for how long?

"What are her injuries?" Theo held his breath.

"They can't say yet. She's still unconscious."

"You've seen enough accidents, Aiden. What did it look like?"

"It's, um…"

Crap. That didn't sound good. "Tell me."

"A lot of broken glass. And a good amount of blood."

He swore, and his hand shook as he held the phone to his ear.

"We'll tow the car to Benji's Auto."

The car? Who the heck cared about the car? "Thanks."

"Theo, I'll check in with you later. Good luck."

"Yeah." Staring at the phone, his brain needed to get moving. Go see how Chelsea was.

The conference room door creaked as he pushed it open, and all looked his way. Norma's business attitude softened and concern crossed her features.

"Sorry. Chelsea's been in a car accident. It's bad." The lump in his throat wouldn't let him get anything else out.

"Go." Norma pointed to the door behind him.

Seeking out Angie, Theo took a deep breath. "Can you pick up Jordan?"

Her head bobbed up and down, and she repeated Norma's word. "Go."

Racing through headquarters, he blew past Dina, ignoring her questions. In the time it took to get to Mt. Desert Island Hospital, Theo's mind had conjured up all sorts of scenarios, most of them devastating. Maybe it was a good thing he hadn't eaten more than that granola bar.

Jamming the truck into park, he flew through the lot and entered the Emergency Department, scanning for whoever could give him information. A few people waited in seats. Luckily, the desk seemed clear.

"My wife was in a car accident, and they said they brought her here."

"Your name?" Often, he hated how small the town was and having everyone in his business, but now he wished he knew more people.

"Theodore Lapierre. Oh, uh…I don't think my wife's license has her married name. Chelsea Woodridge. Do you have any information on her condition?"

"Hold on, Mr. Lapierre." Fingers flew across the keyboard. "She was only brought in a few minutes ago. Why don't we get her information while you're here?"

"I'd really—"

"They'll need time to do an assessment."

"Fine."

Over the next few minutes, he rattled off Chelsea's name, address, birth date, though he couldn't give them much of her medical history.

"Insurance?"

Reaching for his wallet to pull out his insurance card, Theo suddenly realized Chelsea wasn't on his insurance. That would have to be fixed, too.

"Uh, she's not on my insurance yet." Let her think they'd only recently been married.

"Okay, we'll worry about payment later. Let me check what her status is." The nurse picked up a phone. Meanwhile, Theo's eyes flew to Kim and her partner, Pete, who rolled a gurney from the back rooms.

Pushing out of his chair, he straight-lined it to them. "Did you see Chelsea back there?"

Kim nodded, her face solemn. "We brought her in."

"How is she?" That granola bar threatened to come back up.

"They're still assessing." Her gaze roamed the room, and she moved closer to the door as Pete continued outside with the gurney. Theo followed.

"No apparent broken bones. Definite head trauma. They'll most likely do a CT scan and a few other tests."

"Aiden said there was lots of blood." The big hole in his chest grew to gargantuan proportions.

Kim patted his arm. "Pretty sure the airbag broke her nose. Much of the blood was probably from there. Until they get her all cleaned up, they won't really know. Broken glass was everywhere."

Something the size of a watermelon lodged itself in his throat, preventing him from speaking, so he simply nodded.

"Do you need me to call anyone or do anything for you?"

"No, no," he replied, shaking his head, trying to get the bad thoughts out of his mind. "Angie's getting Jordan for me. That's where Chelsea was most likely heading." What the heck had happened to cause her to crash?

Patting his arm a few times, Kim said, "You know where to find me if you need anything."

Theo nodded his thanks, then headed for the registration desk again. When the nurse looked up and saw who it was, she shook her head. "I'm sorry, you can't see her right now. Someone will come out and let you know as soon as they can. You can take a seat, and I'll make sure they know you're here."

His "thank you" was weak as he paced the waiting room floor. The sunshine that penetrated the glass of the window did nothing to warm him. The day was gorgeous and bright, and he should be enjoying every second. Instead, he was standing here with his insides twisted into a pretzel.

Chelsea had only been back in town for about six weeks. Back in his arms for about two. The next step had been in his house, his life, and his bed. Would that happen now?

CHAPTER EIGHTEEN

T he shuffling of booted feet had Chelsea opening her eyes. As soon as she did, she slammed them shut again. The glare of the lights stabbed through her head, kicking off a bass drum solo that pounded in her ears.

"How're you feeling, pixie?"

Theo. His deep voice reached inside her and pieced everything together again. If only she could remember what everything was. The doctors had asked quite often if she remembered what happened, and each time she dug in her memory, the events of the accident stayed hidden.

The caress of Theo's callused finger on her cheek coaxed her eyelids open again, slightly. Enough to see his handsome face. His extremely anxious handsome face.

"Hey." Tears filled her eyes at the emotion pouring from him. It wasn't what she deserved. She wasn't what he deserved. Theo should have a woman who was whole and fit to be a mother to their child.

"It's okay, pixie. You're going to be fine. The doc said you'll have a doozy of a headache, but you'll be sticking around a while."

Something niggled in the back of her fuzzy memory. Jordan. She was supposed to be picking up their daughter. The SUV had the car seat, and Theo had let her use it so she could get Jordan early from school today. Had she been in the car? How could she not remember if she'd picked up their daughter or not?

"Jordan? Where is she?" As she struggled to sit up, an IV pulled at her hand.

"She's fine." Theo placed his hands on her shoulders to keep her from rising. "Angie picked her up an hour ago and took her back to the house."

"What time…?" Tilting her head, she attempted to look for a clock.

"It's almost five. It took forever for them to let me in here to see you. I gotta tell you, pixie, you scared the heck out of me." His voice shook as he looked away and closed his eyes for a moment. When he turned back, he had his emotions under control.

"Bandit. I need to get back and feed the animals. Can I leave?"

Theo chuckled. "Not today. The doc wants to keep you overnight for observation. If everything checks out, they'll let you go home tomorrow."

Stay the night. In a hospital. No, no, no. Pulling at her IV, she pushed herself to sit. The bass rhythm got louder and stronger.

"I can't stay here. Can't, Theo." Her heart challenged the drum beat to a marathon.

"Hey, settle down. I'll call Rico and get him to take care of the pets. You need to relax."

Theo stood, fishing his phone out of his pocket as he stepped toward the door. His hushed conversation let her know he was taking care of things, but he didn't understand. Tentacles of panic gripped her as sweat dripped down her back. Getting out of here was imperative to her sanity. If there was any of that left in her.

As she eased toward the edge of the bed, Theo spun and dashed to her side. "Hey, the animals are all set. Rico's going to take them to his house for a bit. If it's not too late when I leave here, I'll pick them up and take them home."

"No, I'm not staying. I can't stay here." Her breathing grew rougher, and she clung to Theo's arms as he leaned a hip on the side of her bed.

"It's only a precaution, pixie. They'll be here in a few minutes to transfer you to a regular room."

"No. No, no, no." Shaking her head back and forth caused the pain to become explosive, and her stomach objected. "Gonna be sick."

Theo grabbed for the basin beside her bed and tucked it under her chin. Not much came out. Understandable after all she'd heaved earlier. Stupid concussion.

After wiping her mouth with a wet cloth, Theo eased her back down. Her energy level was equal to the piece of fabric. He pressed a kiss to her forehead.

"Why are you so freaked about staying here overnight?" He stroked the side of her face. God, that felt nice, calming. Not calming enough to make her want to stay here.

"I don't like hospitals."

Theo's eyes narrowed. "Is there a reason?"

Her lips started to quiver, and she clamped down on the bottom one with her teeth. "I was in a hospital when they told me my baby died. And they wouldn't let me see her." Tears rained down her face as the agony of the past consumed her. It didn't matter that her child was alive and nearby, the memories wouldn't go away.

"Then, I had a nervous breakdown and they—" Her eyes flew to where Theo sat, his face like granite.

"You had a nervous breakdown? Is that what you meant when you said you were sick?"

Oh, God. Now it would start. The excuses for her not to see Jordan. The questioning looks and the microscopic examination of every little thing she did.

The door of the exam room opened, and two orderlies came in along with the nurse who'd been taking care of her.

"We're moving you upstairs for the night."

Grasping at Theo's hand, she whispered, "No. Please." Would he care or simply desert her? Leave her to flail in the darkness that had constantly surrounded her?

"I won't leave you, pixie. I'll stay with you and chase any shadows away. Okay? But you need to let these people do their jobs."

Letting go, she withered back on the bed, her lips quivering and tears sliding down her face. Did he mean it, or was it only a ploy to get her to cooperate?

They wheeled her through the halls to an employee elevator. When Theo didn't get in, she started squirming.

"Your husband said he needed to make some arrangements for your daughter. Don't worry, he'll be right back."

The words didn't assure her like they were supposed to. Her father had given her a million different excuses for so many things and none of them had been true.

Once her bed was placed in her room and her IV checked, the nurse showed her how to use the call button, told her to rest, and that someone would be in soon. Rest? Right. Highly unlikely.

The silence in the room was deafening. Alone. It wasn't the first time, but this time was almost worse. Closing her eyes, she attempted to get her breathing under control. Pain slashed through her head like thunder, but suddenly other aches burst to life. Her ribs, her back, her left leg and arm. Spots on her face burned like ash had been flicked at her. When she attempted to obliterate her rampant tears, the pain in her nose took her breath away, and she cried out.

"Whoa, what are you doing? What happened?"

Theo was back. Was he staying like he said? God, she needed him to stay, needed him to lie to her if only for tonight. There was no way she could make it through a night here by herself.

"My nose. Really hurts."

Moving closer, Theo said, "Yeah, it broke when the airbag hit it. Accounts for all the blood on your clothes." He held up a plastic bag with the hospital insignia on it. "I don't imagine we'll be using these again, as they cut them off you when you got here."

What had she been wearing? Had it been a favorite outfit?

"I don't remember...Theo, why don't I remember what happened?"

After tucking the bag in the corner of the room, he perched on the edge of the bed and stroked her arm, the one without the IV.

"You have a concussion. A fairly severe one. The doc doesn't think you have any bleeding in the brain, which is good." His expression didn't look like it was good. He looked worried. "They're keeping you overnight simply to make sure. It's only a precaution."

"You need to go home and take care of Jordan." Which would leave her all by herself in this hell.

"No." Theo's lips twisted, and the dimples near his mouth winked at her. "Angie's going to stay the night and bring her to school tomorrow."

"Will she be okay without you?" Jordan should matter more than her sanity. "I'll be fine if you want to go." Her trembling voice gave her away.

"Jordan's stayed with Angie on many occasions. They make it a girls' night. Although she is worried about you. Wants to make sure you're coming back."

"If you let me."

Theo's brows knit together. "What does that mean?"

"I had a nervous breakdown before, Theo. Now, I don't remember what happened when I crashed your car."

Cradling her face, Theo stared into her eyes. "Someone told you your baby died. Having some problems after that is understandable. As for this afternoon, the doctor told me it's common for people with head trauma to have loss of memory, especially surrounding the accident. It might come back to you at some point or it might not. It doesn't matter. What matters is that you're okay."

When he pressed his lips to hers, she sighed. God, she hoped he meant all this.

"I thought I might lose you, pixie," Theo said, his voice gruff like he'd swallowed sand. "*I* almost had a nervous breakdown, thinking I'd just got you back only to lose you again."

She stroked his face, the stubble on his cheeks rough against her fingers.

"What if Jordan had been in the car? I could have killed our child, Theo. I don't think I could live with myself if that happened. Maybe I'd be better off not being near her." It would be the end of her, but at least her daughter would be safe.

"Don't even think that. Jordan is fine, and you're fine."

"But what if I have another breakdown? Or keep forgetting things?" Putting her child in danger was the last thing she wanted to do. It would be worse than when she'd thought her baby had died. And that had pushed her over the edge.

"Let's not worry about that right now. You should rest, so you can heal."

"I'm sorry," she whispered as she closed her eyes. The lids were heavy, yet she didn't want to lose sight of Theo. He was her lifeline at the moment. "I'm so sorry."

"Nothing to be sorry about, pixie. Get some sleep. They'll be waking you up soon enough for vital signs and check-ins."

"Your car? Is it bad? They said I crashed into a tree. It must be bad."

"Doesn't matter. It's only a car, and that can be replaced. You can't." He gently kissed the tip of her nose. Fortunately, that wasn't where it hurt.

"I'll buy you a new one. I promise. A nicer one."

Theo's chuckle warmed her inside. "If it'll get you to relax, I'll let you buy me anything you want."

There were lots of things she'd love to buy him. They were married. She could do it, right? Married? Wait, Dina. Dina had been over this morning. Had she been talking about divorce papers? Did Theo want a divorce? It certainly didn't seem that way with how he was acting toward her. He hadn't even freaked out when she'd blurted out her history of having had a nervous breakdown.

No, the papers were for custody of Jordan if anything happened to Theo. That much she remembered.

"Why would you draw up documents to give me custody of Jordan if something happened to you?"

Theo's gaze flitted away, then back to her. "The tree thing got me thinking that I needed something in writing to make sure she'd be with you."

His expression said more was involved, but she didn't push. "I don't understand. I'm her mother. Why wouldn't I get custody of her?"

Theo's mouth tightened. "Your father sent papers to me a few months after I got Jordan. They said you gave up all legal rights to our daughter and that I had full custody."

"What? I never signed anything like that. How could I when I thought my child was dead?"

Theo shrugged. "It looked like your writing. I didn't question it, since it lined up with everything else I'd been told. I'm sorry, pixie. One more thing I should have questioned." His expression showed self-disgust.

"I probably did sign it," she mumbled, knowing what a mess she'd been at that time. "He could have had me sign my life away during those months, and I wouldn't have cared. It wasn't a good time for me."

Theo hugged her, pressing his lips to her hair. She lifted her one free hand and wrapped it around his neck, needing his warmth and strength.

"We'll get it all fixed once you get out of here. Jordan needs both her parents."

Would Theo still think that way once he knew the extent of her mental illness?

———◦———

Theo scanned the words on his cell's screen, stood up and stretched. Chelsea was asleep finally. The nursing staff had checked on her all night long, which made for sporadic slumber. For both her and him. The chair he was in didn't help.

Creeping toward the door so he didn't chance disturbing his wife, he eased it open and moved into the hallway. Angie stood near the elevator, Jordan holding tight to her hand.

As he drifted closer, Jordan tugged, ran, and jumped into his arms. Her sad face clawed at his heart.

"Daddy."

"Shh, peanut. Lots of people are sick here, and we need to be quiet, so we don't disturb them."

"Is Mama sick again?" she whispered. "I don't want her to go away like before."

"She's not going anywhere, sweetie. I promise." Now, he needed to make sure that never happened. They both needed Chelsea in their lives.

"Sorry," Angie murmured, rubbing Jordan's back. "She was distraught, thinking her mom would disappear." Holding up a bag, she added, "I brought something for Chelsea to wear home if she's ready."

"Thanks, Ange. Appreciate it." He looked at Jordan. "I'll take you in to see your mother for only a few moments, but you need to promise to be extremely quiet and don't wake her. She has a boo boo on her head, and it hurts."

"But she's coming home?" Her anxious face mirrored what his must have been like since he'd heard about the accident.

"The doctor said if she was better this morning, I could bring her home. We'll have to be careful because she still doesn't feel well, and too much noise could hurt her head."

Jordan glanced around the hallway. "Are we bringing her to our house?"

"Yes. She'll need someone to take care of her for a little while until she's all better. Can you help me do that?"

Her little head bobbed up and down, her brown hair swinging from side to side. "And then, maybe she can stay with us? Forever?"

There was nothing more he'd wish for.

"We'll see. So only a minute and you can't wake her up." He guided her toward the hospital room and eased open the door. Angie followed only so far and peeked in as they tiptoed near the bed.

"See? She's still here," he said quietly.

Jordan wrapped her arms around his neck and snuggled against him. Leaning closer, she whispered in his ear, "Can I kiss her better?"

"We can't wake her." He knew how much Jordan believed in the power of those healing kisses. "Maybe you can kiss the top of her head. Lightly."

The girl nodded, and he lowered her down until her lips gently pressed against the dark brown hair, so like her own. Only a moment, then he lifted her back up and backed toward the door.

"Blow her a kiss, too. I'm sure that will help."

After Jordan touched her hand to her lips and waved it at her mother, he left the room.

As they approached Angie, still waiting in the hallway, Theo gave Jordan a kiss. "I'll pick you up once I get your mom home and make her comfortable. Love you, peanut."

"Love you, Daddy. Love Mama, too."

Once they left, he checked in on Chelsea to make sure she was still asleep, then hoofed it down to the cafeteria and got a cup of coffee. What he really needed was some good sleep, yet he'd do it all again to keep her from freaking out. The fear in her eyes when she thought she had to stay here had almost knocked him over. And when she told him why, he thought his insides were bleeding. What she went through still rocked through him like a wrecking ball, and the guilt piled higher and higher.

The nurse was exiting Chelsea's room when he got back.

"Let me know if you need anything or if she seems in more pain than usual. I did a quick vitals check, but she mostly slept through it, only rousing a bit. Her doctor probably won't be in until mid-morning, so order some breakfast and relax."

Relaxing wasn't something he'd done much of since his wife had returned. His wife. Even though he hadn't used those words often, he liked them, hoped he could continue using them in reference to Chelsea.

Settled back in her room, he simply watched her sleep. For once, she seemed totally at peace. It didn't last long with the staff coming and taking blood and checking her IV. When they left her alone, he sat and held her hand and smiled at her. It seemed to keep her calm.

"Do you think they'll let me go home soon? I miss Jordan." Her voice was small but determined.

"She stopped by to see you this morning before school."

"What? I don't remember that." Tears gathered in her eyes, and he rushed to put her at ease.

"You were asleep, and I told her not to wake you up. You didn't forget. Last night was rough, and I thought you needed sleep more."

"Will you bring her to my house so I can see her? The doctor said I couldn't drive for a little while."

Pulling her hands to his mouth, he kissed her knuckles. "I thought it might be better if you came to our house. That way I can take care of you, and you can see Jordan all you want. Plus, your house is a bit of a mess right now."

"Don't you have to work?" Her confused expression pulled at him.

"I took the next few days off. I've got plenty of time coming to me. I don't want you worrying about anything."

A dreamy expression crossed her face as she closed her eyes. "You're going to take care of me."

"Always, pixie girl." Too bad he hadn't tried harder to do that years ago.

He kissed the tip of her nose, making sure to keep it light. There was some discoloration around her eyes this morning, most likely from the broken nose, and some tiny cuts from the broken glass. Even with all that, she was still amazingly beautiful.

When the doctor showed up a few hours later, he declared Chelsea fit to go, provided she had someone with her for the next few days and she made an appointment to see her own doctor soon. There would be no driving for a while, and Theo got a whole list of symptoms he needed to watch for, along with a prescription for some medication that would help with the nausea. Over-the-counter pain reliever would help with any discomfort.

After assisting her in getting dressed, an orderly wheeled her to the entrance as Theo brought the car around to the door. Her eyes, when he pulled up, showed her relief. Did she honestly think he'd drive off and leave her?

As he settled her in the car and maneuvered onto the road, he knew that soon they'd have to do some more talking. Her fear of not being with Jordan was understandable, but he sensed deep down there was a whole lot more to discover about his wife.

CHAPTER NINETEEN

"Mama?"

The tiny voice, in addition to a soft tickling sensation against her nose, woke Chelsea from the light sleep she'd been in. A black ball of fur held by her daughter's hands, scampered near her face. Jordan's head rested on the couch cushion in front of her.

"Hey, sweetheart. Did I fall asleep again? I'm sorry. You were reading me a story."

"It's okay. Daddy always say sleep is the best medicine. That means you'll get better faster."

The soft chuckle escaped before she could trap it, but it wasn't as damaging as previous ones had been. Either the pain meds were helping or she was actually healing. Being here with her child and husband was definitely the best medicine.

As she struggled to sit up, Jordan placed…Snap…back on the floor. It had been nice of Rico to take care of the animals last night and then drop them off here today. She hadn't been able to do much besides watch as Theo and Jordan played.

Once they'd gotten home from the hospital—Theo's home— he'd been extremely solicitous. Lots of pillows had been plumped up on the couch, though he'd wanted her to go right up to his room and his bed. Yes, eventually she'd love to be in his bed, but for now, she wanted to be where the action was. They were her family. She had gone too long without them.

"Daddy want to know if you want a grilled cheese sandwich. He makes the best ones."

"Yes," she said. "I've tasted his. They're yummy. I think because he uses so much butter."

Jordan rubbed her belly. "I love butter. I'll go tell Daddy."

"I'm right here, peanut. I heard." Theo lounged against the doorway into the kitchen, his gaze on her. "How are you feeling? Do you need any more medication?"

"Think I'm okay for now. I've been sleeping so much I won't be able to sleep tonight."

"Daddy says we can stay up and watch a movie. Maybe that make you sleep."

"I said *if* your mother was up for it, we could watch a movie. The doctor said not too much screen time for her eyes. We have to be careful."

A pout popped onto Jordan's face, and her eyes misted. "I don't want you get sick again, Mama. I don't want you go away. You needa stay here."

"Oh, sweetie." Chelsea reached out and pulled Jordan into her lap. "I'm not going anywhere. Even if I'm a little sick. Because now I know I have you and your father to take care of me." Stroking the girl's hair, so like her own, calmed her own rapidly beating heart at the thought of not being with her child. And the child's father.

"So, grilled cheese all around. Jordan, why don't you take Bandit into the back yard before we eat?"

"I don't wanna pick up poop," Jordan complained, her face twisted.

Theo laughed. "I'll get it later. Just make sure he doesn't step in it, okay?"

Jordan jumped up and ran into the kitchen, calling the dog.

"I can clean up after Bandit," Chelsea said, attempting to stand. When the room tilted, she grabbed the arm of the couch.

"We'll let you clean up after the dog once you're not so wobbly." Theo wrapped her in his arms and sat down next to her. "For now, rest and enjoy being waited on."

His warm body felt so nice she couldn't help but snuggle closer. "Thank you for taking care of me, Theo. I've never had anyone care for me the way you and Jordan have."

"Oh, pixie. I wish I could make all the bad stuff in your past go away."

Looking up at his handsome face, she stroked his cheek. "I didn't mean to make you feel bad for me. I just like being here with you and our daughter and appreciate how nice you're treating me."

The expression on Theo's face was so forlorn it tugged at her heart, so she reached up and pulled his head down to her. Their lips touched and again, the tiny pieces of her soul began to slowly mend together. His arms crushed her close as his mouth roamed over hers. Heaven. Here. Always. Please, let it continue.

The slamming of the back door knocked them out of their clinch, but Theo kept his forehead touching hers. "Guess I should make that grilled cheese now, huh? If you want to pick this up at a later time, I think it could be arranged."

Her soft sigh floated on the air. "Later."

When the food was ready, Chelsea claimed she was able to sit in the kitchen to eat, but Jordan wouldn't hear of it.

"Daddy said we could eat in the living room, so you don't have to get up." Her eyes grew wide. "He *never* lets us eat in here, Mama, so we *have* to."

"He's kind of strict with that, huh?' she teased and glanced at Theo as he carried in their three plates and placed them on the coffee table.

"Sometimes, I'll allow popcorn if we've got a special movie. But yeah, your daughter can be kind of messy with food. Like someone else I know." His eyebrows rose and his lips twitched.

Color flooded her cheeks as she remembered a few times they'd snacked in this room when they'd first met. Too often, the food had been forgotten or dropped when kissing and touching had taken precedence. The smirk on Theo's face made her stomach flip and desire twist even deeper. It was times like this that she truly believed they could make it.

Jordan picked a movie. Theo had insisted it be a short one to try and stay within the doctor's orders. Chelsea didn't mind. It was simply too wonderful sitting next to Theo, resting on his shoulder with Jordan sprawled across both their laps. Was this what being a family meant? Being together, happy, and loving each other? No doubt she loved Jordan, and her daughter took every chance she could to tell her she loved her back. But Theo? Did he still love her? Jordan had said he did when she'd mentioned the princess story. Was it all talk?

Theo's actions lately had certainly showed he cared. Not only the kissing and subtle touching but how carefully he treated her. How scared he'd seemed when she'd been hurt. The fact he hadn't freaked out when she told him of her nervous breakdown. Could he accept her the way she was? Did she even dare tell him the whole truth? Soon. Soon, she would.

"Okay, peanut, time for bed."

"Daddy," Jordan protested. A yawn slipped out of her mouth giving her away.

Theo grinned. "Caught ya."

"Can Mama put me to sleep tonight, too?"

"I think I'm going to put your mama to sleep right after you. I caught her yawning a few times, also."

"Where you gonna sleep, Mama?"

It did seem strange that she'd stayed over twice, once on the couch, and once in Theo's bed, with him on the couch.

Before she could answer, Theo said, "I thought your mom should sleep in my bed, since she doesn't feel well. It's more comfortable."

Yes. But where would he sleep? "Are you sure? I can—"

Scooping her up into his strong arms, Theo strode toward the stairs. "I'm sure. No arguments. Jordan, head up, and we'll be right behind you."

Their daughter giggled at the sight of her father carrying her up the stairs. Chelsea enjoyed being held close to his hard chest and slung her arms around his neck.

At the top of the stairs, he put her down. Sadly. Being in his arms was far too nice. Addictive even. But he steered her into Jordan's room and had her sit on the bed while he got the child into her pajamas, brushed her teeth, and read her a story. They both gave her kisses and bid her goodnight.

"Your turn now," he said, lifting her into his arms again. Jordan giggled once more, not quite asleep. He stopped at the bathroom and let her down. "Can you do this part yourself, or do you need help?"

Rolling her eyes, she caught his smirk. "I can probably manage."

By the time she'd finished in there, Theo had turned down the covers and had a t-shirt in his hands.

"I can run over to your place tomorrow and get some more clothes. For now, I thought this might work."

Taking the shirt, she sat on the bed and bent to remove her socks. Theo was already there, pulling them off. His gentle hands helped lift her shirt over her head and remove her bra before putting the new shirt on. It was almost clinical, the way he helped her. Did he not find her desirable anymore? Was she too skinny after so many years of inactivity and not eating?

"Lean back," he instructed as he undid her button and slid down her pants, then tucked her feet under the covers.

"Where are you going to sleep?" Her voice rose, hoping he wouldn't make her stay alone.

His eyes darted around the room. "I don't want you to be uncomfortable, pixie."

Biting her bottom lip, she held out her hand. "I will be, if I know you're downstairs all squished on that couch and I'm all by myself."

"You need someone to hold your hand?" One eyebrow lifted.

"I need you to hold me." Was that too needy? Would it push him away?

Instead, he nodded and kissed her on the forehead. "Let me close up the house, make sure the animals are all set, then I'll be up. Do you need me to bring anything up when I come?"

"Just you."

After kissing her again, he went downstairs. She could hear him puttering around, talking to Bandit and the kitties. Too cute. Soon, he was back and closing the door most of the way, leaving it open a bit to listen for Jordan if she needed anything in the night. Such a good dad.

Once Theo had shucked his clothes, leaving his boxers and a t-shirt on, he stepped toward the window. "Do you still like to sleep with the window open a crack?"

It was the middle of June and warm during the day. However, Maine nights could still get chilly.

"Yes, please. If you don't mind."

"I don't mind at all. I've kind of gotten used to doing it myself."

He shut the light off and slid into the bed on the other side. Not touching or coming too close. Did he hate the thought of touching her that much? No, that was ridiculous. He'd been kissing her the last few weeks every night. Before he knew she'd had a nervous breakdown.

Shoving her head in the pillow, she tried to stifle the sniff that automatically came. She couldn't do this. There had to be a limit to how much crying any one man could handle.

The mattress creaked as Theo turned on his side, facing her.

"What's wrong, pixie?"

She reached toward him and touched his chest. "Ignore me. Sometimes I get stuck in my own head. Things that I'd rather forget."

"Can I help you forget?" A hand snaked around her waist and tugged until she was pressed against him. "Does this help? Holding you?"

The strength emanating from him filled her and made her brave. She adjusted until her head lay on his shoulder and her hand rested next to her cheek. "Very much. Thank you."

"We all need a little help now and then."

Being in Theo's arms brought back more memories, ones that settled between her thighs and brought out feelings she hadn't had in many years. Now was not the time. They'd kissed, yes. And she wanted more. But she also wanted to be in better shape when and if they got close again. It had to be perfect. Having Theo snuggled up next to her was the fastest way to make everything perfect.

As Theo pulled Chelsea's car into the parking lot at Benji's auto, Aiden Cavanaugh marched out to greet him. The chief had called him earlier and asked to meet him here.

"Theo, thanks for coming." Aiden shook his hand. "How's Chelsea?"

"A little improved. Bit of a headache still."

"I can imagine." Aiden's mouth twisted in a commiserating smile.

"What's up?" Theo didn't want to leave Chelsea by herself too long. He'd dropped Jordan off at school, much to her dismay. The school was having an end-of-year field trip, so she wouldn't be back until close to five. Next week started summer sessions. Having Jordan go year-round always bothered him, but he'd never had much of a choice. Perhaps with Chelsea around, their daughter could enjoy being at home a bit more.

"I wanted to let you know what we've found out about the accident."

He'd wondered about that himself but hadn't wanted to push Chelsea any more than necessary. "Chelsea still doesn't remember anything. The doctor said that was normal."

"Yeah, it is, and we had a look at the toxicology report. Nothing out of the ordinary in Chelsea's system."

"Out of the ordinary?" Theo narrowed his eyes at his friend. "You mean like alcohol or drugs? I could have told you that."

"Don't get bent out of shape, Theo. It's routine. Let's face it, Chelsea's been out of your life for years. She could have changed."

And she had in some ways. But in so many others, she was still the woman he'd fallen in love with.

"What I wanted to talk to you about was your SUV. Have you had any problems with it lately?"

Shaking his head, Theo thought back to the regular maintenance he did on the car. "I had it serviced a few weeks ago. It's not the newest vehicle, but it's in decent shape. Did they find something broken?"

Aiden glanced around and pulled him over to the side of the building. "Benji did the work himself. He said the brake line was cut."

"What? Are you sure? It was fine when I had it in recently. I think they would have mentioned if the brake line was damaged."

Aiden tapped on Theo's arm. "The brake line wasn't damaged. It was cut. With a knife. Not enough to have the brakes stop working immediately, but in such a way that it would have taken time for the brake fluid to drain out and the brakes to fail."

The words swirled through Theo's head and stunned him. Why would anyone cut his brake line?

"Is there anyone who has a grudge against Chelsea who might have done this?"

"Chelsea? She hasn't even been back two months. Besides, it was my car. We only switched that morning so she could fit stuff from the hardware store in the back."

The line of Aiden's mouth grew tight. "So have you ticked anyone off recently?"

Brett Sheehan. But that was an old feud. Why would the man suddenly decide to hurt him? The other recent incidents came to mind.

"There have been a few other things that have happened lately." He told Aiden about the car almost running him off the road, the rocks falling on the trail, and the suspicious roots that had been cut when he'd been trapped by the tree.

Scribbling down notes and dates, Aiden frowned. "By themselves, they do all seem random, but this brake line thing? I don't know, Theo. Looks like someone doesn't like you. All since Chelsea has come back."

"Well, it's not her if that's what you're thinking. She'd hardly cut the brake line on my car and then go drive it."

"I wasn't thinking it was her. Could be something to do with her return. Is there someone who's upset that she's here with you?"

Dina didn't like Chelsea, but she'd hardly hurt him. More likely, she'd want to hurt Chelsea, and barracuda that she was, he didn't think she was capable of killing someone. The image of her crawling under a car to cut a brake line was laughable. These accidents definitely weren't.

"Not that I know of. The rockslide and running thing were me all the way, but the brake line and even the tree falling could have gone either way. I don't know what to think."

"I'll do some digging into what she's been doing the past few years and see if anything pops up."

Theo wanted to argue. The idea of someone searching through his wife's private life ticked him off. Then again, something was happening, and he hadn't the first clue how to find out what. Aiden was his best bet. Maybe he'd have a chat with Chelsea about her life in Westchester.

"Hey, Theo," Benji called out. He strode from the garage, holding up a purse. "I found this in the car. I assume it's your wife's."

After taking it, he thanked the man and stalked back to the car, Aiden next to him.

"Let me know if anything else strange happens, Theo. And watch your back."

"I will." Not only his own back but that of Jordan and Chelsea. Jordan could easily have been in the vehicle when the brakes finally went. He never wanted to feel what Chelsea had felt when she'd thought her child was dead.

Throwing the purse on the passenger seat, Theo started up the car and stared out the windshield. Who in the world wanted to hurt him? Or Chelsea? Or was someone only interested in scaring them? Any or all of the accidents, except the most recent, could simply have been just that—accidents.

Some of the contents of Chelsea's purse had spilled out, and he picked up a comb, pen, and pill bottle to toss them back in.

There was something about the overly large pill bottle that seemed strange, so he took a moment to study it. Turning it around, he noticed it had the name of the pharmaceutical company Chelsea's father owned and her name printed on it but no doctor name or pharmacy. There wasn't even a date or any of the little warning stickers you usually get, saying not to operate heavy equipment or go in direct sunlight. Weird.

As soon as he got home, kicked off his sneakers at the door, he trotted up the stairs to his bedroom where Chelsea still rested in bed. Her eyes opened when he came in, and a tiny smile danced on her lips. She looked good there.

"How're you feeling?"

"Okay. My stomach's not as queasy. Head's a bit better. I got up and used the bathroom, then I decided to be decadent and stay in bed a little longer. I wasn't sure when you'd get back."

Sitting next to her on the mattress, he dropped her purse on the bedside table. "You can stay in bed all day if you want."

Her eyes twinkled. "Are you going to join me? You called out of work, and Jordan will be gone until dinnertime."

The words and adorable expression hit him right in the ol' thumper, so he leaned in closer and kissed her. Nothing too strong or passionate—she had been up close and personal with a tree recently—but enough to show her his feelings. Her arms curled around his neck, and she pulled him down until he was flush against her. It felt too good.

"Whatever would we do in bed all day?" He knew what he'd like to do but didn't think she was quite up for it.

"You used to be able to fill a whole day in bed with me. Getting rusty?"

Laughing, he rolled over her and stretched out on the mattress beside her. "Unfortunately, yes. Maybe you need to remind me." Put her in the driver's seat. Her pace.

Pink rushed across her cheeks, and she dipped her head. But after a deep breath, she rested against him, her head on his chest. The blanket had slipped and one of her slim legs peeked out and slid over his. The desire to touch it and glide his hand up until he cupped her sweet bottom was strong. He settled for running his fingers down her back in comfort. Perhaps this was all she needed or wanted. For now, he was fine giving it to her. It was more than he'd had for so long.

After a few minutes, Chelsea stirred and eased her head up.

"You said the police chief called this morning. What did he want?"

To tell him someone wanted him dead. No, that wouldn't go over too well. For now, he'd keep that little detail to himself.

"To let me know what happened during the accident. The brake line was damaged, and all the brake fluid had drained out."

"So the brakes didn't work? I didn't just flake out and have an accident?"

"You weren't responsible, no. I'm so sorry this happened. I shouldn't have let you borrow the SUV."

"You didn't know about the brake line."

"No, but I'll be more cautious in the future. I can't lose you now that you're back in my life. And Jordan's."

"I don't want to lose you either."

It was the perfect time to kiss her again, so he did. Then, her words sunk in. She didn't want to lose *him.* No mention of Jordan. Of course, he was sure Chelsea would be traumatized if something happened to their daughter, but he was equally as important.

The kiss continued, and this time he explored the soft skin of her upper thigh. Her leg shifted and her knee moved closer, allowing him to feel more of her. Up and down, so silky and smooth. One hand stayed on her leg while the other got busy, exploring under the large t-shirt he'd loaned her last night.

She wiggled closer as tiny moans floated from her lips, the lips he couldn't stop kissing. They'd been addictive back when they'd first met, and time hadn't lessened that need any. But his hands needed, too. To touch and skim up her back and sides. Chelsea rounded her back so he could tug the shirt off, but when he eased up, they bumped heads. A sharp cry shot from her mouth, and she fell on her back, her hands cupped around her nose.

"Oh, God. Are you all right?"

Her head bobbed slightly. "I forgot I broke my nose."

"I am so sorry." He kissed the top of her head, taking extra care not to go anywhere near the nose.

"Not your fault. I was in too big a hurry to get this shirt off."

A dry laugh escaped. "That was my thought, too. Maybe we need to slow down a little. We'll get there. For now, let me get you something for the pain."

Leaning over, he picked up her water bottle and the over-the-counter pain meds. As she took them, he remembered her bag.

"Oh, I got your purse back from the car. Some stuff fell out when I tossed it on the seat. You've got some medicine in there, too. Is it something you should be taking?"

Her head whipped up as he placed the bag in her lap, but he couldn't quite read her expression. Guilt? Fear? Anxiety?

"What's the matter, pixie?" He pressed his lips to her hand.

With her other hand, she dug into the bag and pulled out the bottle. "I haven't taken these since I've been here."

He fingered the bottle. "Do you need them?"

"I don't know." She looked lost and confused.

"What are they for? Who gave them to you? There's no doctor name on the bottle."

"I told you I'd been sick, right?" Her eyes shone with moisture.

"You said you had a nervous breakdown. Was there something else that happened after?" Please, don't let it be anything fatal. He needed her and so did their daughter.

"It wasn't after. It was before."

Now, it was his turn to look confused. Getting more comfortable on the bed, he coaxed her into his arms and snugly held her, her back to his front. "Tell me, pixie."

"The pills are to help me."

"Help you how?"

"To help me stay balanced. I don't like them. They make things foggy. But my father insisted, ever since my mother died."

"Balanced? I don't get what you're saying. I don't remember you taking them when we got married."

"I stopped taking them that summer, too."

"And you were okay? You were perfect when I met you. A little sad about your grandmother, but you certainly didn't seem foggy."

"I stopped taking them, because I met you and everything seemed perfect. I thought I didn't need them."

"Maybe you don't," he said, kissing her shoulder. "You haven't been taking them the last few months. Have you felt better?"

"I have. Finding Jordan and being with her, being with you again…it's all been incredible."

"Then, I'd say you don't need them anymore."

Her head tipped up to stare at him. "What if I slip? What if it comes back?"

"What is '*it*' that you're talking about? Do you have some disease?" His heart pounded waiting for her answer.

As she nodded, sweat trickled down his back. Not from the summer heat.

"It's a mental illness. My mom had one, too. I thought maybe having my daughter around, loving me, would be enough. But my mom had me, and I loved her immensely. It wasn't enough. She couldn't live that way, so she killed herself."

CHAPTER TWENTY

"**Y**our mother committed suicide? You never told me. Only that she died when you were ten."

No, Chelsea had never confided in Theo back then. It was something she would have eventually told him, but their romance had been a whirlwind, and she'd never found the right time. Hadn't wanted him to back off thinking she had the same problem.

"It was tough on me. At that age, I didn't fully understand what had happened."

Theo's warm chest felt good, but she wondered if he would still want to hold her once he knew what her future might hold.

His arms tightened around her, and his lips pressed to her temple. "I'm sorry, pixie. You certainly haven't had it easy."

A slight shake of her head was all she could manage. Too many images and memories of her childhood assaulted her.

As if Theo could read her mind, he scooted off the bed. "Why don't we get you something to eat for breakfast and then we can sit outside? It's gorgeous weather today. We should enjoy it."

Bending down, he kissed her. "I want to talk more about you and your past. Learn where you came from and what happened in your life."

Her crappy life that people didn't understand, because she grew up in a huge estate with everything a child could ever want. Everything, except the type of family she'd found here with Jordan and Theo.

As she stood, Theo asked, "How about some eggs and toast?"

"Do I get real Maine blueberry jam on my toast?"

The grin on Theo's face could warm the arctic. "You sound like your daughter. Yes, real Maine blueberry jam. Get dressed, and it'll be ready by the time you come downstairs."

Holding out the side of the huge t-shirt, she laughed. "What? You don't like my outfit?"

His eyes gleamed. "I'd like to remove that outfit. How about you put something on that doesn't tempt me so much."

As he trotted down the stairs, she quickly cleaned up in the bathroom and donned a pair of shorts and a tank top, keeping her feet bare. With the shorts, most of her legs were bare, also. Tempting him sounded kind of nice.

Her toast and a plate of eggs were sitting on the table when she got downstairs, but Theo wasn't around. The sound of whistling told her he was in his office. She quickly finished off the meal, then went looking for him. When she stepped in the doorway, he looked up and his smile froze.

"What's the matter?" Had she done something wrong?

"I thought I told you to put something on that didn't tempt me. You think that's it?"

Okay, her shorts were short, but they were old and the tank top had seen better days. As Theo's eyes drilled into her, she realized how snug the top was and that her nipples were quite apparent through the thin material.

Biting her lower lip, she shrugged. "Maybe I wanted to temp you."

His lips twisted as he rose to his feet and crossed the room. "You definitely test my control, pixie. Are you done eating?"

At her nod, he steered her through the living room and sat her on the bench on the porch.

"Wait here."

A minute later, he opened the door and Bandit dashed through and down into the yard. The kittens' box was placed next to the bench. He tipped it on its side, so they could tumble out and play with the cat toys. Theo had been so good about her pets, and he'd taught Bandit to come when he whistled. They spent almost more time here than they did at her house.

"Back to our previous conversation." Theo sat next to her. "I know it's probably not pleasant to talk about, but I need to know everything about you, pixie. The more I know, the better I can deal with things if they arise."

"Like me flipping out again."

"I only want to understand what you've gone through and make sure not to do anything that will hurt you again." Lifting her legs, he draped them across his, then rested his arm around her shoulder.

As she laid her head on his shoulder, she thought about what he said. He had a right to know the truth about her and her family.

"Why don't you start by telling me about your mom?"

Taking a deep breath, she began. "When I was a little girl, I remember my mom being so amazing. Reading me stories, playing dolls, and brushing my hair. But little by little she stopped doing those things and mostly sat in her rocking chair. Sometimes, she'd sing a little song, and I'd dance to it. Or she'd let me climb into her lap, and she'd hold me tight. She used to tell me how much she loved me and that I was her precious angel."

Tears filled her eyes as she remembered these occasions where she'd known love and acceptance. Her father might come in and ask her a few questions about what they'd done that day, then he'd kiss her mother's head, but he rarely spent long periods of time with them. Too busy with his pharmaceutical company.

"I always made sure to tell her how much I loved her, too, but it didn't seem to matter. Each day, she drifted further and further away from me. Finally, one day she wasn't there. My father told me she'd been sick and had gone to heaven."

"How did you know she'd committed suicide?"

Fitting herself closer to him, she said, "I overheard some of the staff talking. She'd slit her wrists, and apparently the blood was going to be difficult to get out of the floorboards."

"God, I'm so sorry." His arms kept her from wanting to dive into that bottle of pills.

"For the next few years, I was kept fairly close to home. My dad arranged any play dates, and they were always children of people he knew. Once I hit high school, he had me tutored at home. I didn't really like it and may have acted out a bit. That's when my father told me I had to be cautious, because my mother had this mental illness, and it must have been passed on to me. I started taking some medication to keep me from going crazy."

"Going crazy? Because you were a typical teenager who wanted some freedom?" Theo's muscles tightened around her.

"He never called it crazy. It was my *condition*. He wanted to make sure I didn't go the same way as my mother. Everyone said how wonderful he was because he hadn't put her in an institution. He made sure to let me know that as long as I took my medication, he'd make sure I could stay in the house, too."

"Medication? The pills you have in the house?"

Shaking her head, she said, "No, not those exact ones. My dad had some of his top researchers specially make those to help with my depression after my baby...Jordan was taken from me."

"But you never had a doctor check you out and prescribe these?"

"I delivered Jordan in a hospital and stayed there for a few days, heavily sedated for the most part. I remember my father arguing with the doctor. Not sure what about. Then, I went home, and someone watched over me for a while."

She tried to read Theo's expression. Was he disgusted with her illness or that she'd needed so much medication? "Honestly, everything after that is a big blur. Losing both you and our baby pushed me over the edge. I didn't care about anything. Eating, sleeping, talking to anyone. I took my pills, occasionally sat in a chair with the TV or radio on, but most of it's a fuzzy mess."

"Which is why you were confused about whether we were still married or not."

She curled into him, hoping he wouldn't shove her off his lap, dump her on the ground, and run away. The opposite happened. He tightened his embrace and kissed her forehead.

"God, pixie, I can't believe what you went through. And I could have done something to stop it, to keep you from basically being held prisoner. I am so sorry. Can you ever forgive me?"

The catch in his voice made her glance up at him. Agony crossed his face and moisture filled his eyes.

"No, Theo, I don't blame you." Reaching up, she stroked her fingers down his cheek.

"I blame myself."

"You shouldn't. My father is the one who wrecked our lives. But not anymore."

Theo threaded his fingers into her hair and palmed her face. "Not anymore, no. From now on, it will all be great."

She wanted to believe that but knew it might not be true. "I can't promise that. I spent lots of time completely anxious and depressed, not to mention in a fog, even with the medication."

After kissing her carefully on the tip of her nose, Theo's face grew hard. "I want to have someone take a look at those pills. Angie's friend, James, works at Paxton Labs and can probably figure out exactly what they are. Until then, we stay far away from them. I have a feeling your father wasn't actually helping you."

"I want to believe you, Theo. I'm still scared I'll turn into my mom, slowly dwindling away until there's nothing left. What good will that do Jordan? I don't want her to lose me the way I lost my mom."

"Whether you have some sort of disorder or not, we'll deal with it. If we have to get the best doctors to help, we will. But Jordan and I need you in our lives, Chelsea. You're imperative to our happiness."

"Thank you." Having Theo by her side and determined to help was amazing. Yet there was still that little voice inside her that said at any time he might get tired of her inability to cope and kick her out of their lives.

━━━━●○●━━━━

"Chelsea Lapierre?" the nurse called into the crowded waiting room.

Theo stood and gripped her elbow. "Hope you don't mind that I used my last name. They know me here."

It had been a few days since the car accident. Chelsea needed to see a doctor, but she didn't have one in Maine. She'd admitted she'd never had a regular doctor that she could remember. After the results James Yoshita had gotten on the pills she'd been taking, he understood why.

"I appreciate your calling your family practice to get me in. I don't know where else I would have gone."

After walking down the hall, the nurse ushered them into a room, took Chelsea's temperature and blood pressure, then said, "Dr. Pasdar will be in to see you in a few minutes."

"Is this your doctor? I noticed there were a few listed on the sign." Her eyes roamed the room, taking in all the pamphlets and medical posters.

"No, she's Jordan's doctor. Figured you might want to see a woman. I usually see one of the male doctors."

"That's sweet to think of that."

A knock sounded on the door, and it eased open. A petite woman with dark hair tied back in a bun entered and smiled at them.

"Good morning, Theo. I see you've brought me a new patient."

"Yes. Chelsea, this is Dr. Pasdar." He rubbed his wife's shoulder. "This is Jordan's mother, Chelsea."

Dr. Pasdar tilted her head and chuckled. "Yes, I can see that. Quite a resemblance. Welcome, Chelsea, and please call me Roshni. I've been trying to get Theo to do that for four years, since I met your beautiful daughter when she was only days old."

Sitting on a rolling stool, Dr. Pasdar—he'd never get used to calling her by her first name—opened a small laptop and started asking Chelsea health questions. He took note of her answers. It bothered him that he knew very little about so many aspects of his wife's life, but he was learning more every day.

"Now, it says here you had a car accident a few days ago. Once you called, I had my staff contact MDIH and get the hospital records sent over. Let me take a moment to scan them."

Her eyes flew over the screen, and Theo rubbed Chelsea's back. If she hadn't seen many doctors in her life, and the only ones she remembered had been instrumental in her father's deceit, it was no wonder she seemed anxious.

"How are you feeling today?" The doctor asked as she leaned in to examine the small bump on Chelsea's head and the scratches and bruises on her face. "Any headache or nausea?"

"A small headache every now and then, but the nausea is gone, thankfully. My nose still hurts, especially if I forget and accidentally touch it."

"Or when Jordan forgets and hugs her mom too hard," he added.

"The nose might take a while to feel fully better. Sorry. I'm going to look in your eyes. The light might hurt a tad."

After checking out her eyes, nose, ears, and mouth, the doctor listened to Chelsea's lungs and heart and had her lie down and lift her shirt enough to check the few bruises on her stomach and sides.

"Everything seems to be coming along fine. Is there anything you're concerned about?"

The doc looked at Chelsea when she asked, but Theo was the one with the concerns. Taking the sheet of paper he'd printed out this morning, he nodded.

"This has nothing to do with the accident. I don't think, anyway. But Chelsea was given some pills that she took daily. I had a friend at Paxton Labs do an analysis of them. I wanted your opinion."

Taking the sheet he handed over, Dr. Pasdar asked, "What are they for?"

"Mental health issues," Chelsea answered softly.

One eyebrow of the doc's rose. "What specific issue?"

Chelsea looked over at him as if for an answer. "I don't know exactly. My father never said. I guess anxiety and depression, but he made it sound like it was far more than that."

"What did the doctor say who wrote the prescription for this?" Dr. Pasdar asked indicating the sheet of paper.

"My father said he had his lab make them specifically for me. He owned MedLab Pharmaceuticals."

"Oh, my. That's a leader in the industry. Nonetheless, I can't imagine any reputable pharmacologist making and giving a drug out without the proper approvals and doctor recommendation."

"You'll see from that analysis that this drug doesn't match any that is currently on the market or FDA approved. Chelsea's father was extremely controlling, and I have a feeling he used it to keep her from leaving him."

Theo explained briefly what had happened with Chelsea's father keeping them apart and then lying to his daughter about her baby.

As Dr. Pasdar listened and scanned the sheet in her hands, her face grew tense.

"Have you been taking these recently?"

"I stopped a few months ago, when I returned to Mt. Desert Island."

"This has the makings of a heavy anti-depressant. The compounds in this drug would make the person taking them quite lethargic and pliant, for sure. They wouldn't have much of a desire to do anything, even eat, let alone have a normal life. The thing that scares me most is there are ingredients on here that, if taken long enough, could make the user forget whole parts of their life. How long were you on this?"

"Since Jordan was born, but he made me take some other medicine since I was fourteen. I don't think it was as strong. I was able to do my schoolwork, and I ate much better back then."

The doctor's brows knit together. "I'd like to do some blood work to make sure this it out of your system and see if it had any adverse effects on anything else. How are you eating now?"

The joy on Chelsea's face was like fresh air and sunshine. "Excellent. Theo's been cooking for me every day, and he's amazing. I never learned to cook."

"She's been here almost two months, doc, and she's put on some weight since then. When she first got here, she was frail, almost gaunt. It's good to see the color in her cheeks now."

Her cheeks bloomed, showing off that color he'd mentioned.

"Good to know. I'll send the nurse in to take some blood, and when I get the results, I'd like to have you back for a complete check-up. You can make an appointment with the receptionist."

As the doctor opened the door to leave, he squeezed Chelsea's hand and said, "I want to ask the doc something while you get your blood taken." He followed Dr. Pasdar out.

"Hey, doc," he interrupted as she leaned against the counter outside the room, making notes in a chart. "Thanks for taking the time with us today."

"Of course, Theo. I always wondered what happened to Jordan's mom but never wanted to ask. The wedding ring on your finger said it most likely wasn't a divorce. The poor woman. I can't even imagine going through what she did."

"I wanted to ask about her supposed mental illness. She's so paranoid about it coming back, especially after what happened with her mother. What do you think?"

"I'd have to do more testing and speak with her about specific symptoms before I could say anything for sure. However, even if she didn't have any biological factors causing it, the environmental factors alone would have been more than enough to cause problems. Maybe now that she's with family that loves her, she won't have as many issues. But we'll keep on top of it and only give her medication if she truly needs it."

The nurse had gone in and now exited the room with a phial of blood in her hands, so Theo thanked the doctor again and entered the exam room. Chelsea looked lost standing near the table.

"Let's go and get Jordan early today. Maybe we can take the animals and have a picnic lunch somewhere."

Her face brightened, and he loved that he'd made that happen. After settling the bill and making a new appointment, they nipped outside to the car.

"Did the conversation in there make you feel any better?"

"It definitely helped me understand why I don't remember so much of the last four years. I still don't know why my father would do that to me."

"It explains so much. Why you never came back for me or our daughter." Leaning close, he placed a soft kiss on her lips. "I kept thinking you'd miss her, eventually want to be a mom to Jordan or at least see her and get to know her. I even painted the kitchen the color you'd picked out and got the appliances you wanted. It was stupid. Still, I figured if you did come back, I didn't want you to have an excuse not to stay."

"I love the color and the appliances. Not that I use the stove all that much. Kind of silly for me to want a specific range when I didn't know how to use it."

"I'll teach you. I'll do anything to keep you here with us. Now that you're back, I'm not going to lose you again."

As he kissed her once more, he hoped to God that he wouldn't.

CHAPTER TWENTY-ONE

C helsea sighed when the warmth of Theo's arms left her as
he leaned forward and shut off the TV, then placed the
remote on the coffee table. Jordan had been put in bed a few
hours ago, and they'd snuggled on the couch watching a movie.
And kissing. God, she loved when they sat here and made out
like teenagers. Not that she'd ever done that. Her father would
have had a cow and probably drugged her some more.

"You all right, pixie?" Theo stopped in the doorway of the
kitchen with the laundry basket the kittens were in. Bandit sat at
his feet, waiting. Her dog listened to Theo better than her.

"Tired is all."

"It's not every day you go car shopping and buy your husband
a new vehicle." His smirk emphasized the dimples near his
mouth.

She rolled her eyes. "Well, I wrecked your other one. It's the
least I could do."

Theo merely raised his eyebrows, then continued into the
kitchen to lock the doors, adjust the windows, and tuck the
animals in.

As he did that, Chelsea checked the windows in the living
room, office, and Jordan's playroom. She was locking up the

front door when Theo came up behind her and enclosed her in his arms. Her favorite place to be.

"All ready for bed, pixie?"

Humming, she turned and threaded her fingers through his hair. They came together for a kiss so automatically it was like they'd never been away from each other. Part of her desperately wanted to pretend they hadn't. Those years away were too painful.

Whoosh. Theo scooped her into his arms and carried her up the stairs. She giggled softly. "I love when the handsome ranger swoops in to rescue the princess."

"The beautiful princess," he filled in.

"More beauuuuuutiful than the lake," they said in unison, then stifled their laughter so they didn't wake up their daughter.

Theo slid her down his body in front of the bathroom but didn't let go. "You can use it first."

"You'll either have to release me or come in with me."

His eyes gleamed. "Tempting. Everything about you is tempting."

Still, he let her go and retreated into the bedroom. At least they had gotten to a point where they were sharing a bed. Could she get him to share more?

Once she'd cleaned up and brushed her teeth, she entered the room. The bedspread had already been turned back, and Theo tossed his dirty clothes in the hamper. Oh, how those boxer briefs molded his butt. She had to clench her thighs together to keep in control.

"Jump in. I'll be right back," he said.

Peeling off her clothes, she slipped into a fitted tank top and nothing else, then lit a lavender scented candle on the dresser. After shutting off the light, she crawled under the covers. Would he get the message? Would she have to tap it out in Morse code on his chest? That could be fun. She did love playing with his chest hair. Too bad she didn't know Morse code.

The door creaked when Theo came in, and his intake of breath was obvious. It clicked behind him, and her lungs stopped working. Normally, he left it open a crack in case Jordan woke up. Which she rarely did.

When he slid in next to her, she suddenly got nervous. They'd been making out for weeks now. She wanted this, but would it be the same as before? Wonderful and new? It had been so long, and she'd gone through so much. So had Theo.

"Hey, I can see the gears turning in your brain, pixie. I know we've been having some fun, and you think you're ready for the next stage, but we won't go any further than you want to."

A smile and tears both fought for dominance. "You're too good to me, Theo."

"Never good enough." Settling in, he reached for her and rested her head on his shoulder. The same location it had been the last few nights. Inhaling, she took in his scent, and her courage came back.

Hands caressed her back. She kissed across his chest, up his neck and to his mouth. This was familiar territory and a great place to start. Theo joined in, and her whole body came to life as their mouths mated and danced. More. She wanted more.

Her courage grew, and her hands went on a journey of exploration over the broad muscles of her older, more buff husband. God, he felt amazing. As did his hands when they started their own travels, over her back, down to her butt, up her sides to palm her breasts through the thin material of her top. Need surged through her, and she whipped her shirt off, tossing it behind her.

The candlelight flickered, exposing Theo's rapt expression as she knelt beside him, her hands still playing in the dusting of hair on his pecs that arrowed down his stomach, then disappeared inside his shorts. Had he changed down there also? Gotten bigger and stronger? Something was certainly getting bigger as she let her hands wander over the stretchy fabric.

"You're going to kill me, pixie. It's been a long time since that's been stimulated by anything other than my own hand."

"I haven't done anything either."

Emotions soared through her as they touched and kissed and caressed every inch. The last few pieces of fabric disappeared, and the sensations almost overwhelmed her. But she still wanted more. Wanted all of him.

"Please, Theo. I need you."

Moving between her legs, he assaulted her mouth and dragged his hands down her body where they were so close to being connected in the most intimate of ways. Then, he stopped.

Her gaze flew to him as his face screwed up in pain. "I don't have a condom."

Did it matter? No. "We both haven't had sex since each other and we're married. It's okay, Theo."

"You're sure?"

"My whole body has been turned off the last few years. Like I've been dead. I need you, Theo. Need you to bring me back to life. Please."

As he thrust forward, he groaned. "My pleasure."

———•◦•———

"I'm leaving now, pixie," the soft voice murmured in Chelsea's ear. "I love you."

Her eyes fluttered open as Theo pressed a kiss to her forehead. Reaching out, she brushed his hand.

"Hey," was all she managed in her morning haze.

"How do you feel?"

"Amazing. Can we do that again?" Last night had been incredible.

He chuckled. "Three times wasn't enough?"

"Never enough." She reached up and pulled his head closer. "We have five years to make up for."

"As much as I'd love to start now, I need to get to work."

Her pout gave Jordan's a run for her money. "Wait, what did you say to me when you first woke me up?"

Theo's eyes gleamed. Heat crossed her face, and she glanced down. Had she heard him wrong?

"Oh, you mean when I said I love you?" His voice dripped his feelings.

"Yes, that." A tear leaked out, streaking a path down her cheek.

"I do love you, pixie. I never stopped."

Holding his face in her hands, she said, "I never stopped loving you either."

"Good. Do you feel well enough to drive today?"

She tilted her head, wondering at the quick change in subject. "Um, yeah, I think so."

"I know you wanted to check on what the workers did at the house. I thought maybe you could pick up a few more of your things while you're there."

"Why would I need more of my things?" It was her turn for her eyes to twinkle.

His face froze for a second, then he tipped so their foreheads touched. "I don't think it's a good idea for you to be alone."

"Because of my injury?" Had she misread his intentions?

"No. Because when you're alone, you aren't with me. Or Jordan. I'm being selfish with the *me* part."

"I like being with *you*, Theo. A lot. I'll get more of my stuff today."

His hands roamed down her arms as he kissed her. "Darn, I really hate to go. Thinking of you, and what we can do in this bed tonight, that'll have to get me through the day."

After one more kiss, Theo reluctantly pulled away and headed for the door. It wasn't long before Jordan woke up and bounced into her room.

"Mama, you here again. Are you staying forever?" The optimistic look in the child's eyes grabbed her by the heart.

"I hope so, sweetheart. Your daddy said I should get more of my stuff so I can stay a little longer. We'll have to see after that."

Once they'd both washed and dressed, Chelsea attempted to make breakfast. She'd gotten good at toast and bagels, not that there was much to it. Loading Bandit and the kittens in the car was also challenging, but Chelsea wasn't sure how long she'd be gone. If there were problems at the cottage, she might need to stay there for a bit. Jordan would be thrilled to play with them in the back parlor that was still cleared out.

Brett's car was in the driveway when they got there, and Jordan carefully lifted the soft-sided kitty carrier out of the back seat while Chelsea grabbed hold of bandit's leash. Brett greeted them at the door.

"Hey. Wasn't sure if you'd be here today," he said, his face neutral. "You haven't been around much the last few days."

"Sorry," she said as they went inside. She directed Jordan to the back room with the animals and closed off the gate. "I had a car accident earlier this week and was injured."

"Are you okay?" His expression showed his concern as he glanced at her. "I see some bruising. What happened?"

"Theo's car had some brake problems, and I went into a tree. I'm okay, but the doctor thought I needed to be with someone for a few days, so I stayed with him and Jordan."

"Why did you have his car? And why the heck didn't he check his brakes to make sure they were working properly?" A scowl crossed his face. Yeah, there wasn't any love lost between those two, but no way she was getting involved in that right now.

"I'm a decent mechanic, if you need anyone to do repair work. Let me know."

"Thanks, Brett. I appreciate it. What are you working on today?"

"Mostly, peeling the tape off the rooms that were painted. The painters did a good job. Do you want to see?"

Peeking back into the room where Jordan played, she hesitated.

"I'll keep an eye on her if you want to walk around and check it out. Better to see now if something isn't to your liking."

"Thanks. I'll take you up on that." She patted him on the arm and headed into the living room. The soft sage that dusted the walls gave the room a cozy feeling. The dining room in a light blue and the office in gray looked great, too. When she entered the kitchen, she sighed. It was the exact color of Theo's kitchen. The exact color she'd wanted all those years ago.

Now, she realized it didn't matter what color the room was, only that she and Theo shared it. Funny how years and hardship changed your perception of things.

The four bedrooms upstairs, as well as the two bathrooms, had cleaned up nicely. The room Jordan wanted was a soft shade of pink. Both the bathrooms already had new plumbing, and the flooring was due in as soon as the walls had been painted. Deciding exactly what she wanted should be next on her list. Would she ever stay here? This house meant so much to her, as it reminded her of all the great times with her grandmother. But if she had to choose between this and Theo, there was no choice. Theo won. After last night, she never wanted to be apart from him again.

"The rooms look excellent, Brett," she said as she peeked into the back room. He sat on the floor with Jordan while the kittens crawled all over him. Laughter completely softened his expression. Picking up her purse, she fished out the envelope of cash she'd prepared for him and held it out. "I want to give you this before I forget."

The intensity returned as he took it and shoved it in his back pocket. Had she done something wrong? Before she could ask, her phone sounded. Retreating a few steps down the hallway, she didn't bother looking as she swiped across the screen.

"Hello."

"Chelsea? Where in the world have you been?"

Frank. Great. Not who she wanted to chat with right now. She felt bad about that, because honestly, he was running her father's business and taking care of so much for her that she should be grateful. But Frank was also a reminder of what had happened to her. Her old life. He still saw her as someone who couldn't take care of herself, and maybe she wasn't proficient at everything yet, but she was getting closer.

"I've been busy, Frank. Sorry I haven't called."

"I was getting ready to send the police to check on you. I've been worried."

"I apologize. I had a little car accident the other day and have been resting and buying a new vehicle. But I'm okay now. No need to worry."

"Not worry? Chelsea, you could have been killed. Honestly, I'll come get you as soon as I finish up with the stockholder's meeting tomorrow. A meeting you should be at, as primary stockholder."

Did he seriously want her there? She'd held stock since she was a child, but her father had never invited her to attend a meeting, had actually dissuaded her from attending when she'd asked once after turning eighteen.

"Thanks, Frank, for your concern. If you let me know ahead of time about the next one, maybe I will make an appearance."

Silence greeted her on the other end of the phone. Funny. She'd never heard Frank speechless before. Perhaps she could get him talking about something else.

"Hey, Frank, do you know who usually provided my dad with my medication?"

"Um, one of the head pharmacologists on staff, I think. I don't know for sure, but I can find out. Do you need more? I can bring some up."

"No, not yet." No sense letting him know she hadn't taken any. He'd only worry. "I brought a huge bottle and still have some."

"I still think I should plan a trip up again. To make sure you're truly all right and bring you home."

"You can come if you want to, but there isn't any need for you to travel all the way here. I'm fine, and I'm not returning yet." If it was up to her, she never would. "Let me know when you find out who usually makes my medication. I'd like to chat with him about it. Gotta go, Frank. Thanks for calling."

Swiping the phone, she ended the call, then silenced the ringtone.

Brett peeked out of the doorway and lifted his chin at her. "Everything okay?"

She nodded. "It's fine. My father's friend is worried about me. He doesn't need to be."

"Well, if you don't need me for anything else today, I'll take off. I have a few other things to take care of."

"You've been immensely helpful, Brett. Thanks so much."

With a nod of his head and a wave to Jordan, he headed out the door. Her daughter rolled around on the floor, giggling wildly with the kittens scrambling all over her. The sight and sound would never get old.

Jordan got a tour of the newly painted rooms and squealed in excitement when she saw her pink room. "When do I get to stay here, Mama?"

"The house still needs lots of work, sweetheart. Not for a while." Would they ever live here? Or in Theo's cozy place? As long as she had her family, she didn't care.

The day was beautiful, so Chelsea and Jordan took the pets and let them romp around the front yard.

"Keep an eye on the kittens, Jordan. We can't let them get too close to the rocks near the ocean. Bandit's been pretty good about staying near us."

As they sat on the lawn, a car door slammed. Was it Mrs. Cullen next door? She had to be close to seventy. Was she still driving?

"Daddy! Uncle Rico!" Jordan raced across the grass toward the driveway.

After hugging their daughter, Theo knelt at Chelsea's side and kissed her. "Hi."

"Hi. This is a nice surprise."

Tossing a bag next to her, he said, "We stopped at The Brown Bag and picked up some sandwiches. We're working around the corner from here this afternoon, so we figured we'd get something for both of you, too."

"Mama, they got us lunch," Jordan shouted as Rico carried her on his shoulders back to them.

"Yes, your father told me. Why don't we sit at the table on the patio?"

They all strolled over, and Jordan began chattering away, keeping Rico's attention solely on her. The thought of how the little girl would be as a teenager scared her.

"Jordan," Theo warned in his best stern father voice. "You need to eat and let Uncle Rico eat, too. We can't snack all afternoon like you can."

When the child stopped to take a bite, Rico smiled at Chelsea. "How are you feeling?"

"Better. It's good to get some fresh air after a few days cooped up in the house. The aches are finally starting to subside, and the headache is manageable. Don't bump the nose. That's still quite sensitive."

As they ate, Theo asked about the house, and Chelsea told him what had been done and what she still planned to do.

"If you want to look around, Theo, I'll keep the munchkin here and her menagerie occupied."

"Thanks, Rico." Theo pushed all his trash back into the bag, then reached out for her hand.

"We won't be long," she promised as they headed up the steps into the house.

Since she'd already filled him in on most of the projects, it was simply a matter of taking him through. In her bedroom, they both grew quiet.

"You know, I was thinking," Theo said, coming up behind her and holding her close. "Once you have this place all decked out the way you want, it's going to be amazing. Quite a place to live."

What was he saying? That they could sell it for good money, or did he expect her to stay here once her injury was totally healed?

"Yeah. It'll be great."

"Have you thought about living here?"

All she did was shrug.

His nose nestled into her hair, and he kissed her birthmark. "Could you possibly consider living here with Jordan and me?"

Whipping around, she clutched his shoulders. "Would you want to?"

"I want to be anywhere you are, pixie." His eyes held her captive.

"That's what I want, too. Here or at your house or...it doesn't matter. You and Jordan matter."

The crooked grin that showcased his dimples appeared. "I've lived in my place for a while now, and it's home, but I have to admit the view here is a darned sight better. Not to mention, there's a ton more space to spread out."

"We could have a room for the dog and one for the kittens," she teased.

Pulling her close, he slipped his hands in her hair and kissed her. Sweet and gentle but with deep emotion. "Or one for anyone else that comes along. Especially after last night."

His eyes blazed with desire, and her cheeks grew hot. "Maybe we should be more careful."

"Maybe for now." He pressed his lips against hers again, his body so close she could feel his arousal. He lifted his head. "While I'd love to have more children with you, it hasn't been that long since you returned. It might be a good idea to take our time. I don't plan on letting you go again."

"I have absolutely no plans to go anywhere. Except your arms."

As his head lowered to nibble on her neck, he said, "I like that. It's a good plan."

CHAPTER TWENTY-TWO

"I owe you a few, don't I, Theo?" Rico asked, his expression odd.

Theo eyed the group congregating at the Wildwood Stables, ready for the sunset carriage ride up Day Mountain. What was his friend talking about?

"Sure, I'll bet you owe me lots." He'd play along. "Is it time for me to collect?"

Looking back over his shoulder, Rico edged in closer. "Yeah, I figure I'll keep Jordan occupied for the night, so you can have a little snuggle with Chelsea on the carriage ride."

Theo smirked as he noticed Dina glancing their way with that predatory look in her eyes. Since he'd made it quite clear he wasn't available, she must be thinking of getting her hooks into Rico. Poor man.

"Okay?" Rico checked, and Theo nodded.

"I'm sure Jordan would love to have your ear all night. As long as you don't mind hearing all about the kittens and the new Barbie clothes Chelsea bought her last week."

"Heck, I'll *play* Barbies with her if it means I don't get caught hanging with Dina tonight."

As Theo chuckled, Rico jogged over to the little girl and scooped her up in the air.

"Hey, munchkin, you get to be my date for the night. How's that sound?"

Jordan giggled and clapped her hands as Rico swung her around only stopping when Dina approached him.

Rico shrugged. "I've already been promised for the night. Her parents need some cozy time."

Dina's disgusted look turned to acid as she stared at Theo. Not his problem. Chelsea was a few yards away, folding a blanket. He hoofed it in her direction and kissed her cheek.

"Seems we've got a babysitter for a while."

"What?"

Theo explained about Rico, then sidled in closer. "So that means I can put the big moves on you tonight."

"Bigger than what you've been putting on me all week?" Her eyes sparkled with joy. God, he loved seeing her this way, almost as much as seeing her in his bed every night and every morning. It had only been a week since they'd reconnected physically, but it had been incredible.

"Okay, maybe not as big as that. We'll still be in public. But the thoughts I'll be having are going to be X-rated."

"I can't wait."

People started getting in the wagons that would bring them to the top of the mountain. Rico helped a few others into one of the carriages and then tossed Jordan up, too. Waving him and Chelsea over, he waited until they got on, then climbed up.

"Had to make sure this wagon was full, so no one else could fit on," Rico whispered as he passed them to get to where Jordan sat on their other side.

After settling on one of the blankets they'd brought, Theo pulled Chelsea between his legs and circled his arms around her. Jordan sat in front of Rico, animatedly telling him some story of the field trip she'd been on last week. His friend blatantly ignored the daggers Dina sent his way as she was told this carriage was full, and she'd need to get on another. Theo was too ecstatic with his wife in his lap to even worry about the redhead.

"Does the Park Service do this type of thing all the time?" Chelsea asked as the horses trotted along the carriage roads.

"They set up a few activities each summer for the year-round staff, so we can all participate in at least one fun event. With so many different shifts, and the crowds during the tourist season, we can't all go on the same one."

"I love the idea of a carriage ride up the mountain." Her smile told him she liked more than simply the ride. "We did this the summer we met."

Her smile dimmed. Remembering the dark years in between?

"The sunset from the top will be great," he said, trying to turn her mind back to the present.

"Will we be able to see the fireworks they're having in town from up there?"

"I'm not sure. We might already be on our way down by then. It's one of the reasons we got the carriages tonight. Everyone will be in town with the Fourth of July events and fireworks."

As the horses trotted slowly up the trail, Theo enjoyed the simple act of holding his wife. A few of the other employees chatted with them and made small talk, but his mind kept slipping back to the conversation they'd had last week. About living together in her house. Having more kids. Being a real family. Something he'd almost given up on when Jordan had been delivered to him with Chelsea's message of not wanting them.

The fact someone had tampered with the brakes on his car also crossed his mind. Far too often. Aiden hadn't come up with any more information on who could have done it or when. The line had definitely been cut but not all the way through. Had the person meant to kill or merely harm or scare? Like the tree incident and the rocks. It could have been basic carelessness or the work of some evil intent. Whatever it was, he planned to keep Chelsea and Jordan safe. It scared the crap out of him that he might not be able to.

Their daughter's giggle got his attention, and Chelsea snuggled closer.

"He's so good with her," she said, tilting her chin at Rico, who had a string in his hands and was teaching Jordan to do Cat's Cradle. Not very successfully, but then she was only four. Still, the little girl seemed to be having a blast. "Why isn't he married with a bunch of kids? He's older than you, right?"

Theo nodded. "A year or two. But he's got stuff in his past." The secrets were Rico's to tell, so he kept them to himself. At Chelsea's concerned look, he said, "He was a Navy rescue swimmer for a while. Can't have been an easy life."

She seemed to understand that he wasn't about to tell her more and went back to staring at their child as she enjoyed herself. The sun sank lower behind the trees, and it grew chilly. Chelsea pulled a sweatshirt out of the bag she'd brought and handed it to Jordan, then grabbed one for her.

"I brought yours, too. Do you want it?"

"You in my arms keeps me plenty warm."

Once she'd zipped her hoodie, she settled back down with her face inches from his. Too tempting.

"Thank you for all you've done this past week, Theo. I'm finally feeling like maybe I'll be okay."

"You mean from the concussion?"

After glancing around, she reached up and stroked the side of his face. "No, I mean with my…condition. For most of my life, I felt out of it and confused, like I'd never be right again and would have to be content with wandering around in a fog, always waiting for the big breakdown. But being here the last few months, I feel alive."

"God, pixie," he mumbled into her hair as he nuzzled her neck. "From now on, it's you, me, Jordan, and the little beasties."

Sneaking his hands under her sweatshirt, he rubbed her belly. "And any others who might come along."

Her smile slipped into a frown. "Not this month. Started this morning, which means those X-rated thoughts will have to be postponed."

His lips zeroed in on her birthmark. "The actions might need to be modified, but the thoughts will still be there, believe me. It's simply the result of you in bed next to me."

Over the next hour, as the horses traversed the carriage roads, Theo tried to sneak a kiss whenever no one was looking. Or sometimes even when someone was looking. They were married, and he honestly didn't care. These people needed to know that he was serious about his relationship with Chelsea. He needed her to know, also, that he wasn't ashamed or embarrassed by her.

Norma had arranged for food to be available once they reached the top and a small fire to be set up with logs around it. It was only sandwiches, chips, and water, but with an hour ride up, an hour ride to get down, plus an hour at the top, they'd need something.

As the sun dipped behind the horizon, Theo picked up Jordan and put his arm around Chelsea. Blue, pink, purple, orange, all collided and swirled together in the sky as the yellow ball finally disappeared. A few minutes later, a call went out to load up the carriages for the trip down.

With the late hour, Jordan grew whiny, and Theo insisted he keep her, so she didn't disturb too many others. In the back corner of the wagon, he leaned against one side and Chelsea leaned her back against the other, her side against him. He swung her feet across his lap, then deposited their daughter there. With both her parents soothing her and the rocking of the horse-drawn carriage, she was soon asleep.

Rico pulled out his phone and snapped a few pictures. A second later, Theo felt his own phone vibrate in his pocket.

"Get it framed and put it on the mantel next to the others." Rico winked and shifted onto his other side. Dina had managed to get on the same carriage this time. However, one of the other office staff had cornered her and started chatting business. Not what the woman seemed to want. Her disdain at their beautiful family portrait was apparent.

Too bad. Today had been perfect, and nothing she could do could ruin this for them.

———●○●———

Sweat trickled down the back of Theo's neck, soaking into his shirt.

"Man, it's muggy today." The weather since the hayride two weeks ago had warmed up.

Rico glanced over as he pulled himself past an outcropping of rocks a few hundred feet from where the peregrine falcons nested. Theo nodded and perched next to his friend, who looked through binoculars at the chicks.

"They look fine, and I don't see any evidence of hikers nearby," Rico said quietly. Lowering the binoculars, he snagged his water bottle from his backpack and took a long swig.

Theo mimicked his actions, enjoying the cool liquid sliding down his throat. "Did the person who called with the complaint leave their name?"

Rico shook his head. "I don't think so. It was a message on the machine, I believe."

"Guess it doesn't matter." Theo replaced his water bottle and pulled out the camera. "We need to document their growth and see how much longer we've got to keep the trail closed."

The Precipice was a challenging trail on the east face of Champlain Mountain that had a thousand foot, almost vertical climb. It was considered strenuous and only for experienced hikers who were quite physically fit. Due to the falcons nesting on the rocks around the trail, it was typically closed for several months, and hiking wasn't allowed until mid-August.

A park naturalist was often placed at the bottom of the cliff to lead discussions and observations during the forbidden hiking times. Today was fairly cloudy, so no one had been sent. The signs at the bottom were quite obvious, but it wasn't as easy to keep people from getting onto the trail from the top.

After snapping a series of pictures, Theo put the camera back and slung his bag over his shoulders, fastening the clip at the front.

"The bathrooms are all done at the cottage," Theo told Rico as he carefully placed his foot on the rock edge of the trail back down. They usually directed hikers to use another, easier trail to get down, but he and Rico didn't want to disturb the falcons any more than necessary. Unfortunately, it made the descent a bit trickier.

"Does that mean you'll be moving in soon?"

"Not yet. We figured we'd redo the cabinets in the kitchen while nobody's living there. Besides, the porches still have some rotting boards."

"I'll probably sound like a girl, but it's good to see you so happy."

"Yeah, you sound like a girl." Theo chuckled. "Not that I wasn't happy with my beautiful daughter, but—"

"There was always something missing," Rico filled in.

"Mmhmm."

As they got closer to the bottom, the trail grew more difficult. Railings lined the narrow walkway, and metal rungs descended the steep cliff. Theo made sure to keep his mind on his hands and feet and step precisely where he needed to. This wasn't the time to let his mind wander.

Grabbing a rung, he swung his legs down to the metal below that descended like a ladder. When he stepped down again, the metal creaked. As he placed his other foot on the next step down, the rung gave way, and his feet lost purchase and swung in the air. One arm held tight, but before he could get the other one back on, the side of that rung broke free, and he was slammed back against the rock.

Oh, God. His life flashed before his eyes as he held tight to the piece of metal still anchored into the rock face. Glancing down, he cursed. It was straight cliff below him, and the broken rung had turned and made him fly back so neither his hands nor his feet could get near the other rungs. Were they broken, too?

"Rico!" His partner hadn't been too far behind him, but they usually gave each other plenty of space when climbing down the rungs.

As his hand held the twisted piece of metal in a death grip, it jolted again. Was the other side pulling out of the rock? His hand slipped further on the rung, and he tried to swing back to facing the cliff wall. Maybe he could find a small handhold in the rock. The momentum only made him slam back and smash his head into the granite surface. The scenery blurred for a moment, but Theo kept his grip tight.

He needed to shift over and find a rung that was solid. When he thrust his free arm to get him back there, he didn't move. Pushing his feet against the rock behind him, nothing happened except the rustle of leaves. His backpack must be snagged on one of the bushes. Crap.

The moss on the rocks made getting any kind of foot hold impossible.

"Theo, hold on!"

Like he could do anything else, except think about Chelsea and Jordan and what they'd do without him. At least now everything was legal for Chelsea to take care of their daughter.

"Grab ahold of the rope." Rico's gruff voice came from above as a thick white rope dangled in front of him. A slip knot had been tied to the end.

Reaching his free hand through the rope, he grabbed hold. Before he could pull himself up, the rung gave way, and he plummeted, his backpack ripping free of the bush.

Heat spiked through his shoulder as the rope caught him, yanking his shoulder from its socket. Quickly reaching up, he grasped the rope with his other hand to ease the weight. They both shook with the intense pain and adrenaline coursing through him.

"Watch out for the rungs," he yelled up to Rico, who had tied off the top part of the rope to one of the railings. "A few of them pulled out."

"I see that. I'm going to loosen the knot and lower you until you reach the next ledge. Hold tight."

Slowly, the rope lowered until he could pull himself to the ledge that led to another path along the rock face. Holding onto the railing, Theo dropped down until he was sitting on the ledge. Rico joined him a minute later.

"Let's see what we're dealing with," Rico said, unclipping Theo's backpack and slipping it off.

"It's a dislocated shoulder. I've done all the first aid stuff enough to know. Let's just get to the bottom, so we can find someone who can push it back in."

Reaching into his own pack, Rico pulled out his phone. "I'm calling SAR."

"No, don't." Theo placed his good hand on his friend's phone. "We don't need the flippin' search and rescue squad for this. By the time they get here and put the equipment in place, we could have climbed down, gotten my shoulder looked at, and gone home."

"Theo, we shouldn't take a chance."

"Look," Theo said pointing down. "It's a few hundred feet at most. Let's strap my stupid shoulder to my chest and go."

Rico wanted to argue, but Theo could be stubborn, too. He knew Rico would be doing and saying the same thing if the roles were reversed.

"Okay, but I'm using some of the rock-climbing equipment I have in here and belaying you down."

Taking a deep breath, Theo nodded and waited while Rico prepped. It took longer than he expected but still less time than it would have been getting SAR involved. Theo's shoulder was on fire by the time they got to the bottom.

"What I want to know is how those rungs came loose?" Theo growled as he pulled off the rope. "They were fine when we went up. We spent, what? An hour or so checking out the birds and path? They certainly couldn't have corroded in that amount of time."

"I got a look at them when I passed by on the way down. Someone took a pick or something to them."

"Clues. See if they left any clues." Theo began prowling around the parking area while Rico searched through the scrub near the base.

"Uh, Theo? This could be our culprit." He held up a hammer.

As Theo got closer, his gut tightened. The handle of the hammer was wrapped in duct tape.

"I don't believe it. That's Chelsea's hammer. What the heck?"

Rico stared at him strangely. "Chelsea? Why would she…?"

"She wouldn't," he snapped. "Do you have a bag, so we can see if there are any prints?"

Rico nodded and tucked the hammer carefully inside his bag. How had Chelsea's hammer gotten here?

Theo clenched his jaw. "It wasn't Chelsea. Besides the fact she has no reason, she hates heights. She gets dizzy being on a step stool. It's obviously someone she trusts in her house."

"I don't like this, Theo. I'll make sure to get this hammer to Aiden and see what he can do."

"Yeah. I was hoping, since it's been a month since the car accident, that it was all a weird coincidence, but this? They may not be in a hurry to get rid of me, but they're darn serious."

CHAPTER TWENTY-THREE

The thumping of Bandit's tail, along with his rough tongue licking her hand, had Chelsea looking around and blinking a few times. Carefully, she placed her mug back on the coffee table and took a deep breath.

The awful fog had come back. The one inside her head and not out near the ocean. Why? Had she taken her pills recently? Getting up, she stumbled to the kitchen and reached inside her purse. The bottle was gone. Theo had taken it and had them analyzed. Yeah, she remembered that now. So that meant…no. Please, no!

The mental illness wasn't only from the medication.

As she dropped into a kitchen chair, Bandit came over and whimpered, then his nails clicked on the new ceramic tile floor as he padded to the back door. She let him out, then stood on the back porch breathing deeply of the clean, fresh air. Maybe she'd been inside too long, and the paint fumes had overwhelmed her.

Except the painters had finished all the rooms almost a month ago. There were no fumes left. There went her last hope.

Glancing down at her watch, she startled at the time. After dropping Jordan off at school—she and Theo had decided one day a week over the summer was enough to see her friends—she'd come to the cottage. There were still things to be done, though much of the major renovations had been finished. After making herself a cup of tea, she'd scrolled through websites looking for the type of furniture she wanted for each room. Yes, they could use some of Theo's, but much of his stuff had been secondhand when he'd gotten it before they'd met. It didn't look like he'd bought anything new since then.

Bandit sniffed around by the rocks near the ocean, so Chelsea went back in to rinse out her mug. But there was already a mug in the sink. Did she drink two cups of tea? Why didn't she remember?

A deep hole opened in her chest, and frigid ice filled it. Would she end up like her mother, leaving Jordan alone? The fact Theo was nothing like her father eased her mind a bit, but how was this fair? She'd only just found her daughter.

Heading back outside to see where the dog had gotten to, she heard Mrs. Cullen singing in her garden. The woman had a beautiful voice. Chelsea had loved listening to her when she'd visited her grandmother as a child.

Bandit trotted back as Chelsea stole across the grass to hear her neighbor sing. The dog's bark made the music stop, but then the woman's head popped over the hedges.

"My goodness, Chelsea. I didn't realize you were out here. Sorry to disturb you with my noise."

"Oh, no, Mrs. Cullen. Your singing is lovely. It's wonderful to hear."

The woman blushed and waved her hand in the air. "Please, call me June. We're all adults now, aren't we?"

She didn't feel that way at the moment.

"How are you getting about since you've been back? I noticed your car's been missing most nights. Is the house still uncomfortable? I know it was left unattended for so long."

"My husband and I decided we'd stay with him until the whole house is renovated, then we plan to move here permanently. It shouldn't be too much longer." As long as she was with Theo, it didn't matter where they were.

"That's wonderful, dear. That husband of yours certainly is a looker. And far nicer than…well, I mustn't speak ill of the dead."

"Are you talking about my dad? I know he did some things I don't understand, but everyone still thinks he was so great because he took care of my mom when she was sick."

"Sick? Bah. Sick of that man, maybe."

"My mother had a mental illness." That wasn't easy to say, but Mrs. Cullen must have known this. "I…uh, I think I have one, too."

Her neighbor's eyes narrowed, her mouth tight. "There was nothing wrong with your mother. Not until she met that man. He was bad news."

"She was always sad and listless. I get that way sometimes, too."

"You listen to me, dear. Your mother lived here until she was a young lady. There was nothing mentally ill about her. Nothing genetic, anyway, yet after living for years with that controlling man—I still hear your poor grandmother lamenting the day they got married—she certainly could have become unstable. The evil in him could make anyone anxious and depressed."

Chelsea's eyes roamed across the yard to the turbulent ocean that rolled under the cloudy sky. Like how she felt today. In turmoil.

Mrs. Cullen's hand on her arm brought her gaze back. The lady's sweet expression exuded calm.

"We all have days where things seem a bit grim, but it's what we do with that time that counts. You have a wonderful man and an adorable daughter who both love you to pieces. Enjoy every second you have. When things start to close in, remember that love you have."

"Thanks, Mrs….uh, June. I'll remember."

Calling Bandit to her side, she went back in the house, washed the dishes she'd used, then gathered up her computer and fabric swatches. After placing everything in the car, she still didn't feel clear enough to drive, so she took Bandit for a walk. Good thing she'd left the kittens at home. At Theo's home.

The wind gusted past, whipping her hair in all directions. After a while, she began to feel better. As Jordan was being picked up at school by a friend and eating dinner at her house, she drove straight to Theo's.

One of the park SUVs was in the driveway, and her heart thudded. It was too late for Theo to be home for lunch and too early for the end of the day. As she hustled into the house, she heard Theo's deep voice growl.

"Stop fussing over me and get back to work."

"What's going on?" she asked Rico's back. The man moved aside. Theo sat on the couch, his arm in a sling. "What happened?"

Rushing to his side, she knelt at her husband's feet.

"Nothing to worry about. A dislocated shoulder. It's back where it's supposed to be." The look he sent to Rico told her there was more to the story.

When she stared at Rico, waiting for his version, he shrugged and said, "Dislocated shoulder. Little accident on the Precipice."

She tilted her head. "Why were you up there? I thought the falcons were still nesting."

"Part of our job is to make sure no one's bothering them and figure out when they'll be gone." Theo adjusted on the seat and grimaced.

"What did the doctor say? What do I need to do?"

"I'm fine. You don't need to do anything."

A snort burst from Rico's mouth, and Theo glared daggers at him.

"He's got some anti-inflammatory meds and should ice it for a while. He can take over-the-counter painkillers if needed, but I have a feeling the tough guy will gut it out. The sling needs to stay on for a few days, and he shouldn't do any heavy lifting for five or six weeks."

"Snitch," Theo muttered. "Go back to work. You're still on the clock for a few more hours, and you already spent the last one with me at the doctor's office."

"Here's his prescription, although they gave him something at the doc's." Rico handed her a piece of paper. "Oh, and he has an egg on the back of his head from hitting the rocks. If you need anything or he gives you too much of a hard time, call me."

"I will. Thank you, Rico." Standing on tiptoe, she kissed the ranger's cheek.

Rico smirked at Theo, who glared at him.

"Next time you get injured, payback won't be fun."

All Rico did was chuckle as he strutted out the door.

"How do you feel?" She took a seat next to him. "Do you need me to get you anything? Should you be upstairs in bed?"

A grin split his face. "Upstairs in bed sounds great." His eyebrows rose and fell.

"To rest, I mean. How exactly did this happen?"

"Doesn't matter. I should have been paying attention instead of thinking about how I woke you up this morning."

Warmth rushed into her face at the memory.

"I can get you some ice."

"I don't need you to get me anything. I'm capable of walking."

"I know you are." She kissed his cheek. "But you aren't supposed to be lifting anything big. No picking up Jordan or carrying me up the stairs."

"You know there is one thing you can do for me that will make me feel better."

"What? Anything?"

His eyes gleamed with mischief. "Kiss me. According to our daughter your kisses heal everything."

"I can do that." Carefully, she maneuvered into his lap until she straddled him. "Anywhere special?"

His shirt was unbuttoned, so she ran her fingers over his neck and down his chest. The sling got in the way, but she still managed to explore. She kissed him, her lips whispering across his, calling his name.

His injury couldn't be too debilitating as he nibbled on her lips and clenched his hands on her hips. Kisses from Theo were enough to get her excited, but when his fingers dove beneath her shirt to caress her back, desire grew to a fever pitch.

"Theo, we're in the living room," she objected though certainly didn't want him to stop.

"You said I couldn't carry you upstairs. Do you want to carry me?"

Glancing back, she saw Rico had closed the door behind him. "No." Her breath caught as Theo nibbled on her neck and unhooked her bra. Wiggling on his lap told her how aroused he was. She wasn't far behind him.

"What time is Jordan coming back?" Theo's voice was rough with desire.

"Not until after supper. About three hours."

"Three hours. Plenty of time. You might have to help me with a few things."

"I can do that. Is this helpful?"

Theo moaned as she lifted her shirt and tossed it on the ground.

———●———

Chelsea strolled into the coffee shop and headed for a table in the back. Frank waited for her, a cup of coffee in front of him and some tea for her.

"Chelsea," he greeted her, taking in her shorts and tank top with disapproval. Her father would never have let her dress this casually, even when she was alone in the house.

"Frank. When did you get here?" He'd called early this morning to arrange a meeting.

"Late last night. I'm staying at West Street." His eyes narrowed in question. "Have you been by to see the place yet?"

"No, I've never been fond of the caretakers."

Relaxing against the seat, he said, "They do an excellent job of keeping the place in great shape. I might want to come stay more often. If I didn't have so much to do back at the company."

"There are plenty of people who work there. Why don't you hire a few new ones to help you specifically? Train them to do some of your job, so you can take over what my father did."

He took another swig of coffee and sighed. "It has been exhausting trying to get everything settled as well as run the company. You could come back and help me."

"I don't know anything about the business, Frank." After blowing on the hot liquid, she tipped the cup for a sip of tea. "I don't want to know anything about the business. It's all yours."

His brows knit together, and he waved the waitress away when she offered a refill. "I appreciate your trust in me, Chelsea, but I want to make sure you're informed about everything."

"Unless it affects me personally, I don't care. As long as you aren't doing anything illegal, it's fine." This comment reminded her of what she'd asked earlier. After swallowing another mouthful, she asked, "Did you ever find out who provided the medication I've been taking?"

Frank had been staring at her cup but now blinked and looked up. "Oh, uh, sorry. I guess that slipped my mind. So much to do, you understand."

He reached across the table and patted her hand. "There is one thing that came to light as I've been going through the finances. An extremely large check you might be interested in."

Why she should be interested in the finances of the company, she didn't know, but if Frank wanted to inform her, she'd let him.

Reaching in his coat pocket, he pulled out a sheet of paper and unfolded it. When he handed it to her, she glanced at the copy of a check and the amount. Half a million dollars. Okay, definitely a good deal of money.

"Why…?" She took in the name scribbled across the top line in her father's familiar cursive. Theodore Lapierre.

"My father tried to pay off Theo. Why? So he'd take Jordan or leave me alone?"

"He didn't try, Chelsea. He did. The check was cashed." He pointed to the scan of the back of the check where it showed it was paid and canceled.

The room spun, and she held onto the edge of the table. Theo had taken money from her father. He'd never said anything. But there was Theo's signature on the back and a bank account number underneath.

"I know you want to get back together with this guy and raise your daughter," Frank said, his fingers skimming the top of hers. "I only wanted to make sure you know what you're getting into. He's not the altruistic father of the year you seem to think he is."

Her throat dried up, so she grabbed her mug and downed the rest of her tea. What did this mean? Theo had lied to her. Or at least hadn't told her the whole truth about how Jordan had come to stay with him. Half a million dollars wasn't something you forgot.

"I can't stay too long, but I wanted you to have this information. I don't want to see you hurt, Chelsea. You mean a lot to me. I hope you know that. If you need me to do anything, you know I'll be there for you."

"Thanks, Frank." She stuffed the paper into her purse. "I'll let you know. Will you be in town for a while?"

He shook his head. "No, I need to head back. Always something to do. But I'll drop everything if you need me. Call." With that, he rose. She stood, too, and he pulled her in for a hug.

They left the coffee shop, Frank heading left toward the house while she headed toward town. As it was early, she'd found a parking spot by the harbor, but her thoughts were too muddled to get behind the wheel. That fog rolled in again, and her stomach knotted tight. It had happened a few times in the last week, and she hated to think it was stress causing it. Maybe Mrs. Cullen had been wrong about the mental illness. Or perhaps all the damage her father had done was permanent.

Should she confront Theo about the money? After his shoulder injury, he'd been put on desk duty. He'd insisted he was fine, but his boss, Norma, took doctor's orders seriously, refusing to let him go back to trail detail for a few more weeks. Instead, he'd been put on the information desk at the Hull's Cove Visitor Center. To say he wasn't thrilled was an understatement. At least he wasn't in the same office as Dina.

Breathing in the fresh air, she finally felt a little clearer and got in her car and drove back. Today and tomorrow Theo was home due to working this weekend, so if she was still ticked off about the money after they'd talked, she could head to the cottage and get stuff done there without Jordan drawing her focus.

Theo's new SUV sat in the driveway, and she gritted her teeth. If he had half a million dollars, he could have bought his own stupid car.

"Hey, Mama. You just in time to play." Jordan rushed over from where she'd been swinging on her swing. Theo was finishing up the portable fencing they'd been using for the kittens while they were outside. He'd said he'd used it when Jordan was a toddler, as it gave her some room to roam but kept her from running into the street.

"What are you playing right now, sweetheart?"

"Daddy setting up a lava pit, and we gonna put pillows in to make islands, so we can save the kitties from the lava."

"Lava, huh?" Her gaze wandered to Theo, who shrugged.

"Some dinosaur show the boys at school were talking about. Apparently, lava is the thing."

"And there are bad guys in the lava, and we need a make 'em stay away, so they don't push us in the lava."

"Lava is bad, I take it?" Chelsea bit her lip at how exuberant and excited Jordan was.

"It burns you," the girl said dramatically, then moved in closer and whispered, "But it only pretend, so you don't need a worry."

"Phew, okay. I won't worry. Good thing I have you to keep me safe."

Theo connected the last section and threw a few old pillows on the grass inside, along with the kittens. Jordan jumped up and down until her father lifted her over the gate.

"Come on, Mama. You need a help fight the bad guys."

"I'll be there shortly, sweetheart. I need to talk to your dad for a few minutes." She staggered over to lean against the picnic table, and Theo followed her.

"Everything okay with Frank? You seem a little tense. Is he saying he can't run the business without you again?"

"He did say he'd like me to come back, but that isn't what I needed to talk about."

Jordan bounced around inside the play enclosure, scooping up the kittens every time they tumbled off the pillows.

Theo crossed his arms over his chest and smiled at her. "What's up?"

"I was wondering about when my dad dropped Jordan off."

Narrowing his eyes, he said, "I told you I never saw your father. He had some flunky deliver her here."

"He just walked in with a baby in his arms?"

"She was in an infant seat, and there was a small bag of diapers and formula with her. Thank God, because I wouldn't have known what to get for her."

Reaching in her purse, she pulled out the crumpled paper. "He didn't give you anything else? Like money?"

As his gaze took in the copy of the check, his mouth twisted. "The check."

"Yeah, the check. For a half million dollars. My father paid you to take our daughter?" Her voice cracked when she thought of her baby only being loved because of the money. It wasn't something she would ever have imagined from Theo.

"He didn't pay me to take her, Chelsea." His voice was gruff and hard.

When she glanced at the check and pointed to his signature on the back, Theo clenched his jaw and his fists.

"I told the guy who dropped her off to keep it, that I didn't want it, but he stuck it in the bag anyway. It was a few weeks before I even realized it was there."

"Yet you cashed it." The fact Theo had taken so much money from her father astounded her. Even after refusing it, he'd apparently given in.

"I was about to rip it up when Angie stopped me. She reminded me how little money rangers make and asked if I still planned to try for the FBI job. I knew with a baby and being on my own, I'd never be able to manage."

"So this was payment for losing the career you wanted."

"I didn't consider it payment for anything," he snapped and stomped away, running his fingers through his hair. When he turned back, his eyes bore into her. "I had a child to think of.

One who would need all sorts of things that I couldn't afford to give her. One that might want to go to college someday."

His hands slammed into his pockets, but he kept his voice low. "So, yeah, I cashed the check. Not for a few months, if you'll notice the date. I put the whole friggin' thing in a trust fund for Jordan. I didn't want her choosing her college by which one we could afford."

A trust fund. For their daughter. Yet part of her was still angry he hadn't bothered to tell her before now.

"I haven't touched a penny. Not even the interest, and let me tell you, it's considerable. Or hadn't you figured that out? Look at this house, Chelsea."

This was the second time he'd used her real name, not her nickname, since she'd gotten here. He was angry, too.

"Does it look like I've used any money for this? Old furniture, bathrooms that need renovating. The house needs a new roof, for Pete's sake. The only thing I did was get you the appliances you wanted. Not that it brought you back."

Turning away, his shoulders rose and fell. "I haven't even taken a vacation in five years. The first year because I was too afraid to leave in case you came back and then because I had a baby to take care of."

"Okay, I understand why you took the money, Theo. What I don't understand is why you didn't tell me. I've been back for over three months now. You've had plenty of opportunity. It's like you don't trust me."

The silence spoke volumes as did his eyes that couldn't meet hers. They roamed around the yard as he took in deep breaths. Her heart chipped into tiny pieces, the way it had been before she'd come back.

"Mama." Jordan's sweet voice reached out and seized her. "Wescue me. I'm falling in a lava."

Somehow, she managed a chuckle and marched toward the enclosure. Swinging her leg over, she got in and pulled the beautiful child into her arms.

"Don't worry, sweetheart. I won't let you go. I'll always be here to rescue you."

As Theo tromped into the house, she wondered who would be around to rescue her if she fell back into the depths of despair.

———◆———

The pillow beside Theo looked deserted without Chelsea's dark head resting on it. Her scent was still strong and pricked at his emotions. What had he been thinking yesterday when he'd gone silent after her question?

Yes, he'd been ticked that she'd thought for even one second he had taken Jordan only for the money. When she'd mentioned his not trusting her, the thoughts he'd had when she first returned had bombarded his mind. He hadn't trusted her then, had been petrified of her trying to take Jordan away from him.

He'd remained quiet because he was stubborn, and a tiny, sadistic part of him wanted her to know how it felt to be doubted. It didn't take an advanced degree to figure out she'd been hurt by his lack of response. Immediately getting involved in their daughter's lava drama, Chelsea had ignored him. Her tight smile and the near-constant view of her back was enough to let him know she was hurt.

Well, he was hurt, too. How could she have thought he'd only taken Jordan because of the money? Hadn't his actions, and the obvious love he had for their daughter, shown her anything?

He got up, dressed, put some coffee on, then began to make breakfast. Jordan would most likely be awake soon. Automatically, he filled the kettle with water for tea, then remembered Chelsea wasn't here. She'd made some excuse about needing to be at the cottage early today for a delivery.

After putting Jordan to bed, she'd coldly told him she would stay at her place for the night. No kiss or "I love you" for him. He hadn't made any move to kiss her either.

Guess they were both a little stubborn. Today, he'd fix that. No way he'd let her get away again. He wasn't delusional enough to think that everything would always be roses. Still, after the last few months, he hadn't expected any problems to crop up quite so fast.

The sound of little feet running down the stairs warned him Jordan was up.

"Hey, Daddy. I'm hungry."

"Morning, peanut. Why don't you let Bandit in? I'll have your scrambled eggs ready in a minute."

The child skipped to the back door and called to the dog, who trotted in and went straight to his water dish. Then, she sat next to the basket the kittens slept in and started petting them.

"Wash your hands," he instructed when the food was almost ready. Jordan bolted into the bathroom, water splashed, and she ran back out, parking herself at the table.

"Where's Mama?"

Digging into his eggs, he gave himself time to formulate his answer. "Remember she said she had to be at the cottage for some things today?"

"Oh, yeah. Can we go there?"

There was nothing he wanted more than to see her and talk or simply gather her into his arms and kiss the stuffing out of her. Would she get the message that he was sorry? Should he bring along some flowers?

"Not right away, peanut. We need to run some errands first. As soon as you've finished eating, head upstairs and get dressed."

The grocery shopping couldn't wait. They'd run out of dog food and the cupboards for human food were pretty bare, too.

The other errands weren't imperative, but he figured they'd give Chelsea a bit more time to do her stuff at the cottage, plus some time to cool off. His anger had dissipated easily enough overnight as he'd tossed and turned, unable to sleep without her by his side. Unfortunately, the deceit of the past still clung to them both, even with the truth of what her father had done. It wasn't always easy to push that aside.

Later, as he checked his phone once more, he clenched his jaw seeing that Chelsea hadn't responded to his text. He'd written that he missed her, and they could stop by with lunch if she was hungry. Nothing. It was late afternoon now and still no comment from her, positive or negative.

"Let's stop in and see if your mom needs any help," he suggested as he turned the car toward Seal Harbor.

When they pulled in the driveway, it was empty. Chelsea's car was nowhere to be seen. He freed Jordan from her car seat, anyway, and climbed onto the porch. She'd given him a key, so he used it to let themselves in. Jordan bolted up to see her pink bedroom again while Theo headed toward the kitchen. There was a mug in the sink. Her box of tea bags sat open on the counter. She'd been here.

Pulling out his phone, he called her. It rang and rang, then her sweet voice told him to leave a message.

"Pixie, it's Theo. Listen, I know I was upset yesterday, and I'm sorry. I'm not sure where you are, but we're at the cottage. We'll be here for a while if you planned on coming back. Call me and let me know. I love you."

Was she honestly so stubborn she would avoid seeing Jordan today? As he wandered around the house, taking in all the renovations that had been done, he couldn't stop thinking about her or the accidents that had occurred recently. The Precipice incident had only been ten days ago. Even though Chelsea had gotten hurt in the car crash, most of them seemed aimed his way. Had something happened to her?

Or was she having another bout of anxiety and depression like she'd had before? A few times lately, she'd seemed distant and almost out of it. He'd put it down to stress of getting the cottage ready for them to live here. Was it more? She wouldn't run off again. Not with how she felt about their daughter.

The tone of his phone sounded, and he swiped his finger across the screen. Chelsea. Thank God.

—*I need time. I'm not sure I can do this.*—

What the heck? Time for what? And what couldn't she do?

—*What are you talking about? Where are you?*—

It was only a few moments before his phone pinged again.

—*I'm going home. I'm sorry.*—

Home? Was she talking about his place? Or Westchester? That wasn't right. Even in her most emotional state, she'd never thought of Westchester as home.

He tapped in the number for her phone and listened while it rang. No answer, though another text came through.

—*Take care of Jordan and leave me alone. This won't work. I thought it would, but I made a mistake.*—

She couldn't mean this. And why wasn't she picking up the darn phone? His heavy footsteps echoed through the house as he went from room to room, wondering what was happening. Not again. His heart had been ripped out and stomped on once before. Her father had been behind it that time. But he was dead.

"Peanut, you okay in there?" How would Jordan react if Chelsea had really left them?

"Yep. Daddy, look. Mama got me that bed I wanted. And the dresser to go with it. I love it." Jordan sat with her doll on a single bed with a princess bedspread. The headboard had small flowers painted on it that matched the ones on the dresser.

What in the world? How could Chelsea buy furniture for her daughter one day and decide to desert them the next? His head spun with confusion as he wandered into what would have been their bedroom. Nothing unusual here. Except...in the corner. He advanced and flipped on the light.

Chelsea's sneakers peeked out from under the bed. The polka dot canvas ones she loved to wear. The ones she'd been wearing yesterday when she left his house. And her purse. On the floor like it had been tossed there. Or dropped. Reaching inside, he found her wallet, license, and credit cards, as well as a good deal of cash. How had she planned on paying for gas for her car ride home?

Cold sweat trickled over the goosebumps that popped up everywhere. The hollow feeling permeating his chest expanded and threatened to destroy him. His hands shook on the bag as he noted her phone wasn't in there. Obviously. Someone had just texted him with it.

That someone had not been his wife.

CHAPTER TWENTY-FOUR

"**W**hen was the last time you saw Chelsea?"
Aiden stood in the living room, flipping open a notepad. Theo had called his friend as soon as he'd found Chelsea's purse.

"Last night. She helped put Jordan to bed and then came here."

"Was it typical of her to stay here at night?"

"Not in the last month, no. Ever since her accident, she's been staying at my place." Theo took a deep breath, trying to calm his nerves. "But we had a bit of a fight yesterday."

"Could she have taken off to cool down a little?"

"That's what I thought at first. Then, I got her texts."

"She sent you a text? Recently?"

Theo produced his phone and scrolled to the conversation. As he handed Aiden the device, he explained, "The first few texts I thought she was still upset. Then, they didn't make sense. Going home? She never thought of Westchester as home. And we were here, so she didn't mean this place."

Theo told Aiden about the purse, wallet, and the shoes.

"Well, my wife has plenty of shoes she could wear. However, not having her license and wallet is another matter," his friend said.

"Look at that last text. I sent it as kind of a test."

The police chief scrolled and read, "What should I do with Eeny, Meeny, Miny, and Moe?"

"Her response is to keep the animals. But those aren't their names. Whoever is using her phone seems aware we have pets but not what their names are."

Aiden gazed around the room, then strode over to the officer he'd brought with him. After a few minutes of talking, he came back while the cop left the house.

"I sent Tom to get the fingerprinting equipment from the car and to call in a few more people to help with evidence. I want to walk through the house. Tell me if anything else looks off."

The front door opened, and Tom came back in with Angie right behind him. She rushed to Theo, her eyes concerned.

"What's going on? You said you needed my help, but I show up here and there's a police car outside."

"I need you to take Jordan home for me. I'm not sure how long I'll be." His gaze roamed the room, and he lowered his voice. "Chelsea is missing. I don't want Jordan to know. She's upstairs in her room."

"Missing? Are you sure she's not at the store or picking up pizza?"

Shaking his head, Theo filled her in.

"I know you've had some accidents happening lately, but they seemed more aimed at you," Aiden said to Theo. "Is there a reason someone would want to abduct or harm Chelsea?"

"Her money?" Angie snarked and headed upstairs to get Jordan.

The chief narrowed his eyes. "Chelsea has money, other than this house?"

Shoving his hands in his pockets, Theo said, "Yeah, her dad owned MedLab Pharmaceuticals. He was loaded. Gave me a big chunk of change when Jordan got here. I never used it. It's all sitting in a trust fund for Jordan. That's part of the reason for the fight. I neglected to tell her about it, and she found out." He was still kicking himself for that stupid mistake.

"How did she find out? It could simply be a coincidence you had a big fight right before she disappeared, but it seems whoever took her could also have instigated the fight."

"I assume it was Frank, her father's right-hand man. She'd just come back from meeting him for coffee. But he'd have no reason to kidnap Chelsea. As the person running the company, he has access to all the finances there. I'd have to go to him to get any money from her accounts. Wouldn't a kidnapper already be asking for money if that's why they took her?"

"Not necessarily. They might want to freak you out first. Get you desperate. What's Frank's last name? I'll check him out."

"I'm not sure. But he wasn't anywhere near here when the other accidents happened."

Scribbling on his notepad, Aiden said, "I'll check him out, anyway."

"While you're at it, check out Brett Sheehan. He has free access here, and he must have some idea how much money Chelsea has. She's been throwing tons of it into renovating this house. Maybe he wants more than she's paying him."

When the girls came down, he picked Jordan up and kissed her cheek. "Auntie Angie is going to bring you home and stay with you. Kind of like a girls' night. I need you to show her how to feed Bandit and the kitties and where they sleep. Can you do that?" He winked at Angie.

"Yup. Where you and Mama gonna be?"

What should he tell her? His mind was so muddled he couldn't even come up with a plausible excuse.

"Mamas and daddies sometimes need to be alone without little girls," Angie filled in, coming to his rescue. "Let's head home, and maybe we can stop and get pizza on the way."

"I like bacon on my pizza," Jordan informed his cousin as they shuffled out. "And Bandit can sleep on my bed with me."

Theo nodded at Angie's questioning look. Now wasn't the time to fight over where the dog slept. If something happened to Chelsea, Jordan would need all the comfort she could get. He would, too.

"Ready to walk through? Anything strange about this living room?"

"No, this room, the office, and back parlor don't even have the furniture moved back in yet." Theo led him down the hall and into the dining room. Two cups sat on the table, one at the head of it and one kitty corner.

"Do you know if these are from today?"

Theo nodded. "Yes. Chelsea always cleans up her dishes before she leaves." He leaned in close and sniffed. "One is coffee, and one is tea. The one with tea is Chelsea's."

"So, whoever she's with, it's a good chance she knows them and let them in."

"That doesn't make me feel any better." His heart thumped loudly in his chest. "Why would anyone want to hurt my wife? She's only been here a few months and before that she never left her house."

Waving at Tom who was sprinkling some dust over a doorknob, Aiden said, "Let's also check the contents of the cups."

As they searched through the house, there wasn't much more Theo could tell his friend. The mug in the sink showed that Chelsea had made herself a cup earlier in the day, yet the box of teabags still sat on the counter. It wasn't like Chelsea to leave things out.

"Now what do I do?"

The apologetic look on his friend's face was not what he wanted to see. He wanted answers. And his wife back. Safely. In his arms, where she belonged.

"Go home to your daughter. I'm sorry, Theo, I don't have any answers right now. We'll finish the fingerprints and run them, but you said there have been tons of people tramping around here lately doing renovations. We'll analyze the tea and coffee, and I'll have some of my men canvas the neighborhood in case anyone saw anything. I'll check on this Frank guy and his whereabouts and see if Brett is around."

"What can *I* do? I want her back, Aiden. What would you do if Katie disappeared?"

"I'd tear the town apart," Aiden confessed. "Regardless, I don't need you running around in a frenzy, especially not during peak tourist season. I promise I'll put a rush on this, even with the texts indicating she left of her own free will."

Theo started to argue, but Aiden put up his hand. "I believe you. I'm only saying some of the evidence suggests she's gone because she wanted to. There's nothing you can do here tonight. I'll lock up when we leave. You should go back and make sure Jordan is all right."

"What do I even tell her?" His little girl would be heartbroken if the mom she'd waited her whole life to see disappeared. He wasn't sure he'd make it either.

Aiden shook his head. "I promise I'll call as soon as I get *any* information. I've got her cell number and will see what I can do about tracing its whereabouts. Don't get too excited about that. Mt. Desert Island doesn't have a whole lot of cell towers to ping off. I've also already put out an APB on her car."

Frozen in place, his fingers trembled as he threaded them through his hair. He couldn't leave. This was where Chelsea had been last. He wanted to stay to see if she'd come back, even though it wasn't plausible. Thank God Aiden believed that something had happened to her. But what? And why?

After shaking Aiden's hand, he slowly trudged outside and stood on the porch. The sun had gone down, and the stars began to make their appearance. So often, he and Chelsea had sat outside staring up at the night sky. Here in Maine, it was so clear and big it had made them see how small they were, how lost they could get in the world. They'd never minded getting lost with each other.

How could he help Chelsea when she was lost all alone?

Her ringtone went off, and Chelsea attempted to lift her head. The fog had wormed its way more deeply inside, and she didn't have the strength to fight it anymore. Why was she so out of it?

As she shifted to get more comfortable, something pulled at her hands and feet. Which seemed to somehow be both in the same place.

That pried her eyes open. She was on her side, knees to her chest and hands tied to her feet. Her bare feet. Why wasn't she wearing any shoes. Hadn't she been over at the cottage? Yeah, they'd delivered Jordan's new bedroom set, and she'd put the sheets on them. The pink princess ones she'd picked up at the store only that morning. Then, someone had come in. Frank.

"Frank." Her voice was scratchy, like it hadn't been used in a while. What time was it? Where was she? It felt like she was lying on a mattress, yet the smell was all wrong. This wasn't her own bed or the one she shared with Theo.

Oh, God. Theo. They'd had an argument, and she'd run off, scared. Of him not trusting her. Of not wanting her. It had been silly, really. So he hadn't told her about the check. In no way did it mean he'd only taken Jordan because of the money. The love he had for their daughter was apparent in everything he said and did. Why had she been so stupid in accusing him?

The room was dark, but as her eyes adjusted, she began to make out some shapes. A few windows with dim light coming in. A table. Some chairs near the far wall. Something was in one of them. Or was it someone?

"Frank?" Had he been taken, too? Her father had always warned her that people might want to kidnap her to get him to pay a ransom. It had supposedly been one of the reasons he wanted her close to home at all times. Had Frank been taken because he could bargain for money with the company? When? How? Her memories didn't go back much further than drinking tea with him.

The figure on the chair stirred and rose. It was Frank. How was he not trussed up like her?

"Chelsea? You're awake." Before he reached her, he stopped at the table and picked up an object. A phone. It had a floral cover on it. Her phone.

"He doesn't give up, does he? He's been texting every few hours."

"Who? What's going on? Why am I tied up?"

Frank took a wooden chair and turned it around before straddling it and resting his arms along the back. "I needed you to cooperate, Chelsea, and this was the only way."

"The only way to what?" Pushing against the mattress, she wiggled until she was seated, leaning against the wall behind her. Her feet were bound together with a short rope attached to her hands, which were also tied up tight.

"You need to come back to Westchester and marry me." His voice was calm but determined.

"*What?* I'm already married, Frank. You know that."

"I didn't know when I made my plans. Your marriage has ruined everything. Everything!" When he stood and slammed his hand on the back of the chair, she flinched. Frank had never shown any kind of anger or violence that she could remember. It was a feature her father had admired in him.

Shrinking back closer to the wall, she glanced around the room. The place was old and broken down. Completely unlivable. How did they get here?

"Where are we?" Keeping the tremors from her voice took effort. Clearly, she didn't know him well enough to understand what he was capable of.

"Still on the island." He shrugged. "I found this little shack one day while I was exploring. It's a bit off the beaten path, being on the west side of Mount Desert Island, but it serves my purpose."

"What is your purpose?" The fact she was tied up told her it wasn't anything good for her.

"To marry you. Weren't you listening?"

"My head is groggy. I don't understand."

As Frank stalked closer, her skin erupted in goosebumps. He sat next to her and stroked his fingers down her cheek. The hair on her arms stood up, and her stomach revolted.

"You were supposed to have a few months to grieve for your father and then I was planning to court you. You have no idea the lovely things I had in mind. Dinner at nice restaurants, dancing, museums. You would have loved it. I probably would have lowered your medication dosage, so you'd actually enjoy it."

"My medication? What did you have to do with my medication?"

"Your father filled me in on how it kept you calm and amenable. At times, a little out of it, if he put too much in your food."

"He put it in my food while I was also taking the pills every day? Do you have any idea what that stuff does? Theo had it analyzed, and it's horrible."

"It made you the perfect daughter. When you took it. He didn't have as much control when you visited your grandmother. Thus Theo. Obviously, your father never knew you'd gotten married or he wouldn't have put that ridiculous provision in the will."

"Frank, I still don't understand what this is all about. You have control of the company. I let you make all the decisions. What more could you want?"

His eyes turned cold as he stood and faced her. "I want it all. To own the business, the estate, and everything that comes with it. Sure, I have a great salary, but it's not the same. Your father made arrangements so it would all be mine."

What was he saying? "You told me the will said I inherited everything."

Frank took a deep breath. "Of course, I told you that. You do. Or you would have. Unless you're married and then control of it all goes to your husband. On account of your *condition*."

"My condition," she yelled. "You mean the one created by my father? The same man who drugged me, so I couldn't remember how horrid my life was, who stole my baby and told me she died? There's nothing wrong with me!"

Frank's mouth twisted. "I'm afraid there is, Chelsea. It all would have been beautiful if only you hadn't taken up with that ranger. You ruined it all by marrying him and having his kid."

"I told you I don't want the business, Frank. I'll sign it over to you, and you can have it all. The estate, the business. Heck, even the house on West Street. I only want to be here with Theo and Jordan. Let me go, and it's all yours." Would he take it? For some reason, he seemed a bit on the unstable side right now.

"You can't do that. Don't you see? According to the will, your husband owns it all. The business, the estate, every penny your father had in the bank. It all belongs to him. You can't sign it away, because it isn't yours."

"Then, I'll have Theo sign it over to you. Please, Frank."

"Oh, sure. He'll do that right after they haul me off to jail for kidnapping. No, there's only one way for this whole thing to play out. He has to die."

CHAPTER TWENTY-FIVE

Theo was up and answering the door before Aiden even knocked.

"Have you found her?' His breath rushed out as his heart hoped for good news. His friend's face told him it wasn't.

"Not yet. But I do have some information." Aiden's outfit was wrinkled, and stubble dotted his chin. Probably how Theo looked. Sleep had not been easy to find last night. The few times he'd managed to doze off, images of Chelsea being tortured or hurt rammed into his skull, jackknifing him into wakefulness.

"Coffee? I made a pot."

The grateful smile on Aiden's face said yes. They moved into the kitchen where Theo poured coffee into two mugs and set them on the table. Aiden plopped the bag he'd carried in on the table.

"Katie gave me some breakfast sandwiches to bring over. Said you probably wouldn't take the time to eat. Course she knew I hadn't eaten either."

"Have you had any sleep?" Theo asked. "You look like crud."

"Have you done face time with your mirror yet, this morning, my friend?" Aiden's eyebrow rose.

"What have you got?"

Pulling his notebook out of his pocket, Aiden flipped some pages. "There were dozens of fingerprints all over the house, so it took a while to narrow them down. We ran any we could, then we checked them against the prints we found on the hammer that was possibly used in your Precipice accident. Some of those had been partial and hard to match. This solidified things a bit."

"What'd you find?" Theo took a bite of the breakfast sandwich, then leaned in closer.

"Your prints, Chelsea's, and Brett's. But we knew you'd all been there. We also found Dina Bannon's prints. Has she been hanging around there, helping to hammer nails?" Aiden knew Dina, and his expression showed his disbelief that she'd hammer anything that wasn't tall, dark, and handsome.

"I know she came by a while back to deliver some papers. I have a hard time believing she'd crawl under a car to cut a brake line."

"Does she have a reason to dislike Chelsea? Or you?"

Did she? Sure. But Dina? "You know how she is. She's after every available male between the ages of twenty-five and forty. She's been putting the moves on me since I've been here. She wasn't thrilled that I didn't boot Chelsea out the door, but do you honestly think she'd kidnap her?"

"Just asking questions. I've got someone headed to her house to get some information from her."

"Has anyone questioned Brett?"

Aiden nodded. "I sent someone over right after you left last night. He was in his apartment with a few friends. The officer he spoke to said he seemed quite concerned about Chelsea."

"I still don't trust him. He hasn't stopped blaming me for his sister's death."

"Possibly, but he has an alibi for all of yesterday and Chelsea wasn't with him. He insisted we search his place. Honestly, the last prints we found are the ones I'm interested in."

"Frank?"

"His name's Frank Haggar. He's the current CEO of MedLab Pharmaceuticals. His prints were not only in a few spots in the house, but we got a partial on the hammer. The interesting thing is that when I called right after talking to you, he wasn't in his office to speak with. They said he was on a business trip."

"He was here Thursday morning, except Chelsea said he wasn't staying. Did they have any way to contact him?"

Aiden grabbed one of the sandwiches and took a bite. Once he'd chewed and swallowed, he answered, "They wouldn't give out any information on him, so we did a little digging. First, you mentioned he'd stayed a few times at the West Street house Chelsea's father had owned. I went there myself last night and asked a few questions. The staff was eager to tell me what a nice, respectable man he was and how he always cleaned up after himself. Seems he's been there quite a few times in the past three months. Probably more than you realized. The dates matched up to the accidents you'd mentioned."

"He was here? Where is he now?" God, what was this guy up to with Chelsea? Was he hurting her? The blood rushed from his face, and the room spun. Dropping his head into his hands, he grabbed his hair and clenched his fingers. The pain from pulling didn't make the ache in his heart any less.

"The staff pointed out his car. It was still in the driveway. A black sedan. Rental. They said he took a taxi when he left Friday mid-day. Checked with the taxi company, and they verified they dropped him at Chelsea's house. But now her car is missing, so we're assuming he took that. With her in it."

"Sure. To make me think she'd left. He must not have figured I'd go inside and look around, hoping I'd believe her texts that she was leaving me."

"Well, whatever he's done, it was planned out. The tests came back from the liquid in the cups."

Theo's head whipped up as he stared at the chief.

"The tea had a large quantity of a drug similar to ones used for date rape. Tracing it back, we found it's produced by none other than MedLab Pharmaceuticals."

"Do you think he plans to…" Theo couldn't even finish the thought.

"I can't possibly take a guess on his motives, but I think we're definitely looking at this Frank guy. Did Chelsea ever say if he was interested in her romantically?"

"No." His voice hitched, and he cleared his throat. "His name only came up a few times, and it was mostly regarding her father's business. He wanted her to come back, but Chelsea never made it sound like he was angry about it."

He was ready to tear his hair out. Where was she? What was happening to her? This was worse than when he thought she didn't care for him anymore. At least then he'd known she was alive and well. Or so he'd thought. More guilt came flooding back for not pushing harder five years ago.

"Where's Jordan?" Aiden asked as he finished the sandwich and crumpled up the wrapper.

"Angie took her to her place last night. They took the kittens and left me the dog, in case I need him to sniff out Chelsea. As if he's a Bloodhound. Any lead on where they might be?"

"We checked her phone, and according to the towers being used, they're still on Mt. Desert Island. Still working on where. We've got people checking out Frank and any connections he has around here. His name and face have been put out as a Person of Interest, so if anyone sees him, we'll be notified."

"What do we do now?"

Aiden lowered his eyes and looked away. Theo had a bad feeling he wouldn't like the answer.

"We wait."

"What do you plan to do?" The pain in Chelsea's heart multiplied at the thought of Theo getting hurt or dying.

"I plan to get rid of him." Frank's eyes were intense and cold, devoid of emotion. Then, he shook his head and anger seemed to replace the cold. "If only the accidents had taken him out, I wouldn't have had to resort to this."

"Accidents? What accidents? Did you cut the roots on the tree?" Is that why it had fallen so quickly?

A sly smirk crossed his face. "I did a lot more than that. Tried to push some rocks down on him shortly after you first got here. Nearly hit him with my car. The tree, though, that wasn't so easy to figure out, and you almost got in the way."

"But Theo did get injured."

"Injured is not dead," he said, his eyes blazing. "I thought for sure I had him at that stupid Thunder thing. But the fog was so thick, I almost slipped and went into the waves myself. I had a tight hold of a tree to keep from being pulled into the ocean."

Chelsea remained silent, wondering what Frank meant by that. Theo had never told her about almost falling in the water at what she assumed was Thunder Hole.

"Then, you had to go and take his car and get in an accident. It was supposed to be him who lost control when the brake fluid spilled out."

"Brake fluid? You had something to do with my accident?"

Frank paced back and forth, hands in his pockets like he was discussing a business deal. "I cut the brake line. Thought I did a decent job, considering I've never worked on a car before. The internet has everything these days. When that didn't work, I had to follow him around a bit and get creative on that cliff path. Unfortunately, his friend was too close and managed to save him before he fell."

"It was your fault Theo had that accident on the Precipice."

"I'm surprised he didn't tell you. They found the hammer I used to sabotage the metal rungs." He shrugged. "Your hammer. But killing someone wasn't what I trained for, so I'm not very good at it. It's too risky hiring someone else."

"But you don't have to kill him, Frank. Please," she cried, tears rolling down her cheeks. "We can get a divorce, then I'll sign it all over to you."

Turning swiftly, Frank stalked over to her and leaned on the back of the chair. "Don't you understand? That isn't going to work. Even if we could convince your husband to do that, without tossing me in prison, he'd still own *everything*."

"I don't understand."

"Your father had you under control most of the time, but he also knew that occasionally you had lucid moments and did stupid things. Like take up with a park ranger while attending a funeral. He knew that if you ever found out about the codicil, you'd likely divorce me. He couldn't take a chance that your new husband would be the right man to run the company."

"What codicil?"

"The one that said your husband got control of the company and all assets, and that even if you divorced him, he'd still remain in control and have ownership. So even if the ranger divorced you, he'd still get it all. Everything. I worked too hard these last years to lose it all now."

Chelsea sunk deeper against the wall. "So you planned to court me and marry me. What if I didn't want to?" She had a feeling she knew the answer.

"That's what your medication is for, Chelsea. To keep you calm and compliant. No one would ever question your behavior since it's how you've been the last five years. Longer, even. Poor Chelsea, so like her mother. Everyone would think I'm as wonderful as your father. Keeping you safely at the estate instead of locked up in an institution somewhere."

"I can't believe you did all this. You knew my father was drugging me. How long? How long have you known?"

"A few years now. I've worked for the company for over ten years, but it was only the last four that your father began training me to take over for him. We were planning to have me start courting you soon, but then he had a heart attack and died. The will had already been amended. I thought we were all set."

"Did you know he stole my baby? Were you in on that?"

Shaking his head, Frank said, "No, though I have a feeling that's what made your father start thinking about changing his will. The fact you had gotten away from him long enough to have a fling and get pregnant scared him, made him try harder to keep control over you."

"Now, you plan to do that, too."

"My plans will depend on you, Chelsea. How much you cooperate. For now, you need to have something to eat. I got some donuts earlier and some coffee and tea. Most likely cold now, but it's something."

Walking over to the table, he opened up a paper bag and pulled items out. "Do you want sugar in your tea? They gave me a few packets."

"No." She didn't want him touching her drink. Wasn't sure he hadn't already put something in there. But she was hungry and thirsty. The donut he brought over was a simple glazed, and even with her hands tied, she still managed to eat it and drink some of the tea. The way he smirked told her she'd made a mistake drinking. She pretended to have the whole cup, then when he wasn't looking, poured the rest behind the mattress. When she finished up, Frank took her trash and tossed it on the table.

"Your life with me will be easy, Chelsea. You'll never have to work and can do anything you want. Around the estate. Like before."

"How is that a life? Being drugged all the time. I barely remember the last four years of my life. Frank, you can't do this. Take as much money as you can and leave. I won't come after you. Please, don't do this. Theo must be looking for me by now."

"Sure, he is." Frank laughed. "If I hadn't sent him a text saying you were going back home. I've ignored all his tries at contacting you. Hopefully, he'll get the message."

"You sent him what?" Oh, God, would Theo believe the texts like he had before? No, no way. "So, you'll take me back to the estate and forget about this place."

"I will, yes." His smile turned evil. "But not until I get your husband out of the way. I'll need to wait until dark. Easier to dump his body into the ocean without tons of tourists around. I'll have to kill him here first. I don't imagine he'll cooperate by allowing me to kill him near the water."

The tea must have had something strong in it, even though she'd only had half of it. Her eyes wouldn't stay open, and the fog had begun to roll in thicker than ever. "What are you going to do?" Her voice was barely a whisper.

"Lure him here. Send him a text saying you changed your mind but got lost on your way back. He'll come to rescue you, then I'll get rid of him."

Arguing with Frank wouldn't get her anywhere, but how could she stop him from killing Theo? She didn't even want to ask what he had planned for Jordan. Her baby. If he had no plans for her, she certainly didn't want to give him any ideas. How could she get out?

As she slid sideways on the dirty mattress, she groaned. "Frank. I'm cold. Is there a blanket? I had one in my car."

He threw her a disgusted look but left the shack. A minute later, he returned with the blanket she'd used to rest the kitten carrier on and draped it over her. Good. Maybe she could start working on untying her hands and feet without him noticing. *If* she could keep from falling asleep. The light coming from the window indicated it was getting to be late morning. How long did he expect her to be out for? Whatever he'd given her yesterday had knocked her out for over twelve hours. If she was out that long again, there was nothing to stop Frank from luring Theo here and killing him.

It didn't matter what she wanted. Sleep took her, anyway.

The next time she opened her eyes, the light was slanting through the windows at a different angle. Definitely lower in the sky. Frank's head leaned against the back of the chair, and his eyes were closed. Getting some sleep for his busy night of murder?

Without a sound, she moved her hands and began the long, arduous task of undoing the ropes. She'd have to do the feet first and hope getting that undone would loosen the bindings on her hands.

Hours seemed to pass, and every now and then Frank glanced her way. She kept her eyelids lowered and tried to work by touch only, so he wouldn't suspect she was awake. As time moved forward, she grew more and more concerned that the ropes would stay tight, and Frank would make good on his promise of killing her husband.

Once the light was all but gone outside, Frank lit a small jar candle and started scrolling through her phone.

With a last look in her direction, he tapped his fingers on the screen. After a few minutes, he read what he wrote, smirked, and tapped one last time. Crap. There wasn't much time for her to escape and warn Theo. The rope was looser on her feet but still not completely off. Whatever Frank had put in her tea was starting to wear off. Still, if she couldn't get out of the ropes, it wouldn't matter.

The day had been exceptionally beautiful. Perfect, cloudless sky, temps in the mid-eighties, a soft breeze carrying the salty scent of the ocean all the way to his door. Yet Theo couldn't enjoy it. Had barely taken a few steps outside in case the house phone rang. His cell sat snugly in his pocket. He pulled it out to check it every ten minutes on the off chance it had gone off and he hadn't heard it ring or felt the vibration. He was losing his mind.

The sun slid lower and hid behind the trees in his yard. What had been happening with Chelsea all day? Where was she? Was she hurt? Still alive? Why hadn't he heard anything? Frustrated couldn't even begin to cover his feelings. Guilt weighed heavy, too. This time not because he hadn't pushed harder five years ago when she left, though that still banged on the back door, hoping to get in. If he'd only said something a few days ago when she'd confronted him with the bank check. She wouldn't have gone to the cottage and been abducted.

Or Frank could have waited until today, when he was supposed to be at work, and grabbed Chelsea here. Would he have also taken Jordan or left her alone? The thought of his daughter being harmed slammed into him, causing him to drop into a nearby chair.

Angie had the weekend off and was keeping Jordan busy. Probably staying up late with junk food and too much TV, but at least the little girl was safe.

The sound of a vehicle pulling up sent Theo racing to the front porch. Disappointment ripped through him when he saw it was Rico. Aiden, with news that he'd found Chelsea, was what he really wanted.

"You okay?" Rico climbed out of his truck and joined him on the front porch.

Theo could only shake his head. *Okay* didn't even come close.

"Anything new from Aiden?"

"Not since we talked last." His friend had checked in periodically throughout the day and had spent a good portion of it driving around the island, looking for Chelsea's car. It was what Theo wanted to do, also, but he was afraid of missing Chelsea if she somehow got away and came here or tried to call the house.

Pacing back and forth the length of the porch, he clenched his fists. "I'm losing it, Rico. Not sure how much longer I can sit around doing nothing."

"Does Jordan know what's going on?"

"Not really. Angie stopped by earlier with her for a short while to grab a few things. I tried to be upbeat, but I'm pretty sure I stink as an actor. Luckily, my cousin puts on a good show."

"When I spoke with Aiden earlier, he said there was nothing in this Frank's background that indicated he was violent. Maybe he's simply being territorial."

"Then, why all the cloak and dagger of making me think Chelsea was leaving me?"

Rico shrugged. "So you wouldn't do exactly what you did and call the police?"

"I want her back, Rico," Theo shouted, hoping his friend knew his yelling wasn't meant for him.

Rico's hand on his shoulder told him he knew. "I'll do anything you need me to in order to get her back."

"I can't lose—" His phone vibrated in his pocket as the text tone sounded. Pulling it out quickly, he glanced at it, hoping it wasn't another friend asking for an update.

Chelsea's name flashed across the screen, and his thumb swiped automatically.

"What is it?" Rico moved closer.

"Chelsea's phone."

—I'm sorry, Theo. I made a mistake. Coming back.—

Another text came right after it. Then, more.

—Took a wrong turn and car ran out of gas. So stupid I didn't check.—

—Pulled off the street at Indian Point Road, I think.—

—There was a sign for Squid Cove maybe.—

—Please, come get me.—

Taking a deep breath, Theo stared at his friend. "Indian Point Road covers half the island."

Rico narrowed his eyes. "Why is he telling you their location? You know it's a setup of some kind."

"I know, but I can't sit around waiting for someone else to fix this. It'll take a while to find her car, especially since it'll be dark by the time I get to the other side of the island."

"Squid Cove is more north," Rico stated. "How about we split up and both search?"

Theo nodded. "I'll contact Aiden and have him head that way." Fishing his keys out of his pocket, he ran to his shiny new SUV. The one Chelsea had insisted she buy for him.

As Rico moved toward his vehicle, he called out, "I'll contact Kim and have her standby. Just in case."

Yeah, Rico didn't have to finish that sentence. Theo didn't want to think of any *just in case* scenario. Starting the car, he put it in gear, and tore off down the street. After calling Aiden with the information, his mind raced as he flew over the pavement toward the west side of the island. What possible reason did this Frank character have for wanting him hurt or dead? And what had he done to Chelsea?

The head lights of the SUV cut through the dark as he drove along. Once he reached Indian Point Road, he slowed down. It would be easy to miss Chelsea's car if he went too fast, especially if it was pulled off to the side.

Time moved on, and Theo grew antsy. He'd gone almost the whole way down the road and was about to turn around when he saw a light-colored sedan pulled slightly off the road, near a broken-down shack that was hidden in the woods. Not wanting to alert Frank that he was here, Theo turned his lights off and pulled over a few hundred feet farther up the road.

After closing his car door softly, he picked his way through the woods and noted it was Chelsea's car. Empty. He quickly sent off a group text with his location, then shut off the ringer, so anything coming in wouldn't give away where he was. A soft light glowed through the window of the shack. Theo headed in that direction.

When he peeked in, shadows filled the room, but he could make out a table with a small candle on it, some chairs, and a mattress shoved near the wall. He didn't see anyone inside. The bright colors that lay in a clump on the bed shouted at him. It was the blanket Chelsea always kept in the car. Peering in closer, he tried to see if it was his wife under the blanket. That could be dark hair at one end of the mattress, but if it was Chelsea, she didn't appear to be moving. Crap. Where was Frank?

"Did you want a closer look?"

The deep voice at Theo's back spun him around. A tall, blond man with a solemn face stood there. Even in the darkness, Theo could see the glint of what he held in his hand. A gun. Pointed straight at him.

Chapter Twenty-Six

"Frank?"

Surprise flashed across the man's face as Theo said his name. It only lasted a second before Frank held the weapon up and smirked.

"So you know who I am?"

"Chelsea's mentioned you. What have you done to her, and what do you want?"

"Let's go inside to chat." He waved the gun at Theo, who considered, for only a moment, trying to disarm him. He had no idea how much Frank knew about weapons or how well he could use them. If Theo got injured or killed out here, who knew what he'd do to Chelsea? Better to play along and give Rico and Aiden time to arrive with trained help. Theo could rappel down the side of a cliff to rescue a fallen hiker or navigate his way out of the thick foliage anywhere on the island. Hand-to-hand combat with an armed assailant hadn't been in his training.

"Open it," Frank said to Theo as they approached the door. The inside was dim with only the candle providing light.

"Chelsea?" he called out, hoping he'd get a response from the lump on the mattress.

"She's sleeping." Frank brandished the gun, directing Theo further into the room.

As he approached the table, the blanket shifted slightly. Pivoting toward Frank, he shoved his hands in his pockets. Could he manage to get a message to his friends? Probably not without seeing the screen.

"What did you do to her?" Theo's gaze moved to the shiny hair spread out on the dirty mattress.

"I haven't hurt her, and I don't plan to. As long as you cooperate. I simply added a little something to her supply of tea bags to make her more compliant, then gave her something stronger to help her relax even more. It'll be a while before she's awake again. Long enough for me to deal with you."

"What do you have against me?"

"It's nothing personal, you understand." Frank's face looked like he swallowed lemons. "You two ruined everything by getting married. I need to remedy that."

"You're going to force her to divorce me?" Theo knew that wasn't the plan, but he needed to buy time.

"No, I need to kill you. It has to look like an accident."

Taking in a deep breath, Theo said, "I don't think a gunshot wound will be anyone's idea of an accident."

Frank scowled. "Which is why I'm not going to use the gun to kill you." He took a few backward steps and lifted a long wooden object from beside the bed. "Sit in that chair over there."

"You want me to sit here while you bash my skull in with a baseball bat?" Theo laughed. "I don't think so."

Frank looked nervously around the room, then waved the gun at him. "Fine. I'll simply shoot you, then dig the bullet out. When I throw you in the ocean, the wound will attract all sorts of fish to feed, and there won't be much left of you to figure out cause of death."

Before Theo could make a move, Frank lifted the gun higher. The colorful blanket behind the man flew off as he squeezed the trigger. Chelsea pushed at the gun as it went off, and Frank reared back. Theo ran forward, throwing himself at the angry man.

"Get out of here, Chelsea," Theo shouted as he and Frank struggled, falling into the table, The candle crashed to the floor, snuffing out the light.

Reaching out, Theo attempted to grab the gun but only managed some part of Frank's clothing. Glass from the broken jar candle cut into his arm as they rolled on the floor. The gun went off again right near Theo's head, deafening him for a few seconds. Had Chelsea gotten out yet?

He pounded his fist into the dark, hitting something soft. A grunt told him he'd hit his mark. Where was the gun?

"Get off me," Frank growled, and a hard metallic object impacted the side of Theo's skull.

His head spun, but he dove back into the fray, his eyes finally adjusting to the dark. He could make out a figure moving near him and grabbed for it. It was Frank's arm. Wrenching it, he managed to swing his arm around the man's neck and hold tight. Frank struggled and twisted, attempting to break free, but Theo held on. Needed to give Chelsea time to get away. There wasn't any other sound in the room, so she must have escaped. How much longer until his friends found them?

One of Frank's arms swung back, hitting him in the head while the other waved around wildly. The weapon fired again, causing a burn to slash through Theo's side. His hold loosened, but he didn't let go.

The door splintered open, and the beam of two flashlights cut across the room.

"Police! Hold it right there."

Perfect timing. The ache in his side started to burn, and the drum in his head began a solo.

Frank lifted his weapon, but when he saw not two but four men with flashlights, all with guns pointed his way, he finally dropped his.

"Chelsea?" Theo yelled. Rico stepped aside while Aiden and one of his deputies cuffed Frank. "Did you get her outside?"

Panic warped Rico's face. "She didn't come out." His light flashed through the room as Theo climbed unsteadily to his feet. Bare feet poked out from behind the tossed table.

"Chelsea!" Theo rushed over, dragging his wife into his arms, waving for his friend to shine the flashlight their way. A pool of blood covered the floor where she'd been. Crimson seeped from a hole in her shirt near her shoulder and dripped down her arm to hands that were still tied together.

"She needs help," Theo yelled, then pulled her closer to him, whispering in her ear. "Hold on, pixie. I'm here. You'll be fine. You need to hold on. I've got you."

Radios crackling and people talking nearby all faded into the background as he held the woman he loved, praying she'd be okay. His fingers felt along her neck, and he exhaled when her blood pulsed against the pressure.

"Let's get her undone." Rico knelt next to them and untied the rope from her hands. "Kim should be here with the ambulance any second."

"Paramedics are here," Aiden called out as Kim and her partner, Pete, rolled a stretcher into the dilapidated building. "Make sure to check Lapierre out, too. Looks like he took some hits."

"I'm fine," Theo said, attempting to stand once the paramedics lifted Chelsea to the stretcher. Rico held out his hand and helped stabilize him. "I'll ride in the ambulance with her."

When they got Chelsea in the ambulance, Rico patted him on the back. "I'll check in on both of you once I'm sure Aiden's all set here."

"Can you call Angie? Let her know what's going on."

"Sure." Rico nodded.

As Kim climbed up after him, Theo overheard Rico say, "Don't let him put off being examined. Not all that blood is hers."

Theo started to object, but a moan from Chelsea had him sliding along the seat to her side.

"Hey there, pixie."

Her eyes floated open for only a second, and a tiny smile came to her face. "Theo."

"Right here."

Kim got to work checking her vitals and adjusting the IV they'd inserted first thing back at the shack while putting pressure on the wound. She flashed a compassionate smile at him.

"What do you think?" He knew Kim wasn't a doctor and couldn't diagnose or even predict if a patient would make it, but he needed to hear something.

"She's lost a lot of blood, but we got there soon after. You know as well as I do, Theo, that the earlier they get treatment the better the prognosis. Remember that."

All he could do was nod as he stared at the pale face of his wife. As pale as when she'd first arrived here several months back. They'd come so far, and it would kill him if he lost her now.

The rest of the ambulance ride was quiet, and Theo prayed more than he'd ever done in his life. More than when Chelsea hadn't come back after their marriage.

It took him a second to make the world stop spinning when he got down from the ambulance. Pete and an orderly helped him inside when he refused to wait for a wheelchair. They led him down the hall and into an exam room.

"What? No, I want to see Chelsea."

Pete tilted his head and frowned. "You know the rules, Theo. They'll get you information as soon as they know anything.

Now, are you going to cooperate, or do I need to get Bruno here to sit on you?"

Theo eyed the large orderly, whose name was Brian according to his name tag. He'd said he was fine yet didn't think his bruised body could take on this guy.

"I'll stay right here and be a good little boy. For now. If it takes too long to find out how my wife is, I can't guarantee anything."

Both men left and Theo collapsed onto the bed, exhausted. He'd barely slept the previous night, and his nerves were raw. Calling Angie, he checked on Jordan, then gritted his teeth through the medical staff cleaning his wounds and pulling several pieces of glass from his arm and back. No one would tell him how his wife was.

Finally, he got word she was in surgery, and the waiting became harder to bear. After signing papers for his own release, he moved to the surgical waiting room. Only after the doctor assured him the procedure had gone well did Theo relax.

When he was finally allowed in to see her, she rested peacefully on the bed. Perching on the edge, he caressed her cheek. Her eyes fluttered, and a tiny sigh escaped.

"I'm here if you need me, pixie," he said softly, not wanting to wake her if she needed her sleep. He wanted to make sure she was all right.

"I do need you, Theo," she whispered, groggily. Her eyes opened. "You're not hurt?"

He shook his head. "Only a few scratches. I was worried about you. You could have been killed jumping on Frank like that."

Tears filled her eyes. "I couldn't let him hurt you."

"He didn't. I'm fine." Running his hands down her arms, he gently touched the rope burns on her wrists. "You'll be fine, too. Doc says you need some rest."

"Is Jordan safe?"

"Yeah, she's with Angie."

Chelsea's eyes roamed the room, her face anxious. "You should probably get back to her, so she doesn't worry."

"It's after midnight, pixie. She's asleep. I know how much you dislike hospitals. I don't plan on going anywhere."

The relief on her face as she closed her eyes made him more determined to stay right here.

———◆◆◆———

Chelsea opened her eyes to light streaming in the window and Theo sacked out in a chair nearby. The events of the past few days drifted through her mind, the mind that felt clear at the moment, even with pain lancing her shoulder.

Shifting in bed, she grunted. Theo opened his eyes and smiled her way.

"How are you feeling this morning?"

"Okay. You stayed here overnight."

He sat on the edge of the bed. "I'm not going anywhere, pixie. Right here is where I belong."

Her hand clenched his. "I'm not going anywhere either. I didn't run away like the texts said. That was Frank."

"I know, pixie. I figured that out. It's why we had the cavalry show up in the nick of time."

Tears welled in her eyes. "I'm sorry I was angry the other day. I didn't mean to make you mad or indicate I didn't trust you. I trust you with my life, Theo."

He pressed a sweet kiss to her nose. "I'm the one who needs to apologize. I should have told you about the check. You had every right to be upset."

"It was just me and my insecurities. Frank knew it would put a wedge between us."

Theo narrowed his eyes. "I still don't understand what he had against me."

"Frank wanted the company, and he had to kill you to get it."

"That doesn't make any sense."

Chelsea explained about her father's will and the codicil and the plan the two men had concocted. It boggled her mind to think how many times the man had tried, and failed, to kill Theo. Thank God he had.

"Well, it's all over now, and we can focus on us and being a family." Theo ran his fingers through her hair and tucked it behind her ear.

"Are you sure you still want me after all this mess?" The anxiety she'd always felt still lingered.

The sad expression on his face stabbed at her soul.

"I love you, pixie. Now, tomorrow, forever, and always." Pressing a kiss to the tip of her nose, he pulled her in for a gentle hug.

Doubt still nagged at her. "But what if my condition—"

"We'll worry about anything that comes along at that time." He kissed her forehead. "If there's truly some imbalance, we'll deal with it. I'm hoping the love of your husband and daughter and all the support we give you will get you through any hard times. I don't plan to ever have you out of my sight for long. You okay with that?"

Her heart lightened as she circled her arms around him. "I'm very okay with that. I love you, too, Theo, and I can't think of any place I'd rather be than with you and Jordan. Forever and always."

"It's a plan then. Once you get out of here, we'll start getting ready to move to the cottage. I hear the ocean is extremely therapeutic. I can't wait to make love to you with the sound of the waves roaring in the background and the ocean breeze drifting in the windows."

Chelsea's insides flipped. "So you only want me for my oceanfront property, is that it?"

Chuckling, he kissed her passionately. "I thought you said I owned the whole business and estate. I could buy my own oceanfront property."

"Guess you could," she responded to his words and his kisses. "Nice to know you don't want me for my money."

"Oh, I definitely want you for more than that." Theo caressed her cheek, then slid his hands down her figure. "I plan on showing you as soon as you're feeling better."

CHAPTER TWENTY-SEVEN

The water of Jordan Pond glimmered like the diamond on Chelsea's finger. Theo had insisted he get her a real engagement ring to go with the wedding band she'd slipped on her finger five years ago. Five years to this day.

The gentle breeze blew hair into her eyes, and she pushed it aside, wanting to see Theo as soon as she got to the bridge. Yup, there he was waiting for her. So gorgeous in his dress ranger uniform and hat. Rico stood beside him, along with a dozen other friends and family they'd invited for the renewal of their vows. They'd all come by way of the boardwalk, while Chelsea and Jordan had taken the easier route on the graded path.

"There he is, Mama," Jordan yelled. "The handsome wanger. Like in the story."

"Yes, sweetheart, and now he has two beautiful princesses to love."

Jordan brushed her fingers down the peach dress that matched her mother's. Lucky for her, Theo had kept her wedding dress. His mom had sewn a smaller, child version for Jordan.

"More beauuuutiful than the lake," Jordan sang, twirling around making Chelsea laugh. She had lots to laugh about these days. Laugh and smile. Life was so good.

As they approached the small wooden bridge, Theo's face lit up.

"You look gorgeous," he said, then patted Jordan's head. "Both of you. Are you ready for this, pixie?"

"Yes," she said breathlessly. Everything Theo did took her breath away

In the last month, they'd moved to her grandmother's cottage, along with the animals, new swing set, and all Jordan's toys. Being on the ocean was only second best to being in Theo's bed every night and in his life every day. Having her daughter with her made so much pain from the past go away, or at least get pushed back to a part of her mind she kept locked up.

Frank was in prison awaiting trial, and Chelsea didn't relish having to testify, but Theo would be with her, and his strength kept her going. His support had been essential the last month when she'd hired investigators to look into the pharmaceutical company and its dealings. They'd found the person responsible for making the drugs her father had given her. He had also been arrested. Another large drug company had stepped in to buy hers, and she'd sold easily. As for the estate, she'd gotten rid of the staff and given use of it to a women's shelter. Putting some of the proceeds of the buyout into an account, she'd given the shelter access to the interest from the considerable amount. Chelsea planned to keep her eye on it and make sure the residents got the kind of support and help they needed. Help she wished she'd had.

During this time, she'd started seeing a therapist to help her deal with all that had happened to her, mentally as well as physically. Theo came to some of the appointments and was being coached on what to look for if Chelsea started to get lost again. With a loving husband and daughter, it hadn't happened often.

Theo crept forward and took Chelsea's hand, while Rico scooped Jordan up so she could be high enough to see everything.

"Dearly Beloved, we are gathered here today to witness this couple pledge their love and devotion to each other in holy matrimony."

The minister continued as Chelsea gazed out at the peaceful water of the lake, then at the man by her side. Nothing could be better.

"Do you, Chelsea…" The words brought her back to the ceremony.

"I do." The look in Theo's eyes when she said it sent shivers down her spine.

Theo repeated the vow, declaring his love, and they were invited to kiss.

As Theo's lips descended on hers, she thought back to all the many other times they showed each other the depth of their love.

"I love you, pixie," Theo whispered as if he could read her mind.

Creeping her hands up around his neck, she whispered back. "Not as much as I love you."

Theo chuckled but didn't debate.

Kim snapped away with her camera, saying she'd add it to the album she'd made five years ago. Rico slapped Theo on the back with a laugh.

"Might want to move aside, or we'll have Norma on our case for holding up traffic."

Theo bent down and scooped her up, carrying her over to the sandy area by the lake with the new bench. Jordan Pond was still open to the public, even though they'd gotten permission to hold the wedding here. A dozen or so people stood to the side of the wooden bridge, waiting to cross. They all smiled, and none seemed upset to be delayed. They took in Theo is his ranger uniform and applauded.

As the visitors moved past, Theo set her on the bench and kissed her once more. "I love you, Chelsea Lapierre."

"You like the sound of that, huh?" She'd changed her name legally and gotten all her documents updated with her new Maine address.

"I like that it says you're mine. That we're a family. You, me, and Jordan."

As he said this, the little girl skipped over and plunked onto the seat between them.

"And the new baby," Jordan chirped.

Theo narrowed his eyes. "What new baby?" His gaze roamed to her.

"When you got married last time, you had a baby. Me," Jordan said. "So now you have to have another baby."

Theo laughed, but Chelsea remained quiet. She had wanted to wait until they were alone to tell him.

Taking his hand, she rested it on her stomach. "Jordan's right. We do need to have another one."

Theo's intense gaze warmed her inside. "Seriously? When?"

"Are you asking when I'm due or when it happened?"

Caressing her cheek, Theo smirked. "When it happened could be any time in the past month or so. We haven't exactly been careful." His eyebrows raised and lowered.

"True." Her cheeks heated when she realized his parents were standing close enough to overhear. "I'm due end of April."

"Excellent. It'll give us time to go on that trip we talked about."

Theo had been able to arrange a few months furlough during the winter months when Acadia was less busy. Since she'd been practically imprisoned at the estate her whole life, he'd wanted her to see some of what she'd missed. They'd travel some of this country first and then head to Europe.

"We might want to do the overseas part first."

"Whatever you're comfortable with, pixie. As long as we're together, that's all that matters."

Dan and Laurie edged closer. "I think we'll head back to the cottage to make sure the food is all set for the party."

"Thank you so much for everything." Chelsea hugged her mother-in-law. "You've been so wonderful to me."

"You've been wonderful for our son and for Jordan," Laurie replied. "Congratulations on the next one."

"I suppose we should head back, also," Theo said. "Not much of a party without the bride and groom." His gaze moved up and down her body. "Are you okay to walk all the way back?"

Chelsea rolled her eyes. "I managed to get here by myself. I'm pregnant, not dying. I wouldn't mind holding my husband's hand while we go."

"I can arrange that."

"I'll escort young Miss Lapierre," Rico said, hoisting Jordan into his arms and setting her on the path back to the parking area.

Theo helped Chelsea up, and she turned and stared down at the bench Theo had arranged to have placed here. It was dedicated to Chelsea's mom. This had been one of her favorite places, too. As her husband took her hand, Chelsea smiled at the inscription on the bench. No truer words had ever been spoken.

A joyful heart is good medicine.

⚬

Take a sneak peek at book 2 in the Rangers of Acadia series.
Rico and Kim's story: Otter Cliffs.

If you liked the book, I'd love to hear about it.

Please consider leaving a review on your favorite retailer.
Reviews help new readers discover a book.

Rangers of Acadia: Otter Cliffs

Chapter One

"Requesting crowd assistance at Otter Cliffs. STAT." The dispatcher's voice came over Rico Montenegro's radio as he steered down the Park Loop Road in Acadia National Park.

"This is Montenegro. I'm on my way. Four minutes out."

The radio crackled with the responses of several more rangers. He was the closest. A few of them asked for specifics, and Rico listened carefully for the reply.

"Body over the cliff. SAR has been contacted."

Search and Rescue. Meaning he'd most likely get a buzz from them, too. What a way to end his shift. Luckily, he always kept climbing gear in his vehicle. But, man, he hated when you knew your were risking your neck to retrieve a corpse. If someone went over Otter Cliffs, there was little chance they'd survived. Those rocks were steep and ended in the ocean. Was this someone who had just fallen or was the body only now snagging on the rocks from a boating accident?

His phone buzzed as he pulled his Acadia National Park SUV onto the side of the lane. Yep, SAR forming a team. He quickly responded his location and grabbed his rescue gear, then loped to where another park ranger was waving cars through.

"Hey, Joe, what do we got?"

Joe Finnegan cocked his head toward the cliffs. "Tourists noticed a body floating in the water next to the cliffs about thirty minutes ago. Take your time. She's not going anywhere."

Rico shivered as he made his way to where the crowd congregated. First task: Get these gawkers away from the scene.

Grabbing a few orange cones from the breakdown lane, he placed them on the perimeter where two of the Law Enforcement Rangers stood trying to calm people down.

"I need everyone to get behind the cones, please." He used his authoritative voice and tapped a few tourists on the shoulder pointing to where they needed to go.

Two minutes later, his buddy, Theo Lapierre, trotted over, his SAR bag in hand. "Just what I needed on my first day back," Theo said as they approached the edge of the cliff and the officer standing there.

Theo and his wife, Chelsea, had just had a new baby boy ten days ago, and the man had taken the week off. Between the infant and their not-quite five-year-old daughter, Jordan, Rico wondered if they'd gotten any sleep.

"Why don't you stay topside, and I'll do retrieval?" Rico suggested, digging his rope and harness from his bag.

Theo eyed him strangely. "You sure?" Theo knew Rico wasn't crazy about doing water rescues and why. Too many beers one night had them sharing secrets better left unsaid.

"Can't imagine you're bright eyed and bushy tailed after ten days with a newborn. Even if Chelsea is the one feeding the baby."

Theo gave a slight chuckle. "You got that right. And of course, Jordan has been crazy out of her mind with excitement. I promise, I won't drop you, though."

Rico glanced around, a smirk on his face. "Maybe we should tie it off somewhere." They almost always did anyway if they had the resources, but he had to give his friend crap if he could. They'd been working together for three years, and Theo was the best friend he had on the island.

Several more of the Mount Desert Island SAR team showed up and set their gear in place. Once that was done, Rico fastened his harness, approached the edge, and peered over. Blonde hair floated on the water next to the body. His stomach clenched, and he had to look away for a second as images of the past flashed through his mind.

An ambulance pulled up, and Rico held his breath until he saw the blonde paramedic in her dark blue uniform saunter out, bag in hand. He knew Kim was working so why had he been worried?

"I'm ready, Theo. Have Kim send the litter down once I'm at the bottom."

His friend gave him slack in the rope, and Rico slowly eased over the edge. The jagged rocks on this cliff were lethal. Inch by inch, he walked his booted feet down the side of the rock face until he finally got within touching distance. The body was swollen, letting him know she'd been in the water a while. This was the part of the rescue he hated. When they hadn't gotten to the victim in time.

Waves from the rising tide crashed onto the rocks buffeting Rico around. He planted his feet as firmly as he could on a ledge below the body and checked if she was snagged on the rocks. Yup, a ripped part of her jacket was looped around a sharp section of stone.

Looking up, he motioned for Kim to send down the litter. As it slowly descended, Rico worked on freeing the fabric. He had to keep his eyes off the body and face of the victim and concentrate on getting her free. Not that it would help her at this point.

The litter hovered above him until he tugged on the line, then lowered again. This was the tricky part. Getting the body in and strapped while the waves battered them from behind. On many rescues, if they had enough SAR team members, two people would lower to the injured victim, but it was far too dangerous to do that in this situation. The fewer people in the water, the better.

The chilly May air wrapped around Rico, causing the ocean spray to be like frigid fingers choking him. He shifted the litter to a better position and used the rolling of the waves to get the victim inside. Shoving his gloves in his pocket, he got a better grip on the straps to adjust them to fit the swollen body and finally clicked them together.

"Okay, all set," he yelled up and tugged on the rope. Slowly it rose and shifted away from him. Theo had a good grip on his rope, and Rico held it tight waiting for his chance to be pulled up. God, it was cold today. To think earlier he'd been thrilled with the sixty-degree weather. Not when the ocean was soaking most of his clothing.

Rico kept his eyes on the litter as it reached the top and hands moved in to grab it. Kim's blonde head peeked over the edge and gave him a thumb's up. When he'd first seen the victim, his heart had stopped wondering if it was her. She was a good friend, and he'd hate to see something happen to her.

His rope tightened, and Rico glanced up. His turn. Grasping the rope, he started to climb, wishing he'd put his gloves back on after connecting the straps. Too late to do it now. He kept his feet against the cliff face as his harness tugged and rose higher and higher. The icy ocean wind blew in, and Rico swayed. His hand automatically flew out, so he didn't bash into the rock face. The sharp sting of jagged granite cutting flesh zinged through his palm and up his arm.

Ow! No sense checking it out now, he had a cliff to climb. Once he got to the top was early enough to assess the damage.

His feet pressed firmly into the stone, and his one hand held tighter than ever. Of course, his good hand was on the arm with the injured shoulder. The one that had gotten him booted from the Navy Aviation Rescue Swimmer team he'd been on.

Focus on getting to the top. Kim peered over the edge again and held out her hand. When he got close enough, she reached out and hauled him by the elbow. He sunk to his knees, the tension of the climb thrumming through his body.

"Where's all the blood coming from?" Theo coiled the rope, then helped him get out of the harness.

Rico held up his left hand, crimson dripping from his palm.

Kim's eyebrow rose, and she cocked her head. "Aww, you knew we couldn't do anything for the victim, so you made it a point to give us an injury to take care of. How sweet."

"Job security, Kim. It's all about job security."

Shaking her head, she knelt next to him and examined his hand. "This looks kind of deep. I'm thinking stitches."

He narrowed his eyes causing her to pat him on the head like a little boy. "You can't just clean it up and slap a bandage on it? What kind of paramedic are you?"

Her face hardened at the slight. "One who knows enough to recommend stitches, but I will clean this up first. Can you walk over to the ambulance, or should I get a gurney?"

Her full lips twitched, and he wanted to do something to make them stop. Before the next thought entered his head, he reminded himself Kim was a friend. A good friend. But that was it. You didn't ruin friendship by pushing anything more on it.

"I think I can somehow manage." His legs had stopped shaking, yet they still felt like jelly when he stood. Luckily, Theo tucked himself close as he stumbled away from the accident scene toward the ambulance.

Kim opened her case and sifted through for the supplies she needed. After pouring some distilled water to clean off any of the salt, she tenderly dabbed disinfectant on the gash. Rico gritted his teeth at the sharp sting.

After wrapping some gauze around his palm, she said, "We'll drop you at the hospital for those stitches when we bring the body to the morgue."

"I've got my work vehicle here, and I don't really want to ride in the back with the victim. I can get there myself."

"I can bring him." Theo sauntered over, folding the harness and tucking it in the SAR bag.

Rico shook him off. "We get off duty in fifteen minutes, and you have a wife and kids to go home to."

"Ready to go?" Kim's partner, Alan, said coming around the back of the ambulance.

Kim stood and brushed off the knees of her uniform pants. "Take her in, Alan. I'll follow with Rico in his park vehicle. He needs stitches."

Alan nodded, got in the vehicle, and started it up. Rico stood aside while Kim put the medical bag back in its compartment.

"I don't need a babysitter, Kim." Rico hefted his gear and slid the bag on his shoulder.

"No, but you shouldn't be driving with that hand until they've stitched up the wound. If you really feel bad, you can buy me a drink after since I get off shift soon, too."

"Perfect." Theo slapped Rico on the back and grinned. "Thanks, Kim. Appreciate the personal touch."

Rico eyed the pretty paramedic. Personal touch. He sighed, keeping his thoughts to himself about exactly what he'd like to touch.

The ambulance took off and he glared at Kim. "Guess I'm stuck with you now. Let me just make sure the LEs don't need me for anything else."

He took a minute to check in with the Law Enforcement Ranger at the scene, then ambled back to where Kim stood by his SUV.

"All set. To the hospital we go." He dug the keys from his pocket.

Kim cleared her throat and held her hand out. "I'm driving."

———◆———

If you want to be notified when Rico and Kim's book is released, sign up for my newsletter at www.karilemor.com

You can also follow me on these social media platforms and retailers.

Website: https://www.karilemor.com/

Facebook: https://www.facebook.com/Karilemorauthor/

The Lit Lounge – Reader's Group - https://www.facebook.com/groups/373521153021256

Last Chance Beach Romance Readers (FB) - https://www.facebook.com/groups/290055732591791

Romance Gems Where Authors and Readers Meet (FB)- https://www.facebook.com/groups/332592250930075

The Corner of Love and Main – small town romance reader's group (FB) - https://www.facebook.com/groups/cornerofloveandmain

Twitter: https://twitter.com/karilemor

Instagram: https://www.instagram.com/karilemorauthor/

Goodreads: https://www.goodreads.com/author/show/9756283.Kari_Lemor

BookBub: https://www.bookbub.com/authors/kari-lemor

Made in the USA
Monee, IL
28 September 2023

43635365R00208